THE IDENTITY GAME

Nathan March

Published in 2009 by New Generation Publishing

First Edition

Published by New Generation Publishing

I am Rose, my eyes are blue.
I am Rose, and who are you?
I am Rose and when I sing,
I am Rose like anything.

- Gertrude Stein

CHAPTER ONE

W hen he woke up all his fears had vanished, and they were replaced by the most wonderful certainty. He was real, totally and absolutely real He got out of bed knowing that now he was more real than anyone else, more real than anything else. Other people were insubstantial by comparison. He could practically see through them. He had acquired an extra dimension of reality. This was what he was born to become. This day was his epiphany.

He dressed slowly, wondering how it would be when he went downstairs and the others saw him. Cautiously, he glanced at his reflection in the mirror out of the corner of his eye. He looked away immediately. He did not dare look directly at it. He might be blinded, as one could be by staring directly at the sun. He was something new in the world. Jesus was said to be distinguished from other men by his holiness. He would be distinguished by his reality.

All those questions:Who are you? Who do you consider yourself to be? What are you? They had been preparation for the one resounding answer that he was ready to give now. It was the one that, thousands of years ago, God gave to Moses from a burning bush: I AM THAT I AM.

::   ::   ::

It was raining lightly when Donald Green hauled his suitcases off the train at Oxford, the raindrops drifting in the breeze. It had been dry when the train left London a little over an hour ago, and as he was not wearing a hat he glanced up at the sky in annoyance. But then he said to himself, "Oh well, it'll christen my Burberry."

He was an American in his late thirties, shorter than average, tending to plumpness around the middle, wearing horn-rimmed glasses, wheeling a suitcase and carrying a small one as well. He carried his case as if it was important and he carried himself in the same way., holding his head back at a slight tilt so that he looked at things and people across a distance, and would decide in his own time whether something or someone was worth his attention. He put down the two suitcases and buttoned up his new raincoat over a herring-bone jacket, plain grey trousers, and a plain shirt and tie. Then he picked up his cases again and continued on his way out of the station..

He passed through the station exit and glanced around for a taxi. There were a few in line but people were taking them and by the time he got there only one was left. Out of the corner of his eye he saw someone else heading for it, so he hurried over. He wanted to get there in time to meet a few people before dinner. Leaning down, he asked the driver, "Do you know the Abbotsbury School? It's a boarding school near Corpus Christi College."

The driver nodded and opened the door. "I have some cases," Green said and waited pointedly. The driver got out and opened the boot. As he was going around to put them in, the other man appeared beside Green and asked, "Did you say the Abbotsbury School?"

"Yes."

"Are you going to the F.I.S. thing?"

"Yes. Are you?"

"Yes. Do you mind if I share your cab?" The man's voice was English.

"Not at all.`" He could hardly refuse, although he would have liked to have spent his first few minutes in Oxford contemplating the city alone.

The other man had one suitcase, which he swung lightly

into the boot. Then, smiling a thank you, he folded himself into the taxi. Green looked across. He was a head taller than him, and he settled into his seat with the air of a man who expects to be welcome.

He decided to introduce himself. "Donald Green. Columbia University," he said.

"Louis Mannion," said the other and held out his hand. Green shook the hand and waited for more information. "I write for the Sunday Chronicle." Green nodded. He did not read the British Press often and knew very little about the Sunday Chronicle.

Mannion wore a beige jacket and a striped shirt open at the neck. Green compared the man's style, casual, fashionable, even flashy, with his own, which he thought of as suitably academic. He turned away and peered out of the window. They were going through busy streets of two and three-storey buildings with shop fronts, devoted to small-scale commerce rather than learning, a stationer's, what seemed to be a fashion shop that called itself a boutique, a café. This was not the Oxford he held in his mind from his previous visit. It could be any English city. He was disappointed. Then they went into the High Street and he experienced a welcome sense of recognition at the stone walls of a college here and there and the Gothic spire of a church, part of an archipelago of dignity and antiquity in the sea of busy, contemporary Oxford.

"You've come over from New York for this?" Mannion asked.

"Not just for this. I've been at the F.I.S. annual conference in London."

"I see."

Green thought he should make conversation. After all, they were going to be together for two weeks. He remarked, "Pity about the rain. Oxford's not at its best."

"True," agreed Mannion.

"Still, it'll christen my Burberry," Green went on. When there was no response to this he added, "Bought it in London this morning." Mannion acknowledged this remark only with a nod so he turned back to the window. Thick traffic had slowed the taxi to a crawl now.

Green turned back and took another look at the other man. He seemed to be about the same age as him and he had narrow, alert eyes behind glasses with transparent plastic rims, dark hair receding from his forehead and the kind of regular, open features that Green thought of as boyish. But he was pleased to see that there were love handles on his hips and a fleshiness developing under the chin.

Mannion asked, "Do you know Oxford?"

"As a visitor. I've dined at high table a couple of times. You?"

"Only slightly," Mannion said.

"Not an Oxford man," thought Green. They rode in silence for a while. Green surreptitiously ran his fingers over the lapels of his new raincoat with satisfaction .He must look in Oxford for something to take back for Lorraine. She would be annoyed if he did not bring her anything from England. She would not say anything but it would be there in her manner. He should also buy a doll of some kind for Jo. He smiled to himself when he thought about little Jo.

He turned his attention back to Mannion. "I don't suppose you've taken part in anything like this before, have you?" he asked.

"As I understand it, there's never been anything like this before," Mannion replied. "It's an experiment. Have you taken part in any crisis games?"

"No, but I helped write a couple for one of the service academies. They're useful exercises."

"I think this one will be rather more. Are you ready to change your identity?"

"I'll play the game. I'm not worried about changing my

iv

identity," Green replied, shrugging off any suggestion of anxiety.

They rode in silence again for a few moments, and then Mannion asked, "What was the F.I.S. conference about?"

"It had what was pretty much a catch-all title: 'International Organizations In a Time of Change.' It was a four-day affair. There were one or two good papers." He was not going to waste time discussing the subject with an amateur.

"Have you specialised in that area?" Mannion asked, still being polite.

"I'm doing some work on America and NATO."

The taxi had broken loose from the dense traffic into narrow winding side streets. It was moving faster now, throwing the two passengers about with tight, fast turns around corners which made conversation difficult. It stopped outside two iron gates.

"Five pounds. Including the cases," said the driver, and he went around to get the suitcases out of the boot. They each gave him three pounds since neither wanted to fiddle with small change so he got a pound tip, and rewarded them with a warm "Thank you very much," aimed at a point midway between them.

The iron gates led to a long, two-storey, modern building which showed a face of glass and mottled stone. Other buildings, similar but smaller, were visible behind. Paved pathways and grassy verges, glistening now with raindrops, ran alongside and between the buildings. Carrying their cases, they walked up the path, where they found a sheet of cardboard with the letters "F.I.S." written with a black felt-tip pen and an arrow pointing to the right, the writing smudged by the rain.

They followed the arrow into the main building and came to a reception desk in the corner of the lobby, with a telephone and cubby-holes behind. At the desk they gave their names. A young woman gave each of them a fat cardboard folder with his name on it and a room key.

"You're in Blue House," she said to Mannion, and to Green, "You're in Yellow House." Then she recited: "You go down this corridor and out the door at the end, and you'll see both your buildings opposite. You can tell which is which by the colour on the front door. There's a map in your folder that will tell you where everything is." She had a pretty, feline face with high cheekbones and Mannion noticed that her russet dress matched the colour of her hair. She gave him a smile along with his folder and key and he returned the smile.

Green leaned over the desk and asked her, "Are there any messages for me?"

She looked down at a paper briefly and then said, "No, nothing, Professor Green."

"I'm expecting one," he said. "You will let me know if it comes in, will you?"

"We'll notify you of any messages," she assured him. "Until Wednesday. From then on, I understand that - ".

"Yes, I know. I'm expecting a message before gether down the corridor and out into the courtyard, which consisted of lawns criss-crossed by paths. Mannion said, "I'm over there. I'll see you at dinner." But Green was already looking around to see who else was about and he turned and said vaguely, "Oh yes. Sure."

Green walked along a path to a yellow door and, following signs, climbed up one flight on a narrow stone staircase. He had hoped there would be a message from Stack-Stevens. He wondered whether he should phone him here. He had put enough effort into entertaining him in New York. He walked along a corridor and found his room number, unlocked the door and let himself in.

He looked around at the single bed, with its patterned grey counterpane which vaguely matched the pale blue wallpaper, desk, chair, cupboard and chest of drawers. There was a basin with two taps in the corner with a mirror over it and a narrow shelf. He noted that there was no toilet or shower. He would be using the communal ones along the corridor. "Pretty damned basic," he thought to himself.

He opened the folder that he had collected at reception. There was a map of the Abbotsbury School buildings, another map of Oxford with the university's colleges and a few other landmarks identified, and a page with meal times and other administrative arrangements.

There were also two large envelopes containing documents, both headed "Foundation for International Security." One of the envelopes was sealed and labelled "Your Role," and it carried the injunction: "Do Not Open Until Instructed." The other was labelled "The Game," and he opened it.

Inside was a five-page document. He scanned it. It was an account of a crisis around the imaginary Caribbean island nation of St. George. Democratic government after recent right-wing dictatorship. Member of the Commonwealth. British connections, he noted. Nationalisation of an American corporation. Strikes. Anti-American demonstrations. An American business executive dead. What would America do? Would the military stage a coup? He put the paper down. He would have time to study it before the game proper began

In Blue House, Louis Mannion found his room, set down his case, hung his raincoat on a hook and looked around. "Seems comfortable enough," he thought.   .

He wanted to speak to Tess. He sat on the edge of the bed, took out his mobile phone and dialled her at her work, the office of a small left-wing publisher. She said, "Hello, Louis. I didn't expect you to call today." Her husky voice made his skin tingle. He envisaged her face next to the telephone, her wide brown eyes, and her soft skin with the phone resting against it.

"I just wanted to say hello."

"I'm glad you did."

"I keep thinking of last Thursday," he said.

"So do I." She stretched out the last word so that it lingered in his ear. Then she asked, "How is it there? Have you met any of the others yet?"

"A surviving neo-con and a couple of generals who want to nuke somebody. And a sexy blonde who's trying to entrap me."

"Sounds like just your scene."

"Actually, I've only just arrived."

"Look, darling, I can't talk for long. I'm about to go in to a meeting. We've got this manuscript about Britain and the arms trade. It makes awful reading. British companies are selling arms to countries which have a terrible record. They're giving it to me to handle because the subject is up my alley. One firm is actually selling handcuffs to the Uzbekistan police, and they routinely torture people. I want to get this publicised."

"Is that new?"

"Some of it is. I've got to go. I hope you enjoy it there."

"Okay. I'll try to call you again in a day or two, before we're locked away."

"Okay. Goodbye, darling."

"Goodbye."

He went back across to his room feeling light-hearted. Talking to Tess usually left him feeling that way. He wondered whether the men sitting in that little office with her felt some tingling of the skin and longed to reach across and stroke her. And if not, why not? What was the matter with them? It was not just that Tess was beautiful. She was lovely but not in a straightforward Miss World kind of way. It always seemed to him that she had an aura of passion, when she spoke and when she moved, that came from within her and permeated the space immediately around her. Even her moral outrage had an erotic quality. This was not something she turned on. She was young and she hardly seemed aware of it..

He sat down at the desk and pulled his thoughts back to the paper in front of him. He opened the folder and then the documents headed "The Game" and started reading about the difficulties on the island of St. George and the problems it was giving to the United States.

This game was supposed to exercise the imagination as well as the intellect so he tried to picture St. George. He had never been to the Caribbean but he summoned up images: tall trees, a sandy beach, a blue sea - no, that was a tourist poster. This was not going to be played out on sunny beaches. Dusty streets. Sweaty faces. A strong daytime sun abrasive on the skin. White, sun-bleached buildings. Government offices with heavy desks and air conditioning that worked only some of the time. Young ministers who had European suits and American cars. The offices of a few foreign corporations in modern glass buildings with European or American managers. Expat staff who drank imported whiskey and vodka in the evenings and let their hair down talking to each other about the locals.

Still trying to imagine St. George, he got up and hung up the spare suit he had brought and unpacked the rest of his things. A name tag in a transparent plastic badge was in his folder and he pinned this to his lapel. The timetable said they were to assemble in the lounge before dinner on the first evening, so he went downstairs and across to the main building again.

The Abbotsbury School was as determinedly modern in its architecture and decor as in its curriculum. Some of the pictures along the corridor were of the school buildings when they were under construction, others were action photographs of pop groups, all crotches and sweat and strained faces. In his mind, Louis compared it favourably with his old school, where the pictures on the corridors were of sports teams lined up for the camera or past headmasters in mortar board and gown.

He entered the lounge cautiously. His encounter with Green, who had not exactly behaved warmly, reminded him that he would be a bit of an outsider here. Most of the others would be civil servants or others involved in government, military men or academics, at home in the think tank world of which this was a part, and many of them would have been at the F.I.S. conference that had just finished in London. He looked around at the armchairs scattered about and decided that in term time this was the staff room. Glasses of sherry and fruit juice were lined up on a table against the wall and he took a sherry. Then he scanned name tags on lapels and identified Ivor Howe, the Director of the F.I.S. They had corresponded after he had received the invitation to this event. He was not going to stand alone so he went over and introduced himself.

"Delighted to see you here," Howe said. "I hope you'll find this interesting."

"I'm sure I will. I'm very pleased to be taking part. Although I admit I have some trepidation."

"I think we all do." Howe was scanning the room in a way that made Louis feel like a ball and chain attached to his leg. Howe greeted another man who approached him and said, "Do you know Jacob Shemtov, from Tel Aviv University? Major Shemtov, this is Louis Mannion. He's a leading British journalist." Then he went to greet someone else.

Louis shook hands with a man of medium height in his fifties wearing a plain grey suit with short black hair that was greying at the temples. His left cheek was pock-marked and twitched occasionally. He had the awkward look of a man trying to seem relaxed.

"Tel Aviv University but you're a Major," Mannion said in questioning tone. Howe was already greeting someone else.

"I left the army a long time ago," Shemtov said. Just then another man appeared at Shemtov's elbow holding a sherry glass. "Hello, Jacob," he said. Shemtov introduced him as Brian Thaxted of the British Ministry of Defence, explaining, "We met at the F.I.S. conference."

Louis said to Shemtov, "I suppose you've played crisis games before."

"I did when I was in the army, although ours were mostly military-orientated. And not like this. I'm sort of looking forward to it."

"Do you think it will be very different? Becoming someone else?"

"I don't know. When we played our games I always had to try to put myself in someone else's place."

"Like who?"

"Oh, I've been a Syrian general. And a Fattah leader planning a commando raid. You put yourself in the enemy's place and try to second-guess him."

"We try to do that at the Ministry of Defence," Thaxted said.

"Who's the enemy these days?" Louis asked.

"The Treasury, as always."

Louis smiled. Given Israel's behaviour in the occupied territories, he was cautious about speaking to an Israeli with a military rank, but he asked Shemtov, "Do you know this country well?"

"Not at all. This is my first visit."

"Really? I hope you've had a chance to see something of it."

"A little. I have an English friend who showed me around London." Then someone else greeted him and he turned away.

Thaxted said to him, "I take the Chronicle and I read your column most weeks." He had a round babyish face with soft skin and round glasses, and thick lips that looked like a permanent pout.

"Uh-huh."

"I find it very witty sometimes. You're a clever writer." He talked in confident assertions, with a hint of a lisp.

"Hmmm." Louis frowned. "Clever" sounded like the beginning of an attack. It implied shallowness. "I try to be serious occasionally," he said.

"If you don't mind my saying so," Thaxted went on, "When you talk about foreign policy you can be a bit too moral for my taste."

"Really? What's your taste then?"

"I think we all have to adapt to the wicked old world. Don't you?"

"I suppose that if I kicked you in the balls now you'd agree that I was adapting to the wicked old world," Louis thought. Aloud he said, "I'm over-compensating. Suppressing my natural villainy." Better not to get serious just now.

Shemtov joined the conversation again and so did a tall, angular, eagerly sociable woman from the German Foreign Ministry. She said she was looking forward to changing nationality without having to emigrate.

"You'll probably change sex as well," Thaxted said.

"Who do you think you'll become?" the German woman, whose name was Ingrid Mundt, asked Louis.

"I don't know," he replied. "I think I'd like to be the American President." He put on a stern voice. "'I've decided to intervene. We can't let things slide any longer. Defence Secretary, make the necessary arrangements. Press Secretary, alert the networks.'"

"Hardly the role for you, I would have thought," Thaxted said.

"Oh, but I want a change," Louis insisted. "Or I could be a St. Georgian general.'Gentlemen, this so-called democracy has gone too far. We have to restore order.'"   Then, while others continued talking, he withdrew for a minute, as he sometimes did in a crowd. He listened to the noise of a dozen conversations as people approached one another with talk, letting the voices blend so that he heard a tone rather than words. He thought he detected a nervous buzz, a forced quality to the laughter. He concentrated on it for a moment. Yes, there was no doubt. People felt anxious about what was coming.

He was reminded suddenly of an evening in Paris, years ago, when he was travelling on holiday with his friend Bob. At lunch in a restaurant they had met an American couple who told them that they were going that evening to a *partouze*, a large group sex session, along with another American couple. They invited them to come along. He and Bob discussed the matter, decided that one should try everything once, and accepted. The six of them met that evening to set out for the *partouze*.

They decided that they would have a couple of drinks first to loosen up and went to a café. They all laughed at jokes a little more than they might have otherwise, and looked away quickly if they made eye contact. When there were silences there was a rush to fill them. The occasionally forced laughter and nervous anticipation around that café table seemed to Louis to resemble the mood in this room now. (Later that evening the younger and plumper of the two American wives would be bouncing under Louis on a bed, gasping and moaning and, reaching her climax, she would cry out her husband's name, which always seemed to Louis to be the epitome of marital fidelity).

::   ::   ::

A gong sounded. Ivor Howe clapped his hands and called out, "Dinner is ready. Can we all go across the hall into the dining room now, please."

They started to move across, some going more slowly than

others, like a herd. Louis decided to stay next to Shemtov. Among strangers, it was useful to find one companion to start out with and Shemtov was a candidate. As a foreigner he presumably did not know many people here. He had an air that did not invite intimacy but he would be friendly.

Walking beside him, he noticed that Shemtov was walking with a limp. Shemtov saw him glancing down and said smiling, " I got it in a few days ago London. I tripped getting off a bus."

In the dining room, the oak panels on the walls spoke of tradition, the tall wide windows and strip lighting of modernity. The twenty-eight diners sat down at two long polished tables. As they filed in Louis found that there were not enough people to fill his table and he was at one end with an empty chair beside him. A bad tactical position, he thought to himself. Must make sure that I'm not in it again.

Shemtov was next to him, and was engaged in conversation with a bulky, untidy-looking man with a patch over one eye whose belly was spilling between open buttons of his shirt. He started on the avocado that was already on the table. He had no choice but to eat in silence.

Opposite him, a woman he identified from her tag as Frances Carr of the Foreign and Common-wealth Office was talking to the American next to her, Michael Munro. He gathered from what they were saying that Munro was shortly going to go to the American Embassy in Uzbekistan, and they talked about central Asia. There was a mention of Tajikstan and "the other stans," as Munro called them. He was saying that he gathered that it was not a bad posting. The climate was pretty awful but the embassy had good facilities and there was a sizeable Western business community. Louis felt that he was letting Tess down simply by allowing this conversation to continue without introducing another dimension.

The woman called Frances saw that he was listening and she leaned across the table and asked him, "Do you know that part of the world?" He was alone and she was kindly drawing him into the conversation.

"I only know what I read about it," he replied. "I gather that they play a big part in America's plans."

"They play some part," Munro said cautiously. "Not so much now, though."

The oil pipeline, and the war on terrorism and all that," Louis said. "But I gather the regime there doesn't have much time for democracy. I mean, stamping on the opposition and torturing prisoners is the norm." They both stiffened. Invited to join the party, he had spoiled the atmosphere.

"True, the Government's behaviour is not what we'd like," Munro said...

"What are you doing about?" Louis asked.

"The Uzbek Government knows our views," Munro replied defensively.

"But you're not going to actually embarrass the Uzbek G-G-Government? Like suggesting they stop torturing people?"

"Yes, as a matter of fact," Munro replied acerbically. "Our Congress condemned Uzbekistan for its civil rights record. And the Uzbek Government threw out our Air Force base as a consequence."

Inwardly, Louis cursed himself. He had forgotten that he had got it wrong. He said, "Yes Congress did, but that upset the State Department, didn't it?"

Frances joined in on Munro's side. "It would be nice if we could only deal with liberal democracies."

"But we do p-p-prefer them?" He raised his eyebrows.

"Certainly," she said. "But we don't always have a clear choice. Foreign policy isn't about awarding points for good behaviour."

He had started this confrontation and now he sought a way out of it. "No," he agreed. "I suppose that's the job of people

xv

like me, writing in n-n-newspapers." He was trying to soften the atmosphere of hostility.

They were all glad when the waiters interrupted them with the meat course. He wished he had not spoken. He was carried away by thoughts of Tess. He knew that they would dismiss him as a type they understood: naive, well-meaning, but emotional, not a serious person, not one of the people who understand how the world works.

Louis usually shut up when he started to stammer. It was, a friend had told him, a lip stammer. The rest of him was not involved; his face did not become distorted and he had no trouble with his breathing. The stammer came, as he had discovered over the years, in moments of difficulty, and particularly of confrontation. He waged conflict gleefully in print but had difficulty handling it face to face.

Frances Carr and Michael Munro were talking about Indonesia now. It turned out that they had both served there in their respective embassies although not at the same time. Louis looked for an opportunity to join in to show that he could talk about other things besides moral issues but he did not find one.

Jacob Shemtov was free now and he turned to him. Louis learned in answer to questions that he had been in the Israeli armoured corps but that was many years ago and now he taught international relations. He had spent two years at a Californian university and had travelled in Europe but had never been to England before, which seemed strange. He told Shemtov a little about his column on the Chronicle. As they finished dessert, Ivor Howe stood up and rapped a glass to get everyone's attention. He waited for a few seconds while they fell silent, and then he started speaking.

"I think everyone here knows me," he said. "I'm Ivor Howe. I'm the Director of the Foundation for International Security and, what is more relevant on this occasion, the director of the project in which we're all going to participate over the next two weeks." He was a tall, large-boned man in his late fifties with a lined, craggy face and a shock of thick, steel-grey hair that fell over his forehead, and he spoke with easy authority.

"This is a unique experiment," he went on. "It is also, I think a unique collaboration between the disciplines of international relations and individual psychology, the first concerned with the functioning of nation-states, and the second with the functioning of the individual mind. I'm extremely glad that you've all agreed to take part.

"Some of you have played crisis games before. I'm sure you all know about them, and the idea of role-playing. You've been told about the novel features of this particular game, and it's been explained what's in store for you. It's good of you to volunteer. I expect it to be an enlightening experience for everyone, and certainly for us on the staff of the F.I.S.

"I think you all know the arrangements by now but I'm going to go over them briefly. The game will take place over five days, starting on Thursday, the fifth. The three days after the game will be taken up with debriefing and what we might call de-programming. Also, we think you might want a little while to recover before you go back to your offices.

"The next five days, starting tomorrow morning, will be the preparation. Now, for these five days, you'll be expected to study the game and, when you get to it, your roles. The preparatory interviews and exercises will take up a good deal of time. But you'll have a lot of spare time and you're free to wander around Oxford if you choose. However, we would like you to have this as your home, eat your meals here and sleep here, even if you find the Randolph more appealing." He paused to allow a few chuckles. "This is because we want you to be thoroughly acclimatised here, and to identify with the environment here rather than anything outside. And of course, when the game begins, you will be on the premises all the time and will have no outside contact.

"You will all have now the description of the game situation, and some of you will have read it. We'll ask you not to discuss it with one another before the game begins. You're all housed now in a building with others on your national team. I'll go over the unusual arrangements that were explained to you when you agreed to take part. From next Wednesday morning you'll remain in that building for most of the time. The teams will live separately from one another during the course of the game. We chose the Abbotsbury School as the venue because it's a boarding school and it has several small buildings housing the students collected around the courtyard. We've put a certain amount of effort into ensuring that all the houses can be maintained separately.

"To increase verisimilitude you will be isolated in your teams, and the degree of verisimilitude is what is unique about this particular exercise. Meals will be brought to the teams in these quarters. You're not to make or receive any telephone calls. You've agreed to hand in your mobile phones. The aim is total immersion in your roles and in the situation." He had a way of bending slightly from the waist when he was emphasising points, first towards one side of the table and then towards the other.

Our basic way of operating will be the way these games are normally run. You will each be assigned a role in your national team. There are three countries involved: the United States, St. George and Britain. You will contact each other by message. All messages will go through the umpires. This will give us a narrative of the game. Messages can be exchanged very rapidly. If you wish to communicate with anyone who is not a player in the game - a congressman, an international organisation, a newspaper or whatever - you can do so through us, and you will receive a reply. You might want to tell something to a newspaper, for instance, and we may be the newspaper.

"We will sometimes inject events into the situation,

throwing in something that is done by someone or something other than the players. Piers Traynor here and I will play the rest of the world, or circumstances, or sometimes, as it's said in these games, God." He paused again in case anyone wanted to laugh.

"As is usual in these games, time will be compressed. The events of the five days of the game will be presumed to be taking place over three weeks. The roles have been assigned at random. There is no attempt to match a role with anyone's background or character or supposed political predilections."

Louis whispered to Shemtov, "That probably means I'm going to be a military dictator." Shemtov smiled in acknowledgement.

Howe went on, "Now we'll come to the new, the experimental feature of this game." He paused for effect. "I hope you will forgive me if I go over just briefly, now that we're all together, what you've already been told separately in letters.

"Normally, in these games, one is given a role and one plays it. The idea is that by doing so, one learns about the pressures that are on a prime minister or foreign secretary, and gets a feel for it. The progress of the game might give an idea of what might happen in certain situations through the principals interacting. But inevitably, what one is really doing is playing oneself. Oneself in a different situation: you are a prime minister or a foreign minister or whatever, but still acting as *you* would act as a prime minister or a foreign minister. If you're an American and you're playing a Chinese leader, you'll defend the interests of China, and your own interest in staying in power, but you'll do it as you would, not as a Chinese would. That's all you can do." Louis was relieved that the faceless, placeless "one" had vanished and Howe had returned to the solid ground of a personal pronoun.

"But in this game," Howe went on, "we're going to try to achieve a deeper kind of role-playing, a degree of identification of you, the participants, with the roles you are to play. With the help of Dr. Manash you'll try to become, for the duration of the game, the person you're playing. So far as possible you'll replace your own identity with that person's. We're not sure how far it is possible. That's one of the things we hope to find out.

"We can't make you completely into someone else from a different background, of course, a Caribbean politician if you are an British academic or an American military officer. But we think that with Dr. Manash's help, we can go a long way towards it. By detaching you a little way from your own present identity, and giving you something of another, insofar as this is possible, we hope to get you to experience the situation through the mind of someone else, through the eyes of the person in the role you'll be playing. We hope this will be a learning experience.

"You've all agreed to submit - I think the word is appropriate - to the interviews with Dr. Robert Manash here. He's a psychiatrist, as you know, and a very distinguished one, practising, he tells me, within a psychoanalytic framework. He's written several papers on the creation of personality. These interviews may be probing. As has been explained, they will be conducted under the rules of medical practise: that is, they will be in strict confidence. Nothing said in them will be divulged to anyone, you may rest assured, and that includes me and the rest of the staff of the F.I.S, and no record will be kept of them.

"The interviews are an essential part of the process. So are the pills you are taking, and the hypnosis sessions in which you'll be engaged with Dr. Manash. And so will your sessions in the immersion tank. I'll leave Dr. Manash to say anything more there is to say about the tank. All I'll tell you is that I've tried it and so have several of my associates, and none of us found it a disturbing experience. In fact I personally found it very relaxing.

"We hope this will be an instructive experience for all of us, and will enlarge our understanding and our sensitivity. And now I'll ask Dr. Manash to say a few words."

He sat down and the man next to him stood up. In appearance, he was a contrast to Ivor Howe. He was shorter, about five feet nine, and compact. He had an olive complexion and soft skin. He was dressed elegantly, in a dark suit, plain blue shirt and silk tie. Howe was a shaggy bear; Manash had a feline smoothness.

He spoke quietly but he held everyone's attention. "I also would like to thank you for agreeing to take part in our experiment and to go along with the rules," he said. "Of course there's a limit to the extent to which any one of us can assume someone else's identity, his or her character, one can even say. Everything that happens to each one of us since we were born goes into our identity. To become someone else, we would have to be born again, literally. But we're going to see how far we can step into another person's shoes.

He paused, fixing his audience with a look as if he were spearing a fish. "I want to set your minds at rest on a few points. The pills you've been taking for the last three days and will continue to take three times a day are new. Their effects are not drastic. I won't try to explain to you in technical terms the chemical effect of this pill on the brain, but I'll say simply that it weakens the ego defences. Or rather, I think a better way of saying it is that it will make it easier for you to drop these defences. Dropping the ego-defence is always difficult. We've spent a lifetime building them up. But dropping the ego defences is essential if another ego is to move in temporarily.

"The pills will help me in the interviews that I'll be having with you, because we will need to reach the degree of relaxed confidence that it normally takes several weeks or even months to attain in the psycho-therapeutic process. The interviews are a crucial part in helping me. Or rather, I would say, in helping you to detach yourselves from your identity for a little while, so that you can go some way towards taking on another. I'll repeat what Ivor has just said: these interviews will be conducted under rules of strict confidentiality.

"You've been told about the tank. It's a sensory deprivation tank. There are several of them, and they have been placed in the school swimming pool that has been emptied for the purpose. You'll be floating there in water at body temperature, with blindfolds on, deprived of outside sensory stimulation. You'll be in it for two sessions of an hour each, and during the second, you will be fed tape-recorded messages about your role through headphones

"As for hypnotism, it's a technique I use sometimes as an aid. I will try it with some of you. With some I may not. I hope you won't be disappointed if I don't do it." A slight smile flickered across his face as he said this and there were a few smiles in response.

"The effect of all this will be limited. It's not intended to make you hallucinate. You won't be living in a world of illusion. You won't be hypnotised into thinking that you're in Washington D.C. and that when you look out of the window you're seeing the Capitol dome, or somewhere else. But you will tend to act as if you were. We'll ask you to pretend and you'll find it easier to pretend. You'll be here playing a crisis game.

"But you'll be someone different. You will, I hope, be living in that character and in your role in the game. During the period of the game, the intention is that you will forget most of what makes you the individuals you are now. Once again, let me say that I'm grateful to you all for agreeing to take part, and I hope you will find it enlightening. I expect to learn from it. I personally am looking forward to it very much."

He sat down and they all left the dining room and headed for the lounge. A coffee urn and milk and sugar were on the sideboard that had held the sherry, along with small china cups and saucers

Shemtov noted that this was delicate, post-prandial coffee, not robust breakfast coffee which he assumed would come in large cups. He took one, and then took out his packet of pills, which were actually capsules, and swallowed one with his coffee. Several other people were doing the same. His sprained ankle nagged at him so he sat down in one of the armchairs, and he chatted briefly with Ingrid Mundt, who was also sitting down.

Most people soon drifted off to their rooms early so he did also. Once there he sat on his bed and picked up the folder marked 'The Game' and took out the pages inside. He had read through them; now he would study the document. But his mind wandered through the events of the evening. Although the people here were from several countries the occasion was British, in the predominance of British accents and British manners and the British setting, much more so than the conference in London where the participants came from all over. In fact, this was almost the first time in the week he had been here that he felt he was really in Britain. In his hotel and in restaurants, most of the staff seemed to be foreign.

He lay back on his bed and his unhappiness poured back into him. When he was with other people he could forget how unhappy he was. He thought about going back down to the lounge and wondered whether anyone would still be there, and whether they would talk to him if there were. But he could not make the effort. He stared at the ceiling with the familiar feeling of wretchedness.

Donald Green went across to his room early. As he undressed for bed he worried about the lack of any message from Stack-Stevens. Of course, he might be away. It had been a mistake to say in his letter that he would be at the Abbotsbury School for two weeks but could only be contacted during five days. Stack-Stevens would not understand that he would be incommunicado. But having written the letter it would be pushy to call him.

He was pleased with the way he had entertained Stack-Stevens in New York. It was one of those occasions when everything had gone just as he had hoped, the food, the company, the conversation. He had skimmed *Pride and Prejudice* as well as Stack-Stevens' own book on Jane Austen and her world, and had dropped references to these into the conversation. He prided himself on being a fast reader. Lorraine had provided a good meal and had been charming and remained in the background. She was not particularly good-looking – he had to be realistic - but she could be a good hostess.

Stack-Stevens had said just before he left his house, "I think we'd like to get you to my college for a year or so, if you'd be interested. There's a fellowship going in international relations that would fill the bill. Of course it's not my field, don't know anything about it really, but I gather that you've published one or two quite impressive things. I don't have the final say but I could put in a word."

He had expressed some surprise and told Stack-Stevens that he would be very interested. He did not say that this was what he had in mind already, that he had already dropped his name in another quarter. A fellowship at Oxford for a year would be the next step for him and it would be a good one.

Once in his pyjamas he did ten knee-bends, ten sit-ups and touched his toes ten times. He could have a better body but he was not entirely dissatisfied. Although he could be called short and tubby, he was agile, and faster on the tennis court than new opponents expected. He picked up his folder and took out the sheets marked 'The Game.' He would read it in bed. He should be able to get through it before going to sleep.

Then, on an impulse, he walked over to the sink and looked at his face in the mirror. Could this Dr. Manash really take away his identity? Let him try. It was only a game. He knew who he was and no one was going to change that..

Louis was engaged in conversation for a while with an American woman called Mimi, who he gathered had recently been a delegate to a conference on climate change and was now a member of a think tank. He half-listened to what she was saying while he reflected on the inappropriate names people are sometimes saddled with, particularly in America, where the range of first names stuck on helpless new-born infants was much wider. "Mimi" was a name for a movie glamour girl. He recalled that a recent White House spokesperson was called "Dee Dee." An English woman so saddled would have adopted another name when she started her career. Or perhaps they wanted these names. "Mimi" and "Dee Dee" sounded like versions of their names that were adopted or assigned in high school.

"I know about crisis games but this is something really different," Mimi said. "It's sort of scary. I mean, God knows who I'll be playing."

"You're worried about being a fascist general?" he asked her.

"I'm worried that I might enjoy it," she said grinning at him.

He broke off from Mimi after a short while and set off for Blue House. He was still angry at himself for talking at dinner about torture in Uzbekistan. "You've come here to meet the people who make things work in the world," he told himself. "You should listen to the language of power, not to shoot off your mouth with your own moral outlook. Can't you shut up for a *moment*? It was egotistic self-indulgence." He forgot for the moment that he had done so because of Tess.

In his room, he decided to make another telephone call. She took a while to answer. "I'm sorry, were you watching something on television?" he asked.

"No, I was just getting ready to have a bath," Sarah replied. "I didn't expect you to call this evening. There's nothing wrong, is there?"

"Oh no. I just wanted to see how you were. And to say again that I'm sorry about what I said early this morning. I shouldn't have been so irritable."

This was not quite true. He was right in what he had said and she was at fault. But he was going away for two weeks and she was pregnant and he did not want her to feel aggrieved.

"That's okay," she said. "I shouldn't have said what I did about your friend Dick."

"Anyway, how are you?" he asked.

"I'm fine. I felt the baby kicking again this evening." When she said this he imagined her sitting back in the maroon armchair in the living room and smiling the way she did as though she were looking at something inside her.

"But you're still feeling okay."

"Oh sure. Sally Birbeck called, they want us to come over to dinner. It's the day after you get back. I accepted. I hope that's all right."

"Yes of course."

"Depending on my condition, of course. They said Tom Barclay will be there. I know the name but can't place him."

"Historian. On the telly quite a bit."

"Oh, that's right. And some m.p. How's it going there? Have you met people?"

"Yes, one or two. Someone told me I should be more realistic and adapt to the wicked world."

"Not for the first time."

"And I told a couple of people they were servants of Satan."

"Louis Mannion diplomacy. I hope it turns out to be as interesting as you thought it would be. Enjoy it, darling."

They spoke for a couple of minutes, and then he said, "I'll call you once again before we're all locked away."

"Goodbye, darling."

He was pleased that he had called her and pleased that

they could smooth over their sharp exchange over breakfast. Sarah was good to him. She had her faults and he was finding out more about them. But she had sweated through the summer as she got heavier and heavier and was stuck at home with two months or so more of pregnancy to wait out and she was bearing up cheerfully most of the time, and she loved him and cared that he met people here and that he found it interesting. The way he felt about Tess was damned unfair to her.

CHAPTER TWO

"He'll ask me about my parents. That's what psychiatrists always do," Donald Green thought, as he helped himself to orange juice. "I'd better get my answers ready." His appointment was right after breakfast. He always liked to be prepared for situations. He prepared his lectures carefully, including the humorous asides, and if he had a meeting with someone he would familiarise himself with the other's latest article or book if that was appropriate.

Some people, having collected their breakfasts at the buffet table, were chatting while they ate. He took a news-paper from the number that were on offer and put it in front of him as a defensive wall, while he thought about what he would tell Namash.

When he had first taken Lorraine home to meet his parents, he had felt proud. The humdrum, middle-class character of their home and their life-style showed how far he had come. He was lecturing and working for his PhD at Brown University and he fitted in easily at the dinner table with Lorraine's father, a corporation lawyer, and his second wife, in their house in Boston. He felt that Lorraine looked up to him more than the other boys she went out with who had been to prep schools and had had it easy, as well she might.

His parents both worked for the city of New York, his father as a welfare worker, his mother as a teacher. His father had never been made head of his department, something he knew he wanted. They lived still in the small house in Queens where he and his sister Harriet grew up. They had met when they were students, at a Pete Seeger concert, as they told him many times. He had worked out his parents' career paths long ago. He saw that they were, like many of their class and generation, warm-hearted, soft-centred and full of love for the world. Leaving college it was natural for them to join the caring professions. His father had told him he would have liked to have gone to law school and become a lawyer working on behalf of the poor. He reckoned that by the time they lost some of their youthful idealism and thought it would be nice to join the affluent society, they were already committed to their careers. They had a collection of views that were, he thought, typical of their age and social group. They demonstrated over the war in Iraq and the plight of the poor and environmental issues, and sometimes their living room was filled with friends who agreed with them noisily.

After he went to college and started meeting other boys' parents, he had begun to look at his own parents objectively. He saw then how smart and young-looking many of the other mothers were compared to his own mother. She had chubby cheeks and she sagged over her waistline like gelatine and her clothes were unnoticeable. His father, a smallish man with a small moustache, was descended from a rabbi in the Ukraine, family name Grunowsky, and Donald sometimes thought he saw a rabbinical solemnity in his dedication to his work and to his family. The name was changed to Green some generations back by the immigrant Grunowsky, anxious to give his children an American name and not realising that Grunowsky *is* an American name.

His mother used to watch him playing with his father and tell him, "You do love your daddy, don't you." He did love his father. When he was still in grade school his parents used to tell him he was clever and he got good grades. His mother would tell people in his presence, "Donald's a great reader, he loves books." He read a lot. He liked hearing his mother tell people that he was a great reader.

] As he came to the door of Dr. Manash's office, a man he

had not met was coming out, looking thoughtful. Manash must start early, he reflected, but then he had a lot of people to get through.

The office belonged to Abbotsbury School's headmaster. It was a large room with a filing cabinet and three chairs and a polished walnut desk at one end. On the desk were a filing tray, telephone and photograph in a frame, all someone's personal stamp of possession, presumably the headmaster's. Manash evidently recognised this for he was not sitting at the desk but was standing in front of it, next to an armchair. He gestured Green into another armchair opposite and then sat down. It was not a deep leather armchair like the ones in the lounge but fabric-covered and with wooden arms. It was an armchair for serious talk. You could not sink into it..

Manash was dressed smartly, even elegantly, as he had been at dinner the evening before, with the same dark blue suit, striped shirt and silk tie. He did not start by asking Donald about his parents. He said, "Professor Green, I'd like you to tell me who you are."

Green frowned. "I filled out a form and sent in my cv, as requested," he said. "The form was a long one, as I remember, with a lot of questions. If you read it, you already know a lot about me."

"Yes, certainly I do," Manash replied and somehow Green believed him instantly. "But that told me what you have done. It even told me what you think about certain things. I would like you to tell me now who you are. How you see yourself." He sat back and put his fingers together in front of him.

Green hesitated. "I'm a Professor of International Relations at Columbia University," he began. Manash sat there, waiting for more. "I was born in New York City and I live there now, in a house in Riverdale. I bought it last year. I'm forty years old. I'm married to a lady called Lorraine. She's part-owner of an art boutique in New York. We have a daughter called Josephine, who's twenty-two months old." He stopped.

xxx

"I see," said Manash. "So you're a professor and a husband and a father, right?"

"Yes, that's right."

"And do you like being all of those things?"

"In the main, yes."

"Are you happy with your career?"

"One again, yes in the main."

"Are you happily married?"

"Yes."

"Do you love your wife?"

"Of course."

Manash frowned. "You say 'Of course.' What does that mean?"

"Well, it's normal for a husband to love his wife."

"But it's not automatic."

"No, but as I say, it's normal."

"So if you didn't love your wife, you wouldn't be a normal husband. I see."

"I suppose you could say that." Green had the uncomfortable feeling that this exchange had put him at a disadvantage.

Manash had a way of pausing and absorbing his reply, waiting for an exchange to settle before going on to the next one. The pause gave Green time to reflect on his accent. He recognised it as British English, but with a trace of liquid consonants that indicated that he had first learned to speak in another language.

"Tell me," Manash went on, "who would you be if you weren't some of those things? Would you still be you? What if you weren't a husband, for instance."

"I wasn't a husband five years ago. I was still me then."

"And if you weren't a Professor of International Relations what would you be?"

"I'd probably be an Assistant Professor of International Relations." He was feeling a little irritable now

"And would you still be you?"

"A slightly different me, I suppose."

"Waiting for promotion, right? So that you could be the 'you' you are now."

"Well, yes, I suppose I'd be looking for a full professorship. I guess I'm quite ambitious, if that's what you're getting at." When the interview began Green had been sitting back in his chair, deliberately assuming a relaxed posture, but now he was sitting upright.

Manash also sat forward now and assumed a didactic tone. "What I'm trying to do, you see, is find out what is the real you, the irreducible you. What is your identity, which things are part of the essence of Donald Green and which are merely contingent. How could you be something else? Perhaps a different kind of husband, or a different kind of professor?"

Green did not feel like stepping out to meet Manash halfway. He said, "That's for you to work out. It's your field. I gather you're going to change my identity for the game anyway."

"I can't change it entirely, rest assured," Manash replied. "But before I take away a little of your identity, temporarily, I want to know what it is I'm taking away. Or rather, helping you to give up for a short time. Have you ever had the feeling that you were had a different identity, or no identity? Just temporarily, I mean."

Green thought for a few moments and then shook his head. "I can't remember any time," he said.

"Well let's try to see when you started being you," Manash said. He asked him some questions about his childhood, and Green talked. He said he did not have a lot of friends in school but he always had enough, and being the class valedictorian at his high school graduation pleased him because he knew it made his parents proud. He said his parents were decent people and good parents despite the fact that they were not very successful in their careers.

"Do you feel comfortable being you?" Manash asked.

"Fairly comfortable, yes. I'm not totally self-satisfied, of course."

"Would you rather be different in some ways? Some small ways, perhaps?"

Green thought about this for a moment. The question was intrusive and not the kind he liked to answer but now, to his surprise, he found himself trying to respond.

"I think I'd like to be - more - I think more sparkling. Wittier. I have a sense of humour but I'm sort of slow." He was speaking haltingly. "No, not slow exactly, I can work things out quite quickly. But I'd like to be brilliant. I'm intelligent, I've got a good analytical brain, but I'm not brilliant. I don't sparkle. Like some others do. The truth is that the papers I've written - they were good, but the ideas weren't at all original. And the writing style was a bit heavy. I know that. They were a synthesis of - well, very few papers have really original ideas. Hell, there are only a few original ideas in any decade, if that."

Despite himself, he warmed to his theme, saying things he had often thought but never said out loud. "Some people get enormous attention just because of slick presentation. They have a clever way of putting things, they coin a phrase that catches on, maybe. 'The End of History.' 'The Clash of Civilizations.' That kind of thing. And some of them go on television and everybody knows who they are and they can command big salaries." He stopped, and looked a little sheepish.

"Anything else?" Manash asked encouragingly.

He had said far too much already, but he found himself going on.. "I'd like to be more successful with women. To have been. In the past. In college most of the others had more sex than me and more choice of girl friends. And even now - " he stopped, and clenched his lips tight. Then he said, "I'd definitely like to be taller. I suppose everyone below average

xxxiii

height would like to be taller. And maybe - no, I'd like to be taller and that's it." He stopped abruptly.

Dr. Manash said, "You're trying hard, aren't you?"

"What do you mean?"

"You're trying hard to become something better."

"Yes, of course. I've always tried to better myself. Doesn't one always try to make oneself something better?"

He was not in good humour when he left Manash's office. He was rattled by all those questions about who he really was, and even more by the fact that he had done his best to answer them. What was it about Dr. Manash? And what was that exchange about loving his wife? Dammit, he thought, it *is* normal for a man to love his wife.

He had held back a bit. When Manash asked him whether he had ever felt not quite sure of who he was, just such a time came to his mind. The memory was disagreeable. He had gone into hospital for an internal examination, an unpleasant procedure, because of the possibility, happily unfounded, that there was a growth in his lower bowel. He was only in the hospital for a couple of hours. He had to take off all his clothes except his underpants and put on a white hospital gown.

It was a skimpy garment that covered him only to the knees and the elbows, and tied up behind it barely came together to cover his buttocks. It made him look ridiculous. He had to walk through the corridor into the x-ray area. There he saw a few other patients in the same garments. They also looked ridiculous but some, taller and straighter than him and with more muscular limbs, looked less so. He saw himself in a mirror at one stage and there was absolutely nothing in the sight to command respect. Nobody could know by looking at him that he was a professor and was buying a house in Riverdale, on a leafy street where houses had trees on their front lawns. He was glad when he had his clothes back on and Lorraine, wearing her smart new Spring coat from Bonwit

Teller that her mother had bought her, was there to collect him and he was himself again.

He decided to go into the lounge and get a coffee. Walking along the corridor, he straightened his shoulders. He was conscious of his walk. He had short legs and he had learned long ago to walk with measured strides so as not to give the impression of scuttling along.

Louis Mannion was in the lounge talking to Thaxted and another man who was wearing a track suit and trainers and with a towel draped around his neck. Green took a cup of coffee and some biscuits from the sideboard and sat down next to them without waiting for an invitation. "I've just come from my first session with Dr. Manash and I need some sustenance," he explained.

The man in the track suit introduced himself. He was Captain Raymond Wade, an American who taught at the National War College..

"You've been jogging?" he asked Captain Wade.

Wade nodded. "There's some nice running along the river bank here."

Thaxted indicated the walkman at his side. "You listen to music while you're running?"

Wade nodded. "The classics mostly. The Rolling Stones, that sort of thing. Not modern stuff, I'm afraid."

Thaxted grinned. "I listen to music when I'm at the gym. The real classics, mostly. It takes away the strain."

"I went to a performance of Beethoven's Fifth at the Kennedy Centre last month that was great," Wade said. "Ordinary stuff I know, but I enjoyed it. It's my wife's influence. I never went to concerts before I was married."

"We go often," Thaxted said.

Louis said he liked opera, and they talked about music for a while. Green was silent. He quite liked some popular songs and he often had music as background, but just sitting down and listening to music seemed to him a waste of time. If you read a book you learned something more to add to your store of knowledge. Even if it was a novel it was a story you carried around with you, and you could talk to other people about it. You had something you didn't have before. With music there was nothing you could take away.

Wade said suddenly, "Hey, you know what? I've just realised that we won't know who's won the World Series. It'll be decided while we're locked away."

"That's a thought," Green said.

"I don't suppose we'll be allowed to get the news," Wade went on.

Louis said, "Anyway, if you're some Caribbean politician or whatever, you won't care about American baseball."

"You don't realise how serious that is, you're not American," Wade said.

"Yes I am," Louis said.

"You're an American?" Wade asked, surprised.

"My mother was an American," Louis said. "And I'm quite a good first baseman."

"Do you have an American passport?" Green asked.

"Do you stand up when they play *The Star Spangled Banner*?" Wade asked. "Do you get white-knuckled over the World Series?"

"Yes, no and I used to," Louis said. "I have dual citizenship. Do *you* stand up when they play *The Star Spangled Banner*?

"Sure. I'm a patriotic American," Wade replied. Louis could not tell whether he was being serious or sardonic. Wade was shorter than average, with a trim, upright figure and a thin moustache that made him look to Louis like a film star of the 1940s.

Louis wished he followed baseball as he once had and knew who was likely to win the World Series. He had even forgotten who was playing. He felt at home among Americans, swinging with their swing, as he put it to himself.

xxxvi

He did not like feeling that Americans regarded him as a foreigner. He wanted to be able to lambast the American President or draw attention to the stupidities of Americans as an American, rather than being regarded if he did so as an anti-American Brit.

He had never played much cricket but he took to baseball when he was in America. It was a slow game compared to cricket. Runs were scored infrequently and one could go some time without even a hit. But he enjoyed the nervy, noisy atmosphere of the baseball diamonds, the constant talking it up, the dash for a bouncing ball along the ground, the race between fielders and a base runner. He had happy memories of the baseball diamond. He would recall with pleasure the few times that his performance drew applause from the spectators, or the adrenalin rush of racing between the bases or leaping to catch a fly ball. But was also happy just standing on first base, pounding his fist into his first baseman's mitt, part of the team as they all called out encouragement to one another – "Way to go!" "Attaboy!" "Let's play heads-up ball!" He felt buoyed up by the banter and the comradeship.

Shemtov came by and saw them. He was on his way to see Dr. Manash and would not have much time but he had an idea that Green was Jewish and he thought it would be good to know another Jewish person here. Louis introduced him and invited him to sit down.

"Just for a moment," Shemtov said. "I'm on my way to see Dr. Manash." He sat down tentatively, on the edge of one of the wooden chairs.

"Donald here has just been," Louis said.

"How is he?" Shemtov asked."

"He dug deep," Green replied.

"Tell me, have these pills had any effect on you?" Louis asked the others..

"Not yet, no, I haven't felt any," Green said. Then the thought came to him that maybe it was the pills that had made him open up to Manash the way he had. "Have they had any on you?"

"I have to go and pee all the time," Mannion said.

"They must have some effect, otherwise we wouldn't be taing them," Wade observed.

Green turned to Shemtov and asked, "What's your area? The Middle East?"

Shemtov replied, "No. I've been working on the international system and theories of the state."

Green asked, "Do you know Ya'ir Levi at the Jaffa Centre for International Studies?"

"Not personally. I've heard him speak."

Green nodded and turned back to talk to Wade. Shemtov said, "I've got to go, my appointment's now. I'll see you later."

Walking towards Manash's office, Shemtov acknowledged to himself that he was still an outsider among these people. He was not yet relaxed enough to talk about going to the toilet, as that Englishman had just done. It was something to do with not being either European or American.

::   ::   ::

`Jacob Shemtov usually told the truth and always felt that he was lying. He knew that what he told people was never really the truth.

`If he talked about growing up and his life at home with his mother, whatever he said, he was leaving out the sight and smell of his mother's bedroom and the myriad other impressions, from the smears of make-up on the bedsheets to the scratches in the wallpaper to the slapping sound her slippers made on the floorboards and the different tones of her voice, which he could recall but not describe. He did not know how to explain all that. He could not ever say everything about the maids they had who seemed to play a big part in his home life when he was a child, the ones his mother liked and the ones she swore at. He did not want to recall the foul, horrible things he and his mother occasionally shouted at each other. Even the things he could put into words he could not say. And there were other things about him and his mother that could not talk about because he was not sure about, things that were not remembered but left as an after impression in his mind, things imprecise and shadowy but that he felt were shameful.

"I teach at Tel Aviv University." But that did not even hint at the web of anxieties that surrounded his position, his work at changing the course material, the personalities of his students, some friendly, some shy, some questing, some pushy, some several of these things, or the clatter of the canteen at lunch-time, or the mixture of camaraderie and competitiveness in the faculty common room, or the dismal sense of failure that hung over him these days when he contemplated his academic status and the number of times he had been passed over for promotion. It sounded fixed and positive, a solid life, but he felt his life was tenuous and negative. He could not possibly explain all these things. He did not know how and it would take a million words to begin.

Or, "I was a Major in the Armoured Corps." This was true, it was a matter of record. Yet it conveyed a false impression of military success, even - since he had taken part in a war - of heroism. It left out his struggles to fill a role that he felt most of the time was not really his, his changes of mind about leaving the army, his doubts about his authority over his men and just about everything else, his failure to be a part of the in-group among the officers of his generation, and the sterile cleanliness of officers' quarters and the *endless* analysis of tactics and operations and his anxious fixation at times on map co-ordinates and the mechanical parts of a tank. Most of all, he could not explain what any of this felt like, being in the army or living with his mother or going to work on the campus.

When he said, "I'm divorced and yes, we do have one child, a daughter of eighteen," this was such a huge part of his life, and he was leaving out so much just telling it like this, that it seemed like an enormous lie. He had not been a husband and Miriam had not been a wife in a way that fitted into the slots that came with those words.

He sometimes wondered whether anyone really fitted into the shaped slots that were this word or that word, like "husband" or "daughter" or "Major", whether seeming to fit into them was not just an act that people put on. He could only use the same words that other people used to recount a life or a marriage or a career, but these things had happened to him and not to other people so it was all different and the words meant something different. Explaining his life in words was like trying to make a statue out of liquid. It was a lie to pretend that he could do so.

To tell the truth he would have to tell everything he could, much more than he could, some of it childish things, even infantile things, making sure there was nothing hidden away. He would have to dig deep into his feelings, root around there, drag up feelings that he did not have words for and somehow explain these. He would have to take off all his clothes, strip naked, show his body, and then go further, peel off his skin, exposing his bones, and finally his blood vessels, his heart and lungs and kidneys and intestines, and then say, "Here it is, this is me, this is what I'm trying to tell you!"

Sitting opposite Dr. Manash he was upright and alert, loose but ready.

"I see that you have some experience of psychiatrists," Manash said.

Shemtov flinched and then nodded. "That's right."

"At one time, you had quite extensive psychotherapy."

Shemtov nodded again. He knew he would have to answer questions about this and he did not mind so long as he was talking to a doctor. He said, "Yes. I told you that on the form because you asked the question. Not many other people know it."

"You don't talk about it."

"Not to most people, no, of course not."

"That was following your experiences in the war."

"In the Yom Kippur War in 1973, yes."

"You fought in that war."

"Yes. I was in tanks. I had a squadron of Shermans."

"I may ask you about that later on," Manash said. "I want to ask you something else first. A preliminary question. Who are you? Who do you consider yourself to be?"

Shemtov shrugged. "Jacob Shemtov. An Israeli. Fifty-one years old. Five-foot-nine. Seventy-one point two kilos. A lecturer in international relations."

"You put being an Israeli first. Would you be a different person if you weren't an Israeli? If you'd been born somewhere else?"

"Yes. A very different person."

"So being an Israeli is an essential part of you."

"Absolutely. I spent two years in America, at the University of California in Los Angeles. I met Israelis who'd emigrated to America and become Americans. I couldn't imag in advance.

"Why is that?"

"I think it's partly a generation thing. When I grew up we were still building a state. We were surrounded by enemy nations. If you left Israel you felt you would be deserting. Younger people don't feel the same way. I suppose it's partly my father's influence also. Although he died a long time ago."

"When you were thirteen, as I recall."

"Yes, you've done your homework. Just after my barmitzphar"

"Was it sudden?"

Shemtov nodded. "Yes. He had a heart attack."

xli

"You mention your father's influence. What was his influence?"

"My father's background was the Holocaust. His parents were Polish. He was sent to Palestine, as it was , when he was young, but his parents and his whole family were wiped out. Israel meant to him salvation. Not just for him but for the Jewish people. I was raised with that idea from the time I could understand anything. I could never think of Israel as a country like any other"

"Would he have been happy about your going into the army and defending the country."

"The regular army, you mean, everyone in Israel goes into the army. Yes, I think he would have been proud. For him, it wasn't just defending Israel, it was defending the Jewish people. Mind you, the army then, the army I joined, was a different one from the army today. It still had its roots in the Haganah. A lot of men still remembered the War of Independence, when only the other side had tanks. And that was before Israel became the world's favourite bad boy."

"And your mother?"

"She was worried that I might be killed. Which is natural, I suppose."

"Did she feel the same way as he did about Israel?"

"No. She was a different kind of person."

"Different in which way?"

Shemtov pondered the question and spoke even more carefully now. "She was probably more selfish than my father. Probably more intelligent. Stronger. I often wondered why they married. She was young when she married him. I suppose she was in love with him. She said he was very handsome."

"She owned a shop, is that right?"

"She had a shop selling Israeli arts and crafts. To tourists mostly."

"And she died two years ago."

"That's right."

"Were you close to her?"

He hesitated now. He had worked out set answers about his parents that he used glibly in conversation, but this was more serious and he was nervous about going on.

"After my father died - she missed him, she was very lonely. She - we quarrelled a lot. Violent quarrels. Well, not exactly violent. I mean– I suppose yes, violent. It's - . sometimes we were close." He was uncomfortably aware that his speech had become disjointed. He had to get back on track. "We quarrelled. But I was an only child, there was no husband, just the two of us, so I suppose we were close."

"You decided to stay in the army after you finished your national service. Why was that?"

"I didn't know what I wanted to do, but I was doing well in the army, which was a fluke really, and that was a good feeling. At least I thought I was doing well for a while."

"They gave you a commission."

"I was good on tactics in school. Not much else. The army offered me a permanent commission. They said I could go to university and get my degree. I went back after university with the idea that it would be temporary, and then came the war. Then later they said I could take up the fellowship at U.C.L.A. and decide afterwards. They like educated officers. I was still undecided about what to do when I came back from California."

"So you stayed in the army because you didn't know what else to do?"

"I suppose so. Looking back, I think I stayed in the army also partly to please my father, who was dead. And to spite my mother.. She used to badmouth my father, telling me what a lousy life she had with him. That used to make me angry. I thought that if I was killed it would serve her right. And I was insecure, there was that too."

"And the army gave you security?"

"Yes. You know where you are in the army. You have a position, you fit into the scheme of things. That can be a good thing if you get depressed and anxious. It may sound odd but I stayed in the army partly out of cowardice. And I had a purpose. I did want to defend my country. It needs defending. You talk to people in other countries, they don't always realise that. That all seemed simpler then than it does now. I don't think I'd like to be in the army now. But I stayed in the army too long. The last year-and-a-half I was lecturing on international relations at the staff college so I wasn't a real soldier."

"And now?"

The university isn't all that different   You have a position, you know where you are. It may not be one you like but at least it's there, other people recognise it."

"You've worked it all out," Manash said.

"What do you mean?"

Manash leaned back in his armchair and pressed his fingertips together in front of him and contemplated them for a while. Shemtov noted his smooth hands and onyx cufflinks. He recognised them as onyx because his mother had a lot of it in her shop. Manash explained, "I'm impressed with how clearly you have articulated a lot of your own psychology. Your attitude to your country and its roots, and to your career and your motivations. It's all wrapped up, all tidy. You'd obviously worked this out before you came here."

Shemtov knew he was right. "Yes, I suppose so," he agreed. "When your life goes wrong you go over it all, and you have to figure it out. A lot of sessions with a psychiatrist also. And what you haven't figured out then, you work out later."

"So there's not much for me to do. You see, Major Shemtov - should I call you that?"

"I'd rather Mr. Shemtov. I've been out of the army for a long time. Or Jacob."

"Okay, Jacob. You've constructed a story out of your life. It's an edifice that's complete. It's like a closed circle. There are no loose ends, nothing for me to grab hold of. Do you understand?"

"You think I'm inventing parts of the story?"

"No. no, I don't mean that. You're telling me a lot about yourself truthfully and frankly. But in doing so you've built a defensive wall with no hand holds. Yes?"

"I don't think I've given a very flattering pictuer of myself."

"No, you haven't built yourself up. If you had, you could be knocked down. On the contrary. You're cutting yourself down before anyone else can do it. You're telling me the story the way you want to tell it. You're giving away a lot, certainly. But I have the feeling that you've decided in advance that you'll give away so much and no more. Am I right?"

Shemtov felt he could concede this to Manash. "I don't think I've exactly decided in advance. But I suppose I'll give away only what I want to give away, you're right about that. I don't like being forced to give things away. Does anyone?"

Manash did not answer. He said, "I notice that you stayed in the army after your breakdown."

"Yes. I'd actually planned to leave then but I changed my mind. I stayed in for three years more. It was easier to get over it in the army. And I didn't have the courage to leave."

"I used the word 'breakdown.' Is that correct? Would you call it that?"

Shemtov clenched his lips tightly, imprisoning the answer inside, and then released it. "The army gave me sick leave for a little while, that was official, so I suppose you could call it a breakdown. I was never locked up in a loony bin. I kept up an act for most people. I appeared to be functioning approximately normally."

"Why did you finally leave the army?"

"I'd decided by that time that I wasn't going to be a

general. Which was actually pretty clear from the start. My breakdown or whatever you want to call it was on my record. Which wasn't good. And there was more. I'd been in combat and I didn't think I could go through that again and do well. I think I would probably go to pieces."

"But you didn't go to pieces when you were in combat before."

"The army said I did what I should have done. I don't understand how. No, getting out was the right thing. I left just before Lebanon '82. I'm glad I wasn't in the army then."

"Why is that?"

"I was against the war. At any rate, the turn it took. I took part in demonstrations against it. The only time I ever took part in a political demonstration. And the second Lebanon war was a disaster. I certainly wouldn't want to have any part of that."

"How do you feel about the occupied territories? The West Bank?"

"Ah. That's more complicated."

"Yes, it is. What's your view? Do you think Israel should get out?"

"Yes. But not just like that. We should get out of most of it. I always thought that. I've no sympathy with the settlers. The army has behaved badly there, which is inevitable. An army of occupation always behaves badly. But some of the things that are happening surprise even me. But there is a security problem, it's not imaginary. Look, there are a lot of things my country is doing that I don't like. But it's still my country."

"So how much would you give up? Most of the West Bank?"

"Yes, most of it, perhaps all of it. But they shouldn't be allowed to force us out. That's important."

"So you'll give away what you want to give away and you won't be forced to give away more."

Shemtov smiled ruefully. "I suppose I walked into that one," he said.

Manash started on another tack. "How do you feel about changing identities?"

"Fine. I rather look forward to it."

"Why is that?"

Shemtov looked away now, out of the window, taking a rest for the moment before tackling the question. He saw an English lawn with the first of the autumn leaves scattered about, curled and stiff and brittle like sea shells. He wanted to go on studying the leaves instead of answering Manash. He spoke reluctantly. "I don't like my identity very much. I'm not a very happy person. I wouldn't mind changing it for another one for a while."

"Do you want to tell me some of the things that you don't like about yourself?"

Now he retreated. He gave a dismissive wave of his hand and mumbled, "Oh, I'm in an unhappy period of my life right now. It would be good to get away from it for a while."

When Manash waited for something more, he added, "I've been writing a paper that I'd like to turn into a book. I mentioned that on the form you gave me. And it isn't – it isn't working out. It isn't really very good. I don't think my heart is in it." Manash waited some more. "A number of other things aren't working out." His voice trailed off.

He left Manash's office thinking over what he had said and what he had not said. As always he felt his smooth articulation was fraudulent and his stumbling half-utterances were more truthful.

"I had a squadron of Shermans." What a lie that was. The sentence had tripped out just the way he had heard others say it. The possessive verb gave an impression of authority, like saying "my men." It implied command of men in battle, leadership, bravery. It was nothing like the terrified figure he remembered himself to be on those days on the Golan, struggling to assess the situation and somehow barking out orders that mostly reflected what he was being told from above, or what he had been trained to do, like a bad actor.

Certainly he had held back things from Dr. Manash. He had not told him how really awful his life was. He had not told him how he had jumped at the chance to take part in this experiment as a possible escape from his situation, a chance to get away from his mind and into another. He had not told him how unhappy he really was. He had not told him that most days, at the start of the day, he wished he were dead, nor that for the second time in his life he was seriously considering committing suicide.

He decided to go and look at Oxford. He forgot about his ankle for the moment. He set out through some narrow side streets. It was a balmy day, warm for September with the last of the summer weather. The leaves on the trees and the perfectly trimmed hedges were beginning to brown but they seemed to be glowing in the sunshine like tiny newly polished shoes.

Suddenly a memory came to him, with unusual vividness. It was so strong that it seemed as if he was reliving the experience rather than just remembering it. His surroundings faded into a blur.

He was in Tel Aviv on a warm Spring evening some years ago, sitting with Meir Birnbaum at a café facing the beach at the end of Hayarkon Street, where the towering beach front hotels, the Dan and the Sheraton and the Hilton, give way to little shops and falaffal take-aways and cafés. They were sitting outside one of these cafés with beers on the plastic table, chatting and watching the strollers, a breeze from the sea cutting the sultry atmosphere.

As a child he had called Meir Birnbaum "Uncle Meir" although he was not his uncle but a cousin of his father's. He had not seen him for some years after his father died but then Meir had come back into his and his mother's life as a family friend. Now that he was older Jacob felt uncomfortable in their relationship. He could not really look on Meir as his friend although he knew Meir wanted him to.

Nonetheless, he found himself talking confidentially, telling him his doubts about whether he should take up the army's offer of a longterm commission. Meir was nodding understandingly and asking sensible questions about the alternatives. "I think you could go a long way if you wanted to stay in the army, Jacob," he was saying. "With a commission you're in a good position. And a few years as an army officer isn't a bad springboard to go into all sorts of things."

"It's an attractive idea, as I say.," Jacob replied.

"You haven't had combat experience, but if you stay in that will come."

"Because there'll be another war."

"There's bound to be. They won't leave us alone."

Meir always seemed to Jacob to be a man pleased with himself and with his place in the world. He was shorter than Jacob and comfortably corpulent, sitting there in a short-sleeved shirt with a silver bracelet on his wrist. In a vague way that he had only half thought-out, the silver bracelet, because it was such a superfluous accessory, represented a surplus that Meir always possessed, beyond the necessities of life. Jacob never had a surplus, he always had a sense of struggling to have just enough to keep going, enough money, enough style, enough friends, enough standing in the world.

Girls strolled by along the beach front in twos and threes in tiny mini-skirts, some with bare midriffs, some with tassels flicking enticingly across their tanned thighs. Meir would occasionally interrupt their conversation to make a cheerily salacious remark about this one's bouncing boobs or that one's ass. The remarks would have been natural enough if Jacob had been sitting with some other soldiers of his own age looking at the parade of sex appeal, but coming from Meir

xlix

they seemed false, a clumsy attempt to establish a male camaraderie.

"I'm trying to suggest some of the options, but in the end it's your choice," Meir said.

"I know, Meir," Jacob said. "Indecision is my big failing. One of my big failings. The funny thing is, I've concealed it in the army."

"If you decide against the army and want to look for something else, let me know. I may have some ideas."

"Uh-huh. And you know a man," Jacob said, grinning.

"I may know a man," Meir agreed, returning his grin.

Meir always knew a man. When he went into the army Meir knew a man who could coach him for his interviews for the officers' training school. When his mother had to find new premises for her shop he knew a man who had a place to let. When he went to Los Angeles Meir knew a man there, a pillar of the local Jewish community, who invited him to his sumptuous house for dinner several times and dangled before him none too subtly the attractions of his daughter and a career in his retail chain.

"Meir has always been a good friend to us," his mother used to say. "And he likes you." Meir Birnbaum had given Jacob's father a job as a manager in his workshop after he had lost his job with a stationery firm. For a while they were regular visitors at Birnbaum's house where his wife Esther cooked splendid spicy meals as her Egyptian mother had taught her. Then Meir moved to Peta Tikva and came to Tel Aviv only occasionally.

Jacob found he had come out into a busy street and the noise of the traffic brought him back to his present reality. Hayarkon Street and Meir Birnbaum faded away. He saw a newsagent's with postcards of Oxford in a rack outside. He went in and bought one to send to a couple who were friends, and one for Shula and after some hesitation, one to Miriam at the same address. He could not ignore his former wife while

I

his daughter was living with her.

He turned back towards the Abbotsbury School, stopping to look through the open gate of a college into the quadrangle, getting a glimpse of flat green lawns and stone battlements. How old and solid the buildings looked, with those straight vertical stone walls half-covered with ivy leading up to towers and spires. How deeply rooted in this English soil, how confident, giving assurance to the students who lived among them. These buildings were how old? Four hundred years? Five hundred years? Israel had roots going back three thousand years. Yet it did not seem nearly as solid. The white concrete buildings of Tel Aviv University were new and like most of Israel they looked new. His country's roots went deep into the land, but the plant was thin and brittle like a reed, and exposed to harsh, hostile winds. For all its faults, it had to be protected and watched over.

And he too, he felt thin and fragile, his continued existence uncertain, a tenant in the world with no security of tenure. For a while the army had given him a uniform, a rank, the guaranteed company of others. Lieutenant, and then, just because enough time had passed and he had been through a war, captain. He had never really been a major: that was a promotion given to him just before he left the army as a gift. His uniform and his place in the army shielded him from winds that could blow him away. In return he had agreed to risk his life. It was a good deal for him.

`His foot started to ache now and he turned back. He met Thaxted, the British Defence Ministry man. "Had to get something from the chemist," Thaxted said

They walked along together, talking about the F.I.S. conference in London and some of the speakers. Thaxted threw out sweeping comments with an off-hand casual manner that Shemtov envied. This one was the worst kind of American academic - "his prose sounds as if it's been translated from the German." That one had just one idea that

li

he keeps banging on about. Shemtov's comments were more tentative.

Thaxted noticed that he was limping slightly and asked, "What did you do to your foot?"

"I tripped over getting off a bus in London," Jacob replied. "Just clumsiness."

Thaxted slowed down to make it easier for Jacob to keep up with him. Jacob was almost glad that he had the limp. He was suffering in ways that no one could see but the sprained ankle was visible. He went on, "British people are really nice when you're in trouble. Several people rushed over to help me up."

"Wouldn't that happen in Israel?"

"I wouldn't count on it."

"Did they treat you well at the hospital?"

"Yes. I had to wait a long time. But they x-rayed it and decided that it was only slightly sprained. They took good care. They were nice to me."

"Good. I'm glad."

CHAPTER THREE

After leaving Cambridge University, Louis Mannion was a social worker for four years, first with a family welfare department in Nottingham, then attached to an inner city council in London. He dealt with society's losers: the poor, the feckless, the drunks, the addicts, the inadequate parents, people who were not very bright and could not cope and many who were just unlucky, men and women, young, middle-aged and old. He sat in his office or in their untidy, cramped, often squalid homes and listened to them and advised them and explained things to them again and again and argued with them. He managed to help some of them. A few were grateful0 to him, some let him down, some lied to him or cajoled him, two women made passes at him and one man punched him in the face.

Secretly, he felt inferior to all of them. These people bore wounds and they kept going. He doubted whether he would be brave enough to struggle on as they did with their inadequacies. Things came easily to him. He had never been unable to cope with life. He had been unhappy but not for long. He had ended love affairs more often than his lovers had. He had never been seriously short of money. He sometimes wondered what it would be like to be poor or crippled or ugly or stupid, to live with the burdens that some of his clients bore. He felt that he was a spectator to other people's struggles. He was riding in a taxi seeing through the window the long-distance runners panting and sweating as they forced their aching limbs along. He was leaning on the rails on a cruise liner watching fishermen in a tiny boat struggling against the battering of the waves for their livelihood.

His humility was not apparent. When people described him, they used words like "witty," "cool" and "urbane." When he first met his wife Sarah she was going out with another man. He challenged her on who she preferred and she smiled at him enigmatically and quoted from the Bible: "My brother Esau is a hairy man but you are a smoooooth man."

"I'm not always smooth," he protested. "I stutter sometimes."

When he was asked about his parents, Louis would sometimes say, "Quintessentially Hampstead middle-class. My father was a history professor, my mother was a psychotherapist and an American and we lived near Hampstead Heath. And my sister is a solicitor." He sometimes thought his temporary career as a social worker had been an attempt to break free of his clichéd background, taking up a job that was lower in social status that one that was expected of him. With his present career as a successful media figure, he was returning to the norm..

His parents were both strong-willed people whose wills nearly always coincided, which he realised later is rare and was fortunate for him. His upbringing was confined to one social class, although not to one country; the changes in his life were on a horizontal plane. He went to a private school and then on to Cambridge, where he studied politics and history. He spent several summers at his grandparents' home in Connecticut, and when he was fourteen and fifteen he spent two years in Ithaca while his father taught at Cornell, and slipped with ease into American high school social life, helped by the fact that girls found his English accent cute, got good grades and played on the school baseball team. Between school and Cambridge he spent nine happy months as an intern at a peace research institute in Washington D.C., and played softball with a local team.

His mother brought something else to his upbringing besides her nationality: she was a Roman Catholic, from an Italian-American Catholic family. In her young years she had marched behind a radical priest in civil rights demonstrations and against nuclear weapons. Her Jesus was the friend of the poor and oppressed, the man who drove the money-lenders from the temple. She told Louis about liberation theology and the priests who campaigned with opposition movements in Latin America, and when he was a teenager she gave him a book about Dorothy Day, the pacifist nun who worked in the New York slums.

Louis's agnostic father and Catholic mother reached a typically modern compromise on their children's upbringing. They agreed that they would go to Catholic Sunday school and learn about their mother's religion but that no pressure would be put upon them.

The Catholic education he received impressed him at the time although it did not seem to affect his sister. He accepted that he was a sinner as all men are, and that Jesus died on the cross to save him from the consequences. This was partly due to a young priest called Father Donovan, who made him feel, unlike most of the others who taught at the Sunday school, that one could be a Catholic and not superstitious and narrow-minded. Father Donovan used to visit his Sunday school to chat with some of the boys, chats that went deeper than just going over the liturgy. He took a particular interest in Louis and for a while, when Louis was thirteen, they used to talk about big questions of religion and morality, sometimes walking in the park and sometimes by themselves in an empty classroom. Father Donovan told him once that he looked forward all week to these meetings. Then one day he did something that Louis understood only much later. He took Louis's head in his hands and stroked his hair and said he would have to give up these chats much as he enjoyed them. There were tears in his eyes. He said he was sure Louis would go on in life to find the answers to the questions they had been discussing. Father Donovan did not come back to the Sunday school after that.

For a while, Louis used to pray. He would pray for help when he had not done his homework, asking not to be found out, and when he was younger, to be spared the attention of a thuggish school bully. He would pray for forgiveness for having upset his parents unnecessarily, or for looking in the windows of houses at night hoping to see a woman undressing, or for some of his masturbation fantasies about rape. He knew he was a sinner. He knew he thought too much of himself and not enough of other people. He would pray for guidance sometimes when the conflicting demands of friends perplexed him. He found it difficult to pray to God. He knew God was capable of infinite mercy, but God was all-powerful, all-knowing, ruling all existence, and it seemed impertinent to pluck at his sleeve and ask him to turn his attention to his problems. Particularly as other people had much greater problems more deserving of God's time and attention. He was not in danger of dying, he had not lost a limb or gone blind.

He would pray instead to Jesus, who died on the cross for his and Mankind's sins. Jesus seemed more real and human and therefor more approachable, even though his suffering was immeasurably far beyond any troubles that Louis could bring to him. He felt humble even addressing him. Or else he would pray to the Virgin Mary, who was a mother and seemed to be available for sympathy and comfort. He learned to address her as "Mother of God"

This all fell away in his late teens, however, and he stopped going to Sunday school and lapsed into the secular environment around him. Sometimes he missed his old religious beliefs, in the way that one sometimes misses as an adult the innocent intensity of adolescent love. If pressed, as he sometimes was in discussion, he would say he was an unbeliever. "Not a doubter, an unbeliever. I don't believe." It seemed obvious to him that for all the sophisticated language with which modern theologians surrounded the concept, God, and particularly the Catholic God, was a person, a projection, a father-figure. God could not be an abstraction. A university chaplain once asked him whether he did not think there was a certain spiritual value in praying whatever one's belief about God, that the attitude of humility it involved was a spiritually healthy one. He replied heatedly, "No. Because whatever you say you're praying to somebody, and *there's nobody there!*"

At Cambridge he wrote for an undergraduate magazine, gaining a reputation with pen-portraits of faculty members, some of them astringent, a few laudatory. He took part in student demonstrations against Government policies in the Middle East and Third World debt.

In his last year he acquired a girl friend who was not at the university but was studying for a diploma in social work and working on a council estate in the town, "trying to help people beat the fucking system," as she put it. He admired her dedication and decided to take up a career in social work. He would not try to fight against evils far away but, like the Good Samaritan, he would help his neighbour. It sometimes pleased him that his occupation would rank lower in social status than those his fellow-undergraduates were aiming at, and then he would rebuke himself for being proud of his humility. In the religious phase of his adolescence he used to think that of the seven deadly sins, pride was the one to which he was most prone, apart from lust, of course.

He took a one-year course and applied for and got a job with the Nottingham Social Services Department. He was aware, could not help but be aware, that his background was more sophisticated and more privileged than that of his colleagues. He tried to dress the part, wearing a jacket with leather patches on the elbows and non-descript shirts and ties. He did not talk about Cambridge or about his London friends. But he could not conceal his background. At an office Christmas party, a young woman in the department who had been flirting with him for weeks stroked his shirt front drunkenly and told him, "You have an image problem, Louis darling."

He wanted to be back in London and he got a job in an inner city council, and here his image problems became more pronounced. Now he saw a lot of his old friends from school and Cambridge, and although he made a few friends among his co-workers, the difference between their social lives was apparent. He sensed that most felt that he did not fit in and that the director who hired him had made a bad choice.

He started writing articles for a national newspaper about the problems social workers encountered, some funny, some angry. He wrote under a pseudonym, but he was pleased with the articles and let people know that he was the author. He was feeling ill-at ease in his office environment, and when his employers objected to his writing articles about his work and told him he had to choose between social work and free-lance journalism, this gave him a way out.

He got a job on a newspaper he had written for, and because of his background they made him the social services correspondent. He learned the reporter's trade on the hoof, acquiring news sense and contacts. He said he wanted to broaden his field and was allowed to join the team covering an American Presidential election. He was a better writer than reporter and he made his mark with some witty features, similar to the things he used to write as a Cambridge undergraduate. A radio current affairs panel game tried him out as a contestant, and he soon succumbed to the temptation to entertain and became a regular, and he also took part in some television discussion programmes. Then the *Sunday Chronicle* hired him and gave him a regular column, promising its readers "Louis Mannion's independent and sometimes quirky viewpoint."

One media commentator, noting that he was known more as a radio and TV personality than a journalist, said when his column was announced that this was one more instance of the quality press going downmarket. "Downmarket? Hell's fucking bells!" he exclaimed furiously when he saw this, and he quoted Aristotle, Byron and Einstein in his first two columns. He was also negotiating to front a TV series on the rise and decline of the welfare state, although there were signs now that the company might get a former minister to do it instead.

He sometimes missed his days as a social worker. The problems he had grappled with then were gritty and down-to-earth: whether this one or that one would get a job, get off drugs, get away from her husband, connect with his children. He occasionally ran into old colleagues in social work and they would chat, embarrassingly aware of the distance between them. They seemed almost to look up to him, which made him feel guilty. So, he thought, I know the people they read about in newspapers and I'm friends with some of the people they see on television. Big deal. They help people. I don't. If I died I might get an obituary but nobody would be worse off.

He worried, in the recesses of his mind, about the rewards that came to him and the ease with which they came. Sarah understood this. She said to him, "Poor Louis. You want to be a prophet, you preach to the multitude about their sins, and you find you're not martyred, you're rewarded handsomely."

His anxieties about undeserved applause often fixed on an afternoon in Washington several years earlier, during his spell with the peace research office. It was the day before the Thanksgiving weekend, and he and three others took off early and went to a nearby bar in a mood of end-of-term jollity. The others were two young men and a girl who had just joined the office, Beth, a pretty blonde with a fresh, toothy, schoolgirl face and breasts which usually nestled behind a loose-weave woollen sweater with the nipples pointing through her bra.

A television set behind the bar was showing a news programme and at one point a scientist came on urging cuts in military spending. A naval officer was sitting at the bar and now, his tongue loosened by drink, he threw out a comment for anyone who wanted to catch it. "That kind of thing gets my goat. They don't seem to realise that we don't live in their nice, cosy, liberal world. There are wolves out there."

"Absolutely right," one of Louis's group said from the booth where they sat. "What's the good of having the finest country in the world if you're not willing to defend it?" His bombastic tone was parody but the Naval officer missed this.

"I'm glad you feel that way," he replied enthusiastically, turning around on his bar stool to address them. "So many young people don't understand that."

Then the four of them started agreeing with everything the man said, picking the idea up from one another, egging him by making more extravagantly conservative statements. They avoided eye-contact with one another so that they could keep straight faces. "We need more good old-fashioned patriotism." "The more the rest of the world is like America, the better it will be for everyone."

The Navy officer came over and showed them that day's Washington Post with an account of a fashionable gathering for a liberal cause. "What can you make of people like these?" he asked "These arty liberals, they tell America what it should do, but they're totally out of touch with ordinary Americans and they don't really care about them."

Going along with the game, Louis nodded understandingly.
"We have people like that at home in England," he said.
The Navy man told him, "We call them the white wine and
brie cheese set."

"Oh, they sound like awful people!" Louis exclaimed, and
the other man nodded vigorously. "No taste at all," Louis went
on. "I mean, what kind of people would drink white wine with
brie? Brie deserves a strong red burgundy, a Beaujolais
maybe, or at least a Côte du Rhone." The Navy man nodded
again but he was uneasy now. He was aware that something
was wrong with the reply but he could not move fast enough
to keep up. Louis kept a straight face.

The butt of their game left a few minutes later and the
others chortled and clapped Louis on the shoulder. He had
played the best. "You *nasty* man," Beth said to him gleefully,
"treating that poor man like that," and the others knew that he
would be the one to sleep with her.

Later, however, Louis saw the scene differently. He saw a
bunch of smart-ass youngsters making fun of an older man,
probably a decent guy, with far more experience of life than
they had, who had probably served his country with
dedication and with some skill, even if he did not know about
Côte du Rhone and Beaujolais. Louis worried about his easy
victory on that occasion and the approbation it had brought
him, as he worried about the ease with which the good things
of life had come to him.

He sat opposite Manash now, his legs crossed, leaning
back. He looked relaxed, or hoped he did, but he did not feel
relaxed. He was worried that that he might not he in control,
that any of his inner thoughts might spill out of him through
his porous skin, which now seemed as weak a container as his
bladder had been since he started taking the pll..

Manash asked him how he had liked being a social worker,
and Louis told him something about it, and then Manash said,

"You've changed professions. You appear on radio and television now. And you're a journalist. Is that right? Should I call you a journalist?"

"Do you mean do I identify myself as a journalist?"

The sides of Manash's mouth twitched in the direction of a smile. "I suppose that word 'identify' is going around. All right, yes, do you identify yourself as a journalist?"

"Well I didn't set out to be a journalist. I didn't study journalism. And I didn't come up through the usual route, starting on a small newspaper. And I don't report things now, I just write. And a big part of my income comes from radio. But yes, I'm a journalist."

"There were an awful lot of negatives there. You seem doubtful. You trained as a social worker. Do you identify with that profession?"

"No, not now. I suppose I never did, altogether. Which is not to say that I wasn't good at it. Somebody once said I was playing a part."

"And I notice that you've kept your American citizenship."

"Yes. I have dual nationality."

"You're an Englishman with a career in England. Do you feel partly American?"

"A bit, yes."

"Do you like the idea of being just a little different from others around you in having another nationality? Or perhaps you haven't thought about that."

"No," Louis said slowly, "I don't think I have. But yes, perhaps you're right, perhaps I do sort of like it." He thought he had himself figured out but he had not thought of this before.

"And the real you, the real Louis Mannion, is not altogether a journalist, not a social worker, nor altogether an Englishman nor an American nor a - what?"

"A bit of all of those things, I suppose," Louis replied.

"Do you find that a comfortable position to be in? Not

fitting into one category?"

"I think so, yes."

"You have the feeling that you can't be pinned down."

"I suppose so. Well no, I'm not sure that thought has occurred to me." Louis was frowning now. Manash paused giving him a chance to say something, but he had nothing to say so Manash went on.

"If you were pinned down, would you feel - say, confined? Confined in an identity, in a role?"

"Perhaps I would, yes. Though I don't know that it would bother me."

"And limited? After all, it would define you, and therefor limit you, wouldn't it?"

Louis frowned again. "No. I don't know that I ever feel that. Well – maybe, I do, a bit. Perhaps I like not fitting neatly into a niche Being a cliché."

Manash nodded understandingly, and paused again, then said, "You're married. That's a limiting condition, isn't it? It sort of defines you."

"Yes. But I'm not unhappy about that."

"How long have you been married?" Manash was looking down at the carpet, dropping the questions casually.

"Five years."

"Do you love your wife?"

"Certainly. She's pregnant."

Manash looked up sharply. "That's a curious thing to say."

"Why?"

"Well, one doesn't usually love someone because she's pregnant. That's not a reason."

Louis had the feeling that a trap had snapped shut. He shook his head in disagreement. "It's not much fun being pregnant. She's going through it and bearing a baby for both of us. We both want a baby."

"So?"

Louis was taken aback at having to explain what seemed obvious. "Well, I married her because I loved her. It would be pretty shitty if I stopped loving her now that she's pregnant, wouldn't it?"

"Yes, I suppose it would," Manash agreed. "But then, we can't decide who we love and when we love them. We can't love someone because it would be shitty not to." He looked intently into Louis's face now. "Can we?"

Louis was sitting upright. "No, I suppose not. But I do love her."

There followed another of Manash's silences. Louis had spent enough time in the media to recognise this as a television interviewer's trick. You leave a silence and the subject feels he has to fill it by saying something, perhaps something he had not intended to say. He knew the trick but he also knew he was falling for it. He could not sustain the silence.

He said, "Look, this is strictly confidential, isn't it? Because if I'm going to talk about my married life I want to be absolutely sure of that."

"Yes, it's confidential. I'm bound here by the rules of the medical profession."

"But more than that. You won't be making any reports, or put anything on file or anything."

"Absolutely not. This session is just for the purposes of the game."

"And Ivor Howe and the others won't know about anything I tell you."

"Definitely not."

Louis hesitated again but it was only for form. The words were spilling out of him and he could not stop them. "All right, I'll tell you. I love Sarah - that's my wife. We've had some quarrels lately. She can be selfish, in ways that I didn't realise before. But me too, I can be very self-centered, not look at how things seem to somebody else. But I still love her. She's a fine person. She loves me, I know. She deserves my support now."

He paused. He wanted some encouragement to go on but he did not get it. Manash sat waiting. He went on anyway. "But I'm also in love with someone else. So I'm betraying Sarah." Now he fell silent. Saying those two sentences had exhausted him.

After a few moments Manash asked, "Do you see this other person?"

"Yes. We love each other."

"And do you - ?"

"Yes. We're lovers."

"You seem to find this an unhappy position to be in."

"Yes, very. But that sounds as if loving this person is making me unhappy. It isn't. It's making me very happy. It's - oh, if I go on I'll sound like a lovesick schoolboy."

"So? Go on."

"All right. I feel all sorts of emotions with Tess - that's this other person's name - an intensity of emotion, that I thought I couldn't f-f-feel again. I thought it was the sort of thing you only feel when you're young. I do love Sarah. I care about her, I don't want to see her hurt, I don't like lying to her. When I married her, well, we enjoyed each other's company enormously and I had all sorts of loving, tender feelings towards her. I still have. And of course we were attracted to each other physically. But with Tess – there's an enormous physical attraction, but there's more also. I didn't think I'd ever feel like this with anyone. When I married I thought I would always be faithful. But I want to go on s-s- seeing Tessr. G-g-g-giving her up would be like turning my back on life. Like dying."

Louis felt that his insides were wobbling. These were all the things he had never said out loud before.

"So being with her makes you happy."

"Yes. Very. But the situation makes me unhappy."

"Because you feel you're betraying your wife."

"Yes, because I'm lying to Sarah. That's what I h-h-h-hate." He almost choked on the last stuttered aspirate.

Manash let them rest for a few moments, then said sympathetically, "It's a dilemma. So perhaps exchanging your identity for someone else's will be a break from this dilemma. Do you think so?"

"Oh yes. I hope so.".

Louis left Manash's office thinking that it was unfair to Sarah that he should be in love with someone else. He had met Tess, he realised now, at the wrong time, when he had just had a quarrel with Tess. He had never told anyone about Tess, although some of Tess's friends knew they were seeing each other. Saying it all out loud made his infidelity more real. He squeezed his lips tightly and unhappily. Yes, he had not thought of it this way before but it was true. Giving up Tess would be like giving up a piece of life. As he had said, it would be like dying.

He headed for the toilet but sitting on the seat he found that he did not need to go. His bowels were quivering but there nothing there to come out. It was if something inside him was stroking him inside. His skin seemed to be quivering. His skin held his body together and it was being eroded from within. It was a strange sensation. He wondered how far it would go, and how much of himself would disappear when he changed identity, leaking out into the world around him as the words had leaked out of him in Namash's office.

What would disappear? His body would still be here. Was he his body? No, he decided, thinking about it, he was his brain. Or perhaps his mind. He was what he thought and what he felt.in his body. But now this would go. His physical body would still be here but in this game he would leave it, as he seemed to be leaving it now, seeping away through the pores, and someone else would take his place in his body. He became anxious. What would happen to the part of him that was lost? Where would he go? Into some limbo, some form of quasi-existence that was not quite annihilation, like Schrodinger's cat in quantum physics, waiting to be returned to the real world when the quantum wave packet collapsed? Which meant when the game ended. What would happen to his love for Tess? Or for Sarah? Were they a part of him? They seemed for the moment to be entities in themselves, that should be transferred to whatever new person he became, like the shirt he was wearing.

But his feelings for Tess and Sarah, like his opinions of the world, would go when he died. Would losing himself like this be like dying? Would he only be losing his ego, which he over-indulged anyway?

::   ::   ::

He went into the lounge. There were a few leather armchairs in a rough circle, facing inwards, and behind them upright chairs. What looked like a lively discussion was going on so he took a seat on one of the upright chairs at the edge, near enough to join in if he felt like it. After the intensity of his revelation he wanted to have some ordinary conversation, about the weather or the accommodation or the day's news, to steady him in the way plain bread and butter steadies the digestion after rich food.

Green seemed to be doing most of the talking, holding forth on the role of the United Nations sitting with his legs crossed. Louis noticed his shoes; he could tell they were new because of the shine and also because the laces were tied in that special way that only shoe salesmen tie laces. Green was nodding as he made his points and occasionally looking around at his audience, as if he were looking down from a lecture platform. He was in a lecturing mode, it seemed to Louis, talking softly and explaining rather than asserting, as if to students.

Ingrid Mundt said,. "But the U.N. has to take sides if it's going to achieve anything". She was sitting next to him, perched on the edge of her chair, leaning forward as if she was anxious not to miss anything.

Green said, "Where its operations have been successful, it's because it's served the purpose of the big powers. Then it can intervene usefully."

"When you say the big powers, you mean America," Campbell Davies said. Louis remembered the plump Canadian with an eyepatch from the first evening.

"No," Green said. "America can take action unilaterally but then it won't do so through the U.N."

"You think the U.N. shouldn't take sides in arguments where the big powers are involved?" Davies asked. "It should stay aloof? Preserve its virginity."

"Exactly," Green replied, in the quiet, satisfied voice of one who has been understood.

Frances Carr spoke up. "But surely," she said, "virginity is only of value if you're willing to lose it. If you preserve it forever, it's a negative virtue at best." She looked around, with a trace of a smile on her face.

"Do you want the U.N. to jump into bed all over the place?" Wade asked.

"Oh no. I'm not in favour of promiscuity," Frances said, still with the trace of a smile. "One should be discriminating." Louis decided that her flirtatious talk was fake. He noticed that she was dressed the same way she had been the day before, with her frilled blouse buttoned up to the neck and pulled in at the waist so that it was tight over her well rounded breasts. It seemed to him to be sexually ambiguous.

"So when should the United Nations take sides?" asked Davies.

"When the interests of the big powers require it and when they agree," Green replied, looking over his shoulder. "The

United Nations is a part of the international system. It doesn't stand outside it."

Louis saw suddenly that Green needed to talk, needed to have an audience. He seemed to be one of those people who can only maintain contact with people verbally, can only exchange emotions when they are articulated. In fact, he thought, Green could probably only *feel* emotions when they are articulated. He needed a caption to go with the picture. He would always have to ask, "How was it for you?"

Ingrid said,. "So what would the United do in the St. George situation? There are - "

"Ah-ah." Green turned to her and wagged a finger admonishingly. "We're not supposed to talk about the St. Georgian situation."

Davies spoke forcefully. "How about the UN's humanitarian role? What's called humanitarian intervention? All my work has been in the Third World. Often in disaster situations. When you've seen the kind of suffering I've seen, you don't look for reasons for governments to stand back and do nothing. I mean actually seen it, children starving, or who have had limbs cut off, women who have been raped holding their dead babies. Anyone who works for a government should see what I've seen."

After a pause France said, "There is often a case for international intervention, agreed. And I'm sure you have done very good work. Perhaps more people should be doing what you're doing. But if someone is a government servant, he can't follow his own moral inclinations. He represents the interests of his government. Some people don't understand that."

"You mean do-gooders," said Davies sarcastically.

"That's not the kind of language I would use," Frances said.

Louis saw an opening to try out an idea. "It sounds as if you belong to the realist school of international relations.," he said, addressing Green.

"I suppose that's right," Green replied.

"Which probably means you talk in abstractions," Louis went on.."I've noticed that international affairs is the one area in which the more abstract a person is, the more realistic he is said to be. He or she. And the more he talks in real, concrete terms, the more he is said to be unrealistic."

"I'm not sure I know what you mean," Green said.

Louis had the explanation ready. "If I write in the newspaper about some international situation and focus on a few children starving to death, or individuals being tortured or blown up, the kind of thing Campbell here has been talking about, then I'm usually told by some people that I'm just being emotional. The professionals won't take me seriously. The people who actually conduct international relations, they don't talk that way. They talk about national interests or alliances or power blocs - you know, NATO, China, the World Trade Organisation, things like that. Or issues: globalism, terrorism. So long as I talk about these things, they'll take me seriously. But NATO, the WTO, the European Union, they're abstractions. So are countries really. That doesn't mean they don't mean anything They do, of course. But ultimately, they mean something only so far as they relate to the hard facts of individual lives. An individual being happy or unhappy or in pain starving, that's the only hard reality."

Frances said, "That sounds like a newspaper column."

"Perhaps it will be," Louis admitted.

Davies, evidently in an aggressive mood, brought the discussion back to the specific. "You talk about intervention. What about Indonesia? The UN intervened there before, in East Timor. Now the country seems to be breaking up, massacres in some places. I've worked there. It's a big country. It's also a big customer of America and Europe. Should the UN just stand back and let things happen?"

Green, still in the role of self-appointed chairman, said,

"Frances, you were at the British Embassy in Indonesia, what do you think?"

"Oh, I've been away a long time," Frances said. Louis could see that she did not want to be drawn into an argument with Davies. "Why don't you ask Michael here? He had a posting in Jakarta." She indicated Michael Munro, the American who had talked about Indonesia over dinner the previous evening. He had just walked into the room and was sitting near the door.

Green said, "Well, Michael? Do you think the U.N. has a part to play in Indonesia?"

"Indonesia?" Munro looked startled.

"Yes. Does the U.N. have a role there?"

Munro looked surprised at the question. Then he said, "I was thinking about Indonesia this morning, as a matter of fact. Lying in bed." He looked as if he had just got out of bed. His hair was uncombed and he had the vague, unfocussed expression of someone who is not fully awake.

Green said, "Oh really?" in an encouraging tone. Munro hesitated. Everyone looked at him.

"About the Achada situation?" Davies suggested, to break the silence.

Munro said, "I was thinking about Mama Li's."

Green said, "What?"

Munro suddenly started talking, like an engine that has been switched on, addressing Green as if the others were not there. "That's a whorehouse in Jakarta," he explained. "Some of the girls there are from - what's the name of the place? - I can't remember but it's one of the Celebes Islands. The girls from that island have specially strong vagina muscles. They're taught to exercise them from the time they're infants. They're all taught to do that apparently." He was staring ahead, concentrating on the memory. `

Davies chuckled quietly. Green looked disconcerted and started to say , "Er, Michael - " But Michael was oblivious and went on...

"Anyway, when you get your dick inside one of them, she can squeeze it. And I'm talking real muscles. Apparently, they practise squeezing pencils. You meet a female from that island, they say, she's got a really athletic snatch. What's the name of the place?" He shook his head in annoyance. "I can't remember."

Davies said wickedly, keeping a straight face, "Perhaps you can help him, Frances. You spent some time in Indonesia."

"It's not the kind of information that came my way," Frances replied stiffly. "I can well imagine that some of my colleagues patronised Mama Li's but they didn't share their experiences with me." Munro shook his head in annoyance.

After an awkward silence, Wade said to him, "That's what you've been thinking, is it?"

Munro looked around the room as if he was noticing all the others for the first time. He seemed shocked. "I'm sorry," he said. "I shouldn't have - I don't know what happened. I apologise. I think maybe it's the pills I've been taking." He got up and left the room.

There was a few moment silence. "Well go ahead and cap that," Davies said, chuckling. "Do we go back to talking about the United Nations?

Just then Thaxted walked into the room accompanied by Jacob Shemtov. "Some of us are going to take a stroll before lunch. Who wants to come along?" he asked.

Several agreed. "I'll just get a raincoat," Louis said. Frances begged off, saying, "I've some things to do."

As they got up to go, Louis remarked softly to Wade, "Perhaps our friend Munro took a couple of pills too many."

I think we're all loosening up just a bit," Wade replied.

Some curious things are spilling out."

"It's not so curious. What do you think about lying in bed in the morning? European monetary union?"

You're right," Louis replied smiling. "Sometimes I think

about female flesh."

Frances walked out and across the courtyard troubled. She was worried about Munros's outburst. If he could lose control of what he was saying and make a fool of himself like that under the influence of the pills or Manash's treatment, what might she do?

She was also troubled by that Canadian Campbell Davies' talk of suffering. The words nagged at her. She heard this kind of thing from time to time when she was sent to receive a delegation from some protest group. They often sent her for some reason. She had to sit and listen to accounts of atrocities perpetrated by some government whose head was visiting London. Women being raped, that kind of thing. Sometimes the accounts of torture were very upsetting. Yes, we should all try to reduce that kind of thing. But foreign policy means working with the world as it is. These protesters never made the world better.

She recalled a scene with her father, when she was seven or eight years old and the family were watching television, and saw film of starving children in Sudan. She was very upset and wanted the family to send some of their food to Sudan. She said she would give up chocolates and they could spend the money on food and send it to the hungry children. Her father took her on his lap and said, "You're a very sweet, kind little girl, Frances. But we can't take on ourselves all the troubles of the world. We do what we can. Your mother helps in the charity shop. We give some money. But we can't take on everyone else's difficulties."

Other thoughts came to her, and she could not fight them off. She remembered the time her grandmother, her mind wandering, was taken away to an old people's home sobbing piteously. She watched with tight lips. But there was not much else they could do, as her father explained to her. They could not give her the care she needed. There was a lot of unhappiness in the world, a lot of suffering. There were people with terrible troubles all around. There was that man in her department sacked after repeated warnings about his drinking. She had a picture of him in her mind now, and his humiliation, embarrassing to see, as he gathered up his things and said the briefest of goodbyes. She had felt sorry for him, she wondered what he could do with his life now, but she had not looked him in the eyes.

You had to lead your own life and look after yourself, just as a nation had to look after its own interests. You should try to help others, but your responsibility was to yourself and to your immediate family if you had one. Those were your frontiers, your boundaries. Everyone had boundaries. It was the same with a nation. It had its boundaries and other nations had theirs.

Now something seemed to be happening to her. She imagined her boundaries crumbling and the troubles and needs of people all around her flooding in, the drunk in her department who was sacked, the beggar she passed in the street, a cousin who had committed suicide, the starving family in the Sudan, the tortured prisoners that the protest groups told her about, all this suffering pouring in over her, *into* her. She shuddered mentally. It was a terrifying prospect. Abruptly, she decided that she did not want to be alone. She hurried downstairs and joined the others as they started on their walk.

CHAPTER FOUR

There were a dozen of them, in three and four groups, dissolving and re-forming as they went along. Being outside the confines of the school, they found that their involvement in the project provided some social glue, so that they walked along the street looking at the strangers around them like a group of soldiers on leave.

They talked about their meals. "I thought it would be boarding school fare but they've got in outside caterers. It's not bad," Thaxted said.

"The pork chops with apple sauce last night was very palatable," Louis agreed.

They calculated that the bottles of wine on the table at dinner time allowed for just one-and-a-half glasses each and considered jokily sneaking in a few extra bottles. They speculated that since the cleaners came around to make the beds early in the morning, usually when they were at breakfast, they might be assigned to report on whether everyone slept in their own beds.

Donald Green frowned as he walked along. He resented the throng of people brushing up against him and the busy traffic. Oxford, the ancient university town, should be quieter, slower. It had been taken over. In the early Nineteenth Century the population of Oxford was a fraction of what it was today, like the population of Britain. The increase since then due to better hygiene and a reduced death rate had filled Oxford with people and swamped it as a seat of learning. Green saw all these newcomers who had arrived in the last two centuries as unwanted immigrants.

Frances found herself walking next to him. He was not saying anything but she had not come for silence so she looked up at the dust-coloured clouds and remarked, "We'd better get in the strolling while we can. It looks like rain."

Checking that Louis Mannion was not within earshot Green replied, "Oh well, it'll christen my Burberry."

"You bought that in London?" she asked him.

"Just before I came down here."

"I buy Burberry's sometimes," she said. "Usually in the sales. I have a Burberry suit."

He told her that he also bought Church's shoes when he visited Britain. They talked about shopping, and then about Oxford colleges and their architecture. He was pleased to find that she had been an undergraduate at Oxford. He liked being with her. She was quite good-looking but not so much so as to be intimidating, she talked sensibly and quietly and she carried herself with some dignity. He told her about the conference on international organizations and about his own project. She found him uninteresting but was content to keep up a patter of talk with half her mind while she thought about her days as a student here in Oxford.

They turned into Christ Church Meadow. It might have been a meadow once but now it consisted of smooth, well-kept lawns and wide gravel paths, and the deer, foxes and badgers that had once roamed here were replaced by tourists from several countries, no less colourful and rather noisier. They passed some Japanese photographing one another against the ivy-covered walls of Christ's Cathedral, and then a group of pubescent French school-children, most of them wearing sweaters representing American colleges.

Frances found that this place had a memory for her. It

was walking along this path that she had had an argument about sexual behaviour with two girls at her college who she had thought were friends. She had started to explain reasonably why she did not want casual sexual encounters but the others had descended rapidly into a dissection of her behaviour with men with disagreeable implications. "You're just a cock-teaser," one of them had told her finally.

"Oh, fuck off!" she had retorted. She was proud of saying that. It had not come easily and it had impressed them. She could handle that kind of situation better now.

Her standards of behaviour were a part of what made her Frances Carr. They were as much a part of her as her voice, and the sharp-pointed little nose that had worried her when she was an adolescent peering anxiously into the mirror and the growing breasts that had reassured her. The idea of becoming somebody else was beginning to trouble her. What might her behaviour be in her new role? What would this other person's standards be?

"Let's go see the river," suggested Thaxted, and they branched off away from the landscaped area down a dirt path. After only five minutes they seemed to have left the city of Oxford. They were in rural surroundings, walking past ragged fields with three cows staring at them morosely across a wire fence, and then a thatched roof house. They could not hear the noise of traffic from here.

The American woman Mimi started a conversation about developments in the American Administration and then realised that no one was in a mood to talk about this so she stopped.

Louis asked, "How do you find our Dr. Manash?" It was a question thrown out to anyone.

"I had a session with him this morning," Wade replied. "He's got very good target acquisition."

"He's got a manner," Thaxted said. "When he asks a question you sort of have to answer it. Does anyone else feel that?"

"I know what you mean," Green agreed.

"He's supposed to be doing some pretty extraordinary things to us," Louis said.

"And I thought of something this morning," Thaxted went on. "Manash's name is an anagram of 'shaman'."

"Hey, that's right," Wade said.

"You've just worked that out?" asked Louis.

"A shaman has magical powers," Thaxted pointed out. "Can our shaman perform magic?"

"Does the idea worry you?" asked Louis.

"Perhaps a bit," Thaxted said.

Green asked, "Has anyone been hypnotised by our shaman yet?"

"I'm rather looking forward to it," Louis said. "It'll be a new experience. And the immersion tank."

"The CIA uses these immersion tanks as part of its interrogation technique. To dis-orientate people," Wade said. "The others looked at him. "I read about it. It's not my area," he added.

"I'm due to go in the tank this afternoon," Green said.

"So am I," said Frances.

"They're individual tanks," Green added hastily.

Wade chuckled. "I don't think anyone's thinking about any hanky-panky in there."

They reached the grassy river bank and gazed across. A few dirty motor boats were tied up nearby. The river was a few dozen yards wide and on the other side there was stubble along the bank with untidy fields behind. There was no sign of an urban landscape, no sign that the city of Oxford was anywhere near. After a while they turned back.

When they reached Christ's Meadow Thaxted pointed to the building that dominated the street side and suggested, "Let's be tourists and look at Christ Church Cathedral."

"Why not, since we're here," said Green.

Shemtov said he would give the cathedral a miss because his foot was beginning to nag at him and he wanted to sit down for a while. This was true but it was not the only reason. He did not feel entirely comfortable walking around a cathedral with a group of presumably Christians. Over the years he had sloughed off his father's picture from Poland of a Jewish people surrounded by hostile Christians, but he knew he was related by something more than kinship to those Jews who regarded the Christian churches as their persecutors and built the tiled floors of their synagogues in such a way that the lines never met to form a cross. He sat down on a wooden bench beside the path.

Soon memory came to him as it had the day before. As before it was so strong that it took him over and he was hardly aware of his present surroundings.

He was no longer middle-aged, no longer sitting among English greenery with the buzz of conversations carrying across the lawn and bird songs coming down from the trees, no longer a worried unhappy academic. He was on a beach in Tel Aviv on a hot Spring afternoon and he was a few weeks past his nineteenth birthday, with his mother and Meir and Meir's Egyptian-born wife Esther. He was on his first leave from officers' training school, and he was feeling pleased with himself. He still felt a fraud when he snapped out orders, but he had the pleasant feeling that he was carrying it off.

Esther was putting out the picnic food on a plastic tablecloth spread out on the sand: houmous sprinkled with chives, spicy meatballs on sticks, aubergines stuffed with mashed chick peas and semolina decorated daintily with coriander leaves, chopped green salad topped with radishes, pitta bread, and, his mother's contribution, a fruit salad. Esther was wearing a halter and shorts, and he reflected that she was running to fat as most Egyptian women seemed to once they had passed thirty, her cheeks bulbous, her hips rounded out from a waist that was hardly slimmer.

His mother was talking to Meir about her business worries. She dug one foot into the sand and worked it around as she told Meir, "I always paid that bastard on the nail. When he was starting up I gave him advice. I put up with his late deliveries and his stupid excuses. And now when I need some credit. Hah!"

"He's being a bit hard," Meir agreed.

"A bit hard? God, I could kill him." She kicked the sand with her toe.

"I know a man," said Meir, and she smiled.   Louis decided to go for a swim and stood up. He noticed that two girls sitting nearby looked across at him and he was pleased. Meir noticed it also and said to his mother, "That's some handsome son you've got there, you know?"

"Oh, yes!" she agreed, and walked across and put her arm around his waist. "My officer-cadet."

He pulled away from her and said, "I think I'll go in the sea before we eat."

"Me too," said Meir.

They walked across the sand and when they reached the surf Meir said, "I'll race you to the raft." Jacob was surprised. He did not swim often and was not a good swimmer but he was fitter than he had ever been thanks to army training, and Meir was a good twenty years older than him and verging on plump.

"Okay," he called back. He struck out powerfully, splashing the water heavily as he drove himself along. But as he approached the raft he lifted his head and saw that Meir was just ahead of him, propelling himself with smooth measured strokes. When he reached the raft Meir was already hauling himself out of the water to sit on the edge, breathing hard and grinning. He allowed Meir to help him up with an outstretched hand..

` Back on the beach he told his mother. "Meir beat me to the raft. You know that?"

"Uh-huh." His mother did not seem surprised. "Your father couldn't swim at all," she added irrelevantly.

The sun was so strong that it dried the wetness off his skin even as he started to towel himself. "Here, are you thirsty?" Esther asked, holding out a thermos flask of cold fruit juice and a plastic cup. She smiled at him shyly. He was a little embarrassed at the way Esther smiled at him so often. Later, he decided that she would have liked to have had children.

The memory faded and he was back on a bench in Oxford. The vividness and power of these memories worried him. He must ask Manash about them. They must be due to the pills.

He took in the sounds of conversation in the distance, the wind in the trees, and the dark clouds gathering ominously over his head. This was England. To assure himself that he was out of the dream, that he was here and not in Israel, he thought of differences. Israel had churches but no gothic cathedrals like the one facing him. The conversations would have been more likely in Hebrew or Russian than in English. He had never sat on a river bank in Israel. He remembered pictures of young men and girls punting on the river at Oxford. Where were the punts? Where were the young men rowing? This must be a different part of the river. The trees were not Israeli trees. He did not know anything about trees but these looked English.

However, despite himself, his return to the present was only brief. He was like a traveller calling home just for a change of clothes. Before he was aware of what was happening another memory carried him away.

He was hurrying along the street and stuffing his yarmulke and talus into his pocket after the rabbi's announcement. The dramatic news had punctured the God-seeking solemnity of the Yom Kippur service which was the occasion of Jacob's one annual visit to the synagogue. His mother was hurrying alongside him. He could see that she was forcing herself not to cry and he was grateful. They were going to her flat so that he could telephone.

` When he got there he called the camp but could not get through so he phoned Moshe. "You've heard? The Egyptians have crossed the canal. We've got a war."

"The Syrians are in it too," Moishe told him.

"Oh shit!"

"Where are you?" Moishe asked.

"At my mother's." He told him the address.

"I'll pick you up," Moishe said. "I'm just leaving."

After he hung up his mother put her arms around him and put her head against him. Anxiety raced through his mind, anxiety about what dangers lay ahead and how he would perform, along with a thousand thoughts about where they would be going and what they would have to do and how many tanks would be operational. Then one thought stayed there. Damn, damn, why did it have to happen just now, before he went into Centurions? His was one of the few remaining squadrons of Shermans, the oldest tanks in the Israeli Army, American battle tanks of World War Two. The last of them were going to be replaced. Thin armour and no infra-red sights for night fighting. The Egyptians and Syrians had the T-55s from Russia. Damn and fuck-damn! It would be the British-built Centurions that would win the war, the Centurions and the American M-48s, not the Shermans. He might as well be sitting in a cardboard box for all the protection he would have when the guns opened up.

Eighteen hours later he was on the slopes of Golan, bumping along on the rocky, uneven ground in the metal cell of his tank with that bone-jarring motion he knew so well, taut, his stomach churning with anxiety. He was standing up in the turret of the tank as he had been taught the leader of a squadron should do. "You can see the whole battlefield. It's the Israeli way. Sit up tall, let them know we're coming," their instructors used to tell them.

The three others in his tank were also tense, talking very little. They were driving straight ahead between and over scrub bushes and small, twisted trees, into a cloud of dust. This was what all his training had prepared him for. He was worried about the weakness in the left track that they had not had time to repair and what might be wrong with the others in the squadron and how some of the men would perform and particularly about little Benjamin, his radio operator sitting next to his left foot who was always nervous, and whether they would obey his orders under fire as they did on exercises. He was worried most of all about how he himself would behave. He was frightened,.He should not be here, he felt, he had only pretended to be an army officer..

He was consulting his map grid and giving orders over the radio to the other tanks about taking up positions on the ridge ahead in the second line of defence that was being set up. But just as they started wheeling to get into position he saw Syrian tanks ahead of him in the distance, in a dust cloud, dozens of them, a terrifying number. He had never seen so many tanks together..

"Fuck standing up tall! They know we're coming," he said to himself, and dropped down and closed the hatch.

The sensation of re-living the past faded. Those three days on Golan were too frightening and too intense to re-live. He had learned then as he had never learned before the power of fear, how it can take over a man and transform him, driving out every other aspect of his person. He felt fear taking him in its teeth and shaking up as a dog might shake a rag doll. It was said that he behaved well and did what needed to be done so presumably he had, but he found it difficult to believe. Some things he did not remember. He had pushed away his feelings rather than face them. When people praised his behaviour in combat he felt a fraud.

He was back in Oxford. But he recalled - remembering now, not re-living - some of the consequences of those hours on the Golan, and dwelled on them for a few moments He remembered the sense of victory at the end, the mixture they all felt of elation and relief. He remembered sitting in Moshe's kitchen with a cup of coffee, Moshe's wife of a few months, white-faced, paralysed by grief, and assuring her that Moshe had died instantly and had not suffered, which was probably not true as his tank had gone up in flames.

These vivid memories that came to him were all from long ago. Why? he wondered. Why not the intervening years?

He tried sometimes to draw on his behaviour in those times for strength. Evidently, he had done what he was supposed to have done. In the officers' training school, he had somehow learned how to lead men, at least some men for some of the time. Supported by his rank, he had sized them up as individuals and had made them do what he told them. He reminded himself of this from time to time..

He was jerked out of these thoughts by Frances, who came over and sat beside him. Frances was saying, "I saw the cathedral a few times when I was a student here, that's enough. I hope you don't mind me joining you." He was surprised but he agreed.

They talked about England and what he had seen and what he should see. He told her that an old friend in London had spent a day taking him to the usual sights: the Tower of London, Westminster Abbey, the London Eye. "She's an Englishwoman who used to be married to my cousin," he explained. This was a half-truth at best, he reminded himself. He had left out their lively conversations and also some of the awkward moments, and particularly their last moments together after dinner, when she had suggested that they come back to her flat and he had declined abruptly and hurried her into a taxi.

"Have you seen the English countryside?" she asked. He shook his head. "But you should. England is at its most English in the villages. Like some around here."

He nodded. "Even coming down here on the train, I got the impression of England as a series of farms and gardens, all laid out."

"Yes, there's not a lot of wild countryside in this part of England," she agreed.

They talked about places. She had served in the embassies in Brussels and in Jakarta. She had been to America but only to the East Coast. He had visited Washington once but had not been to New York. "You've spent two years in America but you've never been to New York. And you've been to Europe but you've never been to England. How strange."

"You make it sound as if I've spent my life on the periphery," he said, smiling. "But I was born sixty kilometres from Jerusalem. In maps in the Middle Ages, Jerusalem was the centre of the world."

"That's true," she said.

"Of course, we know Jerusalem isn't really the centre of the world," he went on. "Tel Aviv is." She smiled.

It was casual, friendly small talk, no more, the sort of thing she was good at. But while she was talking to him she found she was taking in his dark brown eyes and his black hair, cropped so close that it seemed like a skull cap, greying at the temples. He was a good deal older than her. She wondered how much older.

She suddenly realised that she was listening to him in a way that she did not normally listen to people. She was not just examining the content of his speech but she was hearing the timbre of his voice, his hard, foreign consonants and the strange lilt to his vowels. She was looking at the lines on his face and watching the movement of his lips as he was talking. And then something else. Her hand was resting on the bench, and she was noticing the feel of the wood under her hand. It was untreated wood and she felt its roughness.. She pressed down her palm so she would feel it on her palm also. For a moment she almost lost the thread of what Jacob was saying because she was concentrating on the feel of the wood on her hand. This was a new sensation.

In the entrance hall to the cathedral, Wade considered the white marble slab with an inscription in Latin commemorating one Johannes Fell. "Born in 1625. Boy, that's old," he said. "Back then there was no America, just a few English settlers. I wonder what the world was like without America."

"It didn't know what it was missing," murmured Thaxted.

They stood there for a few minutes looking down the aisle and up at the vaulted ceiling. The ruby reds and rich blues of the stained glass windows glowed vividly even though it was a cloudy day outside with only a pale sun, so brightly that they seemed to be creating their own light.

Inside their footsteps echoed against the stone walls. They were the only visitors but the setting imposed respect and they talked in muted tones. Ingrid likened the cathedral to some late gothic cathedrals in Germany. Mimi remarked that people seemed to be less church-conscious in Britain than in America. Thaxted pointed to a scene on one of the stained glass windows of a saint in heaven. "I've never seen the point of heaven and hell in a religion," he remarked.

"It seems a bit old-fashioned today but traditionally, it's an essential part of the Christian religion," Ingrid said.

"But it seems such a selfish pitch," Thaxted said. "Do good and you'll go to heaven. Do bad things and you'll burn in hell. You might as well say you'll be paid if you do good and fined if you do wrong."

"That's what the law does say," Wade said.

"Exactly. But the law isn't religion. The law is just a set of rules for society, for this world."

"Religion is the same sort of thing plus God," Wade

replied.

"But it should be more than that," Thaxted insisted.

As the others went on Louis hung back at the nave and contemplated the white *bas relief* sculpture of Christ on the Cross. In a spirit of experiment he tried to feel something of Christ's suffering as he had felt it years earlier, during his Catholic adolescence. He thought as he had done once before of the limbs straining against the nails, the hot sun beating down, the flayed flesh. He tried now to summon up some of the reverence he had once felt when he prayed to Jesus, the reverence for Jesus's pain and sacrifice and love, a love so strong that it could perform miracles.

He strained but it did not come to him. He was disappointed. He was an unbeliever now but he would like to feel again what it was like to be reverent, just for a moment, to know that he had the capacity to worship, to find a spiritual dimension to life, like an elderly infirm man who longs to run or play squash one more time, or an elderly woman who longs to flash her eyes and flirt just once again. He did not believe, he could not believe, but for the moment he almost regretted the belief he had lost.

They left the building still talking about religion, and Jacob and Frances joined them but said little. As they arrived back at the school and strolled into the lounge, Thaxted took up the point again about heaven and hell. "People believed in it in the Middle Ages but somehow it didn't seem to make them behave better," he said.

"I wonder whether it really makes a difference," Louis mused as he sat down. "In the days when most people believed in heaven and hell, did the idea that they would go to heaven make them any less afraid to die?"

"People seem pretty keen on not dying at every period of history," Green remarked dryly as he took an armchair..

"I don't know. We have suicide bombers," Wade pointed out. "They seem to think they're going to go to heaven."

"Not all of them," Louis said. "Some of them just want to do something great and noble."

"Like killing some people," Wade said.

"That seems to be the way they look at it."

"How about reincarnation?" Thaxted asked unexpectedly. "That would mean you don't really die but you come back as someone else. A lot of people in other parts of the world believe in that. Would that make you less afraid to die?" When no one said anything he added, "I've been thinking about reincarnation."

"Have you been getting flashes of past lives?" Wade asked. "Banging Shirley McLaine in ancient Egypt? Something like that?" He spoke in short, staccato sentences.

Thaxted ignored his question and pressed on. "Suppose you knew that when you died you'd come back as someone else." His pink round face was screwed up now in a thoughtful expression

"You mean," said Louis, "a person. Not a cocker spaniel or a mosquito.

"Yes, another person.. If you knew that was going to happen, would you be any less worried about dying?"

"No, I don't think it would matter."

"But your soul wouldn't be dead. It would come back."

"But I wouldn't know it. How would you feel about it, Brian?"

"I don't know."

"But you raised the subject."

"It doesn't mean I know what I feel about it. I think maybe that if I was going to come back as someone else, it would mean something to me. If I knew it, that is.". Louis saw what was worrying Thaxted even if he did not. He was thinking of the game. In the game he was going to die temporarily and become someone else.

Donald Green usually had little time for this kind of speculative talk and he had been scanning a newspaper, but he did not want to be left out of a conversation so now he put down the newspaper and took up this point. "If your character and personality are dead, then you're dead. What's left?"

Thaxted pursed his lips thoughtfully. "Something," he said. "The little bit of life you were born with."

"And what's that?" asked Ingrid.

Wade stepped in. "The thing that was there before you started being you in particular. Look, imagine everybody in this room as new-born babies. Right now, we're all different people. All individuals with our own personalities and minds and all that crap. But if we were all new-born babies, as we all were once, all lined up in a hospital room, we'd all be just about the same. No nationality, no rank, no personality, no opinions. Just lying there yelling our little heads off. That's the pure stuff. Everything since then is just detail."

Louis found this surprising coming from Wade. "Have you ever tried to get in touch with it?"

"What?"

"The little bit of life. That thing you were born with. Whatever it is."

Wade shook his head. "Not allowed to. Enlisted men can but not officers. We've got to be officers all the way down."

"How about battle?" Jacob said suddenly. He was surprised at the sound of his voice. He had not intended to say anything.

"What about battle?" Wade asked.

Jacob had to say something more. "I was just wondering whether some people get in touch with it in battle. You're in touch with very basic fears then. Like Hemingway said about bullfighters. He said they live all the way down."

"Have you been in combat?" Wade asked.

"Yes."

"Well what do you think?"

"I don't know." He did know. He had shrunk away from the reality, that he was vulnerable and could be killed. He would not remember. It seemed a lie to say he had been in battle.

Frances did not join in but she thought the subject had something to do with the way she had felt the wood and the ground, and had listened to Jacob's voice. What she had felt then was something like her real life. How often did she feel that? Some worrying thoughts were coming to her.

Green said, "Maybe women feel it when they give birth. My wife told me that giving birth was the most marvellous experience you could ever have. She said men can't imagine anything like it."

Louis decided to take off with this. "That's a thought," he said. "Creating life could be the only point to life. We men are just adjuncts, perhaps, with enough sex drive to make us impregnate women. The rest is superfluous, character and achievement and all that. We spend most of our life farting around anyway. Pollen that go from plant to plant would do just as well at keeping life going if they could get through the complicated business of getting into a woman's inside.

"Men would be the pollen. Think how simple it would be. We wouldn't have to worry about whether women like us or being clever or accomplishing things or any of that stuff. We'd just be those tiny stringy things drifting around. We'd float around in the air until we found ourselves in some woman's whatsit - it wouldn't matter which one - and that's it. Bingo! We're totally fulfilled. That's our life's work all done."

Thaxted chuckled. "Another Louis Mannion monologue," he said..

"It would be a boring life," remarked Wade.

"But at least not spent on trivialities," Louis said.

CHAPTER FIVE

At the lunch table Louis found himself seated next to Campbell Davies, the Canadian with an eyepatch. As they helped themselves to the pasta he said, "I heard what you said to those foreign service people that first night at dinner, about Uzbekistan. I liked that. Somebody ought to be saying it."

"I lost my cool and came over all moral," Louis said.

"I just about lost mine this afternoon, when we were talking about the U.N.," Campbell said. "I don't usually talk like that. Mothers with dead babies, that kind of thing."

"Maybe it's the pills," Louis suggested.

"Maybe it is that. I got carried away by morality," Davies said, grinning. "I try to keep it under control."

"Shake hands."

Davies ate a few mouthfuls and then spoke again. "The sort of thing I spend my days telling young people."

"Not to get carried away by morality?"

"Something like that. Not to be guided by a bleeding heart. I teach NGOs."

They were silent for a few mouthfuls. Louis was interested and wanted to pursue the subject. "What sort of things do you tell them? Idealism isn't enough?"

"Uh-huh. Mind you, a lot of them are careerists, just like any other profession."

Half to himself, Louis echoed again Thaxted's words of that first evening. "Adapt to the wicked old world."

"Yes. I tell them I spend most of my time in the field appealing to people's selfish instincts in order to get things done, not to their altruism."

Again he seemed to be finishing with the subject but Louis pressed on. "How you do it?"

"For one thing, I give them scenarios."

"What kind of scenarios?" Louis could see a column in this.

Campbell paused, as if wondering how far he should get into this. Then, evidently having made up his mind, he launched into an exposition: "There's a civil war, lots of complications. You want to get food to a disaster area in rebel-held territory. The central Government says this will relieve pressure on the rebels and prolong the war. This is probably true, but there are people starving there right now. What do you do? You want your Government's help in getting the food there. Your Government doesn't want to offend the central power. You have a meeting with an official of your Government. What do you say to him? Forget about humanitarian arguments, he knows the official policy and he's got his career to look after.

"I confront them with these situations. Sometimes, sending food to an area which is suffering starvation reduces the price of food on the market and means that local farmers will grow less. It could do more harm than good in the long run. But people are hungry. I ask them, 'What are you going to do? Come on, I don't want to know what you *think*, what you're *uncomfortable* about doing, what are you going to *do*?'"

"Yes, I'm sure aid is a complicated business." Louis was encouraging him to talk more. "Help the hungry. I guess you have to deal with some dodgy situations, and dodgy characters."

"You do indeed. Including among the hungry. I tell them that in order to do good you sometimes have to be more devious than the people who are doing evil."

Just then, a figure appeared in the doorway of the room, a tall broad-shouldered man in his mid-thirties wearing a suede jacket and a sports shirt open at the neck, unusual dress for this company. He had straight sandy hair and his eyes were hooded, almost like a gargoyle's, and were such a bright blue that even men noticed them. Louis thought he looked familiar but he could not place him. He decided that he was probably a pundit who cropped up on television from time to time. The man stood there for a moment fiddling with the plastic name tag as he tried to pin it to his lapel and looked around the room as he did so. He was clearly uncertain about what to do, yet he did not seem discomforted either by his difficulty with his name tag or by his uncertainty.

He spotted Ivor Howe seated at the top of the table and having finished affixing his tag, he walked over to him. Howe stood up and greeted him effusively, shaking his hand. They spoke for a few moments, and then Howe brought the newcomer over to the empty seat next to Thaxted at the end of the table and introduced him.

"Gentlemen, this is Stephen Darrow, who's also taking part in this exercise. Professor Green of Columbia University in New York, Campbell Davies, who's a foreign aid specialist, Louis Mannion, a columnist on the *Sunday Chronicle*. Brian Thaxted, Ministry of Defence. And over here Frances Carr, of the Foreign Office. Louis recognised the man when Howe said his name, with some surprise.

Darrow took his seat saying to the table, "I'm sorry I've come a couple of days late but I explained to Ivor that this was the earliest I could get here. I haven't missed a lot, have I?"

"The briefings about the rules of the game and some pills," Thaxted told him.

"I've been taking the pills. And I know about the briefings." He had a flat Midlands accent with clipped vowels. It was a gritty, sharp-edged voice, different from the other British voices at the table, which were more rounded and smooth. Thaxted asked, "You're from?"

Darrow looked blank, apparently perplexed by the question. Thaxted pursued the point. "Ivor told us your name but nothing else."

Frances spoke across the table. "You're obviously not much of a filmgoer, Brian." Then she said to Darrow, "I saw *Night Work* last month and I did enjoy it. Your performance particularly." The newcomer acknowledged the compliment with a brief nod. A waiter brought Darrow his main course, which was a seafood pasta, and Darrow settled down to it.

Louis recalled newspaper stories about him. He made good copy. He was said to be a film star in the tradition of the young Albert Finney and Peter O'Toole, rough-hewn and from a working-class background. Newspapers and magazines told the story, and Louis remembered some of it. How he had been a building worker and van driver, had bummed around on the Continent, and worked as an extra in some French films. Then he had been taken on by Peter Brook's International Theatre Company in Paris, where the director had recognised his talent and nurtured it.

They talked to him about the game and it turned out that Darrow had not yet read the folder and knew nothing of the St. George situation. He shrugged off the difficulty. "I'm pretty good with scripts. I learn quickly," he said.

He said no more for a while but concentrated on eating, measuring out the right proportions of pasta and sauce on his fork before putting each forkful into his mouth. He gave every sign of being more interested in this than in anything anyone else might say. Conversation started up again around him tentatively. People were uncertain about how to treat him.

After a while Louis decided to venture in and ask what he knew everyone was wondering. "Tell me, Stephen, if you don't mind my asking, how did you come to be taking part in this? I mean, most people here are involved with international politics in one way or another, or at least writing about it."

"I helped set it up," Darrow said briefly.

"How was that?"

Darrow waited until he had finished chewing on the food in his mouth before replying. "The game. Ivor called on me for some advice in the early stages."

"They wanted your professional advice?" Thaxted asked

" Uh-huh. About role-playing. How you put yourself into a part. And what you do with the rest of you while you're in it. I talked to Manash also. We had a couple of sessions."

"You know Ivor Howe?" Green asked. Darrow seemed either unaware of the curiosity he was arousing or else indifferent to it.

"His daughter was my girl friend for a while. She's an actress."

Thaxted joined in. "And he asked you to take part?"

He finished another mouthful and then spoke. "That was my idea. I said yes, I'd help if he let me take part."

"Are you, um, interested in international politics?" Thaxted asked.

"Sort of. I read the newspapers sometimes." No one tried to pursue this point.

Dessert was fresh fruit and cheese. Darrow ignored th cheese board and took a banana and peeled it. As he did Louis said to him, "You come from Nottingham, I seem to recall, from what I've read."

"That's right."

"I used to live in Nottingham."

Darrow turned to him with interest now and they talked about Nottingham. Louis knew the council estate on which Darrow grew up and he had walked its walkways. He remembered groups of feral-looking youths hanging around the stairwell and throwing out the occasional obscenity as he brushed past them, trying not to show his nervousness. He wondered whether Darrow might have been among them.

"If you know the estate, you'll know why I got out," Darrow said with a grin, and asked Louis about his time in Nottingham.

Green heard some of this but did not take part. But when they got their coffees in the lounge and Louis and Stephen Darrow sat down next to one another, he took the next armchair. He could see this actor becoming the centre of attention and he did not want to be far away. He said to him chattily, "I suppose you find this kind of thing less daunting than the rest of us. Playing a role, playing at being someone else."

"I've done it," Darrow acknowledged. He was sitting forward, reaching out occasionally for his cup on the low coffee table in front of him. He seemed absorbed in his coffee as he had been in his lunch, and the conversation moved away from him.

Thaxted said to Louis, "I heard you talking to Stephen here. I didn't know you were once a social worker."

"I don't know that I was a very good social worker," Louis replied.

"My wife's a social worker," Thaxted said. "She trains family welfare workers." Then he asked, "How did you move from social work into journalism?"

"I drifted into it," Louis said. "I started writing about social work and went on from there. Why did you become a civil servant? That's not the sort of thing you drift into."

"It seemed like a good career. I thought it would suit me." Thaxted turned to Raymond Wade. "Since we're all trying to be Dr. Manash for a while, why did you join the army?" Louis realised that Thaxted did not want to talk deeply about his motives either. They were playing pass the parcel.

"The idea of making a difference in the world," said Wade thoughtfully. "Also, I like the idea of serving my country."

"I suppose being in the military, you have some power," Green said.

"Yes, I like that idea. I don't mean personal power, giving orders, that kind of thing. I mean American power in the world.".

"You mean being a part of it," suggested Louis, interested.

"Yes." He thought for a few moments and went on, "I like the idea of having some small impact on the world. That whether I do my job well or not matters. It was either West Point or the State Department. I think I'm more suited to the army. America influences the world. I don't think I'd want to be in the military in a smaller country."

"Like Britain," Louis suggested mischievously.

"Well, yes. No offence. It was different when Britain governed an empire. As a matter of fact, I wrote my master's thesis about the British Empire. Or part of it."

"What part was that?" Thaxted asked.

"Africa. How Britain wound up its African empire." He had held the stage for long enough and he turned to Darrow and asked, "Why did you become an actor?"

Darrow's eyes flicked in Wade's direction. "You get a lot of money. Best paid job I ever had, and the cushiest."

"You didn't always want to be an actor?" asked Green.

Darrow shrugged a negative. "It never occurred to me. I wouldn't have known how to go about it."

As often, there was an awkward pause after Darrow had spoken. Louis broke it. "I suppose most of us took up our jobs at least partly because they're cushy and well-paid," he said, linking Darrow to the rest of them. "Isn't the civil service cushy? Or academic life?"

"I suppose academic life is sheltered once you've got tenure," Green acknowledged.

"This is an easy life, isn't it?" Louis agreed. "We sit around in agreeable surroundings and talk about the great issues of foreign policy. And let's face it, the diplomatic life is not usually a strenuous one."

"John Galbraith said something like that in *The Contented*

Society," Green said. "He talked about 'recreational foreign policy.'" Green mentioned a popular author rather than an academic one for Darrow's sake.

"He sort of gave the game away," Louis agreed.

Green asked Darrow, "Have you read any of Galbraith?"

"He writes books?"

"Well, yes. Have you read any of his books?"

"No. I don't read books," Darrow replied.

"What?" Green was startled.

"I don't read books," Darrow repeated. "I read newspapers. And plays, and scripts and things. But not books. They're too long for me."

Green was nonplussed. He was aware that there were many people who did not read books, and even some who admitted it, but it was a long time since he had had a conversation with one. . He was at a loss as to how to continue. He felt as if he had been talking to someone and suddenly discovered that the person was a woman and not a man, or was someone who did not understand English.

Louis said to Thaxted, "Do you find the civil service cushy?"

"Not as much as a lot of people think," Thaxted replied. "We have our crises."

Darrow got up from his seat saying. "I'd better go up and read the story line," he said. "And I have to make a phone call."

He put his cup on the sideboard, gave a brief nod to the others and left. He crossed the courtyard and went up to his room, sat down on the bed, took out his mobile phone and dialled a Nottingham number. His mother answered.

"You're at that meeting in Oxford," she said. "That's marvellous, Stevie."

"It's going to be interesting."

"I'll bet they're pleased to have you there."

"These people aren't impressed by me. And I explained to

you, it's nothing to do with the university."

"I had another phone call from Dad today," she said. "He is enjoying himself. He and Arnold are visiting Arnold's brother-in-law in Melbourne. He says it's the best present anyone ever gave him."

"Good." He assured her that he was well and remembered to ask how Uncle Ralph was doing in hospital..

Then he telephoned a London number and got an answering machine. It said, "Hi, this is Kerry. I'm not here now. If you're a producer or my agent leave a message and I'll get back to you. If you're a member of my family call me back later. If you're anyone else bugger off, unless you're inviting me to a party."

He said, "This is Steve. I'm in Oxford, long story. I'll be back in London Saturday next week. Let's go out Saturday evening. Save it. I'll call you in the afternoon." He put the phone back in his pocket. He would be spending two weeks without sex and Kerry was a good prospect.

He took out the folder, put it down on the desk facing the window, and read it through. Not many good parts there, he thought. He hoped he would be playing a big one. He went through some of the characters and tried on a few attitudes. Strong and authoritative. Strong and resentful. Strong and worried. Weak-willed and resentful. Changeable.

He stood up and stretched and stared out of the window. He looked down on a straight path, lined with trees, slim and straight like sentries. An early autumn wind was taking off a few leaves with each gust. People were walking along the path. A little girl in a striped dress walked alongside her mother with a brown and white puppy on a lead. The puppy pulled at its lead this way and that, and the little girl pulled it back, laughing with pleasure. Then she knelt down and ruffled the puppy's head and it jumped up to her with its little stump of a tail wagging so fast that it was just a blur, child and puppy bonded in joy. He watched them, smiling at the scene, until they walked on and disappeared from view.

Then he turned back to the room he was in, a small, functional room designed for privileged schoolboys and schoolgirls. "What am I doing here?" he asked himself. The question embraced not only the room and participation in the game but also the city of Oxford, and the suit in the cupboard and the smart suitcase on the bed.

"What am I doing here?" He had asked himself that standing in a coach station in London and looking at the strange surroundings and wondering where to go next, or heaving crates of wine around a Paris pub, or begging a stale sandwich from the Geordie manning a kiosk at Cologne railway station, his stomach rumbling with hunger. He had asked himself the question sometimes sitting in a taxi or in a hotel room. He had asked himself the question standing in the wings, waiting to go on stage. Always in one part of him he seemed to be detached, looking down at Stephen Darrow and at what had become of him.

It was if he were always travelling, away from home. But where was home? What was the place he was travelling away from? He knew what it was although he did not know why. It was his family's flat when he was nine and ten years old, when he was working on a model aeroplane kit or watching television in the little living room with the rest of the family. He could recall the exact feel of the coarse carpet material scraping against his elbows as he lay on the floor, the shine and scratches on the dining room table, the smell of tea and of model airplane glue.

He did not look back on his childhood as a happy time. He was glad to get away from home. He had no deep affection for the other members of his family, apart from his mother. He remembered his father as a distant figure, trying occasionally to be a good father and taking them on outings but living mostly in his own world of pub and fishing and pools syndicate. His brother was a bully, his tormentor at home and a lout outside. He had been fond of his young sister but frustrated by her wilful stupidity, choosing the most mindless companions at school, getting pregnant and marrying at eighteen. He could recall a few happy moments: all of them laughing at the same comedy programme on television; he and his brother teasing his sister, good-naturedly for a change, about a boy in her class; the three of them falling on the iced buns their mother had brought back as a treat. He remembered his uncle and aunt visiting when he would entertain them all with imitations of other family members and of some of his teachers at school, making them laugh out loud, happy to be doing that. But there were not many times he remembered with pleasure..

Nevertheless, if Dr. Manash asked him, as he had said he would, "Who are you really?" he would have to say, "I'm someone who used to be a ten-year-old boy sitting on the floor in front of a TV set in a a council flat in Nottingham." That was the truthful answer, Everything else was just things that had happened to him.

::   ::   ::

Early that evening Donald Green floated in the immersion tank. It was supposed to be perfect stillness, he reflected, but it was not. His body was moving a little, bobbing slightly, with his breathing, he supposed..

His mind wandered into the past. It wandered erratically, down paths it had not trodden for years, into forest glades of his childhood. There was a birthday party with people cheering as he blew out candles on a cake, children and grown-ups both. He was the centre of attention and he loved it. He was on a boat on a lake ringed with pine trees, his father teaching him to row, his father's large hairy hands over his own little ones as they pulled the oars together, he loving being there with his Daddy. "That's the way, Donald," his father said. He went over the phrase again in his mind: "That's the way, Donald" and remembered his father's hands over his.

His mind strayed further and into what he always thought of as the Jewish part of his family. Actually they were all Jewish apart from the occasional gentile in-law but some were more Jewish than others. There was Uncle Ed. A big, red, jutting-out nose, an outcrop on a craggy cliff of a face. "Hey, Donald, you're a college teacher, huh? Take after your mother, the brainy one of our family. You're teaching international affairs? That's great. Make sure you put people right about Israel." His jokes. "This'll make you laugh, Donald. Get this. There's this little tailor, Izzy, and he's knocked down by a car...." Uncle Ed's jokes were always preceded by a promise. "Here, this'll kill you." Or, "You'll love this one." He liked going to Uncle Ed's house in Forest Hills, even though his two daughters were older than him and snooty and hardly talked to him, because his uncle made barbecues and it had its own basketball court and swimming pool.

Further along the same memory path was Auntie Leah, really his great-aunt as he realised when he was older, small, wizened, with bad breath. She would shove her wrinkled face close to his and he would recoil from the odour coming out from between her yellow teeth. Fortunately, she did not speak to him often. There were people he saw regularly at family occasions: a barmitzphar, a wedding, an engagement party. Uncle Nate, his father's only brother, a large man, an observant Jew unlike his father. He was a doctor, who lived in an apartment in Manhattan with his wife and adopted daughter, and was quiet and serious and patient and played checkers with him when he was a child. His cousin Herman, several years older than him, with his flashy clothes and oily skin, who lived in Atlanta where he had a jewellery shop, and his gentile wife. She was a fading blonde Southern belle who used to talk to him because, as he sensed, she was uncomfortable with most of the adults in the family, and her bare arms and legs in her sleeveless dresses and short skirts used to set his adolescent hormones racing.

When they all came together there was a lot of noise and talking and exclaiming and arguing. They set up a force field as if they filled, not only the spaces their bodies occupied but the space between them and around them as well.

He had been pressured into inviting his loud joke-telling Uncle Ed to his wedding. "He's always been so fond of you!" his parents insisted. He could not bear the thought of them in the same room with his sophisticated in-laws whose Jewishness was decently contained, but Lorraine told him reassuringly, "We've all got an Uncle Ed in our family." He felt then that he had made the right choice of a marriage partner.

He came into the present suddenly, sharply, as if woken from sleep by a loud noise. What was he doing thinking about these people, uncles and cousins and smelly aunts? He had nothing in common with any of them. Even his father and mother did not have a lot in common with them, and he did not have all that much in common with his parents. He was two stages removed from commonality.

He seemed to be reverting to childhood. His whole adult life was seeping away. Things were being taken away from him, things he had earned with hard work. He waggled his arms and legs, making splashes, to reassure himself that he was here, taking up the space of an adult. He forced his mind back to the present. He wanted to get out of this tank quickly, out into the world where other people would know him, the world in which he belonged.

He brought to his mind a paragraph of his from his paper *Western Security Organizations After the Cold War.* "NATO in the 1990s found itself in a changed situation for which it was ill adapted. Set up to fight the Cold War, it faced different challenges. It was like a football team who line up in formation on the field and then find that the field is being transformed into a baseball diamond and they will be playing baseball." That was one of his few similes in his writing, which he knew generally tended towards the plodding, and it pleased him. The paper had nothing to do with his Uncle Ed and his Uncle Nate and all the rest of them.

He ran through some fantasies in his mind, simple, modest exchanges.

"What do you do?"

"I'm a Professor of International Relations at Columbia."

And:

"Do you have the corner house with the elm tree in the front yard?"

"Yes."

"I see your little girl playing there. She's so cute."

Imaginary exchanges like this reassured him. They could all happen. Like his writing, they validated him.

Frances Carr floated. She enjoyed the sense of being buoyed up by the water. She liked swimming, and when possible, she swam two or three times a week.

Her mind went back to the time that the deputy head of her department, Oliver Smith, had told her about this project and invited her to take part. "They want someone from here to take part, and Tony and I thought you might be suitable. You're not involved in anything urgent here, you can take the time off. It'll stretch the imagination a bit. It could be very useful." Old smoothie Smith was sitting at his desk with his hands folded in front of him, talking in his office voice, earnest yet informal and friendly. He paused and then added, "It's up to you, of course. You don't have to do it."

"You bastard," she thought. She said to him, "I can see that it could be interesting." She was sure that among themselves they had dismissed the project as some bit of time-wasting nonsense from academia, probably American in origin.

She knew the men in the department regarded her as

uptight and prim. She was not above the occasional flirtatious remark to flatter a male ego, but her stand-offish attitude to office affairs and to jokes about sex was taken as icy disapproval. They would think that the idea of Frances having to loosen up emotionally and shed her inhibitions was a good joke, like giving a novice rider the toughest horse to ride. Bringing in Tony, the head of the department, was a clever stroke on smoothie Smith's part. Tony, the control freak, who would never let a telegram go out from the department without some emendation by him. Who expected any suggestion of his, dropped in the most casual tone, to be acted on immediately. "You don't have to do it. It's entirely up to you" – that was rubbish. If she said she would rather not, this would be remembered for a long time. All right, she would take part and she would show them. She would come and do a straightforward report.

Now another memory came to her, a different kind of memory from a different part of her mind, the feel of a naked man, his hairy body against her, on top of her. She started to block it. This was a dark memory. Thoughts like this, like the act they concerned, belonged in the night-time world. There were things that should be thought about only in the dark, that were not to be thought about in her daytime, workaday world, just as there were things that should be done only in the dark. But being here she was isolated and in the dark and it was like thinking in bed at night, which was allowed, so she let the thought continue. There came a merging of the bodies she had felt. Most of them were American. She remembered kisses all over her naked body, feeling a man's hairy shoulders. She remembered handling a penis, and then feeling it moving inside her, and the excitement. She stayed with the memory, indulging these thoughts for a while, and they went up to the edge of desire.

She had behaved during her year in Baltimore, when she was a graduate student at Johns Hopkins, as she had not behaved in England. There was a price to be paid for surrendering physically and emotionally. The price was not so high in a foreign country where the people around her would not be a part of her future. She told herself that she would not get involved emotionally, but even so she had suffered painful jealousy over Gene. Here in her own country, she did not want to pay the price. One day she would marry. In the meantime every two weeks or so there was James, who returned last year from an overseas posting, a decent man in an unhappy marriage. After America she found that she needed some relationship, that she would be physically deprived if she did not have it. She and James made few demands on one another. No one in the office knew anything about their affair.

Enough of this wasting time, she would take the opportunity to think about the St. George situation. She hoped she would be one of the people in charge of the British end. This would be like her present professional position but it would be a promotion. Well not exactly, because the Prime Minister and the Foreign Secretary were politicians and she was not and would never be a politician, having to win the approval of the voters every few years. It was important to keep things in the hands of the professionals. This should be an exercise in diplomacy.

Louis was floating. He was thinking about his wife, Sarah. He thought a lot about Tess but now, guiltily, his mind went back to Sarah. He ran the film projector in his mind over happy moments in their life together. Sarah reading some of John Donne's poetry to him at night – she had spent a year on Eighteenth Century poetry at university - her eyes glowing when she read certain lines because she loved them so. The first time she met his parents and he watched them connecting and getting on together. Her ready acceptance of his initiatives in their sex life: Their shared delight when the doctor confirmed that she was pregnant. Most of all, the continual conversation that was marriage at its best, in which sex was just a part of the conversation. It would break her in two if she found out about Tess.

He loved Sarah's matter-of-fact approach to the world, the way she presented herself and the way she dealt with other people, sizing them up and treating them accordingly. She knew she was good-looking and what her good points were: "I don't have those big limpid eyes that some men fall for and I don't have a perfect English rose face. But I've got good legs and good hair and splendid boobs." He remembered the matter-of-fact way she told him, after they had started their affair, that she was in love with him. "I find I've fallen in love with you, Louis," she said one day. "I can't stop thinking about you. I can't insist that you fall in love with me, although that would be nice. But treat me gently, please. If you're going to go, try to let me down as softly as you can."

He went over the time he decided that he wanted to marry her. They were on holiday together, in a rented villa on a Greek island. She had gone down to the shops one day in the late afternoon. He was sitting on the porch when she came back down the path, wearing the bare midriff blouse and denim shorts that had the local boys whistling at her. She was carrying meat from the butcher's wrapped in a newspaper.

"Are you going to cook dinner?" he asked, surprised because they ate their meals out.

"No, I'm going to cook this for Plato," she said. "There he is, he heard me coming." And the tall skinny black and white mongrel that had adopted them after they had petted it once on the roadway came lollopping up to the porch on its spindly legs.

She squatted down and rubbed its head and said, "You're going to have a nice dinner, you big handsome brute."

"Handsome? He has an appealing way, I grant you, but he's the ugliest dog I've ever seen." Plato turned his big spotted head to look at Louis quizzically and put his two front paws on the porch. Louis picked up his floppy ears and smoothed them with his fingers,smiling.

"Plato's lovely," Sarah insisted. "Now let's sit down out of the sun and decide where we're going to have dinner."

She put the meat on the table on the porch and they went inside and drank beers from the refrigerator. They decided on Kiprianou's for dinner, agreeing that it was a bit touristy but sometimes fun nonetheless. They were finishing their beers when they heard a rustle of paper on the porch. They darted outside and saw Plato working his way through the raw meat which he had pulled down from the table on to the dusty path, the newspaper shredded around it. Sarah snatched back the remains of the meat. "You fool!" she shouted at the dog. "I was going to cook it for you. You could have had it cooked. You silly dog!"

Her mouth was vexed but her brown eyes were soft with affection. He looked at her and suddenly he found her tender expression heart-wrenchingly lovely. He could imagine her looking at her baby like that. He would never forget her expression and her voice at that moment. He loved the way she looked at the dog and he loved her. He felt at that moment that there was a solidity about his love for her, something that was not transient and dependent on the mood or the circumstances,

He decided then that this was the person he should marry. This was no wild juvenile passion but a love that was a basis for a lifetime together. He could not imagine never seeing that smile again. All his doubts about their differences in temperament and age and his ability to share his life with someone vanished.

He kept this to himself until the following night. In bed he said, "I love you. Will you marry me?".

"Marry?" she repeated.

"Yes, marry. Til death do us part. For better or for worse. The whole traditional shebang."

"You're sure you're not just saying that because we had good sex?"

"I want you to be my wife," he insisted. "Official."

"O.K., yes," she said, and there were tears in her eyes.

Yet his picture of her had changed recently. She was a lovely girl with long legs and long straight blonde hair but she seemed like a lot of other lovely girls with long legs and blonde hair who had been to private school and a good university, who were cool and confident and knew they were destined for the good things in life and could not imagine any other kind of existence. She was complacent and he sometimes thought she was spoiled.

He should not make comparisons, he knew, but he could not help thinking that Tess was not cool and she was not like a lot of other girls. He did not want to think about Tess immediately after Sarah but his mind thrust before him insistently the memory of the evening he met Tess.

He had written something about the immorality of some British arms deals, taking off from a House of Commons committee report, and a small group who campaigned against international injustices had written approving his report and inviting him to meet them. He agreed because he thought he was spending too much time with politicians and men in suits, and not enough with intemperate people who were out of the system and angry at bad things that happened in the world..

They were all in their early twenties and he met them, at their suggestion, in a cheery pub near King's Cross. He was the centre of attention because he appeared on television and wrote a newspaper column and he had the floor whenever he wanted to speak. They listened respectfully to everything he said about newspapers or international affairs or life in Britain.

Tess wore jeans and a black leather jacket and underneath it a sweater pulled tight in at the waist by a wide belt so that it showed off her figure. She had high cheekbones and a triangular feline face, her hair was short-cropped, and she wore no make-up except a faint film of pale lipstick. Her wide brown eyes glowed from time to time, when she spoke about injustice and cruelty or when she was listening to him. When someone made a funny remark she threw back her head and gave a deep strong laugh that he loved hearing. She rarely raised her voice but he sensed reserves of passion within her, the way you sometimes sense the strength of an athlete even when he is just sitting still. He could not take his eyes off her.

Among the four of them she seemed to have authority, and Louis suspected it was because she alone spoke with a cultured middle class voice. Later in the evening when there was only one young man left and he went off to the toilet, Louis asked her whether he was her boy friend. She hesitated and then indicated that there was nothing serious between them. Louis realised that she did not want to appear to him to be attached and found that this pleased him. He wanted to see her again and thought it would be just once. He met her for lunch supposedly to talk about campaigning against World Bank policies in the Third World and also the arms trade, and by the end of that lunch he felt they should go on seeing each other. This was despite the fact that she was only twenty-three years old, sixteen years younger than him.

She was only now discovering her sexual power. When she told him her story he realised that she had not had the usual experience of flirting and dating when she was young. She had dropped out of her private school and run away with a man when she was seventeen, something so brave and independent that he could not imagine any of the women he knew doing such a thing. She lived with him for the next four years. So far as he could make out from her account he was handsome and he was going to be a writer, and running away with him seemed romantic and rebellious. It was also an escape from her insane mother. She supported them while he wrote by working, first in a supermarket – he could not imagine most of the girls he knew working in a supermarket – and then as an office assistant for a left-wing publisher. She was very intelligent and read a lot and she was soon promoted to an editorial position despite her lack of education. Her husband turned out to be feckless, a dreamer, and furthermore a bi-sexual with a preference for homo. As he saw it, she had been propping him up at a time when she should have been leading the carefree life of a single girl.

Soon after that lunch together Sarah became pregnant to their shared delight, and he decided to put Tess out of his mind, and did not call her again. But she telephoned him, a little while later, trying to get publicity for a book they were publishing. He said he did not see how he could help but he agreed to meet her again. They had lunch together again and then drinks, and he did not mention this to Sarah.

He called her and they met again, and she admitted that she wanted to go on seeing him and this made him giddy with delight. Then they made love and she told him that she loved him. She aroused in him passion that he did not know he had or did not know he could feel any more, a raw, youthful, innocent excitement that usually becomes crusted over. Just seeing her walking towards him in the street brought a stirring in his loins.

Tess was still a romantic, he thought, which she was why she allowed herself to be the lover of a married man. If something was right she would pursue it, without regard for convention or what other people thought. She demonstrated for causes she believed in, holding up a placard. She would argue with people on a moral issue rather than allow things to be smoothed over by conversation. This bold independence was one of the things he loved about her. On the few occasions he mentioned his marriage he exaggerated the difficulties.

When they talked about politics they were usually in agreement, but he tried to explain to her that one could not look at international affairs only in moral terms. "You can't dismiss the whole international system. It's too simplistic." Yet while he was saying this to her he was thinking that maybe things were that simple, that they were right or wrong, and that he was only denying it out of cowardice, because he knew that if he talked about it in the simple moral way that she did he would be marginalising himself, cutting himself off from the world of the serious people who made the world work. Even if he was right and the world was not so simple, he knew she was braver than him and a better person.

He worried about the way she would see him, successful and on top of things, at ease in this unjust world. In her mind he must be one of the privileged, commenting from his cosseted position on the struggles of others, one of those people who had compromised away any youthful principles they had. He worried that she would prefer some scruffy young man who could not afford to take her out to restaurants but spent his life working for a good cause. He imagined the sexual appeal of a strong young African who had fled persecution, who spoke little English, but whose soft brown eyes told of suffering. He knew men asked her out, and not only penniless young men, he was sure. She said she was not sleeping with anyone else nor did she want to, and he believed her.

He wished he could play a bigger part in Tess's life. He felt angry at the man she had lived with, who had sponged off her and had kept her from the life of university and boy friends that was her right. Her natural intelligence had not even had the advantage of a proper education. He fantasised about meeting this man and telling him what he thought of him, or hitting him. When he and Tess were together, unspoken questions hovered over them, questions about the future that neither of them could utter.

He had told Manash that he was betraying Sarah. He had

not told him that he was betraying Tess also; he could not bear to tell him because he could not say it out loud. He had never told Tess that Sarah was pregnant. He had intended to tell her but it had never seemed to be the right time. He was afraid that when he told her she would break off their affair even though it would cause her pain. She would know that with a baby coming he must be committed somewhere else. And, decent person that she was, she would decide it would be wrong to deprive a pregnant woman of her husband's attention. His silence on this was another betrayal of someone he loved, and he despised himself for it. The dilemma came into his mind now, and with an effort he dismissed it. He was going to become someone else and escape from these problems or a while..

Captain Raymond Wade floated. He often daydreamed. It was something entirely private. Nobody, not even his wife with whom he confided most things, knew of the varied life he lived from time to time. He regarded his daydreaming as a vice, something slightly shameful since it was a substitute for living in the real world. His father would sometimes dismiss someone as a dreamer.

. He was commanding a battalion and they had been under fire for days; he had not worked out details of where or why. The men were exhausted but his leadership was pulling them through. He was cool, in command, assessing the situation, snapping out orders, and displaying a cavalier disregard of danger. "Boy, you're really cool," one of his subordinate officers said admiringly as shells crashed around them. "That's what they pay me for," he replied in a flip tone.

He was in the White House, receiving a decoration, shaking the hand of the President while Louise and little Matt looked on proudly. The President ruffled the little boy's hair and remarked on what a handsome young fellow he was. He was at a top-level conference to discuss a crisis situation, giving his opinion, and the others were deferring to his realism and his good sense

Now he thought about the slight pain in the stomach he had felt a few times recently. He had put it down to indigestion but it could be something more serious. The doctors' verdict: Only a matter of time, I'm afraid, and not much time. He would respond only with a quip about not starting any long books. He would travel around visiting his old friends and being cheerful company, and write to them afterwards explaining that this had been a last visit. He would tell Louise to mourn him but then marry again – "You deserve love, make sure he'll be a good father to little Matthew," and Louise would cry and say she did not want anyone else, 00that she could never love anyone as she loved him. People would remember how bravely he accepted a cruel fate. He started to think of the words the clergyman would say at his funeral but then stopped himself. This was going too far.

Stephen Darrow floated. He was feeling pleased with himself. He knew he would be an outsider here, among the kind of people he did not know, and he had decided to play it very cool as he usually did in unfamiliar situation, and it was working. He thought about the people he had met here. He was generally good at sizing up people's reactions to him. He knew immediately if someone liked him. He knew it with a woman and if he fancied her he would be quick to take advantage of it, whether she was married or not. He had argued with his agent recently when his agent told him it was a mistake to demand more money. "The buggers want me and they'll pay. Trust me," he said, and he was right.

He reckoned that Ivor Howe had agreed to bring him into the project because he thought he would like it known that he was friendly with a working-class film star; it would indicate a dimension to Howe's life that most academics lacked..Green, the little American professor, was a bit scared of him. That Frances woman kept making eyes at him but she was strange. Probably, if he put his hand on her knee she would freak out. Best avoid her. Louis he could talk to. He'd seen him on television, he was a bit of an entertainer also. He reckoned that some people here thought a film star did not belong with them, that he lowered the tone. Some wanted to be near him because he was famous. Most of them were the kind of people he knew would spent a lot of time talking about how to get from A to B when he would just go straight there. There were the kind of people who, if somebody hit them, they would not hit him back but would call a policeman

These people talked a lot about things in the newspapers. They talked about big subjects, about international organisations and countries, the kind of things he did not talk about. So what was he doing here? Why had he come? He knew why he had come, why he wanted to take part as soon as he was told about this, and why he had pressed Ivor Howe to let him. He wanted to see what happened when he acted a part and went on acting it, when no curtain came down and no director said "Cut!"

In the Peter Brook company, they had talked a lot about what it meant to play a part, and he had found to his surprise that he had something to say. He could feel his way into a part, taking his body and his voice with him. He would pour another's personality and feelings into the way he spoke and moved. He liked the sensation of losing himself in another's life, his feelings, his situation. But he did not like coming out of it suddenly

Throwing himself into the part was an adventure, but it was not a real adventure, like taking off for the Continent with just a hundred euros in your money belt. In a film or a play, you knew what was going to happen. The script was already written. Leaving the part when the script came to and end, or when the director said "Cut!" was cowardice. It was like going to the end of the diving board and then stopping. He did not want to stop. He wanted to go through with the dive, to hurl himself into empty space. He wanted the whole adventure, to stay with the character and see what happened

::   ::   ::

When Stephen Darrow came out of the tank he felt strangely relaxed. He went back to his room and decided to read the briefing paper containing game scenario again. They had been told to make themselves thoroughly familiar with it. He moved the armchair under the overhead light and began to read.:

We tend naturally to believe that in human affairs, important events have commensurate causes. It offends our sensibility and even our vanity to think otherwise. A disaster in one's personal life should not be traceable back to something trivial. If a serious relationship crashes to pieces, we want it to be on the rock of a grand passion and not on the pebble of a misunderstanding. In international affairs we feel a crisis should be brought about by a serious collision of interests, by actions by the movers and shakers of this world, and not by some mere mischance.

Yet the dispute between the United States and the new government in St. George would probably not have become the St. George crisis if it had not been for Dwight Brewster's death from a heart attack. Brewster's kidnappers said his death was an accident and the general opinion is that they were telling the truth, that they had not planned to kill him. Although some people pointed out that if you bind and gag a seriously overweight sixty-two-year-old corporation executive for several hours and then imprison him in a windowless cellar, you must be aware that you are likely to damage his health at the very least.

Without the death of an American citizen, the American public could not have been stirred up about the arrival of a new left-wing government in the Caribbean or give much heed to calls for action. Even with other burgeoning leftist movements in Latin America, Castro and Cuba was no longer a spectre with which to frighten the children. And there was no way that anyone could link the revolution that overthrew the dictatorship there with Islamic terrorism

St. George, situated west of the Bahamas and north of Jamaica, is a part of the British West Indies and a member of the Common- wealth. It was claimed originally by Spanish explorers and named San Juan, but was passed over to Britain and renamed in a shake-out of colonial territories in the Eighteenth Century. In the years after that the population was mostly a mixture of African descendents of slaves, Caribs and Spaniards. The discovery of a gold seam in the 1870s drew adventurers from many countries. The seam was a geological freak and was soon mined out, but the brief gold rush left the island with a population even more ethnically and racially mixed than in most Caribbean islands, so that blue eyes and red hair are found among the inhabitants as well as several shades of skin colour. The mining led to the discovery of deposits of bauxite, which became the most important of the island's exports. Agricultural produce was still exported, but the rocky soil that covered most of the island was not ideally suited and it became less profitable once slavery was abolished and plantation workers had to be paid, however minimally.

Throughout its brief history, both as a colony and, since the 1960s, as an independent nation, St. George has had alternating phases in which British and Hispanic cultural patterns dominated. The government was on the whole democratic in form, although it usually served the interests of the wealthy ruling oligarchy. Occasional bouts of gross mis-rule and corruption were terminated either by a commission of inquiry and constitutional change, in a British phase, or anti-Government riots, in a Hispanic phase. In recent years the political culture of St. George had gone through a pronounced Hispanic period with a Latin-American style *military dictatorship. But some months ago the dictator, General Gomez, was overthrown by the democratic opposition, and he flew out to his condo in Miami as the rebels stormed Government buildings.*

The U.S. Administration initially welcomed the change despite a few anxieties about the professed Socialism of the new regime, as did the British Government. Outside Washington few people in America paid any attention. St. George was one of the smaller Caribbean islands and it was not a popular vacation spot.

The new prime minister was a left-wing academic who had lived for several years in exile in London and Washington and was well-known at international seminars on democracy and human rights. His government soon took a direction that worried the U.S. Administration. It announced that it intended to nationalise the local plant of the American-owned Capital Bauxite Corporation, the biggest industry on the island; it enacted new labour laws that forced employers to pay a minimum wage and empowered unions; it announced plans to break up the large estates, some of them foreign-owned, and distribute land to landless peasants; and it imposed currency controls that reduced the outflow of profits to foreign investors

It ran into economic difficulties, with inflation and unemployment. Workers staged strikes. Left-wingers blamed foreign companies for the trouble and called for them to be nationalised immediately and without compensation. To dramatise this demand, some members of a group called Action for Economic Democracy, the AED, kidnapped the General Manager of the Capital Bauxite plant, Dwight Brewster, and said they would hold him hostage until the Government acted. A week later, they announced with regret that Brewster had died of a heart attack.

The authorities arrested three men for the kidnapping and they were charged with manslaughter. The U.S. Government demanded that they be charged with murder and called for the leaders of the AED to be arrested also as participants in what they said was an act of terrorism. It said the St. Georgian Government was being soft on the AED because its leaders were political allies.

Some media commentators said America should Do Something. After all, the area just south of the continental United States was traditionally a playground for CIA adventurers and the scene of easy interventions by the military. Alternative St. George leaders were said to be waiting in the wings if the Administration should decide that the new regime was to be replaced.

When an American television reporter asked the St. Georgian Minister of Labour why the three arrested men were not being charged with murder, he got a heated response. "Murder?" the Minister repeated angrily. "I'll tell you who should be charged with murder! Your General Frank Benvenista, that's who! Benvenista of Capital Bauxite." He went on to allege that Benvenista, a retired American brigadier-general who was security manager at Capital Bauxite, had conspired with death squads under the old regime to have trade union organisers killed.

Capital Bauxite's public relations staff made sure that the American public knew all about General Benvenista's decorations for service in the first Gulf War, as earlier they had directed media attention to the grieving of Dwight Brewster's wife and two grown daughters and the importance of bauxite from St. George in sustaining the American way of life. A Congressional election was coming up, and some candidates were seeking to demonstrate their suitability for office by demanding that the President declare St. George a terrorist state and take some action. They dropped dark suggestions of dangers on America's doorstep.

This was the situation that was to confront the players in the game. It was recounted, with more details about S.

George's economic situation and about the principal actors on all sides, in their briefing paper, most of it in the formal language of serious political reporting. All the participants in the game were reading it.

CHAPTER SIX

Donald Green had an unpleasant dream that night. He dreamed that he was trying to put labels on ghosts. The labels were attached to cords to be put around the neck so that they dangled in front. He was going from one ghost to another and putting the cord around its neck. But just as he did so the body vanished and the label fell to the ground, This upset him but he went on, going from one ghost to another and putting on the labels, continually frustrated.

The dream came back to him in the afternoon and he could not shake it off. He went down into the lounge and picked up *The Economist* to read and tried to fill his mind with the changes in one part of the world or another and the arguments of the editorial writers. But he found it difficult to concentrate. Even when the details of the dream faded, the sense of frustration that it engendered remained with him.

He looked for a conversational partner to shake him out of it and saw Louis Mannion, who was reading a newspaper. He did not like Louis very much but he would do. However, as he approached him Louis got up and said, "I'm off to see our shaman." He sat down and went back to *The Economist.*

It was Louis's second session. He was not going to say anything more to him about Sarah and Tess. Instead, answering questions about his professional life, he talked about some of his feelings about the people he came across as a social worker, and about the guilt he sometimes felt about his success in journalism.

"I come across as somebody with a lot of self-confidence, and in some ways I suppose I am. But I sometimes have this idea that nothing I do is any good. That what I write isn't any good, no matter what other people say. I look at it and I say, 'Yes, it's true, but so what? It's not worth saying.' I know that's neurotic and silly."

"Why do you say that?" Manash asked.

"Why do I say what?"

"That it's neurotic and silly. Maybe you're right. Maybe it isn't worth a lot."

"But my writing has got me a reputation. I mean, the paper *asked* me to write a weekly column. It's a serious paper."

"So? Does that mean it necessarily has real value?"

"I like to think some of it has. Abeit perhaps transient"

"You said the other day that you sometimes thought that what you were doing was trivial how-ever high-minded it sounded.."

"I was comparing it with what I was doing as a social worker, helping people. And it was just a passing thought, when I was feeling sort of depressed. I don't really think that. Have you read my column?" Louis demanded.

"I'm not saying your writing isn't good, it may be brilliant. And it may be very worth-while. But very few things that appear in newspapers have lasting value. I asked why you assume that it's neurotic to think it isn't seriously good."

"I told you, don't really think that," Louis snapped. "It's just an idea that comes into my head from time to time."

He left Dr. Manash's office in an irritable mood. He had promised to telephone Sarah again and he decided to call her now. He sat down on a bench beside a path and dialled her number.

"It's an interesting experience," he told her. "It's doing something to me already, although I'm not sure what."

"Something bad?" she asked.

"Not exactly. I'm, saying things I don't mean to. It's a little worrying. Some people are behaving oddly."

"How oddly?"

"In the middle of a discussion about Southeast Asian politics, one man suddenly told everybody about a knocking-shop in Jakarta where the girls have special talents."

"Oh really? Anything I could use?"

"It just spilled out of him. He was very embarrassed. And a Canadian civil servant told me about a woman he loved who threw him over. I mean, told me for half an hour. With feeling. Said he hadn't talked about it to anybody for years. I'm struggling to keep myself buttoned-up sometimes. How are you? What are you doing?"

"I'm feeling a bit under the weather, to tell the truth."

"Which way?"

"Oh, headaches. And my hands are swelling a bit. I can't get my ring off."

"Maybe you should tell Dr. Robbins."

"Oh no, I'm sure it's perfectly normal. I'm just a bit jittery going into the final stretch. I can't even do any serious reading. I haven't started the Richard Dawkins book."

"What are you doing? Are you going out?"

"Cynthia came over today for lunch and we talked about her divorce. Mother calls every day to check on my health. Twice a day if I'm unlucky. I'm getting awfully tired of it."

"Maybe you can tell her tactfully."

"Tactfully? You know my mother."

"Well try to fend her off. I'm sorry you're feeling bad. I don't like the idea of your hands swelling."

"Everybody told me the last two months of pregnancy aren't a lot of fun. There's nothing to worry about, I'm sure."

"Okay. But if it goes on and if the headaches go on, do go and see Robbins. He might be able to give you something for them."

"Okay, if it gets any worse I will."

He got up and headed back to his room, thinking about

what a difficult time it was for Sarah with her fatigue and her headache and her hands swelling, and how good she was about it all. He might call Tess later. He could not speak to her right now. There were levels of betrayal.

He decided to read the game situation again to familiarise himself with the details and started off for his room. He saw Stephen Darrow walking along another path and Stephen crossed over the lawn to meet him.

"Do you feel like a drink?" Stephen asked.

"You mean go to a pub?"

"I was thinking of the first floor, Yellow House."

In his room Stephen poured whiskey from a leather-covered hip flask for both of them, adding some water from the tap for Louis. "At home I could have offered you some smack," he said, "but Ivor made me promise not to bring any here. He thinks it might fuck up the psychology part of the experiment."

Stephen sat in the wooden chair turned around so that its back was to the desk, Louis sat on the bed. They speculated about Dr. Manash. Louis asked, "Tell me, how different is this for you from acting a part in the normal way?"

"I don't know yet," Stephen said.

"It must be quite different."

"Yes, but the important thing is that there's no script. That's what's important for me."

"There's a story."

"Only to start with. We don't know what's going to happen."

"But what about the acting," Louis went on. "We're supposed to become the part. Not act but just be the part naturally. Which is what you try to do when you're acting, isn't it?"

"Naturally? You think acting is natural?" Stephen demanded.

There was something in his tone that made Louis think he

had touched a nerve. He backtracked a little. "I mean, no art is natural. But there is naturalistic acting. Isn't there?"

"Balls," Stephen said.

"What do you mean?"

Stephen looked down and seemed to be thinking about whether to reply. Then he looked up and replied with a torrent. "I'll tell you something. Some wanker wrote in a newspaper that I was a natural and a couple of others picked that up. People ask me that in interviews, how natural I am as an actor. Crap! Absolute crap. Acting isn't natural. You're projecting. I had to learn it, and bloody hard work it was. I started on the stage, remember, not on telly."

"How different is that?"

"Very. On the stage you talk so that you can be heard in the balcony. What's natural about that?. Saying a lot of words someone else has written. That's natural?"

"Well, not if you put it like that."

"Okay, so I'm working class and Nottingham and I played a working-class Northern lad in *Along the Canal.* And on the stage I played another in *Billy Liar* - Jesus, that was a real bastard to learn. A natural! As if I was just getting up there and being myself. Just be Stevie Darrow, that's all. You think I'm going to be paid for that? Those poncey, public school critics think all working-class people are the same. Like Chinese, you know. If you're working class you can just be yourself and play a working class lad."

He was leaning forward with his elbows on his knees, his head low, looking up at Louis as he talked. Louis remembered him sitting in that posture in the lounge after lunch the first day he came, only then he was cool and now he was not cool. He was talking faster and he was excited and spittle was coming on to his lips.

"A lot of people in the profession used to treat me as a bit of a freak. Some of those posh girls from university and drama school with their posh little voices too. I'd knocked around the Continent, I spoke some French, but I was still a rough working-class lad who'd worked on a building site. They probably thought I had a bigger prick than their posh boy friends. Some of them might have been disappointed. I'm unusual, you know, someone to show off because I'm different. And you know what? You know what, Louis? That's why I'm here. That's why Ivor said I could come. He thinks it makes him look good that he knows people like me and not just other professors." He leaned back as if he was exhausted by this outburst.

"But you learned to act."

"Yes, I learned to."

"It's lucky you found you had a talent for it." Stephen was silent for a while and Louis thought he was not going to say any more. But then he started speaking again. "I always liked to perform. I loved making the other kids laugh in the school playground. And at home, the family. I wanted to be a stand-up comic. I mean, I didn't think it was really possible but that's what I wanted. Billy Connolly was my idol, a shipyard worker turned comic. I never thought I could be a real actor. I saw actors on the telly but it didn't occur to me that I could be one of those. But somebody in Paris told me about being an extra in films and I thought it was a great idea."

"And then the Peter Brook company."

"Yes. The papers said that was chance that I got a job with them, shifting scenery and stuff. It wasn't chance. I wanted to be around them then. I didn't know why."

"You like acting."

"Yeah. Acting means everything to me." He was speaking softly, as if bringing up thoughts from deep inside himself. "You can put your feelings into what you're doing. They're feelings I didn't know I had, and when I'm acting, somehow they come into it. Even when they're somebody else's feelings. And you make them register with other people, that's the great thing, that's the trick. When the audience follows you. I didn't know there was anything like that. And when you're working off other people on the stage and they're working off you, on the same wave length, it's magic. If I wasn't acting I don't know what I'd do. Just piss my life away, I suppose. Like most people."

There was a long paused after this discharge, as Stephen drifted down from his peak of excitement.

Louis said, "Down there in the lounge, you said you liked ating just because it was a cushy job with good pay."

He shrugged. "Well. That was just something to say, wasn't it. I wasn't going to tell all this to that lot." Then, "How about you? Do you like your job?"

"Most of the time."

"And the rest? Other things?"

"Most of my life, yes. My wife's pregnant."

"You looking forward to being a dad?"

"Yes, I am." Louis found that he wanted to talk and he knew Stephen would listen as he had listened. It was those pills, he was sure. We're like a couple of drug addicts, he thought. You score me and I'll score you. He started slowly.

"I was thirty-three when I got married so I wasn't a youngster. I'd had affairs, I'd had plenty of experience. I'd had one-night stands and I'd had emotional relationships. Excitement, ups and downs. Life has phases. I'd gone through that phase. Now I wanted stability, certainty, commitment. I married for life. I wanted us to share our lives. And now we're going to have a baby. And I'll be committed to the baby as well as to her."

"Commitment, huh?"

"Yes." Now words were pouring out of him and he could not stop. "I didn't have my fingers crossed when I took the marriage vows. I didn't think, 'Oh well, we can get divorced if it doesn't work out.' I didn't think I could always get a bit on the side. I'd had all that. I was going to be faithful to her and she was going to be faithful to me."

cxxvii

"And have you been?" Stephen asked.

"Have I been what?"

"Faithful, as you call it. Nothing on the side."

Louis had not expected the question. "Y-y-yes. Yes. Yes I have."

There was a silence while they both recovered poise. Stephen held out the flask and asked, "Do you want some more of this?"

"Thanks." Louis let him pour some into his glass and went over and added some water from the tap

"Why did you volunteer to take part in these shenanigans?" Stephen asked.

"An experience," Louis said. "I look forward to being somebody else, getting out of my life for a while."

"But you seem pretty pleased with the life you've got."

"Oh yes, I have a good life. I've been very lucky. But I like the idea of a change."

"You mean like a holiday," Stephen said.

"Yes. Well, more than that. When you go away on holiday you get a change of scenery but you're still yourself. I'm going to spend the rest of my life, the only time I have on this Earth, as one person. Just living with my own character and my own history. It's like sitting in your own bath water. It's so limiting. Knowing that you can look at the world only through one pair of eyes. There's so much I'll never know. I'd like to see the world through someone else's eyes. I can never really know what it feels like to be someone else. You get some idea from a good novelist. When I was a social worker I tried to put myself in the position of some of my clients, people having a really hard time, people whose lives were awful. I tried to imagine being where they were sitting. It was difficult. In fact, I couldn't really do it. Don't you ever feel that way? That you'd like to know what it's like to be somebody else?"

Stephen shrugged. "Can't say I've ever thought about it. If things has worked out different, if I'd done something else with my life, I would have been someone else Anybody could be someone else. It's just chance."

"What else could you have been? An industrial worker?"

"Maybe. I could have been a pimp in Paris."

"You mean if you'd been born something different."

"No, no. I mean me, Stevie Darrow. I could have been a pimp in Paris. It was just chance that I wasn't."

"How was that?"

"One night. I was walking back home through this street off the Boulevard Haussman and I saw this bloke beating up a girl. So I thought, well, this isn't right, so I pulled him off her. He wasn't big but the little fucker had a knife and he turned on me. He nearly got me. I knocked him down and because he had a knife I made sure he didn't get up again for a while..

"Well, the lady was very grateful. Turned out she was a tart and he was her pimp. She was good-looking, too. So we went back to her place. I told her I didn't have any money but I guess that was her way of saying thank you. And very thankful she was. Next morning she said she liked me and she needed someone around and she asked if I would like to take his place. I understood enough French then to know what she was about. I might have taken her up on it but I was already working at the company and Brook told me he would give me some lessons. If it was a few weeks earlier but it might have been different. So it was just chance."

Louis said, "You really would have done it? Become her pimp?"

"Sure, why not? It seemed a step up from where I was before. I'd probably have enough money to eat properly."

"But that's you, Stephen. My life's been more limited. I could never have been a pimp in Paris."

"Why not, if the circumstances were right?"

"I just couldn't. I might possibly have stayed on as a social worker, though I don't think so really. I might have been a lawyer, or an academic, or gone into politics. I might have gone into the City as some of my friends did. But I was limited. I couldn't have been a pimp or a gangster or an industrial worker."

"You could be if you wanted to be. I couldn't. I couldn't have been a lawyer or a professor or any of those other things. I didn't have the education. You could be anything you wanted."

"No I couldn't."

"Why not?"

"I just couldn't, that's what I'm trying to tell you. I was going to be a middle-class professional and lead that kind of life." He knew that Stephen, seeing his privileged background, could not understand that it was limiting."That's why I say, I'd like to try being somebody else. Change my identity for a while, like in the game."

"So who would you be?"

"I don't know, just one of the other five billion people on this planet. See the world through somebody else's eyes. Maybe a Bangladeshi peasant or an Afro-American in one of the ghettos"

"You want to try being poor, something like that?"

"Not necessarily poor, no. Maybe an officer in the Coldstream Guards. Anyone else. His outlook on the world, the way he feels when he gets up in the morning, his sense of what it's like to be alive, must be very different from mine. Even if I were an American cabinet minister it would be different. So I'd like to experience that. Just for a while, not for a long. Don't you ever feel that way?"

Stephen paused reflectively, then shook his head. "No, I don't think it's occurred to me."

Across the way in Blue House, Brian Thaxted paced up and down in his room. He was troubled. Every now and again he would stop and stare out of the window looking down at the courtyard, seeking an answer to questions in the paths and green grass and doorways opposite, things he could see and that he knew were there.

Walking back after lunch, he had started thinking about what his family was doing while he was away here, and he realised with a jolt that he could not remember his wife's name. He worked on it as he climbed the stairs, and it came back to him: Paula. What else had he forgotten? The names of his children came to him easily, Tom, Annabelle and Jessica. The family's spaniel was called Sally, that took a little longer. It took him two minutes to get his address. He worked on other names: his wife's parents because they had just been to see them, the people in his department. He knew he would not get his telephone number.

He tried visual memories. He set out to recall incidents of family life. He remembered some from their last holiday, but it got hazy when he tried to go further back, to when one or another of the children were babies. And when he tried to move in closer, to visualise his wife's face, or his children's, the picture became blurred. They were just some people he had known a long time ago.

The things that made up his life were slipping away from him. It was if he reached into his pocket for his keys or his wallet and found that they were not there. He found reassurance in the promise that other things would replace what he was losing.

::   ::   ::

Jacob Shemtov found he was almost cheerful when he got out of bed. Usually the first hours of the day were the worst, particularly when he did not have an early class, struggling out of bed with that heavy weight on him, struggling to choose his clothes and dress. He thought that perhaps those tablets were countering his normal depression. Then he decided that his lighter mood was because this conference was giving him something the army had given him, a place where he was expected, the guarantee of company. He would come down to have breakfast with other people, and people would be around whenever he wanted them. If he did not come down someone would notice.

It was also like the army because he was not really a part of the group here. He had never really felt part of the army, although he needed his place in its structure. When another officer's wife fell in love with him she told him, "You're not like the others." This apartness seemed to be in his nature.Now, as the day wore on he found he was living vividly in the distant past for spells again. He had told Dr. Manash again that he was worried about the way these memories were taking hold of him, and Dr. Manash said this was all right, he could give in to them. So, sitting in his room with the game document on his lap, he let the past come back.

He was in the waiting room of another psychiatrist, years ago, in another country and another language. He could see in his mind the sandy striped wallpaper and two oatmeal-coloured armchairs with wooden arms. A photograph of the New York skyline under glass was on the wall and another one of a Venice canal, presumably souvenirs of holiday visits. On another wall there were drawings in crayon by a child, one saying "Happy Birthday Daddy I Love You." These were signs of a happy and successful life, underlining unnecessarily, Jacob thought to himself, the unhappy and unfulfilled life of most of the doctor's clients..

Inside the office he was sitting in an armchair facing the doctor, trying to answer his questions. "It's just pain. I told you, I feel mental pain. Awful pain. And dizzy spells. I've told you about the dizzy spells. I keep thinking I'm going to faint. But I've never done so."

"What do you feel when you feel this? Do you feel anger? Regret?"

"I feel pain! Pain isn't an emotion. It's not like feeling happy or sad or worried. It's just painful. If somebody's got a

toothache he's got a bloody awful pain. That's what he feels."
He clenched his lips together. A soldier should be able to take
pain. A soldier should not cry. He wanted to cry. Fuck it, he
wasn't a real soldier. He wanted to fall down on the floor and
cry.

"You tell me you've felt this before."

"Yes, I've always had these sort of feelings from time to
time. I've even been to a doctor about it before. I told you, I
had them much less in the army. I think that's one reason I
stayed in. But this is the worst."

That was the really bad time. The army had given him
medical help and written on his report "post-traumatic stress,"
which he reckoned was only a half-truth if that.

He came back to the present and, looking out on the
Abbotsbury School courtyard, he thought about that time, and
about the pain, remembering it now rather than re-living it.
The paralysing pain he suffered all alone, in his room in the
officers' quarters, and in his mother's flat, where he could not
tell her anything, could only confirm for her what was
obvious, that he was not feeling well. He would sit for hours
pinned down in an armchair. The pain had trapped him in a
loneliness that made it worse, that drove him further and
further inside himself. When he read of people whose
neuroses came out in bouts of drunkeness or in violent rages,
he envied them.

On the rare occasions that he had talked about it to anyone
afterwards, he had called it depression. The doctor accepted
that it was depression and that was about as close as anyone
was likely to get. It was a short-hand term. But like all those
other words he used when he talked about himself,
"marriage," "lecturer," "army officer," he knew it did not
begin to encompass the truth. "Potency problem" was at least
more specific and more descriptive. It meant limp dick. That
was something he could not bring himself to talk to anyone
about.

The army gave him medical leave while he had treatment, and he had lived at his mother's apartment, telling her only a little of what was going on in his mind. As it happened she was away some of that time visiting her sister in South Africa. That was the worst time, the pain almost continual. It was easier when he went back and the army gave him part-time administrative duties. Some norms of life were forced on him. Living in the officers' quarters he could not go to bed in his clothes because the effort of changing into pyjamas was too great, or hardly eat for days on end, or not shower or have a bath for weeks. He was forced to make the effort, and having other people around made it easier. Having to get to the office, having to do a job some of the time, having to keep up the appearance of normality, was a terrible strain, and at times he thought he could not do it.. But it was also a source of support.

He had functioned through that time, or pretended to function. He was silent when the others were talking about women and sex, weeping inside because he could play no part in the game between the sexes. Sometimes, when he talked to people, he was amazed at the normal sentences that were coming out of his mouth, when what he wanted to do was cry out, "Help me, somebody please help me!" He had never broken down in public, although he had sometimes been afraid that he would do so. He had an urge sometimes to give up, just sit down in the street and say, "I can't go on, somebody please take care of me!" and sit there helpless and let people come and take him away. But he had never given up, never collapsed completely and asked other people to take care of him. That was an achievement, he reckoned. He did not have much to be proud of in that time but he felt proud of that, although he could not share this feeling with anyone.

He despised himself for being dependent on pills to keep going, for having to look at his watch, anxious for the time when he could take the next one. At the worst times, when it was really bad, he could not reach other people. Even when he seemed to be talking to them it was fake. He had no living flesh that could connect with the world outside himself. He was blocked solid inside, from his head down to his feet, as if he were made of metal, his parts all jammed up, like a watch that was broken, its outside intact but its working parts smashed into pieces inside.

One Spring morning when he was alone in his mother's apartment he was dressing slowly, occasionally looking out wretchedly at the sunshine and at the lemon tree in the front garden of the house opposite and wanting to feel something about the scene, wanting just to feel, wanting something to penetrate the shell of this solid block that was himself. He went into the bathroom and stood for a time facing the mirror, wearing just his trousers and shirt and slippers. He was getting ready to shave, and he was holding a blade that he was about to fit into his razor, the blade in his riht hand, the razor in his left. But he just stood there in front of the mirror, not moving, not even seeing his reflection. Then, without thinking about it in advance, without knowing what he was going to do, he did it.

Blood spurted out of the fleshy heel of his hand to stain his shirt, hurtling him into sanity. He had slashed with the razor blade at the part of his hand that had plenty of flesh and no arteries. He did not want to do himself serious harm. The blood was real and the sharp sting was real. He was sane for the moment and behaved like a sane person and wrapped a handkerchief tightly around his hand to stem the flow of blood and ran out into the street in his slippers and hailed a taxi to take him to the hospital. He felt good now, the pain inside him all gone, the sting in his hand replacing it.

In the hospital emergency room he explained how he had had this stupid accident, slipping and falling with the razor blade in his hand, while the doctor put in three stitches. He was talking normally, and the doctor was saying, "You're

CXXXV

looking a bit pale. An accident like this is a bit of a shock. I suggest some fresh air. Or perhaps get yourself a glass of brandy."

He nodded, and inside he was almost weeping with happiness because he and the doctor were really speaking to each other and he was feeling a part of the world again and not just pretending to be a part.

Back home, an hour later, he lost that feeling and he wanted it back. He wanted to slash himself again, it had felt so good. But if I do, he thought to himself, if they find two razor cuts in the same hand done on the same day, they won't believe it's an accident and they'll take me to a loony bin. I mustn't let that happen. He fought down the desire.

After a while he could go back into active service although it was two or three years before he could really get on with his life. He never worked out how much of it was due to the psychiatrist and how much to the passage of time. The old attacks of the mental pain that he called depression came back from time to time, more frequently and more intensely after he had separated from Miriam. Marriage, like the army, had provided a framework for his life, something that supported him as well as constricting him.

He was pleased when he could tell people normal things, or at least things that sounded normal: he had been in the army but he had left, he got this university post, he was married, he and his wife quarrelled, they were divorced. He could even speak of a period of post-traumatic stress after the war. These things could be in anyone else's life.

He wondered whether his quarrels with Miriam were like other men's quarrels with their wives.

"You ignored me all evening," Miriam would say. This after they came back from a party.

"You were talking to other people."

"You were talking to Hannah. You don't have time for me when Hannah's around. You were hanging on her every word."

"That's crap. Hannah's your old friend, not mine."

"You wanted to go to bed with her once."

"That was before I met you. Anyway, I went through a period when I wanted to go to bed with everyone, I told you."

"You even went to bed with that fat cow Rifka."

"She's not so fat."

"You'd jump into bed with Hannah now if she gave you half a chance."

"What the hell's the matter with you?"

"It's your whole attitude. You don't act like a husband. You don't even know what being a husband means."

He looked across at her. Pain and anger showed in her face. It was easier to respond to the anger. "What do you want me to do?" he demanded.

She looked at the floor and muttered, "You shouldn't have married me. You weren't ready for marriage."

"It's a bit bloody late to decide that. We've been married for ten years. We've got a nine-year-old daughter."

"Well it's about time you started being a husband."

After a while even the gaps between their quarrels were periods of cold war. One subject after another became a field in which to wage coded battle: friends, his teaching career and hers, politics, even television plays that they watched together.

"What a bastard," she would say, as a play ended and they switched off the set.

"Come on, look at the things she said to his mother."

"His mother deserved it. She was an interfering bitch."

He knew he should not reply, he knew where it was going. But he said, "She wasn't that bad. His wife could have been more understanding."

"He's married to her, not his mother!"

"But his wife was being awful."

Politics also.

"The Government's right," she said one evening when the evening news on television had finished. "We've got to defend ourselves."

"But that's just a political move to appease some right-wing idiots."

"Political! Defence against terrorism isn't an abstraction, it's the protection of our people."

"I am supposed to know a little about defence."

"You know about tactics but you don't know about people. You don't have that instinct."

You mean," he said, coming out of code, "deep down, I don't eally care if my wife and child are blown to bits."

She shrugged off his sarcasm. "You lack some feeling. It just isn't there. I'm going to bed."

My wife," he said to a colleague over coffee the next morning in the university cafeteria, "has a Clausewitzian view of marriage. She sees it as the continuation of warfare by other means."

He had got by for a while but then their quarrels became too much for Miriam and she left him and he had to live alone. He missed Miriam, even though whatever love they had for each other had been eroded away by friction over the years, missed having someone around who cared how he spent his days.

Now some of the pain had come back and it hung on him like a weight. He had carried it around London, getting up in the morning alone and forcing himself to go out and look at the sights, not enjoying much of it. The weight was no heavier than in the past, not as heavy as the worst time, but he was older now and he tired more easily

He was lonely. Friends had drifted away. He did not like calling people who did not call him. He had applied unsuccessfully for several academic posts and had been turned down. In the past he had had a couple of articles published in academic journals that he was quite pleased about, that contained some good clear thinking, and one on Israel and the Palestinians that had earned him kudos partly because by chance it had appeared just when the Oslo agreement was signed. He had been invited to speak at conferences, in Israel and in Amsterdam. But that was long ago. He would have to resign himself to being passed over for promotion again and again, knowing some people were saying it was a pity he had left the army.

He hoped that he could turn the paper he was working on, about states and non-state actors and the international system, into a book. But he had begun it long ago and he was always having to introduce new material with the appearance of new forms of international action, such as Al Quaida.. He was relating the changes in the nation-state to classical theorists, but wondered whether he was talking about Hobbes and Hegel because he had nothing to contribute to current discussion. Was he simply keeping the project going as an emotional crutch? Was not the reality that he had nothing useful to do but he had to pretend to be doing something? Pretending to be a scholar as he had pretended to be a soldier, pretended to be a normal human being,

His impotence was not only in the intellectual sphere. Once again he could not approach women. He had had painfully embarrassing scenes and he was not going to risk another. When he chatted with that Australian woman at the restaurant in London, who seemed happy to get to know him, he did not look her in the eye and did not suggest that they meet again. This blocked another path away from loneliness and misery. From now on his sex life would consist of fantasising about women and masturbating. He held himself in contempt.

Too much had been wrong with him for too long, probably for his whole life. Once, browsing in a bookshop, in the section devoted to books on personal improvement, he saw one called *How to Live a Full Life*. How to live a full life? That was easy, he reflected. How about a book on how to live a half-empty life? That was the challenge.

He was quarrelling with his daughter Shula, continuing the quarrels of adolescence that should have stopped long ago. He would blame himself for losing his temper as he yelled at her for her rudeness and hostility. He savaged himself by going over in his mind their worst exchanges. She shouting at him, "You're just jealous of me and Yigal!" her slim little body twisted and tense as she leaned across the table, he shouting back at her, and even as he did so cursing himself for doing so, for allowing this violence to develop between them when he loved her so much. She had always said she would not take sides in her parents' quarrels but he knew she felt more sympathetic towards her mother. It was natural, she was a girl and she was living with her mother. He forced himself to remember that there were good times with Shula also. She liked to cook a meal for him sometimes. She had come to see him off at Ben-Gurion Airport and he remembered the feel of her arms around his neck when she kissed him goodbye. She was kind to him. But this was not enough, not enough to keep him going. Not unless things got a lot better, and he did not see how they could.

. There were fewer possibilities left, fewer years for him to recover. Things that go wrong at this age would probably not be put right. He was like a parachutist in free fall, nearing the ground with not enough time left for the parachute to open.

He knew how he would do it. Nothing violent, he had seen enough of things that smash bones and tear flesh. He would go to his doctor and tell him he had agonising sciatic pains. He had had them once before, as the doctor knew. The doctor would give him some strong pain-killers, stronger than anything one could buy over the counter at a chemist's.

He would go to a hotel in Tel Aviv, one of the big luxury tourist hotels where he could be anonymous and where the surroundings would pamper him and make everything easy. He would register under another name, announcing himself as an Israeli who now lived in America. He would already have dropped hints to Miriam and Shula that he was depressed, so that they would be prepared. He would stay in the hotel room overnight, having arranged to be somewhere the next morning, so that he would be missed. They would have a whole day to worry about him. He would stay there the next day, in his room. He would watch television and read if he could, and look out of the window at the people on the beach, sitting back in his armchair in his shirtsleeves and slippers, enjoying the comfort and the anonymity. Then, in the evening, he would put a note on the dressing table giving his name and address. He would leave a note for Shula; it was important that she should not feel any guilt, that she should not think she had neglected him in some way and had contributed to what he was doing.

He would send down to room service for a light meal , an omelette or perhaps a club sandwich, and a cup of coffee. He would eat the food so that the pills did not go into an empty stomach which might throw them back. Then he would drink the coffee and swallow all the pills, two at a time, and he would lie down on the bed, and close his eyes, and the nagging pain that was living would slip away from him.

Now it was time for dinner. He washed his hands and went downstairs and across the courtyard. It was twilight, and overhead the clouds were dark blue, purple and black with golden hues around the edges, like glowing bruises.

"You're looking serious," Thaxted remarked, as they passed each other in the courtyard.

"I'm thinking about serious things," he replied.

"Getting into practise for handling an international crisis?"

He smiled. "That's right. It's going to be a heavy responsibility.".

In the administrative building, Dr. Manash walked into Ivor Howe's office to collect him for dinner. Howe was on the telephone and motioned him to sit down for a few moments.

When he had finished, Howe asked, "How are the interviews going?"

"Some interesting material coming out," Manash replied. "Those tablets are really doing some good."

"None of them seem to be out of themselves yet," Howe said. "They're still relating to the world around them."

"Of course. They can't get out of themselves yet. They've no place to go. We haven't given them their roles. Which is what's next."

"And then they'll be totally absorbed in their roles?"

"I'm hoping they will be. They'll be playing a game, but they'll accept the rules of the game and they'll be in their roles. I don't know how far they'll lose their present selves. Remember, this is an experiment. From my point of view, the advantage of this game is that we'll find out things."

They started walking towards the dining hall. Howe asked, "Are you finding out anything now?"

"I have the impression that some of them are loosening up a little when they're with one another. Some of them are less firmly fixed in their character than others. Which is what I expected. As I told you, we all create our identities as we go through life."

"What's that line from T.S. Eliot?" Howe said. "'We put on a face to meet the faces that we meet.'"

"Exactly. And not only for others. We create a face for ourselves too."

"I've prepared my announcement about trying on these new faces."

They reached the dining hall as the gong rang. They took their places side by side near the centre of the table. Howe waited until everyone was seated and then rapped his glass for attention.

When the room had fallen silent he said, "After dinner, you may open your file marked 'Role.' This contains an account of the role you will be taking on. You may read it."

CHAPTER SEVEN

A s he dressed, Donald Green wondered whether he should call Stack-Stevens again. He did not want to appear too anxious. But, he told himself, putting on his socks, Stack-Stevens had sounded sincere when he urged him to look him up in Oxford, and held out the possibility of a year's fellowship. He must have got his message. Stack-Stevens had only one more day to reply. As he buttoned up his shirt he reflected that if he did not hear from him he would have to contact him again after the game was over, and he did not want to have to do that. He tied his tie, put on his jacket, looked at himself in the little mirror with some satisfaction, and went downstairs.

After breakfast he went back to his room and, sitting at his desk, he read the paper with his game role. He had read it the night before but now he was going through it sentence by sentence, a furrow in his brow getting deeper as he read. He thought that much of his success in life was due to careful preparation.

"Donald Green is the Deputy Director of the National Security Council, but as the Director is ill he is taking his place. He is a lieutenant-colonel in the Marines. He recently helped organise a covert intervention in Central America. He was given the NSC post to appease some right-wing congressmen. The Administration assumed it was one in which he would be directly under both the Director and the President, and so would have little scope to act independently. They did not count on the Director being ill so that he would be in charge.

"Green believes in the aggressive pursuit of American interests abroad. He has strong views on domestic affairs also, which he inherited from his working-class Irish-American background (his father was a policeman in Boston). He wants strict law and order policies, is sceptical about welfare schemes, is pro-family, anti-pornography. He carries these views into his family life. He, his wife and their two children are regular churchgoers, and on national holidays he raises the American flag on a flagpole outside his house. His 17-year-old daughter has taken to making jokes about his patriotism, which makes him angry. He has just discovered that she is sleeping with a boy in her high school and she has smoked marijuana."

Then followed a detailed biography, beginning with his parents and his high school in Boston, and going on step by step through his career in college, his prowess as an amateur boxer ranking high in the Golden Gloves, his promotions in the service and his move into the Administration.

An hour later he was sitting opposite Dr. Manash,. "I know this man is very different from you," Manash said. "But I want you to absorb his life story, absorb his views, try to identify with him."

Green shook his head silently. "I'll try," he said. "I can manage a university department, but I can't imagine myself being a good leader of men in combat. I don't think honestly that I'd be a success in the Marines and I can't see myself as a Golden Gloves boxer. On the National Security Council, yes. That I can imagine."

"Try to look for things in this other Donald Green that you can find somewhere in yourself," Manash suggested. "Take patriotism. Surely you've felt a surge of patriotic feeling sometimes." Green looked hesitant and he pressed on. "No?"

Green said, "I pledged allegiance to the flag through my schooldays. I sang the patriotic songs. I was patriotic in a simplistic way, like most children."

"And now? Don't you ever get angry at people who sneer at America?"

"Of course I get annoyed at simple-minded anti-American prejudice."

"So work on that. Try to imagine getting angry at the breakdown of standards. You have a daughter."

"Yes, like this man, Colonel Green. He has a son and a daughter."

"Surely your daughter's welfare, her moral behaviour, means a lot to you."

"She's just coming up to her second birthday. I don't have to worry about her sex life just yet."

Manash pressed on. "But you will have to. Haven't you thought about the standards you'll teach her?"

"I suppose so, yes."

"Her standards will depend to some extent on the standards of the society around her. Think about people who encourage an anything-goes attitude. Imagine your daughter rejecting all your ideas of moral behaviour under the influence of some teenage boy with long hair. Like the Colonel's daughter seems to be doing. Imagine what she might be doing with him and his friends. Drugs and all the rest. How does that make you feel?"

"Of course I wouldn't like it."

"Wouldn't you feel angry?"

"Yes, I'm sure I would," Green acknowledged.

Manash had been pushing him and getting only a limited response and he dropped this line. He asked, "Do you know anybody who was anything at all like this man? Anyone you might identify with him just a bit?"

Green knew the answer to that one immediately. "Tommy Gibbons."

"Who's he?"

"He worked at a summer camp where i worked one summer, the year after I finished high school, just before I started at Cornell. He was a swimming coach. I was a junior counsellor. That's what it's called in America. It means helping take care of the younger kids and in my case giving them tennis lessons. My mother got me the job through someone at her school. Tommy Gibbons was an older counsellor." He paused. He was not used to autobiographical forays and he was surprised at how easy it was to go on. There was something about Manash.

"For some reason, Tommy Gibbons was friendly to me. I was younger than most of the other counsellors. I didn't enjoy it much at the camp. The atmosphere among the counsellors was pretty macho. You know, these guys who were good at sports, at diving and swimming, talking about sex and having a great time with the girl counsellors. I spent a lot of time by myself reading when I wasn't with the kids. I don't know why Tommy spent so much time with me. I suppose he didn't know many people like me and he was curious. He used to ask me lots of questions about going to Cornell and my parents and my home. We'd talk a lot. I think his way of looking at things was rather like this Colonel Green. Although I don't think he would have made lieutenant-colonel. Sergeant, more likely."

Manash nodded approvingly. "Good. Think about Tommy Gibbons and the way he looks at things. Now, I'm going to try some hypnotism. I told you last time we might try it." Green nodded in agreement.

He picked up a silver chain with a metal disc on the end and held it up. "I want you to look at this," he said. "Concentrate on it, and listen to what I'm saying. Your eyes are going to become heavy. You'll feel sleepy. That's right. Now when you leave here today, you won't remember anything that I say to you. Gradually, you're going to stop being Professor Green. You're going to become somebody else. Not right away but gradually. Soon, you won't be a Professor of International Relations. You won't be married to

Lorraine. You will be someone else...."

When Green walked away from the office he was thinking about Tommy Gibbons. There had been boys like that in school but he had avoided them. But that summer, he had relied a lot on Tommy for company, and also for protection against the sneering attitudes of some of the others.

Tommy tried to teach him what he called street smarts. Often they would talk in the empty wooden dining hall, open on all four sides with mosquito screens instead of windows, while the crickets chirped outside in the darkness. He recalled now, without much effort, Tommy in his shorts and t-shirt squatting down in front of him when he was sitting on a camp chair, or sitting across the table from him, puffing on a cigarette. Tommy looking him straight in the face with an earnest expression across his freckled face with his turned-up nose and blue eyes as he explained the facts of life.

Tommy on women. "Girls want to get laid just like guys do. Remember that, Don. Only sometimes they feel they got to put up a show. They want to be persuaded, y'know? They want a bit or romance. Like, you got to kiss them a lot before they let you fuck them, that kind of thing. But always remember that they want it too. And if they complain afterwards if you dump 'em, then tough titty. They did it of their own free will."

Tommy on America's place in the world. "We're the greatest country in the world. Every other country in the world wants what we've got. They all want to take it away from us, and if we're not strong they will. So we've got to be strong, That's the price you pay for being number one."

Tommy on international organisations. "If the United Nations had their way, a bunch of ragheads who don't know shit would be telling us what we can do and what we can't do. Stands to reason. Most of the countries in the world are poor and uneducated, and they're the majority of the U.N. Same with the International Financial Whatever-the-fuck-you-call-it. I saw something about it on TV the other day. They want our money."

Tommy on Britain: "They think the world should look up to them and their snotty, stuck-up ways just because of Shakespeare and culture and all that shit. Well the Queen of England can kiss my Royal Irish ass."

Tommy walked differently from him, Tommy and his friends. Their bodies carried their confidence and assertiveness, as if their flesh were armour and they did not have to worry about collisions. They were proud of their biceps and their pectorals, and like Tommy, they wore tight t-shirts with very short sleeves that showed them off. He could never hold his body as Tommy did, never walk the way Tommy did. He shrank from collisions.

Let's try to think like him, he told himself. I'm Donald Green and I think like Tommy Gibbons although I'm more intelligent. Tommy Gibbons would not be a lieutenant-colonel, nor on the NSC. So let's see, I believe in the Marine Corps and the American flag, I'm suspicious of intellectuals. Suddenly he was frightened and brought himself up with a start. What is this? I'm not narrow-minded. I'm Professor Donald Green, my wife is Lorraine, my daughter is Josephine. I've worked to be where I am, I've earned it. No. I should play the game. I promised I would. Let's start again. I consider foreign policy issues. I'm a marine officer. I'm suspicious of intellectuals because they analyse things like patriotism that should come naturally. We need intelligent people who can analyse things but they have to think in the right way. They have to have the right motivation. This other Donald Green thinks in words like 'motivation' First and foremost I'm a marine."

Frances walked into her second session with Dr. Manash with some anxiety. She had been worried about her first session, but she had answered all his questions about her identity without difficulty. She was sure of who she was and how she got that way. She had told him, in answer to one of his questions, that she had no worries about slipping out of her identity for a while because she was sure she would have no difficulty getting back into it. "I'll be playing a part. I 'm aware of that" she told him.

She was not comfortable with self-exposure. She knew who she was and she did not need to share this knowledge with others. What worried her now was that she found she was looking forward to his questions, and looking forward to answering them. She was rushing into something when she should be keeping her distance. She sat in the armchair with her arms on the wooden sides leaning forward despite herself.

He asked her, "How do you feel about being American Secretary of State?"

"Fine. I'm quite comfortable about it. I thought I might have something much more difficult.".

"Why do you find it easy?"

"Because it's the sort of thing I do, the sort of thing I've been trained to do. Diplomacy, if you like. I'll be defending the country's interest. It'll be a different country, that's all."

"This other Frances Carr Dowson is a different kind of person to you. When she was a student she was part of the peace movement. She went on demonstrations in favour of minority groups and against American Government policies. That's going to be you. Do you have trouble imagining that?"

"Not really. She was young. That kind of thing is characteristic of intelligent but naive young people. It's past her now."

"You weren't naive when you were young."

"Oh I'm sure I was. Although not as naïve as a lot of others."

"But you didn't go out into the streets and demonstrate."

"No, I suppose that's not the kind of thing I would do. And I didn't believe that moral protests would make the world better. As I say, I wasn't that naïve."

"Frances Dowson Carr has a somewhat glamorous past. She was married for a while to John Dowson, an academic celebrity twenty years older than her. After they were divorced she had a long affair with a television newscaster."

"You mean I'm not glamorous and I'm not likely to have had an affair with a TV newscaster. Yes, I can accept that." Her modesty was self-assertion. It was saying that she knew exactly who and where she was and nobody else could tell her.

"That's not quite what I meant. I'm pointing out the differences in your lives."

"You mean with different standards."

"In some ways, yes." He paused, giving her a chance to go on, but she did not take it. Then, "You spent a year in America, at Johns Hopkins University."

"Yes. As a graduate student. It was near to Washing- ton so I got to know it a bit."

"Could you picture yourself as an American?"

She pondered. "Mmm, not easily. The students - the people I associated with - were a little different from British students, I suppose. More open about themselves. More self-analytical. More ambitious, or more openly ambitious."

Were you different when you were in America?"

"Mmm, maybe."

"Different in which way?"

She leaned back and now she licked her lips nervously. She knew she was going to tell him.e had "In America I had several affairs. I was quite promiscuous, in fact." She thought she might be blushing.

"Promiscuous? You slept with a lot of men?"

"Not a *great* many."

"But a different one every week."

"Oh certainly not!" This was annoying.

"Well how many then?"

"Four. Five if you include one that was a mistake and

didn't even last one night."

"Four in a year? I don't think most people today would call that promiscuous."

"Well I would. I have standards about how people should behave." She had straightened her back and now she was sitting upright.

"I know."

"And I don't just mean about sex. I mean about integrity. Which is a part of the same thing so far as I'm concerned. And other things. I've told you."

"You're not promiscuous now. I mean not even to your American level."

This was an invitation to supply more information and she supplied it. "I have a relationship. With a maried man. It's not what it sounds like."

"Is it a passionate relationship?"

"It's a physical relationship, if that's what you mean."

"It wasn't, actually." When she did not respond to this, he asked, "Where do you think your standards come from?"

"I know where they come from. They come from my father. He was a man of integrity and he taught me its importance."

"He was a civil servant, as I recall."

"That's right, I said that on my questionaire. He could have gone farther in his career if he's been dishonest. He knew he was expected to doctor a report for political reasons. He refused to do so. That made him unpopular with his department head. I admire his stand."

Manash said, "You have a strong character, you know. No, don't smile. Your character is a defence."

"You mean I'm protecting myself against falling in love with you? Transference?" She thought she might show him that she knew some psychoanalytic jargon.

He did not answer but asked, "What do you think you're defending yourself against? Something outside? Or something inside?"

"I don't go in for deep self-analysis. I don't find it useful."

He did not respond to this but said, "At our next session, I want to try some hypnotism with you. Is that all right?"

"Yes," she replied. "I can't say I look forward to it."

"Because you think someone else will be controlling you?"

"I agreed to take part in the game and to go along with that if it was required."

She left Manash's office and walked briskly down the corridor and into the lounge. At the entrance to the lounge she passed Jacob, who was heading for Manash's office and they nodded to each other.

Ingrid Mundt had a cup of coffee in her hand and was taking one of the armchairs. "I've just been chatting with him," she told Frances, indicting Jacob's retreating form. "Have you met him?"

"I was talking to him yesterday for a while."

"He's quite attractive. That Jewish type with those sad, intelligent eyes appeals to me."

Ordinarily Frances would have ignored a remark about a man's physical appeal but now she replied. "I don't find him attractive," she said.

Ingrid said, "By the way, I was going to ask you a favour. Have you got a hair drier with you that I could borrow this evening? Mine seems to be *kaput* and I won't be able to borrow yours once the game starts."

"You don't think they'll allow government-to-government exchanges on the subject?" Frances asked smiling. "Yes, I have one and I'll bring it over."

She sat down next to Ingrid. Her talk with Manash and the prospect of being hypnotised had brought back some of her earlier anxieties. She remembered Munro's outburst about whores in Jakarta when he clearly did not know what he was saying. Something might happen to her that could be horribly humiliating. Some other people seemed to be behaving a little oddly.

"Are you nervous about this game?" she asked Ingrid.

Ingrid shook her head. "Not really," she said. "But I think it will be interesting."

"You're not worried about losing control?"

"It will only be for a little while and nothing awful will happen. Why, are you worried?"

"I like to be in control of myself," she replied. Ingrid nodded and sipped her coffee but did not say anything so Frances went on. "When I was an undergraduate I had this friend. Well, she wasn't a close friend but a friend. A Welsh girl, from Cardiff, doing English lit. Anyway, she didn't normally sleep around or anything like that. But sometimes she used to drink too much at a party. Then she'd flirt with some man and wake up next morning in bed with him. She told me that. I couldn't stand being like that."

Ingrid nodded understandingly. "I knew someone like that once. Very inhibited. She couldn't go to bed with a man unless she was drunk."

Green walked by. He seemed to Frances to have a peculiar gait. His back was unnaturally stiff and his shoulders moved from side to side while his hips were rigid. In a taller man it would have been a swagger. She wondered whether he was suffering from haemorrhoids. She suffered from them herself during hot weather and knew what they could do.

Green watched the two women talking. The German one is skinny and getting on a bit but she looks as if she's up for it, he thought to himself. The Brit has got nice tits, big and firm. A bit thick around the hips. But stuck-up and distant..

Wade and some others were sitting around near the two women and Wade threw out a question to anyone in earshot. "What do we think of our roles?"

'Frances said, "I'm not sure we're supposed to talk about them."

"We're not supposed to talk about the situation," Wade

said. "St. George and America and all that. I think we can talk a little about our roles. Are you happy in yours?"

"I think so," Frances answered. "It's what I do now, only it's a big promotion. How do you feel about yours?"

"Quite cool. The Prime Minister of Great Britain is not a bad thing to be. I sort of feel I belong in Ten Downing Street. I've read about my role and absorbed it. I've been through a long struggle to get there. Stephen, I gather you're going to be the President of the United States. Have you ever played a part like that before?"

"No. And it's different," Stephen said. "I don't have a script. Nobody's telling me what to say."

"Well they are in a way. I mean, you're not just any old American president. You've got your character and your background and your viewpoint given to you."

"Yes, but I don't know what other people are going to do. That's what makes it interesting."

"Doesn't anyone feel," Davies asked, "that they're going to be just a wee bit out of their depth? I mean, none of us is exactly prepared for the highest office."

"We're being prepared by Dr. Manash, at high speed," Louis said. "Isn't what this has all been about?"

"You feel a bir out of your depth occasionally when you're in command," Wade said, "The trick is not to let anyone know it. That's one of the first things you learn about exercising authority. Let people think you're swimming along splendidly. That you've got things under control."

"When really," Stephen said, "you're not waving but drowning, as the bloke said."

"The bird," said Louis.

"What?"

"Not the bloke, the bird said it. Stevie Smith."

"You mean Stevie Smith is female?" .

"That's right."

Wade asked, "Wasn't she the broad that knocked herself

off?"

"No. You're probably thinking of Sylvia Plath, another poet," Louis said.

Jacob Shemtov sat in Manash's office. He was sitting forward on the edge of his chair, hesitating before speaking each sentence. When he did speak the sentences were pre-packaged, with thoughts that he had worked out before, but they came spitting out propelled by emotion.

Manash was saying, "It was after the 1973 War that you started seeing the psychiatrist."

"Yes. Well, that wasn't the first time but that was the first time for a long period. The war was an awful time. I'm not saying it was worse for me than for anyone else. But I was very frightened. For one thing, I thought for a while that we might lose, and you don't know what that means for an Israeli. Maybe not lose altogether but lose territory, have the Syrians in our towns. That would have been a bloodbath. I was afraid I wouldn't do the right thing. And I was frightened for myself also. So frightened that I didn't think I could function."

Manash said, "But you did function, didn't you?"

'"I seem to have somehow, but I was very frightened." Now he started speaking quickly, in tense, terse phrases. "When other tanks are hit and on fire, you know the same thing could happen to you. You have this terror with you. Somebody's killed or burned alive, you may be next. You may be killed, snuffed out, your life brought to an end. But you have to function, so you keep it away. You hold off the terror. You pretend it can't happen. It's always there, knowing that it can happen to you, threatening to overwhelm you, but you hold it off because you have to keep going so you pretend it can't. It's a tremendous strain, holding it off, while you think what to do, take in the situation, command your tank, command your squadron. Most of the time I didn't know what I was doing, I was giving orders but it seemed as if there was someone else doing it. I wasn't in my skin because there I could have been killed. Then when it's over, it all comes rushing at you, all the feelings, everything you've held off. That's when it hits you."

"So the time after a war, or after combat, is a bad time."

Jacob relaxed his limbs, the tension discharged. "Yes. Everyone says that. Even though we won. That was important too."

"And after the 1973 War, that was a bad time for you."

"Yes, it was."

Manash's next pause was a long one. Then he said, "Now tell me what led to your breakdown."

Jacob straightened up in surprise. He had been found out. After a while he said, "You don't think it was the war?"

Manash shook his head. "Not that, no, I don't think it was the war." He paused. "Was it?"

Jacob said, "I don't feel like talking about it now. I really don't."

"All right, you don't have to. We'll talk about Prime Minister Shemtov. And the situation in St. George."

When Jacob left the doctor's office, he thought he could be on the way to becoming the Prime Minister of St. George, through some process he did not understand. He looked forward to it. He would escape for a little while from the dungeon of his self. The Prime Minister was dealing with a situation. He was out there in the world, acting. He was not punching the air, pretending to do things, he was making things happen. He was not even thinking of committing suicide. Why should he?

He crossed the courtyard to his room, sat down at his desk and re-read the role paper. "Jacob Shemtov, the Prime Minister of St. George, is forty-eight years old. He is a mulatto, the son of a doctor and descendent of a Russian seaman who deserted his ship in St. George at the turn of the century to join in the gold rush. He had loving, supportive parents. He went to Victoria University, St. George's only university, and did a post-graduate degree at Cambridge. He returned to St. George to a post as a lecturer in Caribbean history at Victoria University and joined opposition and human rights groups. He wrote polemical articles attacking the Government. When General Gomez seized power in a military coup after economic disruption, he was sacked from his post and left the country.

"In New York, with financial help from a liberal foundation, he finished his book *The Caribbean Road to Social Democracy.* After that he took up a teaching post at London University and remained there, interrupting his tenure with two sabbaticals at American universities and attendance at international conferences. He was in contact with rebel groups within St. George. When agitation began to threaten the Gomez regime he returned in secret after eight years in exile, and two weeks later, when Gomez fled to Miami in his private jet, he was the unanimous choice of all the opposition groups as the new Prime Minister. Revolutionaries wanted someone more radical but he was deemed the most widely acceptable. His government is a coalition of parties..

"As a young man he was angered by the cruelties committed by the police even under a nominally democratic regime, and it was this that first impelled him into politics. He himself has never experienced violence. He is awkwardly aware of the gap in experience between him and those of his political colleagues who remained in St. George and suffered under the previous regime.

"He values St. George's British connection and membership of the Commonwealth. He believes in the democratic norms. He is worried about the AED, Action for Economic Democracy, the extremists on his left, because they undermine the rule of law and could de-stabilise his government. He has not had much experience as a practising politician. He is not used to dealing with opposition.

"He has frequent quarrels with his wife. She is the daughter of a wealthy Hispanic-American family who spoiled her. She enjoyed her status as the wife of an admired intellectual exile in London and Washington, but chafes at her present life in St. George, where she has few friends and does not even see much of her husband. She often visits to New York and Palm Beach and dresses in designer clothes paid for by her parents. They have two sons, one a student at Victoria University, the other an intern at a law firm in New York." There was more about his family life and his intellectual preoccupations.

"Well," he thought, "I may not know much about the Caribbean, but I believe in democracy, in the democratic norms, as this paper calls it. I've commanded men, I've directed operations, although I haven't run a country, or a revolution. And I know academic life, like he does. Miriam never dressed in expensive designer clothes but she was a bit spoiled, and she could certainly be bloody quarrelsome."

His brow furrowed some more as he thought about the problems of St. George, which were mainly economic. They were going to need a foreign loan soon, or if not a loan, then foreign investment. And the Americans were not likely to be friendly. Considering these problems, he felt his muscles loosening up.

::   ::   ::

Louis had decided already that he would like to be an American in the game. At one time he had toyed with the idea of emigrating to America and starting his career there. He was not too serious about it; his family and most of his friends were in Britain and he felt he was probably more British than American. Also, he had doubts about living in the most powerful country in the world that threw its weight about. It was easier to take a critical stance from outside. But part of him was American, and he would like to have let that part out and let it take over for a while.

Withdrawing here from his day-to-day concerns, he recalled some of his happiest times in America: his first high school dances in the gymnasium at fourteen when he discovered that girls liked him and wanted to dance with him; the darkness of a cocktail lounge, as the most downmarket bar often described itself, laughing with friends, when going out drinking was still a youthful adventure; standing on the softball field pounding his fist into his first baseman's glove as he waited eagerly for the play to begin, and the exultation the time he made a three-base hit that clinched the game, hearing the cheers as he raced into third base and another man made the home plate. When he opened the folder he was disappointed. He was not to be an American. He lay on his bed reading.

"Louis Mannion is a leader of a trade union in St. George and the Labour Minister in Shemtov's cabinet. He is one of five children who grew up in a poor family. His father worked as a porter in a smart hotel and relied on tips from foreigner guests for much of his income. He spent a lot of his money drinking and playing cards. His mother held the family together, made sure the children got to school and kept the boys away from crime. She became ill, refused to visit the doctor on the ground that it was an unnecessary expense until it was too late, and died of peritonitis. Louis was twenty-one at the time.

"Although he left school at sixteen he continued to read, and went to meetings and educated himself. He read novels and some modern political writers, particularly Franz Fanon and Noam Chomsky. He worked at the bauxite extraction plant for eleven years, nine hours a day amidst tremendous noise and heat. He worked on the sifting machines and then he learned to operate the machinery controlling the chemical extraction process, a skilled job. He joined the small union and became its leader and helped to extend its power. He is a good speaker; he can convey his own passionate feelings about issues to a crowd and he can sense when an audience is ready for his message. He was batoned by police during a strike.

"When Gomez seized power he was arrested as a trouble-maker, beaten up in a detention cell, his nose broken and hearing damaged temporarily, but later released. He worked as a labourer on building sites for a time but then got his job back at the bauxite plant. He kept up a network of underground contacts and they formed a nucleus ready to take to the mountains and start guerrilla warfare, taking Fidel Castro's guerrilla campaign as their model. In the event the Gomez regime collapsed after weeks of urban agitation.

"His aim in entering politics is to raise his fellow-workers out of poverty. He believes in democracy but as a means to that end. His loyalty is to these people and to the individuals who took part in the revolution with him. His entire political experience has been in the trade union movement and the illegal opposition in St. George. He has never been out of St. George.

"With his union background, he rates loyalty highly as a virtue. He has friends in the AED, and one of the men who kidnapped Brewster was a close ally in the labour movement and shared a prison cell with him. But he was angry at the kidnapping because he felt it was disloyal to the Shemtov Government and its policies. He enjoys being a minister, enjoys taking decisions, but he worries occasionally about the corruption of power, and whether this will separate him from the workers.

"He is a Catholic, reflecting his upbringing. This does not play a big part in his shaping his outlook, but in a time of crisis he will sometimes go to church and pray for guidance." Some details of his political associates followed.

So he was to be Louis Mannion, a St. Georgian labour leader. How, Louis thought, am I going to get a handle on that? Not for the first time, he reflected on his abysmally limited experience of the world. He had never worked at anything other than a white-collar job. He remembered a conversation about politics in somebody's room in Cambridge, when one student talked about more power for the workers. A girl who was the daughter of a barrister and went hunting at weekends rounded on him. "The workers! What do you know about the workers? You mean those dreadful men in the pubs on the housing estates in Cowley? They're friends of yours, are they? They want more power? You know what they want?"

He thought about hard physical work. He remembered his muscles aching, from a long-distance walk or a hard session of squash or when he was moving house and carrying a lot of things, but that was not day after day, in heat and dust. Loyalty he could understand. He remembered when his friend at Cambridge had got drunk and groped a girl in a pub disgracefully, and they had hustled him away before she could summon help. His friend deserved to be punished but they had protected him. He could understand this other Louis Mannion's loyalty to the workers of St. George. He could understand his ambition. He had imagination. But to place himself in the position of someone who had never been to Europe or to America, whose experience was so limited, that was difficult.

He should be able to relate to Louis Mannion's Catholicism. He cast his mind back to his adolescent years when he was preoccupied with sin and redemption and Jesus, and it came back to him very easily. He had prayed to Jesus, and to Mary, and for a while even to some of the saints also. He had revered St. Peter for his achievement and his martyrdom, and St. Francis for his gentleness.

He could certainly understand this other Louis Mannion's anger. His days as a social worker helped here. He had met many people then ground down by debt and anxieties, whose lives would be made immeasurably easier by even a small amount of money, the kind of money that other people spent freely without thinking, the kind of money that most of Capital Bauxite's shareholders would spend in a weekend. The Government should channel the flow of money away from those shareholders to the workers. Of course it should.

Somehow, he seemed to be sinking into the role even as he was reading about it. It was almost as if he could remember the noise and the heat of the factory. He felt anger for his beating by police.

He was not finding it difficult moving away from his other life. Writing a newspaper column, chatting wittily on the radio, socialising with friends, all seemed distant, as if he had been away from all that for several months and it was fading in the memory. He did not think of either Sarah or Tess all day.

Stephen Darrow was sitting in Dr. Manash's office and he was grinning. "I can do it!" he said. "I'm half-way there now. I can feel it in my bones."

"I'm sure you are," Dr. Manash said. "But you won't be playing the part of somebody taking decisions, you'll be taking them. Are you going to be happy about that?"

"I don't know. Maybe I'll feel out of my depth. You'll make sure I won't be, right? That I'll have the character I need to cope. I think I'm feeling some of it now."

"Good."

"Because I won't be playing President Stephen Darrow, I'll *be* him. I'll rely on my staff, of course, but I'll take the final decisions. I can be authoritative. Or sound it. Because a President, someone like that, is always putting on a bit of an act."

He walked out of Dr. Manash's office with a bouncy step and a slight wobble of nervousness in his stomach. The adventure was starting, the adventure he had been looking forward to. The writer could not stop the world and tell him get off because the last page of the script had been reached.

He would stay in the part, whatever happened next. He would dive off the diving board, sailing into the air, hurtling towards the unknown.

::   ::   ::

Jacob Shemtov went into the TV lounge and watched the nine o'clock news without interest. There was nothing about St. George. Ingrid Mundt started a conversation about one of the reports but he excused himself and went across to his room. He was preoccupied with his last talk with Dr. Manash, and with what he had not said.

He almost wished he had told Manash what happened at the end of the war. He thought he did not want to talk about it but now the recollection lay heavy on his mind, and since he had not let it out in words he found he had to go over it again. He had forgotten a lot in these last two days and was worrying already about St. George but he remembered what he had held back from Dr. Manash.

The brigade was finally stood down at the end of the war and most of the enlisted men were sent home on leave. He and some other officers had to stay. But then on Saturday morning he was told unexpectedly that he could leave. Mordecai offered him a lift into Tel Aviv but he was going immediately. Jacob wanted to telephone his mother to say he was coming but the number was busy when he rang and Mordy said he could not wait, so Jacob just threw a few things into his kitbag and jumped into the car.

It was a hot day. They drove south along the coast road, the sea a motionless dark blue out of the right-hand window, heat haze shimmering above the surface. They did not say it but they were both nervous, heading back from the company of men who had shared violence and terror and loss into a different world, a world of civilians. He knew that even Mordy was nervous.

"What if your mother's not in?" Mordy asked.

"She's quite likely in. It's Saturday, her shop's closed," Jacob said. "Anyway, if she isn't I can wait next door, the neighbours are friendly. You didn't give me a chance to telephone again."

"I'm sorry but my girl friend's waiting at a café, I told you," Mordy said. He accelerated libidinously at the thought.

He dropped Jacob off outside his mother's block of flats and Jacob shouldered his kitbag and took the lift up to her floor. The curtains were drawn.

His nervousness came back to him as he stood there and his heart started thumping in his chest. He rang the bell and waited. He stood in the corridor and rang again and waited some more. Maybe she had the television on loud and could not hear. He rang once again. No answer. He picked up his kit bag and was turning away to try the neighbours when the curtains twitched, so he waited.

A moment later she opened the door and cried, "Jacob!" She seemed shocked as well as surprised She was wearing a wrap-around dressing gown although it was three o'clock in the afternoon.. Then she 'hugged him. "Oh darling," she said, and pushed him back to look at him as if to assure herself that he was all in one piece. Tears came into her eyes and rolled down her cheeks, and she hugged him again.

He kissed her on the cheek and followed her into the apartment. She was disconcerted, shaking her head as she said, "I-I hadn't expected to see you. Do you want something to eat? You must be - I didn't think you'd be back today. Why didn't you telephone? I mean, I thought - ."

"I didn't know I could leave camp until this morning," he said. "I tried to phone you but you were engaged for a long time. Were you taking a nap?"

"Have you eaten, Jacob? Would you like something? Coffee?" She was gazing up at him fixedly as if she might lose him again if she looked away from him fror a moment..

"I've had lunch. A cup of coffee would be fine," he said.

She turned to go to the kitchen and he started to follow her. She put coffee and water into the percolator and switched it on, then turned to look at him again, staring at him as if she were reassuring herself that he was here without any flaws. "I was praying for you when the fighting was on, praying that you would come back. And here you are."

He began to tell her about Mordy giving him a lift and not being able to wait. He had the idea that if he went on talking about things that had happened after the war ended, he would not have to talk about the war.

He was explaining why he thought he would have to stay in camp when he heard a sound behind him. He turned around, and Meir Birnbaum came out of his mother's bedroom.

"Hello, it's great to see you back," Meir said, and came over and clapped him on the shoulder.

He was rooted to the spot. He could not speak. Eventually he replied in a weak voice, "It's good to be back." He managed an unconvincing smile.

"I bet it is," said Meir.

His head was spinning. In the months that followed, he went over that moment and that whole afternoon again and again in his mind. What came back to him most strongly, the particular point of shame, was his passivity, his inability to do or say anything other than utter conventional phrases. He had let Meir set the tone all the way

"Your regiment was in the thick of the fighting," Meir said.

"Yes, we were there," Jacob acknowledged. He could not think, could barely articulate.

"You stopped the Syrians," Meir went on.

Meir said they had all worried about him and talked a little about how the war had turned out. . Jacob acknowledged his words and made minimal response in the same weak voice.

Then Meir said, "I'm sure you and your mother want to talk so I'll leave you." His mother walked with Meir to the door and they spoke softly for a few moments before he left.

She went into the bedroom and dressed and then he talked to her for the rest of the afternoon. He told her just a bit about the war and heard her news. They talked about people they knew. She told him that his cousin Chaim had had his foot blown off in Sinai. All the time his mind was in a turmoil. He could hardly believe that he was sounding normal. The news about Chaim was the only thing he could remember later about the conversation.

In the early evening when she was in the kitchen making him some supper he said he had to go back to camp. He did not know why he said it but he needed desperately to get away, back to the security of the army.

"Oh that's too bad. I thought you'd stay here for a few days," she said.

"Not now. I'll have a week's leave soon," he promised her.

"If you must go, I'll drive you to the bus station," she said.

In the car she said, awkwardly, "Meir was visiting, but we didn't know you were coming. Otherwise - " she trailed off, and he said nothing. He let her wait for his bus and kiss him goodbye when he boarded it.

"What are you doing here?" the duty officer asked when he walked in.

"Difficulties at home," he said.

"I'm sorry. God. they must be really bad if you're back here."

"Yes."

"Feel like a game of chess?"

"No thanks. I'm not up to chess."

That night he had a nightmare. He was a small boy being turned out of a room into an empty corridor. He did not know who was turning him out or why but it made him desperately unhappy. He saw the corridor vividly. It was carpeted but with bare dirty white walls. He had seen that corridor in some film. He woke up in a cold sweat and could not go back to sleep.

The dream stayed with him. The next day the dizzy spells started. He had never fainted in his life but walking down to breakfast he thought he was going to and he had to stop and sit on the stairs. Others asked him what was wrong.

When he came into town next, a few days later, it was to see Ruth, to try to get back on track. He had not called her for some time and did not know whether she would want to see him but she sounded delighted when he telephoned. He supposed she saw him as a returning hero come to claim his reward. He went through the motions over dinner and talked a little about the war and she beamed with pleasure. She was happy for them to go back to her flat, but it was a disaster.

In bed he said, "I'm sorry."

She said, "It's all right, it happens. You've been through a lot."

After a week of sleeplessness and pain and an outburst of sobbing in the army doctor's office, he agreed to the doctor's suggestion and saw a psychiatrist. He asked him, "Why should it affect me that much? That's what I don't understand. I'm not a small child, I'm twenty-four, for God's sake."

::   ::   ::

At the start of lunch the next day, Ivor Howe rapped his glass for silence and made one of his announcements: "Just to remind you, dinner tonight will be the last meal we'll all be having together in this dining room for five days. You'll all be confined pretty much to your own houses after today, and as we said, you'll have your meals there."

Actually, people were already withdrawing from the collective into themselves that day. There was less spirited conversation at mealtimes, and people spent more time on their own. Everyone had a session with Dr. Manash although the sessions were shorter than usual, some lasting only a few minutes. Everyone had a session in the immersion tank, with

clxvii

headphones on, absorbing their roles.

For Donald Green, the day began badly. He woke up troubled, even frightened. He wanted to stay in bed, curled up under the covers. He had to force himself to leave the shelter of his bedclothes. When he did he hurried down the corridor to the toilet and back, trying not to meet anybody on the way. He dressed slowly.

He was frightened and he was unhappy and he did not know why. He searched with his mind for headache, stomach ache, upsetting news the day before, and could not find anything. He did not know what was wrong or what was happening to him. He had heard people talk about anxiety states. He supposed this was one. He had to examine his feelings before he faced the world. When he did he concluded that he was feeling like a little child, a frightened, vulnerable little child. He decided that it must be those pills that made him feel like this.

At breakfast he was nervous about talking to anyone, and he responded to their hellos and good mornings with only a perfunctory nod. He was afraid of them. He knew they were not hostile but he felt fragile, a baby among some large, lumbering animals who, without meaning to, might step on him and crush him out of existence.

He hurried through breakfast and then retreated to his room. He tried to read again the paper outlining the St. Georgian situation but could not concentrate. He certainly did not want to talk to people. The bad feeling did not go away. He had never experienced anything like it.

Only Dr. Manash could have done this to him. Damn Dr. Manash! And his pills and his hypnotism! Manash-Shaman. Shamanism. He had been drugged. That was what was the matter with him. He had agreed to play the game but not to be drugged. Whatever Manash had done he must undo. He must give him some drug that was an antidote. He was not going on with this game.. Fortunately, he had an appointment with

Manash before lunch..

"This feeling will be only temporary, very temporary," Dr. Manash assured him.

"It's the pills, I'm sure. They're having this awful effect. Or maybe it's your hypnotism."

"It will go away."

"You're sure of that?"

"I feel sure, yes."

"Why is it happening? The others don't seem to be in this state," Green responded angrily.

"Different people react in different ways. Anyway, you can't tell what state others are in."

"I don't like this feeling."

"What do you feel?"

Green hated even spelling it out. "I feel like a child. Frightened. I don't know what's happening to me." Tears came into his eyes to his surprise and chagrin. He squeezed them back.

"Were you very unhappy as a child?"

"No."

"So what's so awful about being a child?"

"But I'm not a child. I just feel like one."

"And that's bad?"

Green shook his head, not in negation but in a search for an answer. "I feel as if I haven't grown up. I haven't done anything. I haven't got any further than when I was - I don't know - six or seven years old. It's as if I'm nothing."

"You're not nothing, you're very much something, or you soon will be," Manash assured him. "You won't be Professor Green of Columbia University but you'll be something."

"I feel that I've got nothing inside me," Manash went on, miserably.

Manash said, "You will have something inside you. The last time we talked you were going to think about being Lieutenant-Colonel Donald Green, the Deputy Director of the

National Security Council. And we talked about your old friend - Tommy Gibbons was his name, as I remember. Have you been thinking about Lieutenant-Colonel Donald Green?"

"Yes. Yesterday, for a while, I felt a bit as if I was him. For the game, I mean. I really felt it for a time."

"Did you like being this other Donald Green? Who thinks a bit like your friend Tommy Gibbons?"

"I felt all right."

"Would you like to go on being him?"

" At least I'd be somebody. I wouldn't be like I am now."

"It would be better?"

"Oh yes. I can't imagine this Colonel Green feeling like a child. Even when he was a child I don't think he felt like a child."

"Well he's what's going to be inside you. We're half-way there. Let's see what we can do. I'm going to try some hypnotism again if it's all right with you."

"If you think it will help me. Otherwise I want you to give me an antidote to the pill and I won't go on with the game."

"Yes I do. Now you've done this before. I want you to look at this pendant. I want you concentrate on it.....Now you're not nobody, you're somebody. Do you want to be somebody?"

Green's eyes were closed. He spoke in what was barely more than a whisper. "Oh yes."

"Good. You're Lieutenant-Colonel Donald Green. You knew about Colonel Green. ..."

Frances Carr came out of the immersion tank, took off her headphones, went into the changing room and put on her clothes. She felt light-headed, as if she had just shed a burden. This was odd since she was aware that she was about to take up a burden, that of serving the President of the United States and directing American foreign policy.

She had the strange feeling that she was still not dressed, that she was naked. She hurried through the building and across to Yellow House feeling vulnerable to the gaze of other people. A protective layer had been stripped from her. She went into her room and shut the door. It had no full-length mirror, only a mirror over the wash basin. She stood as far back as she could.. Then she took off her grey dress, and the bright scarf she had been wearing at her throat and put it on a hanger, and then she took off her slip, her tights, her bra and her briefs. She looked at herself naked, or as much of herself as she could see, which was down to her hips and the top of her dark brown pubic hairs.

In past times when she saw herself naked, she usually wished despite herself that some things were different. Her breasts were ample but hung too much, her thighs could be firmer, her skin more glistening. But she did not dwell on this, any more than she dwelled on those advertisements that told you how you could have a better body. She made no judgments now. Looking at herself, she kept thinking that there was something there that she had not seen before and that she should see it now. But she could not find anything new.

She put on her clothes again. Now she felt comfor- table. She was going to be the American Secretary of State. She was going to be Frances Carr Dowson.

She looked out of the window at the straight rows of trees that stretched away from the building, their branches half-bare, silhouetted against the darkening sky, and contemplated them for a few moments. Strange that she had not noticed them before. Then she looked at the wallpaper patterns around the window. The colour was appealing but the pattern was a bit too jazzy for her taste. She had not noticed that before either.

Captain Raymond Wade floated in the immersion tank with his earphones on, with his new British self pouring into his head, pushing out his identification with the American military. Then, late in the afternoon, he went for a solitary stroll.

He stood for a while on the river bank, looking at the colleges, some of them on the other side of the river glimpsed through the curtain of yellowing weeping willow trees along the banks. He remembered vaguely that in a previous life, perhaps when he was much younger, he had jogged along this river bank. He was a different person then. He walked into the high street. Some of the lights in the shop fronts were coming on to meet the twilight. He stopped and contemplated them.

The colleges represented a culture, carried on from past generations and handed on to future ones. They were a part of the history of this nation, part of the back-drop against which the play was acted out. The high street was front stage, where people spent their money and bought the things that made up their lives, in Tesco and W.H. Smith and Next and Argos, browsing and choosing and reaching into their handbags and wallets. This was where a people were prospering or not. This was where a government succeeded or failed in the short run, where he would succeed or fail as Prime Minister.

He passed a pub, another place where people gathered and spent their money, and on an impulse he walked in. Brass and copper implements glistened on the walls, to do with the care of horses and cooking over a coal stove and other pursuits of little relevance to the customers. He looked around him at the half-dozen or so drinkers there.

His gaze focused on a young man sitting on a stool at the bar. He was probably in his early twenties, tall and slender, wearing a woollen shirt open at the neck and a leather jacket and tight jeans. He had long eyelashes and smooth skin, and he had a beer in front of him. Wade found that he was staring at him. He was thinking how handsome the young man was, and how smooth his skin was. He wanted to start a conversation with him. He thought of some conversational gambits.

A pretty young woman with frizzy hair wearing a denim

jacket and a miniskirt came in with a bouncy confident walk.went up to the young man and greeted him and kissed him on his lips. After watching the couple for a while he left the pub and headed back to0 the school. All the way back he thought of the young man. He envied the couple. He wanted to kiss the pretty young woman. Then he realised that that was not what he wanted. He wanted to kiss the young man.

Late in the afternoon, Donald Green floated in the immersion tank with Lieutenant-Colonel Green pouring in through his headphones. When he came out of the tank he seemed invigorated. Still in his dressing gown, he picked up his first briefing paper, the one on U.S.-St. George relations, and read it. He did not read it, as he had the first time, as a detached observer, but with mounting anger.

A left-wing government in some two-bit Caribbean state talking about taking over American industries. An American citizen murdered and they didn't seem to be doing a lot about it. What would America do? What should America do? Certainly America ought to do something. It couldn't let itself be pushed around. There was much too much anti-Americanism in Latin America already. He started thinking about what action America could take.

Despite his time in the immersion tank, he felt the need to wash himself all over, as if there were something to be cleansed. He went into the shower and soaped himself, and enjoyed the tingling of the spray. Then he marched back to his room and started to dress.

As Raymond Wade walked back into the grounds of the Abbotsbury School, he passed two figure walking in the same direction but more slowly. One was short and tubby, wearing a light raincoat, and walking with a slight limp due to an arthritic knee. He was Professor Arthur Stack-Stevens, Professor of English at one of the Oxford colleges, who was known among other things for his work on Jane Austen and for the vehemence of his dismissal of Terry Eagleton and his followers and what he termed "so-called literary so-called theory." His companion was younger and taller, and he was head of the Department of International Relations at the same college.

Stack-Stevens was doing most of the talking, in a thin, reedy, refined voice. "I think we'll just get under the wire, so to speak," he was saying. "Donald said they'll be incommunicado for a few days from midnight tonight, although what that means I can't imagine. But he did leave this message and he'll want to see us. I found him a very civilised American." They walked in silence for a while, and then he went on, "I think he would be a welcome addition to high table. And I gather he's published some interesting papers. Your field, of course, I wouldn't know."

"Yes, I looked up a couple of his articles," the other replied. To himself he said, "'A very civilised American!' Patronising old fart. Why haven't you retired? Still, I ought to meet this Green fellow." They arrived at reception and were directed across the courtyard to Yellow House.

Green was buttoning his shirt when he saw through the window two figures making their way slowly across the courtyard towards his door. One was of them, limping slightly, was distantly familiar. An Englishman, he knew that somehow. They were together so the other one probably was also.

Here were two Brits coming to stick their noses into the St. Georgian affair where they had no business to be. Give them half a chance and they would start working on their friends in Washington. They would be whittling away, probably warning against precipitate action, anything likely to stir things up. They'll say let's discuss it, .maybe go to the United Nations, but don't actually *do* anything. For all the crap about the Commonwealth Britain had no damned business meddling in the American sphere of interest, and it was best to make this absolutely clear right from the start.. He did not finish buttoning his shirt but strode out of his room and hurried down the staircase to meet them at the front door..

Stack-Stevens was saying again to his companion, "A very civilised American. I remember he served a Dow 1987 port after dinner." He paused for a moment, either to catch his breath or to savour the memory, and his companion paused also. "Dow '87," he repeated, and the repetition indicated that he was savouring the memory. He started forward again towards the yellow door.

They reached it and they were about to enter when the door was opened suddenly. A figure stood before them. The light from the hallway was behind him and he they could not see him clearly. Stack-Stevens thought he recognised Green, from his stature and his horn-rimmed glasses, yet the expanse of hairy chest in the triangle of his shirt open down to the navel, and, even more, something about his stance made him look different from the man he had met in New York. For a moment he thought he was mistaken. But then he decided that yes, this was Professor Green, although looking rather strange.

He was about to speak but Green spoke first. "Now look, you two Limey cocksuckers, I've got a message for you. This is Uncle Sam's back yard and you haven't been invited to play in it. So butt out! You understand? Butt fucking out!"

CHAPTER EIGHT

Prime Minister Jacob Shemtov leaned back in his chair, an old-fashioned office swivel chair, and pondered his next moves. He missed his wife. He did not like being alone. He had to take important decisions and he felt lonely and he was annoyed at her for being away. She should be here, supporting him, listening to his doubts, and appearing in public, smiling at the crowds, charming ambassadors, visiting schools and hospitals.. He knew ministers were gossiping about his wife, vacationing in Palm Beach with her parents, six hundred miles from St. George and a million miles from its problems.

This wasn't really her scene, the government of a small, poor Caribbean country. Truth to tell, he was not sure that it was his scene either. He had been waiting for the time when an elected government would rule in St. George, hoping the time would come, thinking and writing and talking about what should happen. He had thought he would be a part of the change, but he had not, until recently, thought that he would be presiding over it. Now that it had arrived he sometimes missed those other times when he was a respected exile in academia, the club-like atmosphere of the faculty lounge, the pub lunches in London, the faculty cocktail parties in Washington, the students. Perhaps he was better at planning a government than running one. But now it was his responsibility.

He looked around him. He had a desk in front of him

containing only a computer, a keyboard, monitor and printer, and a filing cabinet, and an armchair and several other straight back chairs. Bookcases, mostly empty, were against the wall facing him. This was the house master's study, turned into the Prime Minister's office for the duration of the game. It did not look like a place from which to govern a nation but he would invest it in his imagination with the dignity which it lacked. He would imagine also the outer offices and the secretarial and support staff. He knew this was part of a game he was playing. He could not remember anything else.

He had an idea for a bold move. It was based on an old military maxim: one shot fired first is worth a great many fired second. It had been quoted in a discussion a long time ago, sitting around a table, somewhere indoors where they were sheltering from a hot sun. In the same discussion, someone had said, "We should fire the first shots and all the other shots, and then we should make peace." That's what we'll do, he thought. Shoot and then make peace.

First he needed to consult with two of his ministers. For one thing he was not sure of the financial implications, although it seemed to him that it would bring into the economy some of the capital it needed badly. Also he needed their backing. He called his Foreign and Finance Ministers into his office.

"It's going to upset everyone all at once," the Foreign Minister said.

"Yes, and get it over with. The take-overs, the trial of the AED men, all that will happen in the next few weeks. Then it'll all be sweetness and conciliation from us."

He turned to the Finance Minister and said, "Ingrid, I'll need your advice on how it's going to work out economically. It seems to me that it'll give us some capital we need in the short term since we're not getting any inward investment."

Ingrid spoke confidently like a schoolgirl who knows the answer. "From that point of view, yes. It'll give us some breathing space."

And John, I'd like you to sound out our High Commissioner in London on the likely British response."

Shemtov met with other ministers two hours later in the common room that was named the cabinet room. There were seven of them, sitting around in armchairs and on a grey-green couch that was losing some of its colour through wear. He was pleased by what he had learned from his Foreign Minister and from Ingrid. He told them the plan.

"We nationalise Capital Bauxite immediately. We take it over and put in a management team. We announce that we're also nationalising the two other big foreign-owned enterprises in St. George, Dalling's, the food processing plant, and DGT Mining. We'll have Capital Bauxite's considerable working capital. At the same time, we'll propose setting up joint commissions for all three companies to discuss compensation. The commissions will be composed of representatives of our Government, the owners of the plant and the other government concerned. One thing we'll do right away is expand DGT's mining activities - they're not doing much at present. Apparently, that's a practical proposition. This will create more jobs."

"Wow," someone said, and that was the only comment for a few moments.

Then someone observed, "DGT is a British company."

"That's an advantage. The Americans can't say our quarrel is only with them. John here has just talked to our High Commissioner in London. He thinks they're not likely to take as tough a line as the Americans."

"They've been friendly so far," someone else said.

"The High Commissioner," Shemtov went on, "thinks Wade would like an issue on which to distance himself from America, in order to please his European partners. We can give him one."

"But the Americans are angry. The AED didn't kill a

izen," someone pointed out.

Yes, the trial will cause a lot of problems," Shemtov agreed.

"Not so much if the AED three go to jail for life," someone said.

For life? Are we going to lean on the courts?" This from the Agriculture Minister, Ben Devoe.

"No one is suggesting that," Shemtov said.

"A St. George court won't send three men to prison for life for manslaughter," Devoe insisted. "Nobody thinks that bloody man's death was intentional."

"Anyway, that's why we're getting all this over with soon," Shemtov went on, ignoring him. "Once the trial is over I hope things will calm down a bit and they'll be more reasonable."

"The American Congress can pile on a lot of pressure," someone said. "Look what they did over trade with Cuba. And Chavez in Venezuela. They'll stamp on IMF credit."

"The IMF conditions would be unacceptable anyway," Ingrid pointed out.

"The nationalisation move isn't risk-free," Shemtov said. "But it'll get us some capital we need immediately. We can't afford more labour troubles. Ingrid here will talk to us about that." He turned to her. "Right?"

"When you're ready," Ingrid said.

"The great thing is that we'll get the arguments over all at once, and after a little while we can play the international good boys. We can tell the Americans we want to be friends. Comments please."

"You all know what I think," said Devoe. He was sitting hunched forward, his elbows on his knees. "The Americans don't like what we're doing and there's no way they're going to. We've just got to make damned sure that we carry through our programme. It's our bauxite. It shouldn't be used to make others rich."

Louis Mannion spoke up. "I'm worried about this idea of joint commissions. I think we should just decide how much we'll pay and tell them." He took off his glasses and wiped them with his handkerchief.

"What we're doing is not very different," the Foreign Minister replied. "We're just making it look a bit different. We'll pay them compensation, but - "

"Why should we?" Devoe interrupted.

"But it will be spread over a period of years," the minister continued.

"But they'll have a majority of two-to-one on every commission," Louis pointed out. "A representative of the company and a representative of the foreign government concerned."

"But the final decision on what we pay is with us," Shemtov replied. "It won't do them any good to come up with figures they know we won't pay."

"It will if the Americans want an excuse to intervene. That's exactly what they could do. Pick a high figure and then yell when we reject it. There are some disgruntled people around here who would take American dollars to stage a coup.."

"That's possible," Shemov admitted. "But we'll have to count on the St. Georgian comissioner to stand firm against pressure to name a figure that's too high. Any agreement has to be unanimous."

"He'll have to be tough," Louis said.

"He will indeed," Shemtov said. "That's why I'm going to ask you to be the commissioner on Capital Bauxite." There were some grins around the table at this. "You're the right man for it. If you could be tough representing the union, you can certanly be tough representing the government."

Louis was about to express some doubts but Shemtov had put him on the spot with this appointment. He decided that it would be better to keep his mouth shut and save his objections until later but he found himself voicing them anyway. "By my reckoning we don't o-o-owe them anything. The A-A-Americans have taken enough out of our country. I've said this before."

Shemtov realised now that he had made a mistake in not bringing Louis into the discussions when he was working out this move. He had confided in him in the past. He would keep him back after the meeting and seek his advice on worker reaction, which would mollify him.

The cabinet agreed on the plan and then someone said, "What do we do now?"

"We've drafted a statement. If we all approve the wording, we feed it into the web site," said Ingrid. "It's a public announcement."

When they had heard the statement and sent it out, the meeting broke up. Shemtov motioned Louis to stay behind. They sat down together and Shemtov told him that he had discussed the plan with the Finance and Foreign Ministers before him only because he needed their expert advice. "It'll give us some breathing space financially," he said. "And I'm hoping it'll head off some of the discontent at Capital Bauxite. What do you think, Louis? No one knows the workers there more than you. How will they react?"

"They'll like the sound of nationalisation. But then they'll ask what they're going to get out of it."

"You have some influence there. Welfare payments are the first priority. Out in the countryside too. We agreed on that. The unemployed, to start with. Welfare and jobs. Pay rises could create inflation and knock our programmes on the head."

"Yes of course. The unions understand that. But they don't want to see foreign companies taking out any more money."

"I think we're seeing eye to eye, Louis."

"Yes. After all, in the end, we're the Government. We

have the power."

He left and walked along the corridor. Louis lived in a world of powers. He always had, although the powers had changed over the years. First there was his father, seemingly all-powerful at first, controlling, supporting, punishing. He looked up to his father and he feared his anger. He looked up to his mother but she had a different kind of power, which he did not altogether comprehend. It seemed the most important power in his life. His father had power over her. There was Capital Bauxite, the power that had controlled his working life, later the power he did battle with as a labour leader.

He found that he had power when he led the union. Now he had more power, he was a Government minister, but Jacob Shemtov had more power than him, he was the head of the government. The United States had more power still, its money and its agents and its military might ever-present, always to be considered, sometimes to be feared. As you went through life, you tried to move up the power ladder, to have fewer people above you and more below you. The ultimate power, as he had known almost as long as he had known his father's power, was God, the creator of all things. Before God all other powers counted for nothing and all people, his father, the Americans, even the greatest, were as little children.

Walking along the corridor he passed an office with an open door and Devoe beckoned him in. "Are you going to enjoy being tough with your old employers?" Devoe asked him..

` "Well, yes. But I'm in the Government now. I can't just let fly."

"You'll talk to them politely." This was said in a sarcastic tone.

"Not just talk. Negotiate."

"Make sure you remember the old slogans. 'Wages Not Dividends.' 'Power to the Workers.'"

"I remember the slogans, Ben. But we're not protesting now. I'm negotiating on equal terms. More than equal terms because we're the Government."

"Okay, I know you've got to talk respectable now. You can't call them capitalist thieves and Yankee bastards. But remember that that's what they are."

"I'll remember," he promised.

In the Prime Minister's office, a machine murmured and gave Shemtov a piece of paper. He read it quickly. The Secretary of the bauxite workers' union had just made a fierce anti-American speech in which he called for the arrest of General Benvenista, the American security manager at the Capital Bauxite plant, on charges of murder. He repeated the accusation that Benvenista had collaborated with death squads to kill union leaders under the Gomez dictatorship. He wished the man had not made the speech. Mannion had started this off with his outburst in that American TV interview. He remembered reading in a confidential briefing paper that during the Gomez days some people had plotted to assassinate Benvenista. He wished now that they had done so.

But his new move should go a long way towards satisfying the radicals. He was quite pleased with himself. An hour-and-a-half ago, he had been wondering whether he was up to the job. Now he felt as if he were born to be the St. Georgian Prime Minister. He felt grounded, with a feeling of solidity that seemed to be new.

This thought was followed immediately by a doubt, as if from a contrary voice inside his head, a doubt that he could really be an effective prime minister. The doubt was not based on anything solid, anything he could put his finger on. It was a dark cloud in a blue sky. There was never in his life a blue sky that did not have a dark cloud somewhere. It was like the skull in the corner of a Renaissance pastoral painting, a *memento mori*, a reminder of our mortality. Or in his case a reminder that doubt and melancholy were present in his life and would come back.

There was a knock at his door. He glanced at his schedule. Ah yes, his Defence Secretary, Brian Thaxted. Thaxted, a lawyer by profession, had been one of the bravest opponents of the Gomez regime, jailed for his outspokenness, and one of his supporters from his earliest days of political activism. He ushered him in. "Jacob," Thaxted said when he was seated, "I'm worried about some of the people in the army. How far we can trust them."

"We sacked a few of the real bad guys," Shemtov reminded him.

"But not all. For instance, do you trust General Murillo to be loyal to our government?"

"He promised he would be. You deal with him. What do you think?"

"Oh he comes over all loyal, a professional soldier, no politics. But he did Gomez's dirty work. He's a brute by nature. And he's devious. I look at his record under Gomez. He was the Americans' favourite St. Georgian general."

"I don't want to sack any more top officers now," Brian. "It wouldn't do to antagonise the army any more at this stage."

"I don't trust him."

"So keep an eye on him."

::   ::

::

Over in Yellow House, Frances Carr Dowson was alone in the small lounge, finishing her late lunch of quiche and salad. She was thinking about what she would say to the President when she met him shortly. She knew he relied on her heavily for foreign policy advice. She also had to keep in mind that he was under pressure from congressmen running for re-election.

Donald Green came into the room, poured himself a coffee from the percolator and took some biscuits, then came over to where she was sitting in front of a low table and asked, "Mind if I join you?"

She could hardly refuse so she indicated an empty chair silently and he sat down, and since he was going to sit down anyway she gave him a friendly smile. "What do you think is going to happen down in St. George, Frances?" he asked, speaking casually, one professional to another.

"I don't know," she replied. "I'm about to talk to the President about it. And one or two other things."

He bit into a biscuit and wiped some crumbs from his mouth. "Yes, you've got quite a bit on your agenda for the moment," he said.

"It goes with the job."

"How do you get along with Darrow?"

"We have a good working relationship," she replied. She was not going to share confidences with Green.

They were silent while he sipped his coffee and then he said, "You don't have children, do you, Frances?" She shook her head.

"I do. A daughter. I'm worried about kids today. I'm also worried about my daughter. Young people today don't seem to have respect for anything. No values. That's a cliché, I know, but when it's your own daughter you really feel it." This sounded like the opening of a conversation and she did not want one. She nodded politely rather than sympathetically, finished her coffee and then said, "I have to go now to my appointment with the President."

He was disappointed. He had wanted to go on from kids to the importance of respect for the Government and the flag, at home and abroad. He watched her go, her skirt swaying as women's skirts do, and wondered whether her smile indicated some interest in him. He hoped so. The cabinet would discuss St. George, he was sure. An aggressive solution to the St. Georgian problem which involved the NSC would increase his standing in Washington. An affair with the Secretary of State would also increase his standing. For a few moments he fantasised about her taking off her bra as she walked towards him, her hair hanging wild about her shoulders, her usually composed features eager and wanton, and then about the nods and winks in corridors as he walked by identifying him as Frances Carr Dowson's lover.

Frances walked up one floor to the President's office and Darrow stood up and greeted her from behind his desk. When they were both seated he said, "I'll leave you to make a public statement about the new St. Georgian announcement about nationalisation. Make it as strong as you like. Not promising any action, just a first response. Obviously we can't accept this as it stands." He looked at her for agreement.

"No. That's quite right. But do you think it could be a basis for negotiation?

` "Quite possibly. It depends how tough they want to be. Capital Bauxite is not the United States. It's not something to talk about too much right now. There are all sorts of pressures on me with the Congressional elections coming up."

"You know how I feel about Congressional candidates making a noise, Stephen," she said.

"And it follows Brewster's death. And Morgan at Commerce is telling me how much business interests we have in the Caribbean."

"And it's not just business that's affected."

"No, of course not." Darrow talked of trouble but he did not sound troubled and he did not look it either, leaning back in his chair, alert but relaxed.

He put his elbows on his desk and focused his blue eyes on her. "Frances, I'm relying on you heavily in this situation.

You're a lot more experienced in this sort of area than I am."

She recognised the look. It was the look that had won him the hearts and votes of millions of women. It seemed to join them together, to say, "I'm a decent person, I'm trying to do the right thing, help me, back me up, and then you'll feel better, you'll be a better person." She recognised the look for what it was and yet it worked all the same. She felt warm and proud to have his confidence. She would do her best.

The meeting between the two of them was followed by a full meeting of the cabinet. Darrow said little at first but asked questions and canvassed opinions. The Commerce Secretary spoke of the danger to America's Latin American trade. "Is anyone else in the area likely to take this as an example to follow?" he asked. Frances said there no immediate likelihood but it was hardly necessary to point to the other left-leaning governments that have come to power in Latin America.. The Defence Secretary said the CIA had the means, or else could certainly acquire the means, to destabilise the Shemtov regime. However if it did, whatever denials were issued, it would be perfectly clear that this was a US-backed operation. He emphasised that he was stating the capability, not recommending such a move. Frances said this would have repercussions in Latin America, where "Yankee imperialists" was still a potent rallying cry.

After canvassing several opinions, Darrow leaned back and said: "It seems to me from what everyone says is that the best we can do at the moment is to try to keep Shemtov from following a more radical path. Our embassy there tells us that he's got people in his party pushing him in that direction. If we wanted an excuse to intervene, the radicals might give us one. But we don't. I don't want to see a situation in which we have choice between suffering a big setback and engineering the overthrow of a Caribbean government. Nevertheless, I think we should be keeping our friends among the opposition to Shemtov just in case we need them.

"I'd like to get the British on-side. They've got good contacts with Shemtov, the Commonwealth and all that, and they're in a position to influence him. Also, they've got business interests at stake. Frances, can you do something about that?"

"I could talk to our ambassador in London. And I could talk myself to Vallon, their Foreign Secretary, or at least send a message to him," she said.

"Good."

She said, "However, we can't count on the present British government to stand by us. It's not like the old days."

"I know."

When she had left, Darrow turned to look out of the window. He thought he had done well. He had sounded authoritative without pretending to be very knowledgeable and he was taking them all along with him. He had concealed his anxieties. Next time he had a cabinet meeting, he would feel confident instead of just acting it. It was a matter of what words to use and what tone to take.

That afternoon Donald Green went to see Campbell Davies. Davies was a CIA veteran, his eyepatch a reminder of his adventurous younger days when he was working in the field with anti-Soviet guerrillas in Afghanistan. He had directed some sophisticated operations which were legendary within the agency. He gave talks and seminars to agents in training, and some of these trainees spoke admiringly of his lectures on covert action. He was a bulky man, careless about his clothes, and, it was said, careless also of authority and the proper administrative channels.

"I've been hearing about this morning's cabinet meeting to discuss St. George," Green said. "Darrow doesn't seem very worried."

"Davies sat with his elbows on his desk. "What do you think?" he asked. It was characteristic of him to ask the other man's opinion first although he very likely had one of his own.

"I think we should be doing something about it," Green said.

"How do you see the problem?" Davies asked.

"I see it a bit like the early days of the Castro regime in Cuba," Green replied. "Washington welcomed Castro. Sure, we didn't like his economic reforms all that much but we weren't going to worry about them. Washington got worried too late."

"Yes. The Bay of Pigs was not exactly the agency's finest hour," Davies agreed.

"I'll say."

On the other hand," Davies went on, "there was another super-power around then ready to step in." He had a judicious manner of speaking, as if he were considering his own words after he had spoken them as well as the other person's, conducting an internal dialogue as well as an external one.

"Okay, there's not that danger now," Green agreed. "But there are plenty of hate-America. groups all around the world. Muslim terrorists will get a boost if they see that some little country in the Caribbean can give us the finger and get away with it. They could even link up with St. George in some way." He paused. Davies' calm had the effect of slowing him down.

Davies nodded sympathetically. "It's not a good example to set. Anti-Americanism is always a good platform for some demagogue stirring things up. I'm sure the Arab world is watching St. George."

"Exactly! They'll take note of what happens. What do you think we should do?"

Davies leaned back in his swivel chair and pressed his fingers together and then spoke slowly. "I think it's an undesirable situation there. It's not a crisis but we don't have to respond only to crises. I've been accused of being too interventionist."

"You mean," Green said, "instead of sitting around on our butts waiting for something to turn up."

Davies did not comment on this but asked, "What alternative would you suggest?"

"A little sabre-rattling in the area wouldn't be a bad idea. Navy manoeuvres off the coast of St. George, a shipload of marines cruising around. And squeeze their balls on trade. We've got to let them know that if an American businessman is murdered and American property is grabbed, something is going to happen, at least. And I think we should prepare the way for an operation to get rid of Shemtov. Just in case we found we wanted to go ahead."

"Darrow isn't thinking in those terms."

"Apparently not. I understand he said at the cabinet meeting that we should keep any friends we had there in place in case we need them one day. That's all."

Davies sat up straight and his tone became more alert. "Did he? Well that gives us some leeway. We'll certainly do that. We do have friends there, of course, and we'll try to see if we can make one or two more." 0

"Good." Green nodded approvingly.

Davies went on, "It would not be inappropriate for us to see whether we can do a little to influence events in St. George in our favour at some time in the future."

Green went away from the meeting feeling a little better. There were others on the same wavelength as him.

Davies started writing a message which, like all messages, was to go through the monitor. He finished it and sat thoughtfully for some minutes, then wrote another, marked "Top Secret," to the CIA station chief in St. George..

Shortly afterwards Frances Carr Dowson walked into Stephen Darrow's office holding a piece of paper. "Have you see this? A transcript of a CBS news report."

He took it from her and read it out loud. "'Informed sources in Washington say the St. Georgian Government is in secret contact with the Cuban military with a view to co-operation between them. These sources say that the U.S. intelligence community has known about these contacts for some time. They say that at present the contacts are low-level, and that no firm measures have been arranged. The present St. Georgian Government came to power et cetera.' Oh shit. Any point in trying to find out who's leaked this?"

She shook her head. "I shouldn't think so. We know the general area it came from."

"The CIA."

"Or Green and the NSC. They might be behind it."

"Whoever it is, we know what they're after. It's pressure on us to act." He looked down thoughtfully."

::

::   ::

Over in Red House, the British Prime Minister, Raymond Wade, was talking with his Foreign Secretary, Pierre Vallon. He looked across his desk with a shrewd gaze at the man in front of him, with his thin, rimless glasses on his thin ascetic face, showing a man driven not by carnal desires but by ambition, his political ally for twenty years and his rival for most of that time, who he knew coveted his job more than anything else in the world.

"It's not good, the St. Georgians nationalising DGT Mining," Wade said. "But we can't get too angry about it. Plenty of other countries have nationalised things."

"The Americans are going to take a hard line. They'll expect us to go along with it. And after all, an American has been murdered."

"We don't have to go along with it, Pierre," Wade replied. "They have their own quarrel with the St. Georgians that isn't necessarily ours. Tell them we're considering the situation."

"You mean just to hold them for a while."

"Yes."

"I'll draft a message expressing our general support for their position but not committing ourselves to anything specific. And I can have a chat on the telephone with Frances Carr Dowson. She'll - "

"Yes. Okay." Vallon agreed reluctantly

"And I don't think we have anything to say to Mrs. Dowson just yet. We should talk to Shemtov in the meantime. Find out what he's up to."

"He seems to be trailing his coat," Vallon said.

"But he's not stupid. He doesn't want any more confrontation with Washington than he has to have. Perhaps he could use a restraining hand. He listens to us. Meantime, you've got the European Union ministers' meeting next week. The new trade negotiations with St. George is going to come up there."

"We're not going to raise objections?"

I think we should discuss that in full cabinet." He would have support when they discussed the EU issue in cabinet and Vallon knew it.

Vallon walked out into the corridor thoughtfully. This could become a serious issue with the Americans. He wondered whether Wade realized this fully. One of his friends in the cabinet came by and Vallon told him, "Raymond is going to be all macho about the St. George affair. I can tell," he said.

"You mean standing up to the St. Georgians?"

"No, that's too easy. Standing up to the Americans."

"Well, remember when we were in opposition. He was slamming the Government for going along with America all the way." He imitated Wade's clipped voice: "'The pillion rider on the American motor cycle.' He's got to act on some of the things he said back in opposition."

"That's a novel idea in politics," Vallon replied.

When Vallon had left, Wade sat rubbing his chin thoughtfully. If he was going to make any difference as prime minister, it was going to mean striking out in new directions. What was that joke about the question put to candidates for the Foreign Office? "What are the three most important things in the world.?" The correct answer, so the joke went, was "God, love and the Anglo-American relationship." Well, he was going to show that other things were more important, including Britain's position in the European Union. He wasn't anti-American, he must make that clear, just independent.

He sent for his Secretary for Trade and Industry. He told him, "I want you to find out what the value of DTG. So we can talk sensibly about compensation. " Then he turned to his keyboard and started writing a message to the German chancellor.

At about the time that this conversation was taking, over in Yellow House, Jacob Shemtov was writing a letter to the British Prime Minister. As he pointed out to one of his ministers, the important thing was to avoid fighting on two fronts.

"Dear Raymond," he wrote. "I remember well your warm message when I became Prime Minister, and your sincere gratification at the restoration of parliamentary democracy in St. George. We here all appreciate the technical help we have received from the Commonwealth in a number of areas. The Commonwealth connection is extremely important to us.

"As you know, we have a programme of economic reform. This could best be carried out in a period of stability and prosperity, but we have to carry it through in the present difficult circumstances. It is in this context that we are nationalising a small British company as well as a larger American one. Our Parliamentary democracy is not yet completely secure, there are forces on the left and the right that could threaten it, and economic hardship could make us vulnerable. We don't think those companies have acted in the past fairly or in the best interests of our country.

"I would appreciate any help you can give us, or the Commonwealth can give us, in strengthening our democracy. Our nationalisation measures are intended solely to strengthen our economic base and establish our economic sovereignty. They are not directed against any other nation, least of all our Commonwealth partners. We'll be discussing compensation in a manner I think you'll find fair. I do hope you will see our policies in this light."

Down the corridor, the St. Georgian Defence Minister, Brian Thaxted, was looking at a sheet of paper in his hand with a mixture of anger and satisfaction. It was a photocopy of a letter with General Murillo's signature at the bottom, and it had been left on his desk. It made him angry because it was evidence of betrayal. But he felt satisfaction because it justified and more than justified the suspicions he had harboured

He made an appointment and went to see Shemtov in his office. "Prime Minister, I think you should see this," he said, deliberately using the formal title to underline the seriousness of the occasion. "It was slipped into the tray in my office."

Shemtov, sitting at his desk, reached out for the paper and read it quickly. Then he looked up. "This is really something," he said. "Murillo in contact with the CIA."

"It's a reply to an approach from them. A very positive reply. I told you I was worried about him."

"You did indeed."

.. Murillo served Gomez well, and that leopard wasn't going to change his spots."

"Brian, you know, we kept him on as army commander for pragmatic reasons, not because we love him. He said he was willing to serve the new government. And the army likes him."

"Yes. Look at what he says. He's willing to sound out more people in the army."

"Yes, I do. This is a surprise, I must say." Shemtov examined the letter." "This is clearly a photo copy. How do you think the original was sent?"

"There's no indication. Probably it was given to the American Embassy to send in the diplomatic bag."

"Any idea who could have passed this to you?"

"No. My guess is that it's someone in the army who's seen what he's up to and intercepted it. Quite likely someone he approached."

"It does look as if you were right about him, Brian," Shemtov said.

"I think we confront him with this," Brian said. He brandished the piece of paper, his eyes shining with anticipation. "Proof of treason."

"Confront him? Hmmm. Perhaps." Shemtov considered this and then said, "Getting rid of Murillo will upset a lot of people. We'll have to time it carefully. I think I'll talk to internal security about this first. They may want to follow him for a while. Find out who his contacts are. Let's keep this confidential for the moment. Absolutely confidential."

"Okay, if that's the way you think it should be done."

Thaxted left feeling mostly satisfied. He would not have the confrontation with Murillo yet, the moment of melodrama he had looked forward to. But his judgement had been proved right. Murillo would be nailed.

Shemtov typed out instructions to his head of internal security on the computer. He frowned as he did so. Murillo had served the Gomez dictatorship and had a nasty record, but as his Foreign Secretary had pointed out to him, nice people don't often become generals in this part of the world. Murillo had said he was a loyal St. Georgian and would serve any St., Georgian government, and Shemtov had believed he would probably do so even if only out of self-interest. Maybe that was a mistake.

As soon as he had finished the computer produced a

message of its own. An AED figure had made a speech warning the Government that there would be more strikes unless economic conditions improved. He expressed scepticism about the joint compensation commissions. Well, Shemtov thought, he would have one more try at reasoning with these people. He asked the head of the AED, Peter Yelland, to come into his office.

"Look, I know you're not responsible for everything one of your hotheads says, but this kind of thing is stirring up trouble," he told him. "Union members think this gives them a green light to go on strike."

"They have the right to strike," Yelland said. "It's one of the rights your government gave us. It came with democracy."

Shemtov noted Yelland's use of the words "Your government" and "us," distancing himself..

"Yes, they have the right to. I'm questioning whether it will achieve anything beyond making it more difficult for the Government to carry out its programme."

Yelland said, "Its programme was to mean bettering the condition of the workers, first of all."

"Their condition is better. They have security of employment, which they won't have if there are more strikes. Thanks to the minimum wage they have more money."

"But inflation is eroding that."

Shemtov went on, "And now we're taking over three foreign industries. Things are better."

"How much better? Some of my people still have to choose between putting food on the table and buying medicine for their children."

Shemtov glowered at him. He did not like to be reminded that he had not suffered hardship and poverty. "There are members of my cabinet who suffered in jail, who suffered poverty. You know that."

"Yes, only now they're ministers and they see things differently," Yelland sneered. "Now they arrest some of their old friends like Gomez's police did."

Shemtov was not prepared for the reference to the Brewster kidnapping and he should have been, and it made him angry. "Well what are we supposed to do?" he demanded. "They broke the law. They kidnapped someone and killed him. Do you want anarchy here?"

"You know his death was an accident," Yelland retorted. "And why should we give a fuck about him?"

Shemtov looked across at Yelland's pinched face with his skin drawn tight so that it looked like a skull and his fierce expression, and he knew he would be impervious to argument. He would make him take responsibility. "Please don't tell me that you countenance more acts like that," he said.

"No, we're against breaking the law," he said, and his voice softened just a little. "You know I didn't have anything to do with the Brewster affair. But I can't say I don't have some sympathy for the people who did it. Don't you have?"

Shemtov followed up his advantage. "No. I would have once. I'd have said their hearts were in the right place, that sort of thing. But there are times when stupidity becomes criminal. You know that that kind of thing plays into the hands of the opposition."

"Yes, I know. But I have to warn you about the impatience of the workers."

"Peter, I called you in to ask you to restrain your hotheads, not to make their case. I know their case."

When he left Shemtov shook his head wearily. Yes, he was the best man to keep reforms going in St. George. But he was beginning to doubt that anyone could do it. He would allow himself moments of missing the time when he was just teaching and writing articles.

CHAPTER NINE

G reen had asked for an appointment with the President. He decided that he had an obligation to give the President his views; the NSC was supposed to give advice. He marched into his office and stood erect before his desk, looking, it seemed to Darrow, a little ridiculous with his tubby frame in a military stance. Darrow beckoned him into a seat and he started talking, keeping his voice calm and even deferential. "Mr. President, I would like to talk to you about the St George situation again. We at the NSC have been looking into it. I believe that things have now reached the point where we should consider taking covert action on the ground. At last make sure that Shemtov is worried and knows what we can do."

"We're considering all courses of action," Darrow assured him.

"We think State is not giving the matter a high enough priority. The Government down there isn't doing anything to stop anti-American demonstrations. The situation is drifting dangerously. We know the Government is in contact with the Cuban military."

"And CBS News knows it too," Darrow said pointedly. Green did not react to this. "Those contact are low-level," Darrow went on. Then he continued in a conversational tone, "They're not too serious. We've had no indication that they've reached the point of negotiating any kind of co-operation. Yes, I'm none too happy with their domestic policies,and we're watching the situation. I don't think it requires us to act precipitately. Shemtov is not another Castro."

"I think we have friends among the opposition in St. George," Green said.

"We do, and we'll make sure we keep them," Darrow assured him.

Green persisted, "I don't think we should wait until the contacts with Cuba or even terrorist groups become serious, Mr. President. We at the NSC are very aware of the attention that's being paid to the St. Georgian Government's actions elsewhere in the world. And the lessons others might draw from our failure to take strong action"

"I'm being kept informed of these things, and I also am aware of the possible implications," Darrow said. Green was too preoccupied with what he was saying to notice the irony in Darrow's voice.

"There are things we can do to change the situation down there, Mr. President," he said insistently.

"I'm aware of our capabilities, Donald," Darrow told him. He was speaking in a quiet tone and a more alert man might have found a reason to pause before going on. "I expect regular assessments of the situation from the NSC and I assure you that they will be taken into consideration."

"With respect, sir, I don't think we're giving the subject a sufficiently high priority, as I said before. As the acting head of the National Security Council, I would not be acting responsibly if I did not tell you this. I feel I have responsibility for the nation's security."

Darrow's next words cracked with authority. "Colonel Green, *I* have been given responsibility for the nation's security. You have stated your view, as you are entitled to do. Indeed, as I expect you to do. However, I suggest that in future you consider carefully the manner in which you voice it."

Green knew he had erred. All he could say was, "Yes, Mr. President." His cheeks were burning as he walked away. He felt that he might have under-estimated Darrow.

To try to regain his self-composure, he thought about what he said. He was right. You couldn't let people see someone walking all over you. People would chop you down in this world if they could. It was not enough to be strong, you had to be seen to be strong and seen to be ready to use that strength. Some people sneered at the idea of a nation looking strong, as if it were just posturing, like little boys in a playground. Yet this was quite right. In the playground, if someone pushed you around because you were the nerdy little kid with glasses and others saw this, then they knew they could all push you around. It wasn't a happy position to be in. If you were strong, other kids would want to be your friend and anyone would think twice before starting a quarrel with you..

The next person to go into the President's office was the Secretary of State. She told him about the standoffish British attitude. Then Darrow said, "I've just had a visit from Donald Green. He was out of line."

"I'm not surprised," Frances said.

"I'll be glad when the Director gets out of hospital and can take over NSC again."

"By the way," she said, "I have an interview with the *Washington Post* scheduled. It's the first one I've given since I became Secretary. St. George is bound to come up."

"I'm sure you'll handle that well, Frances."

"Anything special you want me to talk about?"

"You know the issues. Don't let him talk about St. George all the time. Make it clear that there are plenty of more important issues in the world. Nuclear weapons, NATO in the Baltic and all that."

"I understand."

"On the other hand, I am a bit worried about St. George," he said, rubbing his cheek. "Let's face it, things *could* go into a dangerous slide there. The measures they've taken already hit American business. The labour laws, the block on the outflow of capital. And it's true that an awful lot of people in Latin America are watching what happens there."

"How worried are you?"

"I'd like to get across to Shemtov what the limits are. What we'll tolerate and what we won't."

"We can communicate that to Dirksen, at our embassy there."

"Hmmm. Yes. I'd like to get the message across to him personally. Talk to him face to face. Pity he can't come to Washington. But if we invited him here a lot of people would go ballistic."

` She left reflecting that Darrow had great confidence in his own personal magnetism, thinking things would be solved if he could see someone face to face. She wondered how far he really grasped the realities of national power and international politics, personalising issues the way he did. Not far enough. But that was why she was here. Darrow thought he could create a better relationship with St. George if he could only work his personal charm on Prime Minister Shemtov. Well, who knows, perhaps he could. A pity that they could not arrange a meeting. She had a feeling that Shemtov should not be considered an enemy.

The *Washington Post* reporter was called Piers Traynor. In fact he was Piers Traynor, and he was Ivor Howe's assistant in the direction of the game. It had been agreed that he would play this role.

Frances had spent some time thinking about how she should conduct this interview. Her manner should be warm and friendly, but without losing any authority. She would have to develop a smile: not the patronising smile of a Margaret Thatcher, nor the glued-on smile of Tony Blair. Something warmer, more womanly. She would only smile some of the time. She had already learned to deepen her voice.

She greeted Traynor in her office. He accepted her offer of

coffee, and after a few light-hearted remarks about his paper's declining circulation as they sipped from their cups, he started in. "Madame Secretary, how do you view recent actions of the St. Georgian Government?"

"If you mean the most recent announcement, my department has already issued a statement and I'm sure you've seen it. We regard the seizure of American property as illegal."

"But now they've offered to discuss compensation."

She dismissed this with her tone. "If someone seizes your property, it doesn't legitimize what he has done if he offers to discuss with you how much he might pay you for it."

"Will the American Government be taking part in the proposed commission to discuss compensation?"

"We're still considering the details."

"And the killing of Dwight Brewster?"

"We've already stated our view. We consider it murder and the people responsible should be charged with murder. There's not much more to say until the trial starts."

"Do you feel that we now have a crisis in the Caribbean?"

She relaxed into a more casual tone. "I don't know that I would characterise it as a crisis. It's a problem and we're dealing with it. I'm sorry, I know 'crisis' is a nice headline word." This last was delivered with a smile. "There are other topics on our agenda."

"All right," Traynor said, "let's turn to one of these. The new Lithuanian Government has indicated that it might take the country out of NATO."

"We're having discussions with the Lithuanians about that, as you know."

"It will be the first time any country has left the organisation."

"Nothing has been decided.."

"But aren't you worried about the effect this might have on other Baltic nations? And elsewhere in Eastern Europe"

"I've seen speculation about that, of course. But there's absolutely no indication that any other country is even considering loosening its ties with NATO." Her voice softened as she went on, "Piers, I know the media likes to see things as crises, it makes life exciting. But the international scene isn't full of crises at the moment."

He smiled back and said, "I'm glad to hear that. Mrs. Dowson, can I ask you some questions about your past life?"

"My college grades are a matter of public record."

Traynor smiled, acknowledging the pleasantry. "And very impressive they are. As a college student, you took part in some pretty angry demonstrations."

"Yes, I did."

"You condemned the American Government pretty fiercely for its actions in Central America, and for some other things also."

"Well, you know, young people tend to get very angry about things. And so they should. I hope the day never comes when young Americans don't care about rights and wrongs in the world. But they tend to think solutions to problems are simpler than they actually are.

"Do you think your younger self might have approved of the actions of the St.George Government?"

She smiled. "I think my younger self might not have had as full a grasp of the situation as I and my department have today. It would be pretty sad if I hadn't learned anything since then."

"Senator Clegg characterised you in your younger days as a bleeding heart liberal."

She smiled again, a soft smile of patronising affection for her younger self. "That's not the kind of language I would use. But my heart bled a bit, yes."

"He said he wondered how much you've changed. Has your heart stopped bleeding?"

She leaned forward towards Traynor in a complicit manner.

"I think we all change as we grow older, don't you? We certainly should. I'm in this job to defend the interests of the American people. But do you mean do I now conduct foreign policy without regard for morality? Certainly not. The American people care about moral issues, and so do I. However, that doesn't mean that I'm a softy."

There was a pause after this and then Traynor said, "There's been some Press speculation about your long relationship with Tom Dieterle. Whether you might - "

She interrupted him firmly. "Now that's out of court. I won't be talking about my private life."

Afterwards, she felt the need for some fresh air and she took a stroll out of doors, confining herself to that part of the school grounds that were reserved for Yellow House. She walked along a path separated by a thin row of shrubs from the playing fields. She was pleased with the way she had handled the interview. She was also pleased that Traynor had asked her about Tom Dieterle. Dieterle's was not a bad name for a woman to be associated with. It was good for her image. In fact it was good for her self-esteem as well.

The breeze was cool with a touch of moisture, and it stroked her cheeks and her arms. She felt her pores opening up. The distant sounds of traffic came to her as a reminder of another world out there. From somewhere nearby came the smoky smell of burning leaves. She raised her face and sniffed as she walked along the path, her nostrils twitching. She savoured the scent, and recalled other smells that had given her pleasure: her father's sweet-scented pipe tobacco, newly-mown grass, the mixture of cigarette ash and sex.

The sun was setting behind some buildings leaving behind purple and brown smudges of clouds. She looked across at them. She opened up and let the sights and the smells pour into her. She needed these few minutes alone under the sky when she could be wide open. Then she would close up and get on with her working life.

Back in her office she checked the computer printer. A senior congressional figure had made a strong speech about St. George ."They burn our flag, they attack our citizens with impunity. They expropriate American businesses and threaten to steal more. How long are going to treat this bunch as if they were a respectable government?" There were a couple of other news agency reports, none serious. There was an invitation to speak at a symposium at Georgetown University, along with a number of other international figures. Jimmy Carter would be there, and Lord Hurd from Britain, and several from the Third World, as well as some prominent academics.

She looked at it and suddenly she had an idea. She began to formulate a plan. A half-hour later she was knocking on the door of the President's office. "I've been thinking," she said to him. "Do you really think it would be a good thing if Shemtov could come to Washington and you could meet him?"

Darrow shrugged. "I hadn't given it a lot of thought, to tell the truth because I can't see it happening. It was just something I said off the cuff. But yes, I'd like to to talk to him face to face if it could be managed. Why do you ask?"

"I've got an idea. He was a visiting lecturer at Georgetown University. They're running a high-profile seminar on the state of the world next week, big names attending. And me. If they invited him, I think he might come, even at short notice."

"You think so?"

"It seems to me likely. I'll be at Georgetown some of the time. I could talk to him. And we could engineer a chat with you, so that it would look like a casual meeting. You can suggest that since he's in Washington anyway he might call on you informally."

"And you think Shemtov will come."

"I don't see why not. From his point of view, he won't be going cap in hand to the American Government. And attending the seminar would be good for his prestige."

"Hmmm." Darrow thought about this. "Do you think you

can get Georgetown to invite him? I take it you have some pull there. A distinguished alumnus."

"I think they'll entertain the idea if I put it to them."

He smiled. "Okay, go ahead. Yes, I'd like to talk to him. You seem to think something may come of it. And let's hope you're right."

"I'll get on to my acquaintance at Georgetown," she said brusquely. She turned on her heel so quickly that her skirt whirled around her and left his office.

She sat down and wrote a note to the President of Georgetown University suggesting that Shemtov be invited. When she was told this would be done, she wrote a note to Dirksen, the ambassador to St. George, telling him to let Shemtov know that if he came to the Georgetown seminar, there would be an opportunity for a meeting with her and, if he wanted, an informal chat with the President as well.

::   ::
::

Jacob Shemtov had a bad morning. First there was a report of another demonstration outside the American Embassy. This time, as the demonstrators dispersed, a bomb exploded under an embassy car. Fortunately, two members of the embassy staff had just got out of the car and no one was hurt. Shemtov called in his Interior Minister and asked him do what he could to curb this kind of violence. "And I don't care whose toes you have to step on," he told him. "That bomb was intended to kill somebody in the American Embassy. The next one might."

"Okay. But it's a sensitive area. Some of our old friends - "

"I'm ready to send some of our old friends to jail if we have to!"

The next report was more alarming still. Benvenista, the security chief at Capital Bauxite, had vanished. He had left his home for the plant and had not been seen since. This was really bad. If Benvenista had been kidnapped like Brewster, or even worse, murdered, then there would be hell to pay with the Americans. He called in his Interior Minister again."Sorry to call you back right away but I've just seen this," he said, and showed him the report. He told him to pull out all the stops in tracking down Benvenista. "It could be very serious, or it could be Benvenista himself and some of his friends up to their tricks," he said

Next he had a meeting with Brian Thaxted which he was not looking forward to. When Thaxted knocked at his door he straightened his tie, a nervous gesture in anticipation of the meeting. Thaxted had an eager look, like a dog expecting to play a game.

But Shemtov looked sombre. "Brian, I asked to see you because I've had a report from the security services on that letter."

"The letter from Murillo to the CIA."

"That letter, yes."

Thaxted smiled.. "Good. Did they find out anything more?" Shemtov looked across at him and reflected that his round, pink baby face had a natural look of innocence

He waited before speaking. "What they found out, Brian, upsets me. Enormously. The security services tell me the letter came from your printer. That you wrote it."

Thaxted seemed stunned. He could hardly speak. "But I didn't - that's not true," he stammered. "You think I forged the letter?"

"The security people think so," Shemtov said. "In fact, they're certain of it. You wanted to get rid of Murillo."

Thaxted seemed to be struggling to find words. "Jacob, I didn't do that. I swear. I don't know how this happened. The security services are lying. Or maybe they're just mistaken."

Shemtov shook his head. "They're not lying."

Thaxted went on, "I swear to you - I *swear* to you - I didn't forge that letter."

Shemtov said, "I know you, Brian. I actually believe that you had the best interests of the country at heart. I want to believe that. I don't like Murillo any more than you do. There are reasons for keeping him there. Soon we might indeed get rid of - "

Thaxted rose out of his chair. "This means the security services are protecting Murillo. And they're out to get me. Jacob, who's been telling you these things? Who are you going to believe?"

"It's not a matter of deciding to believe," Shemtov said coldly. "The evidence is clear."

Thaxted slammed his hand down hard on the desk. "For God's sake, I fought for what we've got here. While you were at London University. Do you think I'm going to lie to you?"

"Brian, the security service says there's absolutely no doubt, and I believe them. I wasn't easy to convince, I assure you."

Thaxted's face twisted into an angry snarl. "You were always a fool when it comes to knowing who to trust and who your friends are. I didn't forge that letter. Did you talk to Murillo about this?"

"No, I didn't," Shemtov replied. "I think you got carried away by your feelings. But it was a serious misjudgement. I've got to be able to believe my ministers." Thaxted said nothing and Shemtov went on, "If you resign now, this won't get out. I promise you. You can find a reason to resign, I'm sure. I'm very sorry this has happened."

Thaxted clenched his lips, spun around and marched stiffly across the room and back again before speaking. "Why should I resign?"

Shemtov had prepared his arguments. "If you don't resign I'll have to sack you. Whatever your reasons for doing what you did, I can't have someone in my cabinet I can't trust."

"Damn it, Jacob, you can trust me. I'm telling you the

truth!" Thaxted was shouting now.

"If I sack you," Shemtov went on, "I'll have to give the reason, and I'll do so. You're a popular man in the party and people will want to know why I've sacked you. Quite rightly. You'll be out of politics and in disgrace. The row will weaken the Government. Because you're an old friend, and because of all you've done for the country I don't want to do that. And because I don't want a row in the party. I'm giving you a chance to resign. If you do, I give you my word that I won't tell anyone the reason. Think about it."

"But people will want to know the reason."

"So think of one."

Thaxted slumped down in his chair and looked at the floor and they were both silent for a full minute. Then he spoke, and his voice was bitter. "All right, I'll resign. There's nothing else I can do. But you're wrong, I promise you."

When he had left, Shemtov reflected as he had before on the power of denial. Thaxted had half-convinced himself. He had promised he would not tell anyone about this so he could not talk about this to even his closest political associates. If he did it was bound to get out. But the meeting with Thaxted had been awful and he wanted to unload his feelings. He could have talked to his wife. But she was still in Palm Beach, damn her.

An hour later, the computer screens in all the offices that carried news items reported that Brian Thaxted had resigned as St. George's Minister of Defence because of ill-health.

Over in Yellow House, Campbell Davies looked at the report and smiled. Thaxted must have taken the bait. He could use it as an object lesson in one of his lectures. Darrow had said the CIA could retain its assets in St George. Well, he had just removed a threat to one of them.

   ::   ::   ::

:

After his difficult morning, Jacob Shemtov was very pleased in the afternoon to get the invitation to the Georgetown seminar, accompanied as it was by a telephone call from the American ambassador relaying Frances Carr Dowson's message. He went to a scheduled meeting with four of his ministers in a more cheerful mood and told them he was going to Washington.

He asked to be briefed on the President's domestic political situation and on the Secretary of State. They talked about the attitude that might be expected from the President, and about action the Americans could take on trade. The Finance Minister warned that he should expect a hostile atmosphere. But the Foreign Minister said, "The President wants to talk to you. He wouldn't ask you there just to crap on you."

"He might ask me there to give me a warning," Jacob said.

The Foreign Minister remarked, "There are plenty of people down there whipping up alarm I see that an editorial in the *Wall Street Journal* says our policies make us a threat to American interests in America's own back yard."

The meeting was drawing to a close. Louis Mannion could see that nothing more of any consequence was going to be said so he decided to pick up this last remark and run with it.

"That's a hell of a big back yard," he said. "I mean, even the most powerful gun our army possesses couldn't reach the American coast. And we don't have enough landing craft to invade. But since it seems to worry them, I've thought of a way to reduce their anxieties. A proposal for you to take to Washington, perhaps."

"What's that?" Shemtov asked.

"We ask them to help us, by lending us their army engineers and later on their Navy. They're not doing much at the moment. The engineers tunnel underneath the island. They separate St. George from the sea bed. Then, when they've detached us, American Navy ships tow St. George away until we're far enough from America so that we're no longer in their back yard and they don't have t worry about us. Of course it would have to be to a suitable climate. We don't want them to leave us off the coast of Labrador, or some place like that. But perhaps a few hundred miles southeast of here. Or even somewhere in the South Pacific. Then Americans can sleep safely in their beds."

Shemtov smiled. "Thank you, Louis. We can always count on you to lighten the burden of office.."

In the monitoring room, sitting at a desk in front of a computer screen, Piers Traynor turned to Ivor Howe, twenty-five years his senior, and asked him, "How do you think it's going?"

"Pretty much as it should be," Howe replied. "Your interview was well executed. Everyone has got into the spirit of the game." He asked Robert Manash who was next to him, "What do you think from your point of view? The changes of identity seem to have taken."

"Yes they do, don't they?" said Manash, looking pleased.

Traynor said, "It's extraordinary! It's like watching a neighbourhood amateur dramatic production. Seeing people you know acting as somebody else. Except this is more convincing. Although one or two people seem to be over-acting a bit. Like Donald Green."

Howe said, "People with a weak sense of identity have to assert it more. Haven't you seen that in everyday life?" He could talk psychology also.

"I'm still amazed at the way people accept the conventions of the game even while they're immersed in their roles," Traynor said.

"I thought they would," Manash said.

Howe said to Traynor, "Come on, back to work. I want you to write the reply to Washington from the American ambassador in London. I've got to write a couple of inflammatory sound-bites from speeches to go on the news wires. Remember, time contracts in the game. Weeks are days.."

Over in Red House, the argument going on in the cabinet room reflected the two conflicting strains in British foreign policy which had been present for decades. Prime Minister Raymond Wade represented the European strain, his Foreign Secretary, Pierre Vallon, notwithstanding his name, had always represented the Atlanticist strain, putting the relationship with America above that with Britain's European neighbours. Three other cabinet ministers were present.

There were two pieces of paper on the table between them. One was a cable from the American Secretary of State, Frances Carr Dowson. She pointed to the threat that the St. Georgian nationalisation of industries posed to foreign investors in the area as well as the possibility of further radical measures. She said that in the U.S. Government's opinion the proposed commissions for compensation were an inadequate response to foreign concern. The U.S. Government would probably reject the proposal and would like a united front with Britain since a British company had been taken over also. She also said that Britain, as a fellow member of the Commonwealth, was in a position to influence the St. Georgian Government, and might indicate that it should pull back from what America regarded as a hostile stance.

The other piece of paper was a message from the European Commission. It proposed a European Union trade mission to St. George, indicating the possibility of buying bauxite and expanding trade and industrial possibilities there.

Wade argued for accepting the European Com- mission's suggestion. "Yes, I know the Americans will huff and puff and I know about Darrow's problems with the Congressional elections," he said. "But they've run the Caribbean as their own backyard and they haven't exactly made it a haven of prosperity."

"They're getting steamed up about this and they could get tough," one of the ministers said.

"We're not putting up with any more Helms-Burton nonsense telling us who we can trade with and who we can't," Wade retorted. "We can show the EU that the Commonwealth means something. Look at all the mileage the French get out of their ex-colonies. Shemtov has brought democracy to a Commonwealth country. We support him."

"You mean he's one of us," said Vallon sarcastically. He did not add what the others knew he was thinking, that Wade and Shemtov had attended the same Cambridge college only two years apart

"All right, yes," Wade said. "In a sense, he is."

The others persuaded Wade to modify his attitude. He accepted their argument that a direct rebuff could damage relations with Washington, so he let the Foreign Secretary send a moderate reply to Dowson. This said Britain was sympathetic to the American view and would indeed be talking to the St. Georgian Government. However, it suggested that the St. Georgian proposal on compensation deserved serious consideration, and that St. George's stance should not be dismissed as irredeemably hostile to American and European interests.

"Let's hope that Benvenista fellow hasn't been murdered in St. George," Vallon said. "That would really stir things up."

"Yes," Wade agreed. "Then the excrement would hit the proverbial fan."

When they had gone Wade sat in his chair and looked out of the window. He let the daydreams flow in..

He was in a Britain that counted in the world for more than it did today. He was a pilot in 1940, running to his Spitfire and climbing into the cockpit as the klaxon sounded and a swarm of German bombers approached. Britain stood alone against the forces of evil and the fate of the world rested on him and his fellow-pilots. Then it was another time, and he was standing erect addressing an American President with tightly controlled anger, clenched fists at his side: "Mr.

President, I would remind you that Britain is a sovereign country and does not need to answer to the American Government for its actions."

He was in an English village, in a street of stone cottages with thatched roofs, looking at a little village church with a square tower encrusted with ivy and with centuries of history. He was standing beside a young man, a young Englishman, slim and handsome with sandy hair, with his arm around his waist, holding him close. The young man was looking at him admiringly, as the national leader. He could feel the man's body next to his and he tightened his arm. He stayed with this picture for a while, and then was jolted by the realisation of what he was doing and mentally withdrew his arm. Where had that come from?

He shook his head to shake these daydreams away. He must concentrate on the present, and deal with the real situation.

CHAPTER TEN

Frances Carr Dowson looked down from her office window as Jacob Shemtov walked across the courtyard from Blue House. His limping gait and the overnight bag he was carrying seemed to weigh him down on one side. He would stay in Yellow House until tomorrow and that, the monitors had decided, would represent a four-day stay. She followed him with her gaze until he went into the door one floor below and disappeared from her view. She was due to meet him in half an hour. She wondered in a fidgety way what she would do until then.

Their first meeting was to be a short one, supposedly during a break from a seminar at the university. They sat on hardback chairs in an empty meeting room and talked to one another across the distance. She talked about the killing of Dwight Brewster and the interests of the United States. He talked about his country's requirements and the economic difficulties. He assured her that the three men responsible for Brewster's death would be put on trial. He was speaking quietly and seriously, aware that he was in the capital of an unfriendly nation.

She appraised him as he talked, on several levels. He was committed to his policy, that was clear, and he had moral imperatives, but he was not a fool and he was not a fanatic and he knew the waters he was sailing in. He could accommodate to political reality.. But the people who had brought him to power would not let him make too many accommodations; her briefing paper from Ambassador Dirksen made this clear. He was also not desperate to remain in office. He would be content to hand over to someone else if it was the right person and could maintain parliamentary democracy. But no one else was acceptable to all parties and a change could he destabilising

She also found him attractive. Her body was sending her little signs that it responded to his presence. The thought flicked through her mind that if she had met him in other circumstances she might have wanted the relationship to develop. She had always been attracted to older men. Her briefing paper said he was married but his wife was away from him a lot of the time.

Jacob tried to soften the atmosphere by assuring her that the St. Georgian Government had no wish to spread unrest throughout the Caribbean, nor indeed to export any of its policies. "We're not a regional power," he said. "And it's no part of my ambition that St. George should become a regional power."

"I accept that," she replied. "But some people here are worried about the example you might set, whether you want to or not. That's a factor that we have to take into consideration. Surely you can see that this can cause concern." She paused and then added, "Can't you see that?" She regretted these last words as soon as she said them. 'She should not be pleading for understanding.

But her words opened up an opportunity for him. He leaned forward and spoke with a new earnestness. He said, "I'll try to understand your position, yes. I suppose we could be seen as setting what you would think of as a bad example. This must worry you. And I would like you to try to understand my position. I don't want us to be like a lot of Latin American countries, rich in resources but full of poor people. You talk about American interests and I talk about St. Georgian interests. But to me this is not something abstract. It's the interest of a lot of St. Georgian people in having enough to eat and in having medicines when they're sick. Our policies are about hunger. I'm asking you please to understand this." He paused and then asked her, "Do you know what it means to go to bed hungry?"

She knew she should refuse to allow the conversation to become personal but nevertheless she shook her head. "No, I don't."

"Neither do I," he said. "But a lot of the people who support me do, and some of the people in my government. They're the people I represent. They feel strongly. We don't have all that much room to manoeuvre."

He nodded, then she said, "As our ambassador explained to you, an informal visit with President Darrow can be arranged."

"I would appreciate that," he said. "Perhaps we could continue our discussion after my visit to the White House. There are some specifics we may want to discuss."

The basis of successful negotiating, Frances told herself as she left the room, is to work out how the other person sees things and where he's coming from. She tried to imagine representing, a poor, small country and having to argue in the capital of a great power. She opened up to his anxieties. There was something admirable about him, fighting for these people the way he did. Then she wondered whether in her position she should be going this far in extending sympathies.

Jacob steeled himself for the confrontation with Darrow, for he was sure that this was what it would be. He told himself that he would not be intimidated but would talk as one head of government to another. An injunction came to him from somewhere: "Stand up tall. Let them know you're coming,"

President Darrow received him at the door of his office. He beckoned him to a chair, sat behind his desk, and got down to brass tacks immediately. "Mr. Shemtov, there can be no question of our supporting an IMF loan for St. George when you've just taken over another American company."

"I had no idea you were contemplating support for an

IMF loan for us even before last week's announcement," Shemtov replied.

Darrow smiled wryly, silently acknowledging his point. "There are degrees of unacceptability," he said. "We're also worried about activities on your streets. Even after the murder of Dwight Brewster, there've been attempts on the lives of American Embassy personnel. The bomb under an embassy car. And if it turns out that General Benvenista has come to harm, then we'll have to take that very seriously indeed."

"I assure you," Shemtov said in an even tone, "no agency of my government has any knowledge of Benvenista's disappearance. We're trying hard to get to the bottom of that. And the bomb also. When my Government expressed regrets for that, I assure you it as not just a formal gesture, it was sincere. We're trying to find out who was responsible and if we do I promise they will be prosecuted, whatever their connections.

"As for violence on the streets, there's violence here in Washington. The Hungarian ambassador was attacked by armed robbers a few days ago when he was walking along the street. I don't think anyone took this as an act of Government policy."

Darrow said, "Look, we get pictures on our TV screens of people burning the American flag outside our embassy."

"I have great respect for the United States and its flag. I lived here for a time, as I think you know. I respect American democracy."

"You may, Prime Minister, but what do those TV pictures look like?"

"You have congressional elections coming up, and you have to worry about the feelings of ordinary Americans right now. I understand your position."

"I always consider the feelings of ordinary Americans," Darrow replied, in a tone that carried a note of rebuke.

Shemtov paused to let this pass, and then said, "Mr.

President, we're both responsible people. We both know that random acts of violence and demonstrations on the streets can have adverse effects on policy. I would like to avoid them. But in a democracy, people are allowed to demonstrate. I don't need to remind you of that. In our country we have a recent history of oppression which gives rise to strong feelings."

. Darrow had been leaning back but now he sat upright. "Mr. Shemtov, we know that the AED. is behind some of these demonstrations. Correction. It's in front of them. Its members are carrying the banner. As you know, they're the group that killed Dwight Brewster. They're terrorists."

Shemtov considered this and thought of the reaction of some of his ministers on the Left. He said, "The men charged with killing Dwight Brewster were members of the AED and they will be tried, as you know. But we don't blame the entire organisation. We don't regard it as a criminal organisation."

"You can't. Some members are in your party."

"They don't support terrorism any more than I do."

"I believe that. But if we say we do regard the AED as terrorists?"

"You have the right to take whatever position you like, Mr. President. But I would suggest that you're mistaken. The members who carried out the violent act are under arrest." He was praying that AED members were not behind Benvenista's disappearance.

"You say it would be a mistake if we labelled the AED a terrorist organisation," Darrow said. "But is it a serious mistake?" Darrow paused to let the question sink in, and then went on, "It doesn't affect your Government directly. Only two members of your government are AED members and they're not in senior posts."

He leaned forward now and went on, in a soft voice: "Mr. Shemtov, we're going to declare that the AED is a terrorist organisation. Members of the AED will not be admitted to the United States. And probably former members, even if they are ministers of your government. Are any of them planning to take a holiday in Disneyland? If so, they'll have to cancel their plans. Just between you and me, I don't see that it will cause much more inconvenience than that." He paused to let Shemtov absorb this.

Shemtov was surprised. He saw what he was being offered, and he took it up. "As you know, the AED doesn't represent the policies of our Government, although it was a part of our revolution..".

"We know that," Darrow said. "I'm sure they're causing you some problems." Shemtov acknowledged this silently. Darrow added, "This is a gesture the Administration feels obliged to make at this time. As I suggested, I don't think it will cause you serious harm"

"I think I understand," Shemtov said.

"And it would improve relations between our countries, or at any rate help prevent them getting worse, if you would do your best to curb the anti-American enthusiasm of some of these demonstrators."

"I will try to prevent them getting out of hand," Shemtov said.

Darrow nodded approval, and leaned back in his chair again in a more relaxed mode. "Mr. Shemtov, this Administration isn't totally hostile to you and your Government. There are people telling us we should put a tight economic squeeze on you but we don't want to do that if we don't have to. We'd rather you did some things differently. Taking over American companies is a bit of a bugger. So is blocking the export of their earnings. American business doesn't like that. But I think I understand your reasons. Between you and me, American companies down there haven't always played fair. They haven't exactly run their affairs in the best interests of your people. .

"You can talk over details of policy with Frances. I'll just say this: Don't push us too far. You can throw a little shit at us. We're a big country, we can take it. But not too much shit. Okay?"

Jacob was taken aback at this tone. He smiled in response. Tension was going out of his limbs that he had not known was there. "You've made yourself clear and I appreciate that," he said.

When he left he was almost light-headed with relief. He wondered how he could be more conciliatory towards the United States without giving up anything serious. Accommodation was possible. Although the veiled warning about an economic squeeze was also there.

Darrow got up from his chair and walked over to the window and stared out for a while. He had sounded cool, confident, with nothing much to worry about from a tiny Caribbean country. And indeed, what did the United States have to worry about? He had done well. But inside he had been anxious about his first meeting with the head of another government. Did the other man feel so nervous? he wondered. Almost certainly not or he would have seen it. He had put on a good act.

Shemtov's mood had changed since his meeting in the White House. He no longer felt that he was in enemy territory. He was less worried and more confident. He messaged Frances Carr and she suggested they meet over dinner. He went to his bedroom and accepted the offer of tea and biscuits sent up on a tray, which he ate at the little desk, and read again the briefing paper on her. Background in academia, known to take a hard line on many issues. Darrow relies on her heavily for advice. Long affair with a well-known TV anchorman. Yes, a powerful man could find her attractive, he could see that. She was a spirited woman with a lot of appeal, professional, but, he sensed, imaginative and capable of thinking beyond the bounds of professionalism.

She arrived for dinner wearing a brown trouser suit with

a cream blouse underneath and an amber necklace. She had unpinned her hair so that it lay straight and rested on her shoulders and the ends bounced as she walked into the room with a vigorous step. She seemed eager, rather like, Jacob could not help thinking, a young woman arriving on a date.

Over the first course he reminisced, as he had planned, about his time at Georgetown University. This would establish the link between them. His stay there as a lecturer had overlapped by one term hers as a graduate student, but she had never attended any of his classes or lectures, which were about Latin America. "The students I met were bright, ready to speak up," he said. "A lot of them had ideals. But most were careerist. Planning their career in the Government service or in some kind of academic institution. The students I taught in St. George and in England weren't so practical."

"You preferred them?"

"In some ways. There's time enough to be practical and realistic when you're older."

"I wasn't planning a career in the State Department, you may be surprised to know. I didn't know I'd go this way."

She enjoyed the chit-chat and she indulged herself by letting it go on for a while. But when the main course of baked fish arrived, she decided that it was time to return to business and she asked, "Did you find your talk with he President useful?"

"Yes, very. I found him understanding of our position. Although he told me you're going to declare the AED a terrorist organisation."

"That's right. I should tell you in confidence that there are domestic pressures behind that."

"I realise that, of course. I came away thinking that an accommodation with your Administration's views is possible." He quoted, with an apology for the language, what Darrow had said about throwing shit at the United States.

Frances smiled. "That sounds like Stephen," she said.

They talked about St. George's economic plight and the

IMF. "You seem to feel these nationalisation measures are essential," she said. "Couldn't you achieve the same results by some other means?"

"What do you think my Parliament would say if I announced that we were going back on nationalisation? I wouldn't be Prime Minister for long. And I wouldn't deserve to be."

"I admire your commitment," she said.

"We want friendly relations with the United States. American hostility worries us. We remember the Gomez years."

He was weighing his words, putting the essentials of his Government's position while leaving room to manoeuvre on the details. At the same time he was watching the swaying of the amber beads around her neck as she moved, and the way she lowered her eyebrows and her eyes flickered when she made a point. He had not noticed before how mobile her eyebrows were. And the pale smooth skin of her neck, at the side, where the hair stopped. At one point he wanted to reach out and touch her neck but he pushed the thought out of his mind.

She said, "We welcomed St. George's return to democracy."

"Yes, but you were friendly to Gomez, you sold him weapons. His death squads murdered people for trying to form a trade union, they murdered people who wanted civil rights and left their bodies for others to see as an example. And that was a government supported by the United States! I'm sorry to tell you these things, but my people remember this." Despite herself and despite her concern for professionalism, Frances shivered at the idea of bodies in the street as a warning..

He went on, "I don't like it when people burn the American flag in my country. As you know I've lived here and I enjoyed it. I respect American democracy. But to a lot of people in St. George, those things, the murders under Gomez, are what the American flag represents. And there are people in America, people here in Washington, who want to bring back the Gomez regime or something like it."

"Not any in positions of influence, I assure you."

"But when you talk about America being upset at what we're doing, what's in my people's minds is CIA tricks."

She could only mutter, "I can assure you that nothing like that is planned."

He sensed that he was getting through to her. He did not want to sound too harsh. He softened his tone. The table had been cleared now and they were sitting in upright armchairs angled towards each other. He leaned towards her. "Frances," he said – "do you mind if I call you Frances? – "we talked about some students being idealistic. When you were a graduate student at Georgetown, you took part in a demonstration on the campus about the treatment of immigrant farm-workers in California. In fact, you were one of the leaders. Do you remember?" She nodded.

"I was there too, marching behind your banner. I wasn't there because of St. George, it wasn't about St. George, but because I cared about injustice and cruelty. And so did you. We were on the same side then. Surely our views aren't that different today."

She looked into his eyes. "They're not that different, Jacob," she said. "We don't have to be on opposite sides. We do represent different interests, although they don't have to be opposing ones."

"Our people are poor in the way those immigrant farm-workers were poor."

"We don't want anyone to be poor."

"I don't think the person who led that demonstration as a student wants America to be a bully. I hope you don't find the term offensive."

This was getting too personal. She pulled herself back to

a professional stance`. "We might be able to accept the nationalisations if there were compensation that was considered adequate."

"The companies won't accept any figure as adequate, you know that," he replied. "But I think you'll find they're fair. We'll make an effort."

Neither of them said anything for a while and then he said, "I think we've gone as far as we can this evening on policy matters."

"I agree," she said. But they both knew that their conversation was not at an end. A current was carrying them along..

"Tell me," he asked her, "do you ever miss your days as an idealistic student? The talk, the demonstrations, the enthusiasm and all that?"

"Of course. Particularly the enthusiasm. Things seemed simpler then."

"Yes, it seemed clear what was right and wrong."

"And what should be done."

He smiled. "Oh yes, that was simple. It was certainly simpler deciding how my country should be governed than governing it."

"Did you want to be Prime Minister one day, back then?"

"I don't think so. I'm not sure what I was thinking about my future. I was always politically active. Even when I was an undergraduate."

"So even then you spent most of your time thinking about politics."

"I spent *most* of my time thinking about girls."

She smiled. "Girls or one girl in particular?"

"Girls. One girl in particular for a few terms. And what did you think about in college? International relations and boys?"

"I guess that's it. Not always in that order. I suppose most students think more about the opposite sex than the state of the world."

"Let's hope they always will," he said. "The other way lies fanaticism." Her face lit up now; she agreed with what he said. More than that, she liked what he said.

They talked for a little while about how young people today were different. He felt attracted to her now and at the same time relaxed. He got up and walked over to the window. Clouds scudded across the night sky, now veiling the moon so that it looked a shadowy ghost, now revealing it in its full pale light. "A full moon," he said.

She joined him at the window and looked down at the scene. "The green looks quite beautiful in the moonlight," she remarked.

"When I was young," he said, "I used to look at the moon sometimes, wherever I was, in London or Cambridge or wherever, and think that this is the same moon that's shining on my parents in St. George, and on other places all over the world. Whoever they are, Americans or Chinese or African bushmen or Arabs or Israelis or whatever, they're looking up at this moon. The same moon. Did you used to look at the moon when you were young?"

"I suppose so. I looked at the moon and had dreams"

"Romantic dreams?"

She shrugged. "I probably wouldn't have accepted the term, but I suppose that's what they were."

"Did any of them come true?"

"A few. Bits of them, anyway. But things are never the way you think they're going to be."

He looked down at her and he seemed to feel a welcoming warmth coming from her. It was up to him to say something now. Things came into his mind: "I wish we'd met in other circumstances." "You look lovely by moonlight." "Would you mind if I kissed you?" It all sounded foolish.

He found he did not need to say anything. She turned to face him and they were looking straight into each other's eyes.

Her look shot through him like an electric shock. She was a statement and his presence was the response.

He put his hand on her shoulder and drew her closer to him. That was all that was necessary. Usually, when a man and woman come together, when the relationship becomes physical, there are a number of thresholds to be crossed. There are degrees of physical intimacy to be passed through, of touching here, touching there, kissing, feeling, holding. But here, because they had met as representatives of governments, there was only one threshold. They had crossed it and they both knew it.

He put his arms around her and kissed her on the lips and they stayed like that for a few moments. His heart was pounding with excitement but he spoke calmly. He asked, "Where's your room?"

"One flight up," she said

He followed her up the narrow staircase, holding her hand. For a moment he had a pang of anxiety, a feeling that he should not be going up to her bedroom, as if he were an actor about to go onstage and he did not know his lines. But the moment passed..

She did not turn on the light but the curtain was open and they could see each other in outline by the light of the moon as they started to undress. He sat on the bed to take off his shoes and socks first, always, he remembered, the clumsiest part of undressing. When they were still in their underwear he put his arms around her and felt his stiffness against her.

Something in him told him that he should hurry and do it all before the feeling went away, but he dismissed this thought and started to stroke her body. She pulled back, then moved closer to him. "I'm sorry if I'm awkward. I'm a bit nervous," she said.

Her words surprised him and pleased him. "So am I," he said, and when he said this all his hesitation vanished. They helped one another with some fumbling, but then he stroked her while she reached behind her to unclick her bra, and then he pushed her back on the bed and slid off her panties. Then he kissed her nipples and went into the foreplay he remembered and heard her panting with excitement and he entered her.

She thrust up to meet him. He came sooner than she would have liked, but her pleasure in the intermingling of flesh had never been so undiluted. Afterwards she could not stop smiling.

Hardly knowing what he was saying, Jacob murmured, "Thank you." But he said it in Hebrew so she did not understand.

They had left the curtains open so he awoke with the dawn. He got up and dressed quietly and kissed her cheek gently. She half-opened her eyes and answered when he whispered goodbye and thank you. Then he went back to his own bedroom.

At breakfast, Donald Green said to her. "I hear you met with Jacob Shemtov yesterday. Did the meeting go well?"

."Yes. It was very useful," she replied, careful not to smile.

When she got to her office, there was a news agency dispatch on her computer. It said General Benvenista had arrived in Kingston, Jamaica on a small boat. He told reporters that he had received death threats in St. George and showed them the messages. They were unsigned. One said: "You will die and you deserve to die. You murdered our people and you will pay." The other said: "You will pay for your crimes. We have a St. Georgian government here, not one run by American lackeys who will protect you."

"Oh God," she thought, "this means more talk about danger to American citizens and more yelling by some congressional candidates."

::   ::   ::

ccxxviii

Louis Mannion was worried and as he usually did when he was worried, he was pacing up and down. The two men talking to him were standing still and they followed him with their eyes as he talked. Both were men he worked with and respected. This made what they were saying more worrying.

Ben Devoe, the Minister for Agriculture, was talking now. "Jacob was the right choice after Gomez," he said. "No doubt about that. Nobody's saying otherwise. The important thing then was to get the system going again, Parliamentary democracy and all that. He could get the support of most of the country. But he's not the man to carry through big changes. He's not a strong leader. He's spent his life in universities. You know a lot of people in the party feel that way."

"Yes, I know," Louis acknowledged. They were talking in Louis's office.

"Now he's with his old friends in America," Devoe went on. "What do you think they're telling him?"

"He's not gone there just to listen."

"They're telling him," Devoe continued, ignoring Louis's reply, "that we should scale back the take-overs. Go slowly. Don't give in to extremists. Ban the AED, probably. Extremists! I remember the time when we were all extremists." This last was said with a sardonic laugh. "And so do you.

"The Government," he went on, "is putting three AED.men on trial as if they were criminals. Men like Juan Ortega. We all know Juan. He spent three years in jail under Gomez, and he's still got the scars. How do you feel about putting him back in jail?"

Louis acknowledged that he felt badly about it, but he said, "We're not in a state of revolution, we have a legal government."

"Yes, but whose side is it on? The way things are going, we'll probably end up with an IMF loan, which will mean we'll have to follow IMF rules. Foreign capital will be able to buy our public services."

"That could happen but it doesn't mean it's going to," Louis said..

"But that's the way things are moving."

"You want to ask the party to vote Jacob out?"

Brian Thaxted spoke up. "A lot of us want to. Ben here has agreed to go forward as an alternative leader. We want to put it to the party now. Call a conference to vote on the leadership. When Jacob gets back the conference will already be scheduled."

Louis shook his head doubtfully. "I don't know. I'm not happy about moving against Jacob. It's not just a personal loyalty thing, he was the right man."

"But he's changed," Thaxted said. "I was close to him too. He's got different friends now. He listens to different people. Haven't you found that?"

"Sometimes," he acknowledged. He walked from one side of the room to the other and then turned and suggested, "Ask Ingrid Mundt what she thinks."

"You're temporising," Devoe said. "You know damned well what Ingrid will say. She owes her job to Jacob."

" S-s-so do I," said Louis..

"No you don't," Thaxted retorted. "You owe it to the people here who supported you, the unions and the workers. They wanted you to have one of the top jobs in the Government."

"And so you should have," added Devoe. "Let's face it, Jacob wants you there to keep the workers quiet."

"A g-g-government led by you and me and some of the AEDs will be less acceptable to a lot of people in Parliament than a Shemtov Government," Louis pointed out. "Even if the party accepted it."

"Yes, and less acceptable to the Americans," Devoe sneered.

"And you think you n-n-n-need my support?" Louis felt his stutter was getting out of control. He must he silent for a while, he thought, or else terminate the conversation.

"If you're with us, we've got a good chance of swinging the party," Devoe said. "But if you're not willing to come out with us, if people think you're still with Shemtov, then party people will get cold feet and vote to keep Shemtov. No, we won't go to the party if you're going to oppose us.

"But then what future is there? Shemtov will backtrack. We'll be just another mildly liberal bourgeois party. The workers and the peasants will have been sold out. He won't break up the big estates. We'll still be run by American capital. And you'll be Minister of Labour in a bourgeois government with no power to do what you think should be done Yes, it'll be better than under Gomez. But the country deserves more than that. And you deserve more."

Louis stopped his pacing and stood silent for a moment. The others could almost see the conflicting moods in his face. Then he said, "Let me th-th-th-think about it. Please."

"You'll have to think quickly," Devoe said. "We want to call a party meeting while Jacob is still in Washington."

When they left, Louis went on pacing up and down. He thought about what the workers deserved and he thought about what was politically possible. How much real power did Shemtov have? He was constrained by political pressures. But at present no one person had more. Who had power? He thought about the years working underground with some of the men who were now AED leaders. He thought about political radicalism. Where had Maoism and the cultural revolution got China? Now they were going through a typically capitalist industrial revolution with a big gap between rich and poor. He thought about how he would feel about being Deputy Prime Minister under Devoe, rather than a

Minister of Labour who could be ignored when important decisions were being taken, like the decision to go ahead with nationalisation immediately. That was an attractive thought.

But was he just self-seeking? Was he betraying the people who had elected him their union leader? He paced up and down some more in his anxiety. It was all too much for him. Jacob had spent his whole life talking with people in government, talking about how to govern, in the capitals of the world as well as in St. George. He had no such experience. Indecision and uncertainty flooded into his mind and he sat down and held his head in his hands He needed help. He needed guidance.. Suddenly he wanted to ask his mother. She was long dead and would not have understood the politics anyway but she would have listened sympathetically and understood some of what he was going through.

He stopped pacing and sat down. Silently, but moving his lips, he began to pray to the Virgin Mary: "Holy Mother of God...."

CHAPTER ELEVEN

After breakfast Stephen Darrow went to the toilet as he usually did, and as he usually did he spent a few minutes voiding his bowels and waiting for the after-effects to pass through him. He remembered something he had not thought of for years. When he was a boy he used to wonder sometimes whether the great people of the world, prime ministers and film stars and people like that, felt the same as other people in their private moments, when they were lying in bed or sitting in the bath or on the toilet. At these times, did being a great and famous person make any difference? When they were sitting on the toilet, did the Queen or the President of the United States or Michael Jackson feel the same as him, Steve Darrow? Mr. O'Toole who lived along the landing - who was he? anyway, somebody - used to say, "They've all got arses to wipe just like the rest of us." He heard this as a child and he would try to imagine some of the great people of history wiping their arses: Winston Churchill, Hitler, the Queen.

He finished and washed his hands. He was President of the United States and sitting on the toilet did not feel any different. He had a rash on his feet and it itched just the way it would if he were not President. He found this comforting. He did not have to become a different species of human being when he was elected.

He went into his office and looked at the papers on his desk. The most important was a copy of the message that Frances had received from the British Foreign Secretary. "A bit of a disappointment," she had scrawled across it. It said the British Government had decided to accept the St. Georgian proposal of joint commissions to discuss compensation for the industries they had nationalised., and were taking part in a European Union trade mission to St. George.

"Fine bloody friends," he said to Frances. "I'm not surprised that they've accepted the compensation commissions. Our London ambassador, whatsisname, warned us that they would. Of course, that puts more pressure on us to go along with them. Which I'm sure as hell not going to do until after the congressional election. But this thing about a trade mission is just spitting in our face."

"I don't think they necessarily meant it that way," she said. "The British are on a European kick at the moment. They'll go along with anything European. They're trying to undo some of the damage in Brussels that the last government did."

After she left Darrow read the report about Benvenista arriving in Jamaica, and on an impulse he sent a message to him expressing sympathy with his plight at having to flee from St. George in a small boat, and gratification at his safe arrival. He received a reply almost immediately. Benvenista said he appreciated the President's good wishes. He said that as an old soldier he would have remained at his post even at the risk of his life if this would have served any purpose.

Darrow decided that he needed a break so he went for a stroll, first taking his Walkman from his desk drawer and clipping on the earphones. He walked along the path beside the playing fields with a preoccupied air. He had the autonomous, authoritative stride of the Man Who Walks Alone. An acquaintance seeing him would not casually stop and greet him, reluctant to interrupt his thoughts, knowing his responsibilities. In fact Darrow was listening to a tape of the

Jam on his Walkman. Paul Weller bellowing sentiments in his ear drove his White House worries out of his mind for a while.

In the monitoring room Piers Traynor said to Howe, "Things are certainly rattling along. You've thrown in some nice touches. Like General Benvenista scuttling off to Jamaica and those threats. It's keeping people in their toes."

Howe grinned. "I'd prepared a number of things before the game started." Then he said to Manash, "I'm impressed with how some people are taking to the authority of office. Aren't you, Robert?"

"They're taking to it in different ways, " Manash said. "Darrow is doing well but I think he feels the burden of responsibility. I gather that Shemtov is a natural depressive but the responsibility seems to be a stimulus."

"I think we could still add a little more," Howe said.

"Like what?" asked Traynor.

"Well, let's see. The CIA has been stirring the pot in St. George, and they've been having an easy time of it. Let's stir the pot the other way and see what happens." He typed out a note and fed it into the computer.

"I've got a couple of other ideas. I don't think the British Government should get away with what it's doing scot-free."

Just then a young woman came in and handed him a note. He got up and hurried out of the room. He came back later looking worried. "I've had some bad news," he said. "I think we're going to have to interrupt the game and take someone out."

"Who?" asked Manash.

"Louis Mannion. He's in Blue House. His wife's been rushed to hospital."

"It's serious?"

"Apparently. She was pregnant. She's given birth prematurely. She's ill."

"What is it?"

"The hospital says she's in a serious condition. They say she's had - it was something like clampsia or pre-clampsia," Howe said.

"Pre-eclampsia," Manash said. "Yes, that could be serious."

"The hospital says critical. Oh, Christ! We'll have to get him out so that he can go to her." He turned to Manash. "Can you do a quick de-programming job? In one session? An hour or an hour-and-a-half, maybe."

"Not really. They were going to have three days to come out of it."

"Can't you give Mannion some intensive treatment?" Howe asked anxiously. "We want to get him to his wife in a hurry."

Manash pondered and said,. "It's not just the treatment. It's the de-programming plus the time. Up to three days in which they shake themselves out of their other identity, interact with one another as their normal selves. That's what I'd planned. I don't think it's something you can speed up. I don't know exactly what will happen, this is all experimental, remember."

"We'll have to do something," Howe said, shaking his head.   "At the moment he probably doesn't know who his wife is."

" I'll do what I can. An hour-and-a-half should help. And the news about his wife might shock him partly out of it. Get him in touch with his real life. But I don't really know."

A few minutes later, Louis Mannion was hurrying over to the main building with a puzzled look on his face, accompanied by Traynor.

A news report went over the computer system. "Louis Mannion, the St. Georgian Minister for Labour, was severely injured when his car veered off the highway outside Victoria and plunged down a steep embankment. Mr. Mannion is at present in the Victoria General Hospital in a coma. Doctors say he suffered injuries to the head and the upper torso and is in intensive care. They say there is no question of his resuming his ministerial duties for a long time. He was driving the car himself and was alone in the car."

In an office in Blue House, Brian Thaxted and Ben Devoe looked at the message and exchanged sympathy for poor Mannion with his injuries. Then, after a pause, Thaxted said what they had both been thinking. "Louis was wavering. I think if push came to shove he'd stand up for Shemtov. If Louis is out of the picture, this is the time to make a move."

"We call a party meeting now."

"And put down resolutions. When he gets back we'll be ready for battle. Jacob won't be. He's not really much of a fighter."

Early in the afternoon, Piers Traynor drove Louis to the station. Louis's head was still reeling from his hour-and-a-half of Manash explaining to him insistently and often puzzlingly who he really was and how this had all come about.

Piers bought a ticket for him, and steered him to the platform where the London train was due. Louis looked around at everything, the platform, the empty benches, the rail line stretching away on both sides, the signs. He was seeing it all as if it were in a foreign country and he was familiar with it from pictures.

Piers talked continually, as he had been advised to do by Manash, about things that were happening, keeping Mannion in the present, tying him to the world around him with details. "We could have got a car and a driver but this will get you into London more quickly. The train's due in six minutes. It should take you an hour and twenty minutes to get to London. You get into Paddington, you know Paddington Station, do you? I'm sorry you didn't have time to pack your things but we'll have your suitcase sent on to you, I'll organise it myself.

"Here, I've got you a paper. This is this morning's Times. See, the lead story, they're still going on about the division in the Government over the Euro. Ian and I were talking about it just this morning. The alignment of fiscal policies and all that. And there's this U.N. vote on Palestine. Have you been following that?" Louis was nodding with the minimum of verbal response. "I hope everything turns out all right at the hospital. Your wife's in good hands. You can get a snack on the train. They have a buffet car."

"Yes. I'll get some coffee," Mannion said.

Shemtov came back from Washington feeling invigorated. He had been prepared to fight from a position of weakness. As it was, he had found some common ground with the Secretary of State and the American President had conceded much of his case. As for his night with Frances, even thinking about it brought on such a rush of feelings that he could not sort them out, but happiness and gratitude were among them.

Taking his place at his desk, he saw the motion calling for a special conference of the party. It was signed by Devoe and Thaxted and two others. Pity about Thaxted. After that awful affair of the fake General Murillo letter, it confirmed his view of the man's instability. The conference was to be convened to vote on a proposal for the regular re-election for the post of party leader, which, while it was the majority party in Parliament, meant the Prime Minister.

So he would have to fight for his position, would he? A little while ago he would have been more worried about it, and might have thrown in the towel rather than fight against his old allies. Now he knew he would fight the motion and win. If Devoe and his friends won, there would be economic chaos, unemployment and a collapse of living standards. If things got bad enough the military would take over. And people might be grateful for it..

He thought he could win the party over to him but a public division now would weaken the party and would weaken his standing in the governing coalition. It would be much better if he could get them to withdraw the motion. Devoe was the prime mover and he was about to call him into his office when he paused. Devoe would undoubtedly come in with Thaxted and perhaps some other allies they could find. Thaxted was in an emotional state and the others would strengthen Devoe. Better to see him alone. He went along the corridor and into Devoe's office. Devoe was reading something on his computer. He looked up in surprise.

Shemtov got down to brass tacks right away. "Ben, I'd like you to reconsider this motion,"

Devoe was caught off balance. Sounding defensive, he said, "I don't want you to take this as a personal criticism.".

"How else should I take it?"

"Jacob, you were made Prime Minister by acclamation at the time of the revolution. You were the obvious choice, acceptable to everybody. That's why we have the support of Parliament. Now we think it's time the party had a proper choice of candidates and a choice of policies."

"And if they choose you we won't have the support of the other parties any more."

"That's not certain. But we'll be doing what the party called for in opposition."

"That was when we were an underground party. It's different now."

"Jacob, you know I want to follow a more left line than you. I always did."

"And do what? Promise the workers all sorts of things and have wild inflation? And a go-slow by business. And an illegal outflow of capital and the workers making more demands which you know you won't be able to satisfy. That's what it will produce."

"But what we want to do you can't do gently. You met with the American Government in Washington."

"Yes I saw the President and I saw the Secretary of State."

"And I suppose they warned you of the dangers of going too far."

"They'll make noises about terrorism and they'll argue all

the details of the commissions on compensation and we'll have to make a few changes to keep them happy but they won't do anything drastic to stop us. Darrow is not as hostile as I thought he might be. I know that now.

"Right now we can carry Parliament with us. But a fight wouldn't be good for the party. If your motion comes to the conference I'll take it as a vote of confidence and I'll tell them the consequences of your policies I might also have to point to a few of the things which we tolerate but which it's better not to raise now."

"Like what?"

"Like the behaviour of some of the workers' leaders who would be your allies in this. Like the trade union leader who now has two cars and a chauffeur and lends one of the cars to his mistress. And you know who I mean. There's another who's living high on his expenses. I'd rather not have to do all this. You won't win, Ben."

"This isn't just opportunism," Devoe protested. "It's an honest difference of opinion."

"I'm sure it isn't just opportunism," Shemtov said with a grin. "If it were it would be very stupid, and you're not a stupid man."

"What do you mean?"

"You know that if you lost this vote you couldn't stay on as Minister for Agriculture."

"I'd still be willing to serve under you."

"It wouldn't work, Ben. Not once you've divided the party. Which would be a pity." They had both been standing but now Louis dropped into a chair.

"Ben, you and I have discussed agricultural reform, giving land to the small peasants, and that's one of the most important things we have to do. You're the best person to carry it through. I believe that and I still want to have you as the minister. If you bring this to a vote and lose and you have to step down, you'll set back the programme. But if that's what you feel you have to do - !

He stopped. He knew he had won. He did not need to force Devoe to say the word. "Think about it, ," he said. "Let me know your decision. I know you didn't come into this alone, and perhaps you've got a wiser head than some of the others." That gave Devoe a get-out.

"I'll think about it," Devoe promised. "As I said, there's nothing personal in this. I've always had a lot of respect for you, you know that.". .

Jacob nodded and left, and as he walked back along the corridor to his own office, he felt like skipping.

::   ::
::

Stephen Darrow got back from his walk and found another message on his desk. This was a shocker. It was a news agency report from the St. Georgian capital, Victoria. The St. Georgian police had arrested two men who had confessed to having planted the bomb outside the American Embassy and having sent the death threats to Benvenista. They said they had been paid to do so by the CIA. They were *agents provocateur*. They named the man who had given them the he said. "It plays into the hands of the extremists down there."

"And Shemtov will never trust us again."

"I think," she said slowly, "that if I talk to him on the telephone, I can persuade him that you didn't know anything about this."

"You established a satisfactory relationship with him while he was here?"

She looked across and decided that he did not mean anything special by the question. "Yes, I think we understand each other."

"Okay, then do talk to him," he said. "Tell him it was a rogue section of the CIA. Apologise. Say we're dealing with it. And I want to see Davies. I'll have his guts for garters."

Donald Green was having a mid-morning cup of coffee in his office when he saw the news that the British Government was accepting the St. Georgian compensation plan and would take part in a European trade mission. He nearly choked. The British had turned around and spat in America's face. He knew about the British, with their superior stuck-up ways, cold and calculating. He knew about them as oppressors, as the American colonists knew them and as his Irish forefathers knew them. They were people who starved Irish peasants and sucked up to Hitler at Munich.

He had to talk to someone about this, and thought immediately of Campbell Davies as a kindred spirit. He set off for his office.

Davies was sitting in his office with several messages on his desk, but he was looking at only one, the message summoning him to see the President. He pursed his lips and shook his head slowly in dismay. He had seen the report from St. George and he knew what it would mean. His operation had been blown. He thought about what might have gone wrong. It should not have happened, but this was academic now. He imagined himself before the President's desk, on the receiving end of a tongue-lashing.

Always, when there was a setback, he looked for some way t hat it could be turned to advantage, or at least something to salvage. If nothing else, there were lessons to be learned for next time. But there were no lessons for him to learn because there would be no next time. He would be reprimanded and removed from his post, shunted aside, quite possibly forced into retirement. After a lifetime's serivce.

He was trying to think of what he could say to Darrow or do in the way of damage limitation when Green knocked at his door. He called out "Come in." Green walked in and a question exploded out of him. "Campbell, have you see what the British have done?"

"Yes, I've seen the news from London," Davies replied.

"Those bastards! They've shafted us."

"Mmmm, yes," said Davies. Green was preoccupied with what he was saying and did not notice that Davies, sitting with his elbows on the desk, was only half listening. Davies was thinking about the note on his desk spelling disaster for his career.

"They're supposed to be our fucking allies! Do they think they're going to get away with it?" Green went on. "I don't know what Darrow is going to do about it. I know what we ought to do." He waited for a response but none came, so he went on, "What do you think?"

"Yes, it's unwelcome," Davies acknowledged.

"Unwelcome!" Green repeated, thinking this was typical of Davies' understatement. "You're right about that."

Davies switched focus and looked at the small, agitated figure before him. Suddenly, he saw possibilities, a way ahead. All this fizzing anger could just possibly be useful if it was directed in the right way. Maybe there was a way to avoid disaster. Now he directed his attention to Green. "They've shafted us, all right, Donald," he said. "Do you know about the military aid?"

"What military aid?"

"The British are going to send a new military aid mission to St. George. Part of Commonwealth co-operation, they say. Raymond Wade, the Prime Minister, is very keen on the Commonwealth. We've just learned about it. It hasn't been announced yet."

"Jesus Christ!" Green stood still and clenched and unclenched his fists in anger.

"We don't know what Shemtov has offered Wade," Davies went on. "Perhaps something on trade with the industries the state has taken over."

"So he'll be bribing the British with money he's stolen from Americans! What are we going to do?"

Davies spoke slowly and judiciously. "I'm sure we'll send Wade a note expressing American displeasure in diplomatic terms."

"Displeasure! Diplomatic terms!" Green spat out the phrases scornfully. "That's what those Brits love. They'll get a diplomatic note and they'll send us a diplomatic note and meanwhile they're fucking us up the ass."

"That's the way these things are done," Davies said.

"But they're plenty of ways we can get tough with other countries," Green pointed out. "At least we can speak out."

"Yes, but these are our friends and allies."

"Friends? We ought to tell them something of what we can do to their little country and their European buddies if they go on screwing us this way." He flung himself down in an armchair. Then he said, "I'd like to go over and tell them myself."

"So would I," Davies said. "But we're playing this game by the rules."

"The rules!" Green repeated the phrase, and then shook his head over it..

Davies said. "Donald, sometimes we have accept things. Be good losers." He leaned back in his chair and continued,. "It's a lesson we can learn from the British, actually. They cultivate the art of being good losers."

"Show me a good loser and I'll show you a loser," Green retorted

Davies went on in a reflective mode, "It goes with cricket and their talk about fair play. Curiously, they developed this while they were the world winners, back in the Nineteenth Century. Now they've given up their empire and their world role with a certain amount of good grace and not much unnecessary violence. That's what we can learn. To lose with good grace."

"Learn from the British?" Green repeated incredulously. "Lose with good grace?"

"I know it doesn't come naturally," Davies said sympathetically, "We Americans aren't used to losing."

"Neither are the Marines," Green retorted. His fury propelled him out of his chair and he started pacing up and down again. "Can't the agency do something? Put some real pressure on the Brits? You've got tricks up your sleeve, surely."

Davies shrugged. "I'm sure we could if Darrow gave us the green light," he said. "Britain needs us more than we need Britain. But we can't step out of line. I'm having my knuckles rapped already because of a little bit of initiative I took."

"I've a mind to go over there and deliver a warning myself," he said. "They'd listen, by God!" He was thinking about what he would say and the way he would say it.

Davies spoke warmly. "That would really show them they can't get away with that sort of thing, wouldn't it?" Then he sounded more sober. "But you can't do that, Donald. As I said, we've got to play by the rules. Just accept things."

Green glowered. Wild thoughts were going through his mind. Davies talked about the rules. Accepting things. Accepting being shafted by our so-called allies. Sometimes you have to break the rules..

"Play by the rules. And be good losers. Sure." He stopped at Davies' desk, clenched his fist and held it a few inches above the desk for a moment, then slammed it down in a gesture of decision. Without saying another word he stalked out of the door. Davies listened to his footsteps, and heard him go down the stairway and smiled.

::   ::

::

Donald Green's fury was focused now, and his walk as he strode down the corridor was an angry walk. In his own mind, he was not walking alone. In fact he was not walking, he was marching, as a United States Marine. The marines had not earned their reputation by sending polite diplomatic notes. He was humming under his breath the Marine anthem and hearing the words in his mind: *From the halls of Montezuma to the shores of Tripoli, We will fight our country's battles on the land as on the sea.* Those were the only words he remembered but he went on with the tune.

He went downstairs and out of the door and crossed the grassy courtyard. He arrived at red house, pushed open the door and climbed the stairs to the first floor corridor. Through an open doorway he saw a man sitting at a desk. "Where's the Prime Minister's office?" he demanded.

"Who are you?" asked the man.

"I'm Colonel Green of the American National Security Council."

"I didn't know we were expecting a visit," the man said.

"You're not." Green walked across the room and leaned over him. "Now where's the Prime Minister's office? Are you going to tell me?"

The man was intimidated. "It's along this corridor on the left.".

Green marched along the corridor, a narrow corridor with a wooden floor and doors along one side and windows on the other, just like the one in his own building. He came to a door marked "Prime Minister's Office" and knocked. A voice inside called, "Who is it?"

He did not answer but opened the door and walked in. Two people were in the room. One man was sitting behind a desk, a trim figure with a moustache in his shirtsleeves. The other, sitting in an armchair, was tall and rake-thin with thin glasses and the kind of thin, cold, emotionless face that Green expected to see on a member of the British Government. The two men looked at Green in surprise.

Green addressed himself to the man behind the desk. "Are you Raymond Wade?" he demanded.

The man did not answer but asked in an equally demanding tone, "Who are you?"

"I'm Colonel Donald Green. I'm Acting Director of the United States National Security Council. I've come to talk to the Prime Minister."

The other two looked perplexed. The man behind the desk said, "You can't come in here."

Wade stood up. "We haven't had any communication about this," he said.

"I'm the communication. I'm here in person," Green informed him.

Wade was confused. His mind swirled. He was the Prime Minister and people could not just barge into his office and say they were representing a foreign government. Terrorists came into his mind. This seemed like a terrorist attack. He did not want to be trapped in a sitting position so he got up and walked out from behind his desk. "What do you want?" he asked.

"You're the Prime Minister, Raymond Wade," Green said, challengingly.

"I don't know what's going on," Wade said.

"I'll tell you what's going on," Green said. "I've come to ask what you think you're up to, sitting on these commissions with the St. Georgians. And now with this military mission. And to tell you some of the things that might be in store for you if you go on this way." He knew he had to be firm.

"What military mission?" Vallon asked automatically. "There's no military mission."

"Who are you?" Green demanded.

"This is the Foreign Secretary," Wade said.

Green went on, "I'm talking about the military mission you're sending to St. George."

"We're not – " Vallon began.

Wade broke in. "Go away," he said to Green. He did not understand what was happening. There were channels of communication for intergovernmental messages. How did this man get into his office? Things seemed to be breaking down.

"I'll go away when I've delivered my message and had an answer," Green said and he went on slowly, "Your behaviour is not what we expect from our allies."

Vallon said, "This isn't the way to do it. We can't talk to you."

"The hell you can't," Green retorted.

Vallon walked over and he stood between Green and Wade, so that they were almost touching. He was angry and was breathing hard. "If you have something to say you can communicate it in the proper way," he insisted.

"I'm communicating with you now."

"I'm not hearing you." He was a head taller than Green and he looked down at him

"I want to talk to the Prime Minister. Get out of my way!" Green ordered. When Vallon stood his ground Green pushed him aside. That was the first physical action.

Wade now stepped forward. He did not like this aggressive stranger who was intruding both into his office and into the game. "I don't know what the hell is going on but you'll have to get out of here," he said.

"Do you really think the United States is just going to stand by and let you go on this way?" Green asked him.

"I don't recognise - " Wade started to say but Green pressed on:

"Don't you think there are going to be consequences?"

Wade felt threatened. He sensed that if this man remained in his office it would no longer be the Prime Minister's office and everything would fall apart. He put a hand on Green's shoulder to turn him around in the direction of the door. "You've got to leave," he insisted.

"Get your goddamned hands off me," Green snapped, and knocked his hand aside with his fist.

Wade was confused, anxious and angry and he

responded to Green's blow physically. He said again with more emphasis, "You've got to leave!" and he put his hands on Green's chest and pushed him. He pushed him harder than he had intended so that Green, who was smaller than him and not very strong, it seemed, fell back against the wall. "I tell you - " he started to say.

Green was incensed. His background, his training, everything that made him Lieutenant-Colonel Donald Green USMC dictated his response to being slammed against the wall. He swung his fist at Wade's face. Wade was startled. He bobbed back and avoided the full force of the blow but it struck him on the tip of the nose. He yelled out in surprise and pain. Immediately and instinctively, he darted forward and punched back. The blow caught Green on the side of the cheek.

Green felt the blow, felt the room spin round, and found himself on the carpet, lying on his side propped up by one hand, with his cheek aching. He was hurt and frightened, and bewildered by his fear. He should not be frightened. He was a fighting marine. This should not be happening to him. He sprang to his feet and went for Wade again, swinging his fist wildly. Wade had no idea how this could happen but here was a man throwing a punch at him. He blocked it easily and slammed his fist straight into Green's mouth.

When Green swung his fist for the second time he was still a fighting marine, still a man of action. But at the instant that the other man's fist came at his face he was paralysed by fear, so that he could not duck or raise his hands to block the blow. It hit him on the mouth. Pain shot through him and he fell backwards on to the floor. Blood from his upper lip trickled down his chin.

Somewhere in the back of his mind there was an image of Colonel Green in action. But he was lying on the floor and he was hurt and he was cringing. He could not help it. He should get up again, go at this other man with his fists, a couple of quick jabs with the left and then a haymaker with the right. But he could not get up and face those fists. His body would not let him. He was frightened of those fists. How could this be?

Wade was confused. His last fist fight had been years ago and he had not expected to have another. This sudden eruption had shaken him. For a moment he knew that he was not the British Prime Minister. He was Captain Wade of the United States Army, a lecturer at the National War College. He was in England and he was playing a crisis game and he had taken on the role and the persona of the British Prime Minister. This vision faded and then returned, and it seemed somehow that this man sitting on the floor was playing the part of someone in the American Government.

"You'd better get up," he said to him. Green looked up and shook his head dumbly. He was in pain and he was frightened and he did not know what was happening to him. He took out a handkerchief and held to his bleeding lip and started sobbing, and his nose ran, the snot mingling with tears and blood.. Wade felt sorry for him. He stretched out his hand to help him up but Green drew away.

Green could not get up just now, could not even face getting up. His fear in the face of a swinging fist was replaced by panic. He, Colonel Green USMC, former Golden Gloves boxer, could not be feeling like this. His strength, his courage, his determination, everything that made him Colonel Donald Green was leaking away from him and he was left empty, without even the strength to stand up.

Wade was feeling uncomfortable and felt he had to get back into whatever game they were playing and be the British Prime Minister. He went back to his desk and sat in the Prime Minister's chair. He was feeling himself into the part again. It was difficult with Green s0itting on the floor bleeding. This should not be happening in Ten Downing Street.

Earlier, Traynor had seen Donald Green marching across

the courtyard to Red House when he came back from the station. He went up to the monitoring room and asked Howe, "Is Donald Green supposed to be going on a visit to Britain?"

Howe shook his head. "No."

"Well he's gone. I just saw him walking into Red House."

"Oh God. He isn't supposed to. You'd better go over there and see what's going on, will you?"

When Traynor walked into the room Green was still sitting on the floor with blood, tears and snot running down his face. He was appalled at the scene. He asked, "What happened?"

"He just barged in," Vallon explained. "He started a fight."

Traynor said to Green, "You'd better come back to your office." But Green just looked up at him with vacant eyes. The trickle of blood from his lip had reached his shirt collar now and was starting to spread in a stain. His glasses were askew. He started to sob, shaking his head in what seemed like bewilderment.

"Please come back," Traynor said again. After a while Green allowed Traynor to help him to his feet and take him over to Yellow House, and then to a bathroom where he washed his face. Then Traynor led him to his room. During all this time Green had not said a word.

In Red House, Pierre Vallon said to Wade, "What are we going to do?"

"To tell the truth. I can't think clearly," Wade said.

"I know, I'm a bit confused," Vallon said. "Are we going to go on dealing with the American note?".

"Of course, let's get on with dealing with that note. Give me a minute." His head was spinning.

Trying to get him back to the matter at hand, Vallon handed him the note and asked, "So what do you think?"

Wade looked at it and responded slowly. "As an

American, I think that Darrow has a right to be pissed off."

"As an *American*?"

"No, I didn't mean that, of course. It just came out. I mean, I can see their point of view. But we've got to be firm."

::   ::

::

Early that evening, Howe, Manash and Traynor were in the monitoring room. Manash was looking grave, Howe worried.

Howe said, "I think we have to call off the game a day early."

"No. All sorts of things can still happen," Manash protested.

"Yes, but it's falling apart," Howe said. "Mannion is out of the game. Green is *hors de combat*. The whole British team are shaken up."

"Wade is trying to go on as British Prime Minister," Traynor said.

"Yes, but I'm not sure he's not just pretending now. It's not the same thing. I think Vallon has problems.".

"But most of the others are still in their roles," Manash said.

"Besides," Howe went on, "the whole thing is getting out of control. I'm worried about what may be happening to people. Green has gone to his room and he won't come out. Won't speak. He seems to be having some kind of breakdown. Wade is in a confused state. Vallon seems shaken up."

"But they're going on with the game," Manash insisted.

"As I said, things are falling apart. It's been very instructive up to now. But things are happening to people. Green breaking all the rules and starting a fight. Also, I didn't tell you but we think Frances Carr may have spent the night with Jacob Shemtov."

"Really?" said Traynor with interest.

"Yes. She may decide afterwards that that's something she wouldn't do in her normal state of mind. She might decide to sue us, for God's sake.!

"That's a bit far-fetched."

"Really? What if she gets pregnant?"

"The baby would be a citizen of St. George?" suggested Traynor.

"Very funny," snapped Howe. "No, Robert, I want to call off the game now. Ultimately, I'm responsible for what happens."

"Well, it was an experiment," Manash said. "We didn't know how it would work out. We have a lot of results now."

"You see why I feel I have to do this," Howe said. "Things could go badly wrong."

"Yes, all right," Manash said reluctantly..

Howe now slipped into a brisk, authoritative tone. "We know the drill. We circulate a message telling everyone the game is over, That will shake them a bit. Then you" - to Manash - "will go around and give your little talk to each team."

. "And after that," Manash said. "they'll have their individual sessions with me,"

The announcement that went out said the game was being terminated. It concentrated on administrative arrangements. It said participants in the game were no longer required to remain in their own houses but were free to walk anywhere. It said that starting with breakfast the next day, meals would be served in the main building again. Individual appointments would be made with Dr. Manash.

In Yellow House, Campbell Davies read the message at his desk and smiled. He went over in his mind a lesson in basic tactics for one of his classes, his questions and their responses.

"You're playing a game, say it's a board game, and you suddenly know you're going to lose. Perhaps you've made a blunder. Or you gambled on a move and lost. You're found out. The situation is irretrievable. What do you do? Come on, let's have some answers.

"Cheat? Sometimes, perhaps. But here the situation is such that you can't cheat and get away with it. So what can you do? What's that you say? Break up the game, kick over the board? Yes, that could be a move, it would get you out of trouble. But it doesn't look good. It will reflect badly on you. So what can you do? How about getting somebody else to kick over the board? Yes, that's an idea, isn't it?. But how do you get someone to do that? Well, let's think about it. Let's see what we could do."

CHAPTER TWELVE

Donald Green woke up terrified. Lying in bed with his eyes closed, only half-conscious, he had a sensation of falling. He grasped frantically at things to hold on to. He could not hold on because there was no "he" to do it. He was nothing. He found a name. He had a name. He was Donald Green. He was Lieutenant-Colonel Donald Green of the National Security Council. No, that couldn't be right. Donald Green was a fighting marine. He had been an amateur boxer. But he had been knocked down. Fists coming at his face had made him cringe. He shuddered at the memory. Colonel Donald Green would not have cringed. Colonel Green would have stood up and punched back. Why didn't he do that? Wasn't he Colonel Green? The name Donald Green was not a part of him. It gave him no substance. He was still falling.

He was filled with emptiness and surrounded by emptiness and he could not think. He tried to find a memory he could cling to. He had played a game. He had played at being a marine who was Deputy Director of the National Security Council. But the game was over now. He could go back to being who he really was.

He struggled to recall this, groping for a handhold. The

same name. Donald Green. He was a Professor at Colum- bia University. He had a wife and a little girl, he had a house in Riverdale. Those things should all count for something. But when he clutched them they seemed to be figments that he had dreamed up. Who were they? What did the house look like? He was a drowning man grabbing at the mirage of a lifebelt. He opened his eyes and knew he was nothing, and the universe was cold and empty and there was nothing in it to sustain him.

He looked at his watch. It was seven-fifteen. He had got up at seven-fifteen the last few days and gone down to breakfast at about a quarter to eight. But the fear was paralysing. He could not move. He had no substance, no strength, not enough to get up, even to sit up. He had never felt anything like this before.

He set his mind in motion and knew there were things for him to do. He should get up and wash and shave. He should go downstairs for breakfast. People knew him down there, they would say good morning to him and greet him by name and he would be somebody.

His bladder was full. He had to urinate but he could not get up to go to the toilet. By twenty-five to eight he could hold it in no longer. Desperate to avoid the humiliation of wetting the bed, he found the strength to roll out, put on his slippers and bathrobe and hurry to the toilet. When he got back to his room he sat down on the edge of his bed, exhausted by the effort. Fear pinned him down.

Then he noticed a folded piece of paper on the floor half-way under the door. It must have been put there during last night, perhaps when people were knocking at the door and he did not answer because he could not speak to anyone. With an effort of will, he got up from a sitting position, took one pace across the room and reached down and picked it up.

It was a short note in neat handwriting: "I would like to see you in my office at twelve o'clock. Dr. Robert Manash."

Good. Dr. Manash knew he existed. If he did not turn up his absence would be noticed. Dr. Manash would help him.

He would get up, however difficult it was. He wished Dr. Manash could come and see him here in bed. It was four steps to the place on the floor where he had dropped his clothes in a pile. It was only three steps to the chair where he had put his socks. He would do the easy part first and take the three steps, and put his socks on before the other things and before taking off his pyjamas. Then he would wash at the wash basin. He did this every day. He must surely be able to do it. He willed himself to get up.

He looked at his watch. Nineteen minutes to eight. Let's have round numbers. At fifteen minutes to eight he would stand up. He would have to stand up some time, he told himself, so he might as well do it now. Or at any rate at a quarter to eight.

He could not believe he was in this state. He watched the second hand of his watch go around and around. Then he looked at the minute hand and it was coming up to quarter to eight. He was not ready. He could not do it. All right then, ten to eight. Ten was a round number, the roundest number. He told himself that when he was in the dining room, when other people were about and were talking to him, the pain would be less. Ten to eight. He still could not get up. Breakfast service stopped at eight-thirty. He would set himself a simple, limited task. He would get up from the bed, walk over to the wash basin, take his bathrobe off and wash his hands and face. He would do that at five to eight. At five to eight he managed it all, and after washing he sat down again.

Now he would get dressed. He would put on his socks first because they were within reach. He bent down and accomplished that. Sitting there now in his pyjamas and socks, he worked out the moves involved in dressing himself.. Getting his undershirt shirt and putting it on. Putting on and buttoning his shirt. His drawers, his trousers. He would not put a tie on today. He could get away without one. He would not shave either. He would start at eight o'clock. All right, five-past eight. He watched the second hand go around. Round numbers, a quarter past?. He forced himself up at ten past and with painful effort, he struggled into his shirt and then his trousers. He could hardly believe that he was standing up. There seemed to be nothing to sustain him.

He walked downstairs stiffly, passing a couple of people who greeted him with nods, wondering whether he showed what he was feeling. When he got into the dining room his mouth was dry. He took a glass of orange juice and then forced himself through the normal motions of pouring coffee and taking toast and marmalade. He almost choked when he put a piece of toast into his mouth. He forced it down but did not try another mouthful. He could drink but he could not eat. He greeted a few people, managing to mutter the conventional words. They must, he thought, recognise the state that he was in. He took a newspaper and read a few items. The only thing he could hang on to was the appointment with Manash at twelve o'clock. He could tell Dr. Manash how he felt and Dr. Manash would help him.

He went back to his bedroom and lay on his bed and he got through the morning fifteen minutes at a time.

In Manash's office, he found that he could not speak. He struggled, but he was choked up. He mumbled, "I feel terrible. I - I - I'm very unhappy. I can't - I don't - " He shook his head and could not say any more

"You find it difficult to speak?" Green nodded mutely. "Take your time."

Green started to sob. He had held everything back all morning and now he thought he could let it out, tell Dr. Manash what he was feeling with lots of words. But no words came out, only dry sobs. He took out his handkerchief and put it to his face. It was humiliating. After a while the sobs subsided. He put his handkerchief away and spoke. "I'm sorry," he said. "I think I'm in hell."

"What's hell like?"

"It's emptiness. It's being nobody, nothing. It's – " he stopped..

"You feel like that? That you're nobody?" Green tried to speak, and shook his head in an effort to spill out some words, but he could not say anything, "You're Donald Green, Professor Green. Do you remember?"

"Yes, of course I remember. That's my name. But it doesn't mean anything. It doesn't - " He stopped.

"It doesn't what?"

"It doesn't mean anything." There was a long pause and then he spoke again. "I'll tell you what hell is like. It's being in empty space. It's a baby's sense of falling – you know that feeling a baby has when it's dropped? You see it in the eyes, a moment of pure terror. It's a baby's sense of falling, total loss of security, but with an adult's terror. An adult's eyes wide open. Going on and on, all the time."

Manash said, "You were playing a game. You played at being another man. Lieutenant-Colonel Donald Green. Do you remember that?"

"Yes. I was playing a part. But it broke."

"It broke?"

"The part broke. It was smashed."

"But you're not playing a part now. You know who you are, don't you?"

Green shook his head despairingly. "I'm trying to tell you. I know my name's Donald Green but that doesn't mean anything. I could have some other name and that wouldn't mean anything either. I'm not really anybody. "

Manash went over to the desk and opened a drawer and took out a packet. "Take this pill and swallow it with some water. It should help. I'll give you another one take away in case you need it later. Then we'll talk again."

It was an effort even to get out of the room. Walking

across the courtyard, he tried to feel himself as a body with weight. With each step he hit the ground hard with his foot. He wanted to feel pulled down by gravity. He could not make himself feel it. He was still nothing.

He walked through the door of Yellow House and climbed the narrow stone staircase up to his room, holding on to the banister and pulling himself up step by step. He took the pill with some water in his toothbrush glass and lay down on the bed. After a while the pain was dulled. The feeling of emptiness did not go away but it was not quite so painful. He was able to go through familiar little fantasies in his mind, things that could really happen and that should validate him.

His father speaking, proudly: "Donald has been made a full professor now. One of the youngest on the faculty." That was not a fantasy, that was something he actually remembered. He remembered a man he had called his father, but he did not connect with him in any way. He tried to remember his mother saying something.

He summoned up other things that might be said.

"Didn't you write the chapter on America's options in *Western Security After the Cold War?*"

"Yes, I did."

"I remember it well. It was very interesting."

"Thank you."

They did not do anything for him. He tried some more.

"You bought number 117, didn't you? The one with the ash tree in the front garden?"

"That's right. We moved in last month."

It was all true, these exchanges could all happen. But the phrases were empty. They did not carry the weight that he needed. It was as if he had spent his life amassing money and found that it was counterfeit money and had no value.

The full force of the fear started to come back. He felt the substance seeping out of him and he started to shiver. With an effort he got up from his bed and put some water in the toothbrush glass and took the second pill, then lay down on the bed again and stared at the ceiling. That was all he could do. He did not go down for supper. The room became dark as evening came on but he did not think to turn on the light. He had to make himself real, he told himself. After a while he closed his eyes and slept.

Early that afternoon, Frances was sitting in Dr. Manash's office, in the same armchair that Green had occupied a few hours earlier and she was crying. Tears poured out into the handkerchief which she held pressed against her face. Between sobs she gasped out, "I'm sorry - I'm so sorry. I-I don't know why I'm crying. I just - can't seem to stop." She knew something was pouring out of her. She was surprised that it was tears.

"It's all right," Manash said reassuringly.

"I-I'm not - even - unhappy," she gasped. "I came here to tell you how I was feeling, and the moment I began I started crying."

Eventually she stopped crying and she sat silent for a moment. She noticed now that Manash was dressed less formally than in the previous interviews. He was still neat and stylish, but was wearing a polo shirt under his jacket instead of a shirt and tie, and loafers shined to a gloss. The office was still unchanged by his presence; they were sitting again in armchairs in front of the headmaster's desk.

"I think I'm me again," she said. "Frances Carr. But I'm not sure. I feel different in some way." She spoke slowly and analytically, like one puzzling her way through a problem.

Manash nodded. She expected him to say something, to ask a question or invite her to continue, but then she realised that this was one of his silences so she went on. "You said I had strong defences. I don't think they're strong now. You saw the way I was crying. I couldn't stop."

"Does that bother you, not having strong defences?"

"A bit. I don't know what will happen."

Manash nodded understandingly. "It must make you a bit anxious. You're so used to having these defences."

"I worry about other people," she said.

"What?"

"I worry about other people. What's happening to them."

"What people?"

"People who are suffering. Victims. Actually, any people. Terrible things happen to people. I worry about them."

"Is that bad? Surely we should all care about the people around us."

"Yes of course. I do care about other people. But this is somehow different, worrying. It's as if they're getting too close." She paused and then went on, "I think I'm mostly me, again. But maybe it takes a little time."

He nodded. "Yes, I think it may take some time."

She knitted her brow in concentration and went on: "One's defences, one's boundaries, are what defines one, aren't they? The way a country's boundaries define it. So if my defences are not what they were - I don't know. I find I'm talking in your language."

He ignored this and said, "Maybe being you is not quite what you thought it was. Is that possible?"

"Yes, perhaps. I'm not sure. It's a matter of where the boundaries are."

When she left Dr. Manash's office she went outside. She did not want to go beyond what seemed like the safety of the school grounds. She spent much of the time walking alone. She stopped occasionally to listen to a bird song. She thought it might be nice to learn about birds, to know one song from another.

She started towards the lounge but changed her mind and turned back towards Yellow House. She would have to join the others when the bell sounded for lunch but not before then. She felt too vulnerable to want to be among people now. Her defences were crumbling, no doubt about that. Whether from inside or outside, feelings were coming into her that she was not used to, and could not handle.

She passed Donald Green. She nodded to him but saw that he seemed to be skulking along, avoiding looking at anyone. She did not find it surprising. Everyone was in a bit of a strange mood after the game.

In the dining room that day, at lunch and later at dinner, conversation was subdued. People did not speak a lot and they addressed one another cautiously when they did. No one was quite sure how anyone else was feeling. Some ate by themselves and did not talk to anyone. A few turned up late or did not turn up at all.

Raymond Wade was talking a lot, trying to draw others into conversation. "I miss being Prime Minister," he said cheerily. "An army captain - that's a hell of a come-down. What was it some Roman emperor is supposed to have said? 'I'd rather be head man in a village in Spain than number two in Rome.'" His voice had a brittle, nervous quality.

"You were one reason it ended early," someone said, not to seriously. "Getting into a fist fight."

"Hey, it wasn't my fault," he retorted. "This guy Green barged in to my office. He was supposed to be in the American Administration. He broke all the rules. Came across to our building and just marched in."

"He just barged in?"

"Yes, and he was very belligerent. Next thing I knew he was throwing punches at me. So I hit him back. I don't know what got into him but I know prime ministers don't get into fist fights. " He paused and continued eating and then, to get attention away from himself, he asked, "How about you, Campbell? How did you get along as a top CIA man?"

"I was so good I scare myself," Davies said. "Looking back, I'm glad I came a-cropper."

Ingrid Mundt joined in. "I was sorry when the game ended. I was enjoying myself."

"You enjoyed being Finance Minister?" Wade asked her.

She nodded enthusiastically and talked as she was chewing. "Mmm. things were beginning to go well. I think Jacob could have pulled it off. We'd get away with the nationalisation, we'd buy some time with the unions, and we could - " she stopped. No one said anything for a while.

Davies said, "Stephen here made a great President. He had real authority."

Stephen looked abashed. "Being President of the United States isn't as easy as it seems," he said. "And I had a good Secretary of State." They looked at Frances who was two places away from him but she continued eating and did not say anything..

"I never thought being President of the United States was easy," Davies said.

"Well I suppose I thought it was," Stephen said. He continued eating in silence. He had always thought being somebody else, someone with a good background and good schools behind them and the right sort of parents, would be easy. "They have it easy," he had always told himself. Not like himself, he did not have their advantages. But other people did not always have it easy.

At the other table, Jacob Shemtov found he wanted to talk to the man next to him about St. Georgian politics. This was clearly not possible so he searched his mind for another topic of conversation but could not find one. He ate in silence.

After lunch Stephen Darrow went for a walk. Sticking to the habit of the past few days he remained within the school grounds and even in the area reserved for the Yellow House team. He walked along the path beside the playing fields, looking downwards and talking to the world.

"I'm sorry. I know I come across as an arrogant bugger. Coming on strong. As if I don't give a shit what anyone else thinks. But what else could I do? I was among these people, actors and producers and people who live in their smart world.

I didn't know how to behave. I had to say I didn't give a fuck about the rules because that was all I could say, I didn't know the rules. I'm sorry if I upset anybody."

Jacob Shemtov had a session with Dr. Manash after lunch. Manash reminded him who he was, his Israeli nationality, his position at the university. Like a master builder reconstructing a house, he put the key bricks in place and then built upon those. They talked about his past fits of depression, his time in the army and his marriage. He came out remembering it all, but it was still as if most of it had happened to someone else.

He went back to his room in Blue House and lay on his bed and looked at the hairline cracks in the ceiling and talked to himself. Or rather, his two selves talked to one another. His lips were moving and his expression changed with the words, although he was not talking out loud

"You're not the Prime Minister of St. George. You're Jacob Shemtov. An Israeli, a rather unsuccessful academic, divorced and lonely and depressed. That's who you are."

"That doesn't sound like an attractive move. I'm much better off being a Prime Minister of St. George.

"But you can't be Prime Minister of St. George because St. George doesn't exist. If you go to an airline and say you want a ticket to St. George they won't give you one. If you telephone your wife in Palm Beach no one will answer. She doesn't exist either."

"I made love to the American Secretary of State. That certainly happened."

"She isn't real either."

"She damned well is. "

"Well yes, she's real but she's not a real American Secretary of State. The Secretary of State is someone else."

"But we made love. I fucked a woman. I hadn't done that for a long time. I'd rather go on being Prime Minister."

"The game's over. You're just talking air. You've got

more as me than you had as prime minister because you're real."

"What have I got?"

The pronoun switched. It was no longer a conversation between you and I but between I and I. "I've got a real daughter. I've got a real job. I teach people. Real students come to my lectures and write papers for me."

"What's so good about that?"

"I'm not saying it's good or not good but it's real, it's not something invented for a game. Look, the Prime Minister's life and character were contained in six pages. Could all of my life be written in six pages?"

"No."

"Of course not. Not in six thousand pages. A million pages. Things happen to me every moment. I'm alive."

"But I'm neurotic and a failure."

"So? I'm neurotic and a failure and alive. The Prime Minister isn't even dead. He isn't anything. Being alive is a kind of success."

"Anyway, I've got a few things going for me. Some students like my teaching. They've said so. Some have said I gave them understanding. My daughter likes me although we have our difficulties. In fact she loves me. I'm her daddy. And yes, I'm alive."

The conversation ended. Lying on his bed with one arm underneath his head, Jacob traced the cracks in the ceiling. Three cracks radiated out from a single point, each one a crooked line. They were streams, meandering downhill from a single source. They were the beginning of a Paul Klee painting. They were the beginning of a star. They were pretty

::   ::

::

Louis Mannion sat on the train with the newspaper on his lap unopened and looked out of the window at fields flashing by, some with cattle, some with sheep, demarcated by long, straight hedgerows. Then they passed some cultivated fields, with rows of plants he did not recognise. These were large fields. These were not peasant smallholdings. The people who owned this land still had power and that power should be broken. These estates should be broken up, somehow, while retaining their efficiency. Ben Devoe was right about that. But Devoe replacing Shemtov as Prime Minister, no, that would not be right. Devoe could not see the big picture, he could not handle a democratic opposition, he liked power too much.

He let his mind rest for a while as he watched the scenery. Now he remembered sitting in Dr. Manash's office, coming out of hypnotism. He recalled Manash telling him again and again who he was, insisting that they talk about Sarah and his newspaper column and university days, pulling this person out from the St. Georgian Minister of Labour. His mind turned back to Sarah. The baby was not due for another two-and-a-half months. Something must have gone badly wrong.

Sarah was ill. Sarah could die. He kept telling himself that. It seemed like a situation he was reading about in a novel, that did not involve real people let alone someone he loved. It was if Sarah were on the other side of a window, like people in the fields flashing by, and had nothing to do with him. He repeated her name like a mantra: Sarah, Sarah, Sarah, Sarah, Sarah. It worked. He began to get a picture of Sarah, to remember what she looked like, what it was like eating supper with her, going out of the house with her, lying in bed with her. He felt for her suffering. By the time the train pulled in he was frightened at the thought of Sarah dying.

He hurried out of the carriage into the throng of Paddington Station and waited impatiently in the queue for a taxi. Sitting in the taxi, he fumed as it slowed to a crawl in the traffic, looking out at the grey, grimy streets of Paddington. Then, for a few minutes, he forgot where he was going. He knew he would not be there for Jacob when Jacob got back from Washington. Jacob might need his support against Devoe's challenge. And Devoe would challenge Jacob if he were not there, he was sure of that. He saw before him Jacob's face with its usual worried frown. He was a good man but not a strong man,and he needed all the help he could get, buffeted as he was from several sides. Then he remembered that he was going to his sick wife's bedside in the Royal Hospital, Richmond. But he must get back to his office in St. George to deal with things as soon as possible.

The taxi stopped, he got out, paid the driver and hurried into the hospital and over to the reception desk. A young woman sitting behind a glass screen said, "Yes?"

He stopped and looked at her blankly. He could not think what to say or what he was doing here.

She spoke again. "Can I help you?"

Then he remembered. "I want to see Mrs. Mannion. She's in the private wing. I'm her husband."

She pressed some keys on a keyboard, looked at a screen and told him the room. He hurried to the lift, an old-fashioned one with iron gates that you pulled shut with a clang, and went up to the floor, and spoke to a nurse at the desk. "Mrs. Mannion is asleep," she said. "You can go in there."

He went and looked at the figure on the bed. Sarah was lying on a bed, her eyes closed. A needle was taped to her arm and a tube led from the needle to a container of colourless liquid attached to a metal pole. Her face was white and drawn. Illness had transformed Sarah into an object, a mechanism of breathing and blood flow of which the tube and the needle were another part. Her blonde hair was untidy and matted. He knew she would hate to have her hair looking like this.

He pulled up a chair and sat down at the bedside and watched her breathing. Memories of their life together started to come back. He wanted to go on with their life together. He wanted to see her come back to life, he wanted to see her skin fresh and her hair combed and her face animated. He loved her and he sat there, unhappy and frightened.

A nurse came into the room, checked the drip and said to him, "Mr. Mannion?" He nodded. "Dr. Clarke will have a word with you in a moment."

Dr. Clarke was tall and thin with rimless spectacles and reassuringly grey-haired. "She went into full eclampsia," he said. "We've had to sedate her." He waited to see whether Mannion had any questions, then talked about her condition. He used the words "pre-eclampsia" and "eclampsia," and high blood pressure and protein level.

Mannion forced himself to ask, "Is she in danger?"

Dr. Clarke looked grave. "We're hopeful," he said. "It depends on whether we can keep the blood pressure down."

Louis shivered. He cou.ld not think how to phrase the next question. There were things he could not say out loud. "What's going to happen?" he asked.

"It's a serious condition," Dr. Clarke said. "But as I say, we're hopeful." Then he added, "The baby is in our Special Care Unit."

Louis was startled. "The baby?" He had forgotten about the baby.

"Your daughter."

Daughter? The word went through Louis like a shock. A baby was one thing, an expectation, something due to come into being. But a daughter was a living person. Louis saw the doctor was waiting for him to say something. He recovered himself and said, "I didn't know I had a daughter.".

"Oh good Lord, you weren't told? I'm sorry."

"How is she?"

"Well, she's very premature. She's in the Special Care Unit, as I say. In an incubator."

"Is she all right?"

"There's a problem with the lungs. They're not fully

matured."

"What does that mean?"

"It means that at the moment she has to have help with breathing. Would you like to see her?"

"Yes, yes of course." Dr. Clarke called over a nurse and she led him along a corridor and to a little room with glass walls. He looked through the glass and saw a cot..

The sight struck him dumb with wonder. The baby was a tiny thing with a thin tube leading into its nostrils. Another thin tube led to a black pad on its back. The baby was so small that he could hardly believe what he was seeing. It could fit into the palm of his hand. He did not know a baby could be so small. It was curled up in the shape of a comma, its skin pink and wrinkled, like an overripe peach. Its head was oval-shaped, set back against its tiny wrinkled neck like a duck's head, and covered with a few thin strands of hair. He bent over and peered at it and saw the features: a nose, ears flat against the head, eyes tightly shut, amazingly, tiny legs and tinier feet, and most amazingly, tiny fingers on a tiny clenched hand. He thought he could even make out minuscule knuckles.

This was a little human being, a girl. This was his daughter. As he stood and stared at the tiny still figure attached to a life support system, he realised how frail she was. Dr. Clarke's words came back to him: "a problem with the lungs." She might not live! With this realisation new emotions swept over him, catching him by surprise: love, fear, and a desperate concern that the baby should go on living. Tiny and fragile, the baby was kept alive by those tubes, by the mechanisms of medicine. He wanted it to live, he wanted to protect it. He wanted it with his whole being.

He hardly knew what was happening to him. A few moments ago he did not know this tiny creature existed. Now its life was as important to him as his own. He had looked forward to having a baby but he had not expected this. He peered at the baby's face but could not see any sign of breathing although it must be breathing. He willed it to breathe. He willed it to breathe without any help from the machinery. He stood there for a long time, staring at his baby daughter. Then he went back down the corridor to his wife.

It was dark outside now, and there was only a bedside light on when he went in, and he sat in the semi-darkness. Some of the time he held Sarah's hand. Every fifteen minutes or so a nurse came in and checked the drip and felt Sarah's pulse. Occasionally, one would make an adjustment. Four times during the night a nurse wrapped a strap around her arm and took her blood pressure. He stared at Sarah anxiously, and then at the colourless liquid in the flask, which seemed to be reducing gradually, looking for some sign of change, of something happening. There was little movement outside in the corridor. The hospital was quiet. Sometimes, as he sat through the night, his mind would wander off and he would be back arguing with Devoe and Thaxted, wondering how Jacob was doing in Washington, wondering how he would cope on the joint compensation commission with Capital Bauxite. He wanted to get back to his government office, but right now he had to be here.

Once Sarah opened her eyes. She had no expression and he could not tell whether she knew he was there. He said, "Hello, darling," and stroked her arm.

A nurse suggested that he get something to eat in the staff canteen but he would not leave. However, he let her bring him a cup of coffee and a ham salad sandwich in cellophane wrapping and he ate half the sandwich. He went back down the corridor from time to time during the night and stared at the baby. He saw it now as a baby girl, a beginning, a being projected forward in time. The baby should go on. She should start to make cooing noises and wave her little arms and crawl and toddle. A whole lifetime was starting here. It would unroll over the years, a long full life. This must happen. She must go on living.

He wanted desperately to keep death away from this tiny creature whose grip on life was so tenuous, and away from Sarah also. He wanted to protect his wife and his baby yet he was powerless. There was nothing at all that he could do to help them. He remembered feeling something like this helplessness another time recently, when he could not make up his mind what was the right thing to do. But it was obvious. He should stand by Shemtov, and refuse to join Devoe and the party rebels.

Then he realised that there was something he could do. He could pray. He could pray for help as he had prayed for guidance earlier. He could pray to God who was all-powerful, more powerful even than Capital Bauxite or the American Government, and he could play to the Virgin Mary, who was herself a mother. He clenched his hands together and bent his head and prayed silently. "Holy mother of God...." The words came to him unbidden, words he did not know he remembered., and his lips started moving. "Hail Mary, full of grace, the Lord is with thee. Blessed art thou among women, blessed is the fruit of thy womb, Jesus." He asked the Virgin Mary to intercede as a mother and save this mother and baby. A nurse came into the room and he ignored her.

He walked along the empty white corridor and stood and looked at his baby again, and God was in his thoughts so that thinking about the baby was the same as praying. He peered through the glass as a nurse came in and readjusted the tubes going into the baby's arm and nostrils. Then, as she went away, he remembered something and asked her, "Is there a chapel in this hospital?"

"On the fourth floor," she said. He found the lift and took it up.

The chapel turned out to be a small room with white stucco walls and a few plain wooden chairs arranged around a lectern. The only signs of a spiritual function were three

Bibles stacked neatly in a corner and a small unadorned wooden crucifix on a plain table. Two sprays of artificial flowers were also on the table and, incongruously, a half-empty bottle of ginger ale. He knelt before the crucifix and prayed.

Memories of Sarah and of their life together moved in and out of his mind., mixed up with the St. Georgian's awe before God's power. At one point he had anxieties that belonged to the columnist on the Sunday Chronicle. He had been lucky in his life and successful at most things he did. Perhaps this loss would be a compensation for his good fortune, to balance things out, so that he would not have so much more than other people. He should have had more failure. Please God, he prayed, don't let Sarah and my baby pay for my success. He wished there was something he could offer God in return, but God did not need anything from him.

Then it came to him that he had something he could offer God in return. So he offered it. Sitting on one of the wooden chairs, he bent over as he had done as a boy when praying in church, and spoke in his mind, thinking the words rather than saying them out loud, "God, if you let Sarah and my baby live, I promise I will not be unfaithful to Sarah any more. I will not lie any more. I will not see Tess again. I will care only for my wife and my baby. I promise."

He went down to look again at Sarah and at the baby. The sky outside the window was lightening to a pale blue-grey liquid. The hospital was coming to life with sound and lights, a clanking of trolleys, rustling of starched material and brief conversations. A woman wheeled a breakfast trolley into Sarah's room and he took some coffee and a roll and butter. The first bites of the roll stuck in his stomach and he left the rest but he was grateful for the coffee for his mouth was dry. He repeated to himself the promise he had made to God in the chapel. Let Sarah and my baby live and I will not see Tess again.

Nurses and then a doctor came in and out of the room. One nurse checked Sarah's blood pressure. Another removed the needle from her arm, changed the flask containing the drip and reinserted the needle. Sarah did not stir. A doctor came in and suggested, "Why don't you take a break? Nothing is going to change for a little while. Take a little walk and get some fresh air. You'll be in better shape when Mrs. Mannion wakes up"

Yes, he needed some fresh air. He went down in the lift and out into the road and walked up to the corner. The noise of traffic affronted him. He was on the edge of Richmond Green so he walked into the park away from the road. It was a crisp autumn morning, the sky now cleared to a sharp blue. The main part of the green was a wide grassy plain criss-crossed by paths. Tall trees grew in rows along some of the paths and in clumps here and there. This was not a place for issues of life or death, for desperate prayers. It was a place for people to walk their dogs and for joggers to take their early morning exercise, and these were about. But he could not stop praying. Now that he had made contact with God and spoken to him, his hopes were the same as prayers and he had to keep hoping He felt humble before God, humble and powerless, which was as it should be.

He walked along a path and it came to him that he was not really humble, that he was still wilful, desperately wilful. There was one further step he could take, one further surrender of self, one more thing he could give. He would say it in the chapel. He turned on his heel abruptly, getting in the way of a young woman in a grey track suit jogging along the path, hurried back to the hospital, and took the lift up to the chapel.

In that little room with the white stucco walls that could do with a cleaning, he sat down and bent over and spoke in his mind again. "God, I do not understand your ways. I am too small and have only human wisdom. I do not understand why you cause to happen all the things that happen in this world. If it is your will that Sarah dies, or that my baby dies, or that they both die, then I will accept it. I will suffer, I will think it is the most terrible tragedy, I will not want to go on living. I will not understand, but I'll accept it as your will." He stayed there for a while. When he left he felt purified, cleansed of all will, all ego.

He went down and sat with Sarah for a while. A doctor said they could find an empty bed for him if he wanted to take a rest and he could be called if there was any change. He thanked the doctor but said he could not rest. He was glad he had said that because a few minutes later Sarah opened her eyes and turned her head. Her eyes showed anxiety. He reached out and touched her face gently." Hello. You're going to get better," he said. She showed no sign of hearing. He said, "I've seen the baby. She's beautiful." Sarah seemed to understand this. She smiled at him gratefully and closed her eyes again.

Around mid-morning a young doctor came in and wound the strap around her arm and checked the blood pressure again. He went out and came back a few minutes later with Dr. Clarke. Dr. Clarke said to him, "We're seeing an improvement in Mrs. Mannion's condition. Her blood pressure's on the way up. I think she's rounded the corner."

Louis nodded. He could hardly speak. Then he asked hesitantly, "And the baby?"

Dr. Clarke smiled. "I understand her lungs are starting to function normally. That baby wants to go on living. The longer she goes on like this the better it looks."

Louis managed to say, "Good."

Then Dr. Clarke said, "I suggest you get some rest or we're going to have you as a patient. One of the nurses can find a place for you to lie down if you don't want to go home."

"No, I want to be here when she wakes up," he said.

"Well perhaps we can get a more comfortable armchair

in here for you," Dr. Clarke said.

It was done and he sat in the armchair and leaned his head back and closed his eyes. He was tired but tense with anxiety. He dozed but woke whenever someone came into the room.

In the late afternoon Sarah was awake and talking to him. He lifted her head and held a glass of water to her lips. Then a nurse brought a cup of tea and he gave her a few sips of tea. Characteristically, Sarah made a feeble attempt to straighten her hair before closing her eyes again. A young doctor told him, "The blood pressure's coming right down. She's doing very well."

"I want to see my baby," Sarah said. With the doctor's permission and a nurse's help he got Sarah into a wheelchair and wheeled her down the corridor, holding the drip feed, and they looked through the glass together at their baby daughter.

::   ::
      ::

Frances was having another session with Dr. Manash. She sat up straight in Manash's armchair with her hands in her lap. She was dressed as she had been on the first day, with a frilled blouse and skirt and with her hair tied in a bun. She talked in a confident, earnest voice, the words pouring out in a continuous stream.

"I've decided what I want to do with my life. I'm going to resign from the Foreign Office and study medicine. I'm going to become a medical scientist. There's one thing Mankind needs, one thing more than anything else, and I'm going to find it. It's come to me.

"You see, people suffer too much pain. People shouldn't be born with such a capacity for pain. It's a fundamental design fault in human beings. I know pain has an important function, it's an indication that something is wrong with the organism and corrective action needs to be taken. Some discomfort is necessary as a prod to repair the damage. But the capacity for pain has gone far, far beyond what's necessary

"I read when I was a girl - I was about thirteen - about the police in some African country who killed a girl by shoving a hot poker up her vagina. It must have taken her some time to die. I tried to think about how that must have felt. It would be much, much better for that woman if she'd never been born. No amount of happiness could balance against that pain. After I read that, for a while I thought of committing suicide because if I lived there was the possibility that that could happen to me. It was not likely but it was just possible. I imagined ways that it could happen. I could somehow find myself in one of those countries and be captured in a civil war or something. Or I could be kidnapped by a sadist, because things like that happened elsewhere also. It seemed to me at the time that so long as there was even the remote possibility that that could happen, or something equally horrible, it would better not to be alive. Rationally, I should kill myself to remove the possibility. Incidentally , much later I read that some white soldiers in what was then Rhodesia did the thing with the poker. You don't have to be among Africans

"Other things. In Algeria the police use blow torches on people. Have you ever been burned, even for a moment? It hurts like hell, and you put some salve on it, and cold water but it still hurts. Try to imagine what it's like with no salve, being burned a lot, the pain going on and on and getting worse. For days. Imagine having your fingernails pulled out. I mean really imagine it, think what it must feel like. One by one. This is done to people. It's possible, it must be possible, to make a person suffer the most intense pain, more than we can imagine, constantly, without dying. By twisting the joints, for instance. For days, weeks, maybe even months, continual. I could go on with the terrible things that are done to people.

We turn our minds away from this sort of thing because it just tears the heart to think about it, but it happens, it's part of the world. Imagine being boiled alive. In South America some people scoop out people's eyes with a teaspoon. And people suffer the most terrible pains without anyone doing it to them. People who are burned by accident in places where there are no anaesthetics of any kind. People die of thirst in the desert, slowly. or they're buried alive in a sandstorm with the sand in their nostrils.

"So long as people can suffer this way, it would be better that the human race didn't exist. That suffering - even one person's suffering of that intensity - is much too high a price to pay. We shouldn't have been born. If there's a God, we're his terrible mistake. You may remember in *The Brothers Karamazov*, Ivan says that God and his world are not worth the suffering of one tortured child. He says he wants to give God back his entry ticket. He's right.

"And the truth is that in a world in which these things can happen, in which people can do these sort of things to people, I don't want to live. But committing suicide would be walking away from the problem. My training says you solve problems. Other people won't commit suicide. I can give back my entry ticket but the rest of the world isn't going to. The human race does exist, we can't do anything about that. So we have to do something about the capacity for pain.

"What's needed is something to correct this. A vaccine, like a smallpox vaccine. You could inject every baby in the world with this at birth. It would preserve a certain capacity for pain, so that it would serve its purpose, it would come as a warning signal to show that something is wrong with the organism, but there would be a threshold. People couldn't suffer very intense pain the way they can now. I want to become a medical scientist and devise such a vaccine. It should be possible. Scientists know the parts of the brain and the nervous system that transmit pain. I'm going to start studying medicine and then work on developing a vaccine like that.

"Perhaps we could go further, and manipulate the genes in the whole human race so that people would be born with less capacity for pain, and they wouldn't need a vaccine. I don't know about genetic manipulation, but it should be possible. But at least a vaccine. It's just got to be done. It's *got* to be."

Dr. Manash nodded. "I see," he said.

CHAPTER THIRTEEN

R aymond Wade sat in Dr. Manash's office. He was sitting upright, on the chair, sounding chirpy. "Everything's okay," he said. "I'm back to normal. Captain Wade, United States Army."

"You seem to have made a very quick adjustment," Manash remarked. "But you started coming out of your role early. Prematurely. That wasn't your fault."

"No, I was sort of knocked out of it," Wade said. "And now I've readjusted."

"Good. I hope you've profited from the game"

"I found out what it's like not to be an American. It's given me some things to think about."

"You feel now that you acted as the Prime Minister of Britain would?"

"Yes. Well, perhaps there was some of me left in the person. I was pretty hard-line."

He walked out with his usual vigorous gait, in fact more vigorous than usual because he had lied. He was troubled.

He forced himself to be reasonable. "If you go back to that pub," he told himself, "it's very unlikely that the young man will be there. There's no reason to suppose he's there every day. And even if he is there, he's not going to be interested in talking to you. He has a girl friend." No, he would resist going back to that pub.

He passed Donald Green in the corridor. He greeted him with forced joviality. "Hi. No hard feelings about that fight, huh? Neither of us were our usual selves." Green responded to this with only a brief nod and walked on towards Manash's office. Wade reflected that something weird must have happened to Green.

When Green got to Manash's office, he sat down awkwardly in the armchair and waited for a while. Dr. Manash, sitting opposite him in the other armchair, also waited, and finally said, "Well?"

Green tried to work out what he should say. He knew in the back of his mind that he had some claim on Manash, that Manash was at least to some degree responsible for his condition. But he could not feel resentment, or anything other than misery.

"I still feel terrible.," he said finally. It was not saying much but it was all he could think of.

"You still don't feel like yourself?"

"I still have this feeling that I'm nothing. I'm not real. I'm frightened to face the world."

"You seem to be having trouble getting into yourself again. It'll come back."

"When I was Colonel Green it was all right. But I can't go back to being him."

"No, you can't. You've got to go further back, to being Professor Donald Green."

Green pondered this for a while, and then said, "I know all about him. I know I'm supposed to be him. But those are just words."

"I can help you," Manash said. "I'll try you on another pill. It's a new one. Here, I want you to take this when you leave here. And we'll have some more hypnotism." He picked up the pendant and chain from his desk. "Now look at this.

Watch it closely."

After a while he started speaking softly. "You're Professor Donald Green.. You have a history. You are somebody. You do exist. You are real."

Early in the afternoon Louis Mannion, assured now that his wife and baby were on the mend, telephoned for a taxi on one of the direct line phones in the hospital lobby and went home to his house near the river in Richmond. He had spent thirty-six hours in the hospital and he had gone without anything approaching proper sleep for two nights. He was exhausted.

When he opened his front door and walked into his living room it seemed as if he had been away for a long time. He had almost forgotten the look of his own home. He wanted to get back to his normal life. He liked his normal life and the prospect of resuming it with a baby. Tragedy had been averted and now he wanted Sarah and their baby home so that he could protect them.

He was tense with strain and fatigue so he went to the drinks cabinet and poured himself a whiskey and added some soda from the kitchen, and sat in his favourite armchair. He noted the newspapers scattered around the couch and reflected that Sarah must have been taken ill suddenly and left in a hurry. It was not like her to leave a mess. He took in again the familiar titles of the books that lined most of one wall, and the pictures on the walls, mostly modern paintings and a colour photograph of the Washington skyline at twilight. He collected the newspapers and arranged them neatly.

He picked up the mail and three days' newspapers from the mat. He telephoned his mother and told her what had happened at the hospital and that she was now a grandmother, and he took in her happiness. He asked here to pass the news on to his sister and said he would call her soon. He had called Sarah's parents from the hospital and they were on their way to see her. He telephoned a couple who were good friends and told the wife all about Sarah and the new baby. His life was coming back to him. There were two messages on the answering machine. They could wait.

He thought about Sarah and wanted to bring her closer to him. He loved herso much that he wondered why he had ever thought their quarrels were important. He went up to his office and took out from a drawer an old folder containing a number of letters. He took one in Sarah's handwriting, dated, a few weeks before they were married, and started to read it.

"Louis, my darling. Until I knew we were going to be married, I didn't dare tell you how much I loved you. I didn't dare tell myself. Now I'm waiting for you to come back and I can't wait to see you. I had no idea I'd miss you so much after only a week. I think of you coming through the arrivals gate at the airport with that half-smile of yours and your untidy hair and you coming up and putting your arms around me and your glasses bumping against my forehead when you hug me. I ration myself to thinking about it not more than once an hour.

"That doesn't sound like me, the cool chick, as you once described me, does it? But there you are. Every now and again I get wild, nightmarish fantasies. The airplane crashes in flames. You come back and tell me you've changed your mind about our getting married. Or you've met somebody else. Something I couldn't bear. Oh darling, I want you to arrive back well and I want to make you happy for ever." He did not deserve that much love.

He picked up another letter. It was dated a little earlier. She had sent it to him when he was in England, and they were talking most days on the telephone if they did not meet.

"I don't know whether I'll send this to you," it began. "Perhaps I will, or perhaps I'm just writing it for myself. It's nearly midnight but I know I can't sleep so I won't even try. I'm looking out over the wet wintery rooftops of Hampstead. They're grey and not at all pretty. Would I rather be looking at palm trees and a starlit summery sky? I don't think so.

Right now that seems like fairyland and this is reality, and with you here I'm content with reality. The big reality is that you and I are in the same city.

"Louis, Louis. People see you as sharp and on top of things, with your intellect and your wit. Sometimes people are a little afraid of you. I was when I first met you. Did you know that? I'm pretty sure I didn't let on. I can see why people are a little afraid of you. You sometimes have sharp, angular edges. But I can also see something soft inside you. Very deep inside you, something soft and warm. I think you're a little afraid of letting it out, as if that would make you more exposed, more vulnerable. So you cover it up. But I can see it and I think I can reach in and touch it.

"You shouldn't bury that thing so deep. It's soft, like the 'v' in 'give,' but although it's soft it's strong, and it gives you strength, even where you don't think it will, when you think something soft will weaken you. It will give you strength and help you grow. You can still grow, we can all still grow. You will grow in ways you can't imagine. I think I can help you reach into it. If I love you, and I think I do, it's because of that part of you. Even more than then fact that you can always make me laugh, and that you can make me go weak at the knees by running your fingers up my arm."

He read the letter through, and then he put it down and he started to cry. Sobs shook his body and he did not try to stop. Tears pour out of him unbidden, as if from a fount, and with them went what was left of Louis Mannion the tough, anxious, fiercely loyal Carribbean labour leader. He wept from exhaustion. He wept for the St. George trade union leader, and his struggles with his own ambition, and his struggles also on behalf of poor people among his fellow countrymen. He wept for the poor people with their stunted lives, in St. George and here, the ones he met as a social worker and the ones he knew. He wept for himself, for loving and being loved, for the kind of person he could be and the kind of person he was not and ought to be. And he wept for Sarah, with her capacity for love, and he wept for the little bundle of life in the respirator tent. He mopped up the tears with a handkerchief, and then more tears came pouring out. He had no control over the process and he did not try to control it. After a time the sobs subsided..

Slowly, his daily life seeped back into his mind. He thought about home and work and the weekend. And then he thought of Tess. He should speak to her. But what he could he speak about? Not about the baby. Perhaps about the game. He never telephoned Tess on his home telephone line even if no one else was in the house. The number would appear on the telephone bill. He would have to phone her from his mobile

The thoughts came automatically, and then he ran up against the promise that he had made like a car slamming into a brick wall. His mind spun for a moment. He had promised God that he would not see Tess again if Sarah and the baby were allowed to live. Only it was not really he that had promised it.

He got up, for this was too powerful a thought to take in sitting in an armchair, and started walking up and down. What he had said to Dr. Manash was true. If he gave Tess up, a part of him would be giving up on life. It would be like dying. He did not have to keep the promise. He would not have made a promise to God, he did not believe in God. There was no God to make a promise to. He had made that promise at least partly in the persona of someone else, a Caribbean trade union leader who had never been to university and had never travelled abroad and who prayed to the Catholic God and the Virgin Mary. He was, literally, not himself when he did so. He had made the promise to a God who did not exist, in the person of someone who also did not exist.

But he had asked God to let Sarah and the baby live because he wanted that more than anything in the world, and they were both alive. God did not exist, he reminded himself.

Logically, he did not have to keep his promise. But he knew that he did have to.

His daughter was a new life, a new life for him to take care of. It would have to make up for the life that he was giving up.

::   ::

::

Jacob Shemtov came down early to breakfast the next day and found Frances already there . He joined her and she smiled a welcome. "You're up early also," he said to her.

"I woke early and couldn't get back to sleep," she explained. "I'm still coming out of being Frances Carr Dowson."

"Yes, I know the feeling."

"And you? Are you back to being the old you?"

"I think I'm out," he said. He noticed that she was taking it as natural that they would talk now as good friends. "How are you feeling?"

"I don't know. I said some pretty crazy things to Manash yesterday," she said.

"What kind of things?"

"I told him I was going to change the world. I talked about all the suffering."

"That doesn't sound crazy."

She paused thoughtfully. "Well maybe not crazy. I said I didn't want to live in a world in which people's fingernails are torn out." She squeezed her lips in distress before going on. "The trouble is, there isn't any other world. I haven't figured that one out yet."

"It's a difficult one," he acknowledged.

"Yes indeed." She smiled, switching moods visibly, and said, "What about you? Has it done anything for you?"

"As I said, I'm back to being the old me." he said. He took some toast and spread honey on it and spoke in the tone of a practical man who is getting on with his breakfast. It was enough talking about himself without digging around for his soul.

"Are you happy with that?"

"Not really."

"Why not?"

He shrugged away most of the question. "I'm not in a very happy situation. But I feel a little differently about it now. I was a successful prime minister of St. George. I've made one decision anyway."

"What's that?"

"I'm going to drop my paper on the nation-state."

"Oh why? Maybe you're just feeling depressed about it."

"No, I'm not feeling depressed at all about it. It's just isn't worth going on with. In my heart of hearts I've known that for a long time. I just wouldn't admit it. I don't need that paper. I'm a good teacher. That's enough."

"If you're sure," she said. "You'll do the right thing."

He was thinking now about their night together and the confidence with which he had approached her. He wondered whether any of this would remain. It was important now that she did not expect too much from him. He looked down into his coffee cup and spoke hesitantly.

"You know, the night before last - it was great, but we were different. Things were different."

"Yes. You were the Prime Minister of St. George."

She said this with a smile. She was hiding her feelings. She guessed now what was coming. It was something women often talked about. The morning after. Would the man walk out saying casually, "That was great. I'll call you some time"? She had seen women increasingly tearful as days went by and no telephone call came. Jacob had a good excuse. They had not been themselves. They had been playing a game. She braced herself..

He said, "I'm due to go back to Israel the day after tomorrow."

"I see."

"But I could stay a few days longer. I'd like to see you again."

She was so relieved that she could not speak for a few moments. Then she said, "You could stay in my flat in London."

"I'd like that," he said.

They both sat in silence for a while, sharing a sense of relief that this was settled, and at where they had arrived. His relief was tempered by anxiety. He had to tell her something. "I was different then," he said. "Now I - I'm not sure. I'm not exactly sure what I'll be like. But I'd like to be with you in London anyway."

"Good."

"You know," she said, speaking tentatively, "You know - it's been said - I think people have said - that I'm inhibited."

"No-o, I didn't find you inhibited," he said.

"I'm not. Well I am but I wasn't. That's what I'm saying. That I wasn't so much so when I was Secretary of State."

They finished their breakfast in silence. That was as far as she could go. Her stream of thought went underground, and so did his.

Jacob asked, "Want to come for a stroll?"

Freed from the constraints of the game, they walked out of the school grounds, in silence for a while. He indicated left and they headed into Christ Church Meadow, where they had walked with the others before, away from the traffic sounds.

"Tell me some more about yourself," she said. "I've a right to ask you now."

"You mean me and not the Prime Minister of St. George?".

"Yes, Jacob Shemtov, Israeli, Major, Professor."

"Not professor, only lecturer," he said. "Also, I wasn't a real Major. That was a rank they gave me as a leaving present when I was going to resign. But I was a real Captain. I helped defend my country. And I'm a lecturer, and I'm quite a good teacher. Some of my students have told me that when they've finished my course. I try to make connections between theory and what's happening in the world. But I haven't published much. Younger people have been promoted over me. I have a daughter, she's eighteen and she's about to start her army service. She thinks she's going to be a medical student. We've quarrelled a lot, but it's been difficult for her, living with her mother while we were getting divorced. And I wasn't always as understanding as I should have been. I think she loves me. She likes going to the pictures with me and she likes cooking me a meal. She's a lovely girl and she's very bright. I don't like my government but neither do a lot of people, I don't like a lot about what's happening to the country. I'm an old-fashioned Israeli. Another generation." He paused.

"It's not bad so far."

"Then I couldn't have told it right. I haven't been a success, either in the army or at university. And I've had difficulty with relationships. Perhaps it's my army training. Being on the defensive. Defending the country's borders."

"What do you mean?"

"We're taught that we have to defend the country at its borders. You can't be flexible. We don't have room for defence in depth. We can't afford to give up any ground. There are good reasons for that if you look at a map of Israel."

"Tell me," she asked, "do you sometimes advance beyond your borders?"

"In our situation that's not easy," he replied. "If you're going to cross one of our frontiers, it had better be in a tank."

"That's not what I meant."

"I know."

They walked in silence for a while. Then he said, "Okay.

Now tell me about yourself. I know about Frances Carr Dowson the American Secretary of State. I read a briefing paper. I don't know much about you."

"Well, I was born in London and brought up in the better part of Wandsworth. That's in South London." She was speaking slowly, looking down at her brown felt shoes as she walked along with precise steps, as if choosing carefully where to take each step as she was choosing each word. "I'm an only child. My father was a civil servant. In the Home Office. He was a decent man, a man of great integrity..He was a tall, handsome man. People respected him. My father and I were close. He died two years ago. He'd been ill for some time."

"And your mother? And you?"

"My mother was my mother. She was a good wife to him. I joined the Foreign Office out of university. This place, as a matter of fact. Oxford. It seemed like a more interesting part of the civil service.."

"Boy friends?"

"Some."

"Now?"

"No."

"So what's your future? Her Majesty's ambassador to somewhere?"

"That's what I thought. I don't know now."

They walked in silence again for a while, and then on an impulse she put her arm through his and said, happily. "Do you know Oxford?"

"He shook his head. "No, not at all."

"I'll show you some of the sights before we leave. Starting with my college, New College, which is just across the High. It's called New College because it's only six hundred years old." She turned them around and they back towards the street arm in arm.

When Donald Green woke up that morning, all his fears

had vanished., and they were replaced by the most wonderful certainty. He was real, totally and absolutely real. He was of a special substance. He got out of bed knowing that now he was more real than anyone else, more real than anything else. Other people were insubstantial by comparison. He could practically see through them. He had acquired an extra dimension of reality. This was what he was born to become. This day was his epiphany.

He dressed slowly, wondering how it would be when he went downstairs and the others saw him. Cautiously, he glanced at his reflection in the mirror out of the corner of his eye. He looked away immediately. He did not dare look directly at it. He might be blinded, as one could be by staring directly at the sun. He was something new in the world. Jesus was said to be distinguished from other men by his holiness. He would be distinguished by his reality.

All those questions: Who are you? Who do you consider yourself to be? What are you? They had been in preparation for the one resounding answer that he was ready to give now. It was the only answer. It was the one that had been given thousands of years ago to Moses from a burning bush: I AM THAT I AM.

He went down the stairs, out into the courtyard, and across to the dining room to get his breakfast, smiling to himself all the time. In the dining room people spoke to him. He saw their mouths moving but he did not hear their words. They came from a great distance, for these people existed in fewer dimensions than him. He did not hear their words and he did not need them. He ate alone and he was content to do so. He was a whole universe, complete in himself.

:: ::
::

When the last of the participants in the game had packed

their suitcases and left, and the men from the catering firm had loaded their equipment into the van and shared out among themselves the left-over food and wine, Ivor Howe sat in the monitoring room, typing at his keyboard. He would write a sentence, look at it, and then sit thoughtfully for a while before writing another,

The heading on the screen was Preliminary Notes. He wrote:

"A first assessment of the game indicates that there were ways in which the attempt to achieve a greater degree of realism than in other crisis games succeeded, others in which the degree of realism was no more than in other games. Some preliminary thoughts present themselves:

"1. It was intended that the participants should bring to the situation the predilections and value systems of the role assigned to them. This was largely achieved. However, they were less aware that they were role-playing than participants in a game as normally run. This was as intended. However – this is just an impression that I have - many of them exercised less control over these personal predilections than they otherwise would have, and personal inclinations became strong factors in the action..

"2. The degree of participants' identification with their roles varied. In a few cases, certain characteristics were exaggerated so that the role-playing became caricature. In others, the identification with the role seemed to create confusion in the individual. However, this is not my field and I will not comment further on this.

"3. As tends to happen in crisis games, there was an over-emphasis on individuals as a determinant of events, compared to real-world international situations. The particular way of organising this game did not overcome this."

He stopped and thought about this. He was trying to sort it out in his mind when Piers Traynor walked through the door carrying a pile of papers.

Traynor said, "Oh, sorry. Are you working?"

"Just getting some thoughts down, for my paper. While it's fresh in my mind. He swung his swivel chair around and looked up at Traynor. "Tell me something."

"Yes?"

"If we did this again, would you take part? After what you've seen?"

Traynor shook his head. "No way. Would you?"

Howe frowned doubtfully. "I'm not sure. I think it might be an interesting experience."

"Bloody terrifying, I would say. You don't know how you're going to behave." He began putting the papers into cardboard boxes.

In the headmaster's office on the ground floor, Dr. Robert Manash sat at the desk typing on his laptop computer. He typed at a steady pace, pausing only rarely. When he paused he would stare at the wall opposite for a few moments constructing some sentences. He wrote:

"Although individuals' alienation from their own selves is not specific to our culture, the experiment pointed to a considerable degree of uncertainty about personal identities. This is engendered partly by the individualism of modern society, and also by the increased social, familial and even occupational fluidity. This despite the fact that most of the participants were in clearly defined professions and with a clearly defined status within these professions.

"Because of the environment in which the experiment was conducted, the subjects were drawn from a fairly narrow social and occupational spectrum. They were people whose apprehension of the world is primarily intellectual rather than experiential, with developed verbal skills, sometimes compensating for emotional limitations.

"The experiment has thrown up some useful material on character formation and the role of the ego and super-ego. In general terms the experiment demonstrated powerfully the role of character as armour, to use Wilhelm Reich's formulation (which I personally have always found one of the more useful of the metaphors that make up the classical psychoanalytic canon.). This character armour protects the individual against the instinctual demands of the id and the practical and social demands of the external world,

` "The exercise pointed up the absence of any clearly definable distinction between authentic emotions and those deriving from expectations imposed by the social and cultural environment. In this respect one should note an attitude which I believe is characteristic of our time. One might call it a line of defence, an ironic and detached mode of approaching the world, which has as its first reference points representations of life or commentaries upon aspects of life rather than life itself, these being less demanding of strong and direct emotional responses.

"In this experiment, where the suit of armour, to continue with Reich's terminology, has carried out its functions of protection and repression efficiently, it proved possible to remove it and substitute another quite smoothly. This was achieved with the use of psycho-active tools, including psycho-analytic interaction enhanced by psycho-pharmaceutical agents. It is important that everyone was required to function in their new character immediately, to interact with others and to respond to the pressure of events, without having time to sit and contemplate their situation, which might have allowed the new character to leach away.

"In a few cases the individual was able to transfer to another character with considerable gain in ego satisfaction and a release of libidinous energies even while transferring also some negative characteristics.

"There are certain personality types in whom the release of libidinous material from the id that follows the removal of the character armour can be threatening. The subject should be watched, and might possibly require therapeutic support for a time. Other people in whom the character formation was developed late and in whom the sense of identity is weak and excessively dependent on externalities, ie, socially agreed status and recognition by others, may find it difficult to revert to their original character formation. It may be that such a person should not take part in an experiment such as this.

"I will expand on all of these individual reactions later in this paper. I hope at some point in the future to carry out a similar experiment in identity transfer in a different situation with a group of people drawn from a different background."

Dr. Manash paused, then switched off the computer and closed its case. There was a lot more to be said and he would continue when he got back to his office. He picked up his laptop and started for the door.

::   ::

::

` It was a mild winter in the last months of that year, but towards the end of December an Arctic cyclone swirled in an easterly direction around a 2,000-mile stretch of Northern Canada and Greenland. These icy winds drove a cold front south, where it pushed up the warmer winds rising from the land masses of Europe and North America. Descending, it brought frost, and then snow, and the proverbial white Christmas to both sides of the Atlantic.

In a flat above a shopping street in the Highbury district of London, its plain stucco walls adorned with some photographic portraits and a poster about Third World aid, snow flakes blew against the window panes and cold air seeped through the gaps. The two small radiators in the two rooms did their inadequate best to keep the cold at bay. A young woman wearing a sweater and jeans sat in an armchair, a much-used piece of furniture with its colours fading and the fabric on the arms worn thin. She was, leaning back, her brown eyes apparently focussed inwards. In front of her another young woman was walking up and down, propelled by frustration, and talking, punctuating her talk occasionally with impatient gestures.

` "Okay, they're not the most scintillating people in the world but it's a party, and who knows who you'll meet there. Jeffrey will be there, you know, that doctor who was asking after you. You said you'd go. Now you suddenly say you want to spend Christmas Eve here alone. You're in a blue mood. Come on, get out of it. I know, you're still in mourning for that affair. Right? Okay, it's easy for me to say you've got to move on, put it behind you. But you do have to. I thought you were getting over it. You haven't talked about it for a little while.

"What gets me is that you're not angry at him. You get angry at the Government, at the Americans, you get angry at some poor businessman just because he sells machine-guns to people to massacre some natives, but you're not angry at this man who didn't tell you his wife was pregnant while you were having an affair with him, and then dumped you when his wife had a baby. Yet you still say he was a good guy at heart and that he really loved you. Just maybe a bit weak. You were in love with him, I realise that. But making excuses for him. You're such a softy. You even said once that – "

` "I saw him." The young woman in the armchair spoke.

The other woman stood still. "What? Where?"

In Richmond High Street. I was going to visit my uncle."

"When?"

"Yesterday. He and wife and their baby. She was tall, blonde. Good-looking. Smartly dressed." She paused to recollect before continuing in a soft voice, "She was pushing a pram along.. They both looked so fucking pleased with themselves. He didn't see me. I scooted down a side street."

"Oh."

"So it hurt. It brought it all back. I don't talk about this to anyone else, but I can tell you. You know, I never thought of the baby as a person. It was just a secret he'd kept from me. And then I saw it. I mean, I didn't actually see the baby but I saw the pram, the baby was presumably in it. I don't begrudge him his happiness, if he is happy. But as I say, it brought it all back."

There was a silence when the other woman absorbed this, then she started talking again. "Well that's all the more reason to get out and be among people and not sit alone and brood. Take drastic action. Come to the party. Get drunk. Get laid. I can't leave you here. Come on, get up and put on something sexy. Show some cleavage. You've got great .boobs. I'm going to take you to this party if I have to drag you by the hair."

The young woman looked up and smiled for the first time that day..

Six miles away, in Barnes, on the other side of the river, snow flakes fluttered down on to Frances Carr's window sill. She was lying on her bed wearing only a dressing gown, and looking out of the window at the snow flakes and at the thin sheet of white that was being created on the sill. Her flat was comfortably warm. She had just come out of the bath and the dress she was going to wear was on a hanger on the cupboard door in front of her. After staring at the snow for a while, she sat up, picked up the telephone next to the bed and telephoned Jacob Shemtov.

"I've just come back from a class," he told her in answer to her question.

"I thought I'd call you because it's Christmas and we get in touch with old friends at Christmas," she said. "Do you know about Christmas?"

"I lived in America, remember? In America, even Jews celebrate Christmas." She smiled hearing his voice again.

"It's snowing here. What's the weather like where you are?"

"Raining. And they say there might be snow in Jerusalem.

What are you doing?"

"I'm going over to my mother tomorrow. I always spend Christmas Day with my mother. This evening I'm going out to dinner with my boy friend."

"That sounds good. I'm going to the theatre with my girl friend tomorrow night."

She did not know whether he was telling the truth or whether he just felt he had to match her. She hoped he was telling the truth. "Are you well?" she asked.

"Not bad. I've been a lot worse. And you? How's life at the Foreign Office?"

"It's okay, but I'm leaving."

"Have you made up your mind?"

"Yes, it's definite. I've handed in my notice. I decided I'm not really going to spend my life defending the quote national interest unquote."

"What are you going to do?"

"I'm not sure. Something different. My experience should be useful to somebody."

They talked for a little longer and then said their goodbyes. She lay there for a few moments thinking of Jacob, and then got up and started to get dressed, taking from her drawer the lacy underwear she had brought the week before.

On the other side of the Atlantic, snowflakes propelled by gusty winds swirled around in Washington D.C. and the surrounding area. In Alexandria, Virginia, a dormitory suburb of Washington. The snow flakes were striking noiselessly against the bay window of a pink brick house and laying a thin coating on the lawn in front that glistened in the street lights. Inside the house, a four-year-old boy lay sleeping upstairs, and a Christmas tree festooned with lights stood in the living room in front of the bay window, a celebratory spectacle for passers-by.

The atmosphere in the living room was a grim contrast to the warmth and good cheer that radiated out through the window. Raymond Wade and his wife Louise stood beside the Christmas tree facing one another. She was standing with her feet apart, her body erect and tense, her hands quivering. He stood with his head bowed in pain.

"How long have you known?" she demanded.

"I think I knew when I was fifteen. Sixteen. But I forgot."

"You *forgot*?"

"I put it out of my mind." He turned towards her. "Things happened. But I thought it was just a passing phase and I put them out of my mind, as I say. I wanted to go to West Point. I forgot that I'd ever felt that way." He had turned his face half-away from her, as if he was flinching from a series of blows.

"I don't know what - I just don't know." She screwed up her face in perplexity and pain. "Have you talked to a doctor about it?"

He looked up at her and made an empty gesture with his hands. "Louise, I still love you. I want to be with you."

"But you want - other things also. I don't think I can handle that. I can't come to terms with it. If only you'd told me before."

"But I didn't really know. And if I told you, you wouldn't have married me, right?"

"I suppose not."

"And now?"

"I don't know. I just don't think I can go on."

"But our marriage – little Matt – " He stopped and shook his head.

She sat down and they looked at each other in silence, both of them weighed down by loss.

In New York City the snow came down in blobs to settle on to the soft white carpet several inches thick that already covered the ground. In the road, traffic was churning the snow into dirty slush as it fell, and cars moved along slowly, one occasionally skidding as it pulled up at the traffic lights On the pavement people trudged along and struggled to keep their feet, some of them laden with packages.

From a window in Mount Sinai Hospital. Lorraine Green stared down bleakly at the scene, and then turned back to the doctor. "He seemed to recognize me today," she said. "He didn't speak of course but – well, I've an idea that he recognized me."

"I think he may be responding a little to the treatment." The doctor tried to make this sound convincing.

"He seemed to know Josephine. Our little girl. Tears came into his eyes when he saw her."

"That's good. Encouraging." Then he said, "We're going to try him on Olancapine starting next week."

"What's that?"

"It's one of a class of anti-psychotic drugs that we haven't tried yet."

"If you think it's the right thing."

"Olancapine occasionally produces results where other things have failed. I can't promise anything of course. We can only try."

She nodded. "I understand. I'll come and see him again tomorrow."

"All right. I won't be here until after the holiday, Mrs. Green."

She turned to go. He was going to wish her a merry Christmas but it did not seem appropriate.